"THIS WASN'T A DATE," SHE SAID.

Tag's hands cupped her face, thumbs brushing her cheeks. His palm felt like feathers dancing across the sensitive place on her neck. He leaned in for the kiss, and Nikki went up on her tiptoes.

She had been kissed before. She'd had long-term relationships. She'd had her heart broken more than once since she'd lived on her own. She'd made mistakes and learned from them. But nothing prepared her for the way she felt when Tag's lips met hers. The whole world disappeared in a flash, leaving only the two of them standing on a small upstairs porch with the moon and stars above them.

When the kiss ended, Tag took a step back and braced himself on the railing. "If that affected you the way it did me, then, darlin', this was definitely a date."

High Praise for Carolyn Brown

"Carolyn Brown makes the sun shine brighter and the tea taste sweeter. Southern comfort in a book."
—Shelia Roberts, *USA Today* bestselling author

"Carolyn Brown is one of my go-to authors when I want a feel-good story that will make me smile."
—Fresh Fiction

"Carolyn Brown writes about everyday things that happen to all of us and she does it with panache, class, empathy and humor."
—Night Owl Reviews

"I highly recommend Carolyn Brown as a go-to author for all things sexy cowboy."
—Harlequin Junkie

COWBOY BRAVE

"Sizzling romance between believable characters is the mainstay of this whimsical novel, which is enhanced by plenty of romantic yearning."
—*Publishers Weekly*

"Warmth, humor and sweet romance...Carolyn Brown always manages to write feel-good stories."
—Harlequin Junkie, Top Pick

COWBOY HONOR

"The slow-simmering romance between Claire and Levi is enhanced by the kind supporting characters and the simple pleasures of ranch life in a story that's sure to please fans of cowboy romances."

—*Publishers Weekly*

"Friendship, family, love, and trust abound in *Cowboy Honor.*"

—Fresh Fiction

COWBOY BOLD

"Lighthearted banter, heart-tugging emotion, and a good-natured Sooner/Longhorn football rivalry make this a delightful romance and terrific launch for the new series."

—*Library Journal*

"*Cowboy Bold* is the start of a new and amazing series by an author that really knows how to hook her readers with sexy cowboys, strong women, and a bunch of humor…Everything about this book is a roaring good time."

—Harlequin Junkie, Top Pick

"Everything you could ever ask for in a cowboy romance."

—The Genre Minx

Also by Carolyn Brown

The Longhorn Canyon Series

Cowboy Bold
Cowboy Honor
Cowboy Brave

The Happy, Texas, Series

Toughest Cowboy in Texas
Long, Tall Cowboy Christmas
Luckiest Cowboy of All

The Lucky Penny Ranch Series

Wild Cowboy Ways
Hot Cowboy Nights
Merry Cowboy Christmas
Wicked Cowboy Charm

Cowboy Rebel

A Longhorn Canyon Novel

Carolyn Brown

FOREVER

New York   Boston

Forever
Hachette Book Group
1290 Avenue of the Americas, New York, NY 10104
read-forever.com
twitter.com/readforeverpub

First Edition: May 2019

Forever is an imprint of Grand Central Publishing. The Forever name and logo are trademarks of Hachette Book Group, Inc.

The publisher is not responsible for websites (or their content) that are not owned by the publisher.

The Hachette Speakers Bureau provides a wide range of authors for speaking events. To find out more, go to www.hachettespeakersbureau.com or call (866) 376-6591.

ISBNs: 978-1-5387-4871-8 (mass market), 978-1-5387-4870-1 (ebook)

Printed in the United States of America

OPM

10 9 8 7 6 5 4 3 2 1

*To my cousins
Marthanna Goshorn and Brenda Long,
who love cowboys as much as I do!!*

Dear Readers,

As I finish *Cowboy Rebel*, fall is arriving in Sunset, Texas, where the Longhorn Canyon Ranch is located. Y'all will be reading it just as summer is starting, so grab a glass of sweet tea, curl up on a porch swing, and enjoy the story. I was privileged to get to see the cover for this book before I even began to write it. Tag Baker was exactly as I'd pictured him in my mind—blue eyed, hair just a little too long, a slight cleft in his chin, and a swagger to his walk. That last part I couldn't actually see in the picture, but my imagination is very good when it comes to cowboys!

As always, I have a bushel basket of thanks to pass out today. The first one goes to all my fantastic fans who continue to support me by not only buying my books, but also by recommending them to their friends, talking about them at book clubs, writing reviews, and sending notes and messages to me personally. Please know that each and every one of you is precious and appreciated more than you'll ever know.

If my thanks were medals instead of heartfelt gratitude, Leah Hultenschmidt would get a gold one for everything she does to help me take a rough idea and turn it into an emotionally charged book. And my team at Grand Central/Forever, who do everything from copyedits to covers, promotions to sales, would have medals hanging around their necks for all their hard work behind the scenes.

As always, there are no words to truly say how much I appreciate my agent, Erin Niumata, and the staff at Folio Literary Management. Y'all are simply the best and deserve a bushel basket of thanks all of your own.

Last, but never least—thank you to my husband of fifty-two years, Mr. B. He's stood beside me through the thick and the thin of this writing career and continues to be my biggest supporter.

Keep your reading glasses close by after you finish *Cowboy Rebel*, because there's more on the way. Maverick tells me that he's feeling the magic of Christmas in the air, and Paxton and Hud are trying to convince me that they're not ever going to fall in love. Shhhh...don't tell anyone, but I know better.

Until next time, happy reading!
Carolyn Brown

Cowboy Rebel

Chapter One

"What can I get you, cowboy?" The cute blonde whipped a towel from her hip pocket and wiped down the bar in front of him.

He tipped his cowboy hat back just a little so he could see her better. "A double shot of Knob Creek. Where's Joe tonight?"

"He works Saturday. I get Thursday and Friday," she answered. "Haven't seen you before."

"I only moved here a couple of months ago. My brother and I usually come in on Saturday nights. But we might change our days." He winked.

"Oh, and why's that?" She set his whiskey in front of him.

"You're prettier than Joe."

"I've heard that line before." She moved down the bar to draw up another beer for the woman sitting at the far end and then worked her way back down to him, her ponytail flipping back and forth as she went from customer to customer.

"Ready for another?" she asked when she was in front of him.

"Not yet. This stuff is sippin' whiskey, so I enjoy it a little at a time."

The folks between him and the woman down on the end were quick to leave the bar when Jake Owen's "Down to the Honkytonk" started playing on the jukebox. They soon formed a line dance, and the noise of their boots on the wood floor competed with the loud song.

He motioned for the bartender to bring him another drink and had just taken the first sip when a big, burly man burst into the bar and stormed across the floor with his hands knotted into fists the size of Christmas hams.

"I knew I'd find you here," the guy yelled above the music and dancers when he reached Tag.

The man bumped Tag on the shoulder when he passed by him. Tag spilled the rest of his whiskey down the front of his shirt. In Tag's way of thinking, it was a shame to waste even a drop of good Knob Creek.

He spun around on the barstool. "Hey, now."

"I'm not talkin' to you, so turn around and shut up. I'm talkin' to my woman down there." He pointed to the other end of the bar. "When she gets mad at me, she always shows up here."

"Well, you spilled my drink, so you should buy me another one," Tag said.

"I ain't buyin' you jack shit." The guy took a few steps and grabbed the woman by the arm. "Come on, Scarlett, we're goin' home."

She slid off the stool, shook off his hand, and got right up nose to nose with him. "I'm not going anywhere with you. If you want a woman, go get Ramona. I'm goin' to finish my drink and then have another one or two."

"I told you that she was a mistake. I broke up with her weeks ago, so don't give me that old shit." He drew back his hand as if to slap her, but instead grabbed a handful of her hair and jerked her to his chest. "I said you're coming home. I made a mistake but so did you. I wasn't the only one cheatin', and I damn sure wasn't the first one."

A bouncer who looked more like a strutting little banty rooster hurried across the room, got between them, and demanded that the guy leave. Tag could see from the fire in the bigger man's eyes that he wasn't going anywhere. And the stance that the bouncer had taken said he wasn't backing down either. It wasn't one bit of Tag's business, but the man had caused him to spill whiskey on his favorite shirt. While he slid off the stool, the jukebox began to blast out Trace Adkins singing "Whoop a Man's Ass." Now, that was an omen to Tag's way of thinking, especially when the words said something about cussin' and roughin' up a lady.

He took a few long strides and stood beside the bouncer. "The lady says that she's not going home with you," Tag said. "It'd be wise if you just scooted on out of here."

The big fellow put his hands on Tag's chest and pushed. Tag grabbed for anything that would keep him from falling and got a handful of a shirt. The bouncer fell into the woman and they fell into a pile. Before Tag could get out of the tangle of arms and legs and find his hat, Scarlett kicked the man in the knee about a half dozen times. He went down like a big oak tree, landing to one side of the pile.

"You bitch," he growled as he popped up to a sitting position and grabbed a beer bottle from a nearby table, slammed it on the floor, shattering the bottom half into a million pieces. "You know that's my bum knee." He drew back the bottle to hit her with it, but she ducked.

The bottle slashed right across Tag's chiseled jawline.

Tag had always considered himself a lover, not a fighter, but there was something about his own blood dripping on his new Western shirt that brought out the anger. Then he noticed that his best cowboy hat was now ruined with beer splatter and cast-off blood drops. He popped up on his feet, hands clenched in fists, ready to fight, but the bouncer had brought out an equalizer in the form of a Taser. A picture of David in the Bible came to Tag's mind as the man dropped to the floor and began to quiver. Amazing what a rock and a slingshot or a little jolt of electricity in today's world could do to a giant.

"You've killed my husband! He's got a bad heart," Scarlett screamed. "I'll sue the whole damn lot of you! Call an ambulance!"

"No!" the big man yelled from the floor, where he was still twitching. "Take me home. Cops will haul me into jail for assault on that cowboy."

Through a red haze of anger and pain, Tag could see that the bartender was already on the phone. He picked up his hat, settled it on his head, and slipped out of the bar before anyone could rope him into testifying or giving his story.

"Glad I didn't drive my motorcycle tonight," he grumbled as he got into his black Silverado.

He removed his plaid shirt and held pressure on the cut with one hand while he started the truck engine with the other. The hospital emergency room was the first place he'd checked out when he'd moved to Montague County the previous month. That information was pretty damned important when he lived by the words of his two bumper stickers. One said ONCE A REBEL, ALWAYS A REBEL. The other was the title of Tim McGraw's country song LIVE LIKE YOU WERE DYING.

He'd barely gotten out on the highway when blood started

to seep through his fingertips and drip onto his snowy white T-shirt. He hoped that the doctor would throw some super-glue and bandages on it and that it would heal up without too much of a scar.

The only parking place he could find was all the way across the lot. By the time he made it to the door in the heat, he was getting more than a little woozy. The walls of the empty emergency room did a couple of wavy spins when he stepped inside. A nurse looked up from the desk and yelled something, but it sounded like it was coming through a barrel full of water.

Then suddenly someone shoved him into a wheelchair, took him into a curtained examination area, helped him up onto a narrow bed, and turned on a bright light above his head. He expected to see his whole life begin to flash before his eyes any minute, but instead Nikki Grady, his sister's best friend, took the shirt from his hand.

"Want me to call Emily?" she asked.

"Hell no! Call Hud. His number is on the speed dial on my phone. It's in my hip pocket," he muttered.

"What happened?" she asked. "Looks like you were the only one at a knife fight without a knife."

"Beer bottle." Tag tried to grin but it hurt like hell. "Just glue me up. Give it a kiss to help it heal and call my brother Hud."

"Honey, with this much blood loss and the fact that I'm lookin' at your bone, it's goin' to take more than glue and a kiss," Nikki said.

*　　　*　　　*

Taggart, or Tag as the family called him, was one of those men who turned every woman's eye when he walked into a place—even a hospital emergency room. The nurses, old and young alike, were buzzing about him before Nikki even got him into the cubicle. With that chiseled face, those piercing blue eyes, a cowboy swagger, and a smile that would make a religious woman want to drink whiskey and do the two-step, it's a wonder he hadn't already put one of those "take a number and wait" machines on the front porch post of his house.

"The doctor is on his way. He just finished stitchin' up a patient with a knife wound. From the looks of you, I'd think you'd been in on that fight." Nikki applied pressure to the cut with a wad of gauze.

The curtain between the cubicles flew to one side, and a white-coated guy came over to the bed. "What have we got here? I'm Dr. Richards." He gently lifted the edge of the gauze. "Knife?"

"Beer bottle," Tag said.

"Well, the first thing we have to do is shave off that scruff. Deaden it up and then shave off the area around it, Nikki. I'll take care of the kid who thought he could ride his skateboard down a slide, and I'll be right back," Dr. Richards said.

"Yes, sir." Nikki nodded.

The doctor had been instrumental in getting Nikki her first job as a registered nurse, and she really admired him. An older man with a white rim of hair around an otherwise bald head covered in freckles, he was the best when it came to stitches, in Nikki's opinion. Tag was a lucky cowboy that Dr. Richards was on call that night. It could have been an intern doing the embroidery on his face, and it would be such a shame to leave a scar on something that sexy.

"You still going to go out with me even though I'm clean shaven and got a scar?" Tag asked her as she prepared to shave part of his face.

"If I don't work, I don't eat, and I'm real fond of cheese-burgers," she answered.

"What's that supposed to mean?" He winced when she picked up a needle to start the local anesthetic.

"That I don't have time to take a number and wait in line behind all those other women wanting to get a chance at taming you," she answered.

He wrapped his hand around her wrist before she started. "I'd move you to the front of the line, darlin'."

"Well, ain't that sweet." She patted his hand and ignored the heat between them. "But, honey, you're way too fast for this little country girl. Now be still and let me get this ready for Dr. Richards."

Without blinking, he focused on her face as she sank the needle into several places to deaden the two-inch cut. Whispers of other conversations penetrated the curtains on either side of Tag's cubicle, but heavy silence filled the space while Nikki put in the last shot.

"That all?" he finally asked, but his piercing blue eyes didn't leave her face.

"Except for cleaning up around it," she answered. "And you were a good boy. I'll tell Dr. Richards to give you a lollipop before you leave."

"It ain't my first rodeo," he said. "Did you call Hud?"

"Not yet," she said.

"Then don't."

"With the amount of blood you've lost and the shot doc will probably give you for pain, you'll need a driver or you won't be released," she said. "So it's Hud or Emily. Take your choice."

"You're a hard woman, Nikki," he said.

"And you're a hardheaded man," she shot back as she carefully shaved the scruff from around the wound.

"We ready to fix this cowboy up?" Dr. Richards threw back the curtain. "What'd the other guy look like?"

"Not a scratch on him, but he was limpin'. His woman tried to kick his kneecap halfway to Georgia," Tag answered.

Dr. Richards chuckled. "And I bet you were defendin' her in some way."

Tag grimaced when he tried to smile. "Just helpin' out the bouncer a little. Seemed like the thing to do since 'Whoop a Man's Ass' was playin' on the jukebox."

"Well, looks like you was the one who got the whuppin'." Dr. Richards chuckled and turned to Nikki. "Good job there, Nikki. Now it's my turn. We could try glue and strips, but as deep as this is, stitches will do a better job."

"You're the doctor," Tag answered.

"It's up to you whether you shave your face clean when you get home, but if you don't, you're going to look a little like a mangy dog."

"Looked worse before," Tag drawled. "And probably will again."

A lady in pink scrubs poked her head between the curtains.

"What do you need, Rosemary?" Dr. Richards asked the nurse.

"Sue Ann just arrived. Nikki handles her better than any of us. Would you mind if I help out here and she takes that job?"

"Go on," Dr. Richards said. "I've got this."

"Where is she?" Nikki asked as she pushed back the curtain. Rosemary had fast become her friend since they both worked the weekend shift. The woman was average in every way—brown hair, brown eyes, but her sense of humor and smile were infectious.

"I'll show you and then get right back in there with Doc." Rosemary led the way. "Lord have mercy." She laid one hand over her heart and fanned her face with the other one. "That cowboy could melt my panties with those blue eyes."

"Sue Ann strung out or drunk?" Nikki liked Rosemary, loved working with her, but she was always teasing Nikki about settling down and getting married.

"Maybe both. Did I hear you turn that man down when he asked you for a date? Are you bat crap crazy?" Rosemary asked.

"You're married and have four kids," Nikki said.

"And I'm on a diet, too, but that don't mean I can't stare in the window at the candy store." Rosemary laughed. "Oh, there's another good-lookin' cowboy out in the waiting room who says he's here for Tag. Want me to let him come on back?"

"I'll get him if you'll keep Sue Ann pacified for another minute." Nikki made a quick right turn.

Tag's twin brother, Hudson, stood up when he saw her. "How bad is it this time?"

She motioned for him to follow her. "Stitches on his jaw. The cut was deep. Doc's takin' care of him right now."

Nikki had had no trouble seeing that the Baker brothers shared DNA from the first time she met them. The cleft in Tag's chin was more pronounced, and he wore his hair longer than Hud did, but those crystal clear blue eyes were the same. Even with those similarities, there were enough differences between them that she could hardly believe they were twins. However, they were pretty true to what she'd heard about it taking two personalities to make one when it came to twins. Tag was the wild and crazy one. Hud, the more grounded brother with a funny streak and a big heart.

"Right here." Nikki eased aside the curtain to Tag's cubicle.

"What'd you do now?" Hud asked.

"Had a little run-in with a beer bottle," Tag answered.

Nikki hurried away to take care of Sue Ann, their regular weekend patient in the Bowie emergency room. Some folks were happy drunks, but not Sue Ann. When she had too much liquor or snorted too much white stuff up her nose, she became the poster child for hypochondria.

"Oh, Nikki, darlin'." Sue Ann slurred her words. "Just take me on into surgery and take out my stomach. It's got an alien in it that's trying to eat its way out through my belly button."

"I need a list of all the medicine you've taken since you were here last week, and whatever you've ingested in the way of alcohol or drugs in the past twelve hours— no, make that twenty-four hours—before we can do that, honey." Nikki pulled a stylus from the pocket of her scrubs and was ready to write before she realized she didn't have her tablet. "You think about what you've had, Sue Ann. Things are hectic here tonight. I'll be right back."

"All done," Dr. Richards said as Nikki slipped inside to get her tablet. "You see to it that you call my office tomorrow and make an appointment for next Friday so I can check this. If you start running a fever, call me. I think Nikki did a good job of cleaning it up, but one never knows when it comes to bar floors and beer bottles."

"I'm riding a bull at a rodeo on Friday night," Tag said.

"We'll see about that." Doc turned to Hud. "Make your brother behave this week."

"That's an impossible job." Hud grinned.

"Then I'll admit him for a week. We've got restraints that we can use to keep him in the bed, and the nurses will love taking care of his catheter." Doc winked at Hud.

"I'll be good," Tag growled. "But I don't have to like it."

"Give me your truck keys. Paxton is out in the waiting room. He's going to drive it home, and I'm taking you," Hud said.

"I'll call if I need you," Nikki said as she picked up her tablet. When she reached Sue Ann's cubicle, the woman was sitting up in the bed. She was as pale as the sheet she tucked around her thin body. One hand was over her mouth and the other was pointing toward the bathroom. Nikki dropped her tablet on the table and barely got a disposable bag to Sue Ann in time.

When she finished emptying her stomach, Sue Ann handed the bag to Nikki and said, "I had a little drop of tequila at the Rusty Spur tonight."

"How big of a drop?" Nikki picked up her tablet and stylus. "Tell me the truth. If we have to do surgery, it'll make a difference in how much anesthetic we give you. You wouldn't want to wake up before we got done, would you?"

"Five shots. No, six, and then maybe four"—she lowered her voice to a whisper—"of those pills."

"What pills?" Nikki asked.

"The ones I bought from that cowboy who was dancin' with the pretty girl. That damned alien got in my stomach. They told me it was just the worm in the bottle of tequila when I ate it with a little lime and salt, but I know better. It looked like a baby alien, and I just swallowed it whole. Then my stomach started to burn and hurt. I saw that cowboy passing some pills to a lady, so I bought some from him."

Nikki thought she'd seen and heard everything when she worked at the nursing home in town, but this would be a story she'd have to share with her best friend, Emily. "Okay, then several shots of tequila and pills of some kind. I think we can kill the alien and fix you right up without surgery."

Sue Ann fell back on the bed with a sigh. "I don't know about that. Don't you need to do one of them TSA things?"

Nikki bit back a giggle. "You mean an MRI?"

"That too. Do all the tests you need to. I want this thing out of me." Sue Ann put a hand on her stomach.

"I'll talk to the doctor and be right back. Are you still taking..." Nikki read off a whole page of prescription drugs. "You do realize that you're not supposed to drink with about half of these or take street drugs with them?"

"I know my body better than you do," Sue Ann declared. "My grandma drank every day of her life and she lived to be ninety-eight."

"Yes, ma'am," Nikki said. "I'll go talk to the doctor and be right back."

She stepped out of the cubicle, tablet in hand this time, and stopped so fast that her rubber-soled shoes squeaked on the tile floor. One more step and she would have collided with Tag.

"It's just not my night." He smiled down at her. "I get in trouble for taking up for a woman, and now one almost falls into my arms but doesn't."

"It might be a sign that you need to peel those stickers off your truck and begin to reform a little," Nikki told him.

"Never." Tag grinned.

Chapter Two

If the next door neighbor's dogs hadn't set up a barking chorus with the landlady's mutts, Nikki might have slept until dark on Monday. That would have been disastrous since her mother expected her to answer the phone at exactly seven o'clock. If she didn't answer, then her mother would call the police station and the hospitals. Any other day of the week, it didn't matter if Nikki was lying in a ditch half dead, but no one had better mess with Wilma Grady's schedule.

"Thank God for barking dogs," Nikki said as she crawled out of bed. She had an hour until her mother called, so she took a quick shower and got dressed. She sat down on the sofa in her tiny three-room garage apartment and called her mother's number.

"It's not seven. My show isn't over, but there's a commercial, so what's wrong?" Wilma said curtly.

"Nothing's wrong. I thought maybe we'd go out, or I'd

bring a pizza or some fried chicken over for supper and we could visit in person," Nikki said.

"I eat at four thirty so I can take my medicine. I don't eat fried foods or spicy pizza. You know that, Nikki. The commercial is over. I'll call you at seven and we'll visit." And just like that she was gone.

Nikki was hungry, and she'd figured out that she didn't have to be in her apartment to talk to her mother on Monday nights at seven o'clock on the dot. She could talk to her anywhere, especially when Nikki's part of the conversation was nothing more than muttering, "Well, that's too bad," or "Bless her heart," now and then. She could do that in a booth at the Mexican place or sitting in the park while she ate a hamburger. With her purse and keys in hand, she locked the apartment door behind her. She made up her mind as she started the car engine that chicken enchiladas sounded really good that evening.

The hair on the back of her neck prickled when she walked into the restaurant. At first she attributed it to leaving the sweltering night air and coming into a cool building. Then she heard her name and turned to see Tag and Hud sitting in a booth, waving at her to join them.

It would be rude not to sit with them. They were, after all, her best friend's brothers. Besides, the place was full and there were no more seats available. She threw up a hand in a wave and started that way. When she got close enough, Tag slid over to the far side of the booth to allow room for her to sit beside him.

"How's the jaw? I see you opted to look like a mangy dog, rather than go clean shaven for a few days," she said.

"Sore as the devil, but it'll get well. Maybe you'll take pity on a poor old hungry dog and go out with him?" Tag cocked his head to one side and whimpered like a puppy.

Nikki grabbed a menu and propped it up in front of her. "You don't look like you're starving to me."

"You've met your match, Tag. You might as well admit defeat." Hud grinned.

"Why's it so important for me to go out with you anyway?" Nikki asked.

"Because he's never been rejected, not one time in his whole life," Hud answered.

Nikki reached up and gently patted him on the cheek. "Poor baby."

He grabbed her hand, brought her knuckles to his lips, and kissed each one. Sparks flitted around her like Fourth of July fireworks. It had been that way since the first time she met him, and then again a month ago at Emily's wedding to Justin Maguire. She'd served as maid of honor. Tag and Hud had both been groomsmen, and Tag had glued himself to her side all evening. As much as Nikki would have liked to be the maid of honor who went to bed with one of the groomsmen like in the movies, she wasn't interested in a one-night stand—not even with the supersexy Taggart Baker. And any kind of fleeting relationship she might have with Tag could complicate her friendship with Emily. No way on the great green earth would she ever do that—Emily meant too much to her.

"Why do you just keep breaking my little cowboy heart?" Tag's blue eyes begged for an answer.

"Darlin', you are way too wild for me." She told him the same thing every time he asked.

The waitress finally made it to their table and took their orders, then promptly returned with their drinks, individual bowls of salsa, queso, and a basket of warm chips. "Orders will be along in a few minutes," she said, and then hurried off to clean a table so another group could be seated.

Nikki's phone rang before Tag could come back with one of his famous pickup lines. She dug her cell out of her purse and checked the clock on the wall. It was five minutes until seven, so she was surprised to see her mother's number pop up. Evidently her mother's clock wasn't in sync with the one in the restaurant.

"Hello, Mama." Nikki would have to talk to Wilma or the world would come to an end for sure. She was about to tell the Baker brothers that she had to take the call and motion to the waitress to make her order to go. Then she would sit on the park bench outside until it was ready. But a long sigh preceded a whisper. "Mrs. Thomas from next door came over with a plate of chocolate chip cookies and asked me to make coffee so we can have a visit. I don't know what she's thinkin'. We visit on Tuesday evening at six, never at seven on Monday. She's getting senile and can't remember anything."

"Where is she now?" Nikki asked.

"In the bathroom washing her hands. I'll have to clean the room when she leaves because she always makes a mess, and all she does is gripe about how her kids never come to see her. I wouldn't go in that house either. She's a hoarder. I bet there's roaches in them boxes she's got stacked everywhere."

"Then you want me to call later?" Nikki asked.

"Lord, no, you can't call later. She'll stay until nine and you know that's when I have to get my medicine and then get ready for bed. We'll just have to talk next week," Wilma said. "She's coming out of the bathroom right now." A long sigh and then the screen went dark.

"You need to take your order to go?" Hud asked.

Nikki dropped the phone back into her purse. "No, Mama has company, so I'll talk to her later. We usually have a catchin' up visit on Monday nights."

"Only once a week?" Tag said.

"The first week we were on our ranch, Mama called twice, sometimes three times a day," Hud said.

Tag winced when he grinned. "Mama missed her pretty babies."

Hud chuckled. "Yeah, right. She's just afraid that you'll kill your fool self. From the look of your jawbone, she came close to being right. I told her this morning that you wouldn't be riding bulls on Friday night."

"Well, if a bull comes through named Fumanchu, you can bet your country ass I'll ride him, even if I've got stitches, a broken arm, and a busted up leg."

"You're crazy," Nikki said.

That was another reason she wasn't starting something with this cowboy—not even a first date. When Nikki fell in love, she fell hard, and the way Tag lived, well, he'd never see his first gray hair. She'd never knowingly put herself in that kind of situation.

"Maybe so, but when I check out of this life, I'll be able to say that I lived every single minute," Tag said.

The waitress brought their food, reminded them that the plates were very hot, and then asked, "Need more chips or dip?"

"I'm good," Nikki said.

"Prove it." Tag nudged her shoulder.

Heat popped out in her cheeks in the form of two bright red circles. "You have got to be the biggest flirt I've ever known."

"Thank you. I do my best," Tag said.

*   *   *

Tag and Hud settled their sweat-stained straw hats on their heads as they stepped out of the cool restaurant into the hot night air. Hud's truck was parked down the block with the windows rolled up. When Tag opened the passenger door, it felt like a blast from an oven hit him in the face.

"Hurry up and get this thing started so it will cool down," he said as he got inside.

Hud nodded, started the engine, and turned the A/C as high as it would go. He pulled away from the curb and headed back toward the ranch that he and his brother had bought. It adjoined the huge Longhorn Canyon Ranch, owned by the Maguire family. Their sister, Emily, had married the younger Maguire brother, Justin, and they were about to get their new house ready to move into.

Hud drove west out of town. "We really should name our ranch and get a brand registered."

"I was thinkin' the same thing." Tag smiled and then frowned. "Dammit! This thing hurts like hell when I grin."

"Serves you right for stepping into another couple's fight," Hud told him. "And you weren't really thinkin' about a name for our place. Your mind was still on Nikki Grady. What is it about her that makes you keep going back for more rejections?"

"It's just a game we play. A man would have to be blind or dead not to be attracted to those big brown eyes. But the truth is that in the long haul, we both know she deserves someone who's grounded and stable, not an old rebel like me," Tag answered.

"Do you feel more for her than, say, you did for all the other women you've sweet-talked into takin' their clothes off?" Hud took the road heading south toward Sunset.

Tag shrugged. "Maybe. Why are you askin'? Interested in her yourself?"

Hud shook his head slowly. "Not me. She's sweet and has a firecracker sense of humor, but there's no sparks between us. Got to admit, though, I see some serious electricity when y'all are flirtin'."

"She's fun, and I like her sass. That's as far as it goes or will go. Like I said, Nikki is one of them good girls who someone with my background don't have a right to." Tag adjusted the vents so the cool air blew right on his face. "This thing burns when I sweat."

Hud made a hard right onto a section line road off Highway 101. "Should teach you a lesson to stay out of other people's fights." Another right hand turn down the ranch lane and Hud pointed ahead. "Looks like we got company."

"Halle-damn-lujah! Maverick and Paxton have arrived. We've got help." Tag was out of the truck the minute Hud parked. He met the two Callahan brothers, distant cousins of his and Tag's, on the porch in a three-way bear hug instead of handshakes. When Hud arrived, it turned into a back-thumping event that looked like football players congratulating the quarterback on an eighty-yard run for a touchdown.

"We're here a day early," Maverick said. "Mam talked about having a going-away party for us. The plans fell through when our sister had to go on a business trip, and our parents had to go to a funeral."

"Well, we're glad y'all are finally here," Tag said. "Y'all had supper? Want a beer?"

"Had supper on the way," Paxton said. "But we're Irish. We'd never turn down a beer. Where are we bunkin'? I'll grab some of our gear and bring it inside."

Hud unlocked the door and swung it open. "House only has two bedrooms, so we set up twin beds in both of them. It's a little crowded but better than bunk beds. Me and Tag got one room. Y'all can have the second one. I hate that y'all missed your grandma's party, but we're sure glad you're here."

"I ain't sleepin' in the same room with my brother," Paxton said. "His snores rattle the windows. I got no problem sleeping on the sofa."

Maverick took a long look around the sparsely furnished house and turned back to Tag. "It'll do just fine. Slept in bunkhouses smaller than this many times. Matter of fact, one winter me and Paxton had to stay in an old line cabin and the whole thing wasn't any bigger than this room right here."

"I was ready to pour honey on him and stake him out in the snow for the fire ants to eat." Paxton grinned.

At just over six feet, both Maverick and Paxton had dark brown hair. Maverick was the oldest by three years, but they looked more like twins than Tag and Hud did. About the only difference was that Paxton's face was slightly rounder and his eyes a lighter shade of green. Their grandmother and the Baker boys' granny were cousins. They always had trouble figuring out if they were fourth or fifth or twice removed, or what the actual kinship was, so they just told everyone that they were cousins.

"So how is your grandma?" Tag asked.

"Mam is feisty as ever. Says if we don't behave out here, she'll get in her truck and come straighten us out," Paxton said as he tossed a duffel bag through the door.

"And she means it," Maverick assured them. "Now, about those beers?"

"Tag, you pop the tops on four beers. I'll help Paxton bring in the rest of their stuff," Hud said.

"Appreciate it." Paxton nodded. "My brother packed everything but the splinters from the boards on the corral."

"You might find those in my bags, so be gentle."

Maverick's drawl was a mixture of West Texas and Irish. His grandmother had come over from Ireland, but she hadn't totally lost her accent, and the brothers had spent a lot of time with her. "So the place don't look as bad as I thought it might. From what I can see from the drive onto the property, the fences are shabby. It's a wonder your cattle haven't broken through and gone visitin' the neighbors before now. I guess doin' some proper fencin' is the first order of business this summer?"

"And plowin' and plantin'." Hud heard the last of the comment as he came inside with a huge duffel bag on his shoulders. "Then we've been workin' with Emily's new husband, Justin, on a design for a bunkhouse so we won't be all crowded up in this little place. We might have the ranch lookin' pretty good in five years and be ready to expand if the neighbors down the road ever want to sell."

Maverick pointed toward a bag that Hud brought inside. "That one can go out to the barn to put in storage. Don't need what's in it until winter."

Paxton came in behind Hud with another load. "Guess this one can too. Where's the barn?"

Hud turned around and headed outside. "Y'all might as well come on and go with us. We still got enough daylight left to show off our new ranch while we drink our beers."

"Just barely." Tag grinned and then flinched. "Ouch!"

"Noticed that you've already been in trouble," Maverick said. "What happened?"

"It's a long story." Tag brought up the rear as they all paraded out of the house.

"That ends in the emergency room with Nikki Grady," Hud teased.

"I remember her." Paxton tossed the bag he'd brought back from the house over into the bed of the truck. "A cute little dark-haired woman with the biggest brown eyes. Emily's friend who was in the wedding last month, right? Seems I remember you hangin' around her a lot at the wedding reception."

Paxton and Hud slid into the backseat, leaving the front passenger seat for Tag.

Maverick got behind the wheel. "I'll drive. You tell me where to go, Tag. You talked that pretty girl into a night out with you yet?"

"No, he hasn't," Hud spoke up. "I think he might have lost his mojo."

"Surely not," Paxton chuckled. "All of us hit a dry spell every now and then, but it will rain again someday."

"I'm beginnin' to wonder," Tag said.

Chapter Three

Nikki was always on duty during the weekend, but sometimes if the staff got in a bind, she'd pull another twenty-four-hour shift through the week. When her phone pinged that morning, she figured it was the hospital calling. She was already headed to the kitchen to jerk her scrubs from the clothes dryer when she answered.

"Nikki, I need help. This is overwhelming me." Emily's voice sounded like she might cry, and that was so unlike her friend, who usually took any bull by the horns, spit in its eye, and then wrestled it to the ground.

"I'm on my way," Nikki said. "Want to stay on the phone while I drive out to the ranch? And am I going to the cabin or to the new house?"

"Cabin and I'll be fine until you get here." Emily sounded relieved.

Nikki slung her purse over her shoulder, slipped a pair of flip-flops on her feet, and locked the door behind her as she started down the stairs to her car. "Should I pick up maple iced doughnuts or ice cream?"

"Doughnuts would be great. I'll put on a pot of coffee. See you in a few," Emily said.

Nikki's pulse settled down a little after she heard that. Ice cream was reserved for big problems, so this wasn't too huge. Most likely, Emily was ready to throw things at Tag for getting into a fight that wasn't any of his business. They'd eat half a dozen doughnuts, drink several cups of coffee, and talk it out. Then everything would be fine.

Even after stopping at the doughnut place's drive-through, Nikki made it all the way to the back side of the Longhorn Canyon Ranch in record time. Emily was sitting on the porch when she parked. Two big mugs of steaming coffee sat on a small table between two white rocking chairs.

"You're smiling," Nikki called out as she opened the car door and grabbed the bag of doughnuts from the passenger seat. "I drove like a bat out of hell because you were crying."

"Yep, but when you said you'd come help me, I knew everything would be fine." Emily motioned to the other rocking chair and then held out her hand for the bag. "There's so many decisions about the house that need to be made, and it overwhelmed me. And my brothers living on the next ranch over doesn't help either. Mama calls me every day for a report on them." She took a doughnut from the bag and dipped it in the coffee. "And last night, the two hired hands from back home arrived, so now it's like having four brothers over there. You remember Maverick and Paxton?" She handed the bag to Nikki and tucked a strand of red hair back behind her ear.

"Oh, yes." Nikki sat down in the chair. "Two tall good-looking cowboys with a little bit of an Irish lilt in their Texas drawl. I didn't know they were going to be part of your brother's ranch. Did you give Tag a dressin' down for those stitches?"

Emily's chair stopped rocking and she sat forward, her blue eyes as big as saucers. "What stitches? What has he done now?"

Nikki wouldn't want to be Tag when his sister found out about his barroom brawl. Emily was a tall woman—plus-size they called it these days—and her temper knew no bounds when she was angry.

"I shouldn't have said anything." Nikki sipped her coffee. "That's his story to tell."

Tag chose that moment to step around the end of the cabin and sit down on the porch steps. "And I'll tell it, but first I'd sure like one of them doughnuts. Been a while since breakfast."

Nikki handed the bag toward him, but Emily reached out and snagged it.

"Talk first and then we'll see if you can have one. Good Lord, Tag! How many stitches are in your jaw and when did this happen?" Emily asked.

"Didn't count 'em and it happened on Saturday night or maybe it was after midnight and Sunday morning. I haven't been around because I knew you'd pitch a fit," Tag answered.

"Keep talking." She set the bag in her lap.

He explained pretty much the same way he'd told the doctor about what happened to get him cut open. "Now can I have a doughnut?"

She handed the bag over to him. "Are you pressing charges?"

"Nope. I shouldn't have meddled in it," he answered. "Maple is my favorite kind. Is there coffee left in the pot?"

Emily started to get up.

"Keep your seat, sis. I'll get it."

Tag's arm brushed against Nikki's shoulder as he went inside. That there were sparks didn't surprise her one bit. She needed to get back into the dating game—just not with him.

"What makes him so wild?" she whispered.

"That's his story too," Emily said. "You'll have to get him to tell you all about his teenage years sometime."

"Okay, then let's talk about what's got you upset this morning," Nikki said. "Are you doubting your decision to leave the retirement center?"

"No, that was a solid choice. I don't regret it one bit," Emily answered.

"What was a choice?" Tag asked as he carried a mug of coffee out in one hand and the pot in the other. "Thought I'd top off y'all's cups."

Nikki held hers up. "Thank you."

"You're just bein' nice so I won't tell Mama," Emily said.

He refilled her cup after he finished with Nikki's. "You want to be the cause of her worryin'?"

"Me? I didn't nearly get my throat slashed," Emily protested.

"Aww, come on, now. My jaw is a long way from my throat," he slung over his shoulder as he took the coffeepot back inside the cabin.

Nikki was jealous of the cabin, maybe even more so than the two-story house Emily and Justin were building on the other side of the ranch. The old cabin was peaceful and calm. Only the noise of an occasional truck or car driving past on the dirt road beyond the trees could be heard, or maybe a cow lowing off in the distance. According to what Emily had learned about the dwelling, it had been there for years and years. One big room housed the bedroom, living area, and small kitchen. The bathroom was tiny and had the world's smallest shower, but Emily, even at her size, loved every square foot of the place.

"Raising my own kids won't be as much trouble as Tag and Hud," Emily growled.

"Are you tellin' me that you're pregnant?" Nikki teased.

"Tell Mama that instead of about my unfortunate accident." Tag grinned as he joined them again. "She'll be so excited about a grandbaby that I won't matter anymore."

"I'm not pregnant." Emily glared at him.

Tag sat back down on the porch and reached into the bag for another doughnut. "What I came over here for is to ask if we might beg, borrow, or rent the cabin after you move into your house? We're findin' that our place is too little for four grown men, and we ain't even got to a weekend yet." He wiggled his dark brows. "It'll be the end of the summer before we can begin to build onto the house or put up a bunkhouse, and we need more room."

"Weekend?" Emily frowned. "What's that got to do with anything?"

"How are four big old cowboys going to bring home a girl if they get lucky on Saturday night?" Nikki answered.

"Well, well," Emily giggled. "I guess you'll have to shell out the money for a motel or else take turns using the tack room out in the barn."

"Come on, sis," Tag begged. "Will you just ask Justin? There'd only be two of us living in it anyway."

"There's one bed, Tag. Who'd sleep on the sofa?" Emily asked.

"Okay, then just one of us. I'll volunteer even though I can't turn around in that shower. Don't know how you do it." Tag touched his wounded jaw and looked at her with sad eyes.

"I'm not going to feel sorry for you, so don't play that wounded hero card with me," Emily declared. "However, if Justin wants to rent the cabin to you, that's between y'all. If he does let you move in, you could always turn the living room over at your ranch house into a bedroom and then the other three could have a little privacy."

"Thank you." Tag finished off the doughnut and took a sip of coffee. "I never thought of that. You're a genius, sis. I'll leave you ladies to whatever you were talking about when I got here. I'm going to see Justin and offer to help any way I can to get y'all out of this cabin and into your new house."

With that, he disappeared around the end of the cabin, and in a little while they heard the faint roar of a four-wheeler somewhere over to the east.

"Must've rode up close to the fence and then walked on over here." Emily sighed.

"I didn't hear anything before," Nikki said.

"Me neither. I imagine the sound of your car kind of masked the noise. But now to my problem, Justin's mama is driving me crazy," Emily said. "She calls every day to see how things are going with the house and wants to add her two cents to every decision. She thinks we shouldn't have carpet. The new thing is vinyl plank that looks like hardwood. And she keeps sending me pictures of crystal punch bowls and candlesticks. I don't like all that stuff!"

"Tell her that you don't," Nikki advised, and finished off her coffee.

"She's only trying to help, I'm sure, but I've got different tastes than she does." Emily sighed. "I don't want to hurt her feelings just when we're beginning to get along."

"Sounds like you're between one of those rocks and a hard place," Nikki said.

"Okay, let's turn this thing around. You've met my mama," Emily said.

Nikki wasn't sure she liked where this might be headed, but she nodded. "Of course I have. I stayed at the ranch out there in West Texas for a week before the wedding and a day afterwards."

"Okay, let's say that you fell in love with Hud." Emily pulled the last doughnut from the bag and took a bite.

"Why Hud? Why not Tag or Matthew?" Nikki asked.

"Tag is too wild for you, and Matthew is too uppity. Anyway, let's say that you fell in love with Hud, and y'all got married. You were building a house just the way you wanted it, and my mama got all up in your business. You know how bossy and tough she is, so think about it." Emily was about to take another bite when Beau, the ranch dog, ran up to her side. She pinched off a big chunk of the doughnut and held it out to him.

Nikki could have sworn that the dog, a mix between a blue tick hound and a Catahoula, smiled at Emily when he'd devoured the doughnut. He wagged his tail and laid a paw on her lap.

"You're worse than my brothers." Emily broke off another piece and gave it to him, and then turned to Nikki. "Well, what would you do?"

"Your mama likes me," Nikki answered.

"It's true Gloria and I didn't get off on the best foot. I want to stay on her good side without having to give in all the time." Emily gave Beau the last of the doughnut. "That's all of it. So all the begging won't do you a bit of good."

Nikki hated confrontation. Always had. Probably always would. "I understand where you're comin' from, and it would be tough on me to stand up to your mama and tell her to butt out. But I'd do it."

"Then you're tougher than you look because I'm not sure I'd tell my mama to butt out if she told me how to furnish my new house," Emily laughed. "But today, I've got to make the decision about where to use tile or carpet. Justin says that he doesn't care as long as it's soft on his bare feet. Will you go with me over to Wichita Falls and help me?"

"Of course," Nikki agreed. "Let's get nachos on our way through Nocona."

"Sounds great." Emily stood up. "I'll get my purse."

"I'll make a dash through the bathroom before we leave." Nikki headed into the bathroom and stood in front of the small mirror above the wall sink. She stared at her reflection and thought about what Emily had said about her being married to Hud. She didn't feel a thing for him. Why, oh, why did she always have to be attracted to the wrong cowboy? Hud was a sweetheart—funny, kind, and almost as sexy as Tag.

Almost, she thought, *only counts in horseshoes and hand grenades.*

*   *   *

Tag found Justin throwing small hay bales onto a trailer over in the north part of the Longhorn Canyon. Chris Stapleton's "Tennessee Whiskey" was blasting from the truck radio. A vision of Nikki flashed through his mind as Tag pulled his gloves from the hip pocket of his jeans and shoved his hands down into them. He picked up a bale and threw it up to Levi, who was stacking the bales on the trailer.

"You ain't got enough work over on your place?" Justin asked. "Not that I'm complainin' one bit. I'll take all the help I can get."

"Got a favor to ask and I ain't one to stand by if there's

work to be done." Tag matched Justin, bale for bale. They were about the same height and weight, and both had blue eyes, but that's where the similarities ended. Justin's eyes were that steely blue that could look as cold as ice. Tag's were the color of the summer sky.

"Hey, remember there's only one of me and two of y'all," Levi said.

"Favor?" Justin asked.

"How much longer until you and my sister move into the house?" Tag asked.

"A week. Ten days at the most. You want to help us move in?"

"Don't mind a bit, but I was wonderin' if I could rent the cabin when y'all do. Maverick and Paxton are over on our place. Man, it's crowded," Tag answered.

"I'd tell you to move your help into our bunkhouses, but the kids will be here in a few weeks. Still, if you need the space until they get here, you're welcome." Justin stopped, took bottles of water from a cooler, and tossed one each to Levi and Tag. "Let's take a break. Trailer is full, so we'll need to take it to the barn."

"Thanks." Tag twisted the top off his bottle and took a long draw.

All three of them sat down on the ground on the shady side of the truck. Levi removed his straw hat and wiped sweat from his angular face with the tail of his T-shirt. His brown hair was plastered to his head. Even his eyelashes had droplets of sweat on them.

"I'll be glad to get this all in the barn. It's supposed to rain tomorrow. Looks like we only got one more trailer full after this." Levi downed half his bottle of water before he came up for air.

"I appreciate the offer of the bunkhouses, but we'd just

as soon stay over on our place. The cabin isn't far from the fence separating the Longhorn Canyon from our ranch, so I thought I could make a gate and"—Tag hesitated and took another drink before he went on—"and kind of go back and forth that way if you was willin' to rent to me. I'd be the only one livin' there and it wouldn't be for long, just until we can get a bunkhouse thrown up over on…" Another pause. "Dammit! We really need to get a brand and a name to the place."

"I can't rent to family. Wouldn't be right," Justin said. "But you're welcome to use the cabin as long as you want. Soon as we get moved out, consider it yours. I can't imagine being cooped up with three other grown cowboys in that little house. And if you want to put in a gate or a stile, just go right ahead."

"Thank you." Tag held out his hand.

Justin shook with him. "Remember, now, that bathroom is tiny."

"I can live with it," Tag said.

"You got any ideas for your ranch name?" Levi asked.

"A few but none we like. We're Longhorn fans, but y'all already got the Longhorn Canyon brand," Tag answered.

"Canyon Creek runs through your property as well as ours," Levi said.

"I like that. Has a nice ring. Canyon Creek Ranch," Tag said. "I'll have to talk to Hud about it and get Maverick and Paxton's thoughts. But I sure like it. Let's get this trailer taken to the barn, and I'll help y'all stack it before I get back to my fencin' business."

Justin stood up. "Thank you. Three of us can get the job done quicker than two. We got our hired help out workin' on fences and doin' some plowin'."

"Ranchin' ain't for sissies," Levi chuckled as he got to

his feet and dusted off the seat of his jeans. "But it gets into the blood and nothing else satisfies a cowboy."

"You got that right," Tag agreed.

After they'd unloaded and stacked the hay, Tag drove his four-wheeler back over to his ranch. He stopped at the entrance, where a wooden sign with JOHNSON RANCH emblazoned on it used to hang, and imagined one with Canyon Creek up there. The brand could be two Cs, back-to-back with a wavy line under them for the creek that snaked through his property. He liked it, but now he'd have to convince Hud, and dammit, his brother had to mull over everything for days before he made a decision.

Hud barely glanced up from driving T-posts when Tag hopped off the vehicle. "Where'd you disappear to?"

"Went over to face the music with Emily." He picked up a post and stepped off eight feet.

"How'd she take it? Is she goin' to tattle to Mama?" Hud chuckled.

"I'm not sure. Nikki had already told her," Tag answered. "I talked to Justin and he said whichever one of us wants to can use the cabin when they move out. It's not that far."

"I'm not living over there," Hud said. "Have you been in that bathroom? You have to practically take a shower on your knees. Besides, me and the guys have been talkin' this mornin'. We think we should turn the house into a bunkhouse until we can get one built. We can use the living room as another bedroom."

Tag drove the metal post into the ground. "Emily suggested the same thing, and I'm willing to move into the cabin."

"All it's got is that little window air conditioner. Remember how hot it got when we went over there for supper with Emily and Justin?"

"I'll take the living room," Paxton said from twenty feet ahead, where he was taking down the old wooden fence posts and rolling up the rusty barbed wire. "But only if I can have the tack room in the barn when I get lucky on Saturday night."

"What makes you so sure you'll get lucky?" Hud asked.

"Just feel it in my bones." Paxton grinned.

"No A/C out there. I guess old Eli Johnson never got frisky in the barn," Hud said.

"I'll be glad to have a bedroom to myself. I'll get rid of those twin beds and put in a king." Maverick stretched new barbed wire between the posts. "And y'all are gettin' too far ahead of me."

Tag finished with the post he was driving and went back to help Maverick. "Guess you are stringing five wires to our every one post."

"Can we store the twin beds in the barn?" Paxton asked. "I'd like to buy a bigger one too. Hey, I just thought of something. You're not doing us a big favor by moving to the cabin. You'll have it all to yourself. Talk about a chick magnet."

Tag's mind flashed on Nikki again, and in this picture, a heart-shaped magnet was glued to her scrubs. When he crooked his finger, it pulled her straight into his arms.

Yeah, right, he thought. *Like she said, I'd have to change my ways. You can't teach an old dog like me new tricks, especially when they mean changing a whole lifestyle.*

Chapter Four

Nikki drove between the concrete pillars on either side of the arched wrought-iron sign for Hogeye-Celeste Cemetery. She always made the trip out east of town to visit her brother's grave on his birthday, September 30; at Christmas; and on May 8, the day he died. She parked on the gravel road closest to his grave and reached over into the backseat for the gerbera daisies she'd gotten at the florist that morning. Flowers for a twelve-year-old boy hardly seemed appropriate, but daisies were better than roses—at least in her way of thinking.

She sat down in front of the small headstone and laid the flowers at the base. She traced his name, Quint Grady, with her fingertip and then the birth and death dates. Not much to say about a little guy who'd fought so hard to live. She could tell stories about his humor, even when everyone finally accepted the fact that even if by a miracle a bone marrow donor did show up with a match, his body wasn't strong enough for the transplant.

She pulled a few weeds, wiped tears away with the back of her hand, and said, "I'm sorry. I promised I wouldn't cry for you when you were gone, but I still miss you." She pulled up the tail of her T-shirt and dried her face. "Let's try this again. You always made me laugh, Quint. We had to stick together to survive all that tension in the house between Mama and Daddy. I missed you when you left us. Daddy left that next week after your funeral and Mama went to bed. For a whole year, Quint, and I was only fourteen. The cooking, paying bills, shopping for food, and all that fell on me. I used to spend hours in your bedroom unloading my problems on you."

The crunch of car tires on gravel caused her to look over her shoulder. It wasn't her mother's fifteen-year-old vehicle, but then Nikki wouldn't expect it to be. She'd never known Wilma to visit Quint's grave even once after the day of the funeral. Wilma was so wrapped up in her own ailments, real or imaginary, that she had little time for anyone else. Looking back, Nikki realized that's the way it had always been. Wilma was always sick or dying with something. When Quint died, she'd convinced herself that she was coming down with leukemia. She'd taken to her bed and only got out of it at meal time and when she had to go to the bathroom. A year later, she declared that she was in remission. Nikki didn't have the heart or energy to tell her that wasn't the way things worked. She was just glad that her mother was willing to take over some of the cooking and the housework again, even if it did mean that they ate at exactly the same time every day and the house had to be spotlessly clean at all times.

The vehicle stopped and the window came down partway. A man wearing a baseball cap and mirrored sunglasses stared her way for a few minutes before he moved on. Most likely he was looking for a specific grave site, she thought, and it wasn't in that area. She moved around behind the tombstone to take care of the weeds back there.

"There now," she said when she finished and stood up. "I've got you all prettied up for another few months. I miss you, Quint. Even yet, I miss you." She wiped a tear from her cheek and blew a kiss toward the big white fluffy clouds in the sky.

When she got into her car and drove away from the cemetery, the same vehicle that had been looking for a grave pulled in behind her. It followed her to the snow cone stand, where she ordered a rainbow with cherry, grape, and orange— Quint's favorite and her own little tradition on the anniversary of his death. On his birthday she bought a cupcake, put a candle on it, and sang the birthday song. At Christmas, she made iced sugar cookies and ate the Santa one in his memory.

She handed the girl behind the window two dollars when she handed her the snow cone and told her to keep the change. Then she drove straight to the park where she and Quint had spent so much time before he got sick. Sitting on the bench under a shade tree, she could picture him over there on the slide. He'd always been small for his age, but he had a big heart and a smile to match it.

Eating the snow cone, she noticed that same car from the cemetery passing slowly on the far side of the park. Had it been a pickup, she would have figured it was Tag, pretending to stalk her as a joke. But it was a fairly new shiny black sedan. Maybe a Lincoln or a Caddy—all cars looked alike to Nikki these days. The window rolled down but only for a moment; then the car slowly moved back out onto the road and disappeared.

Nikki looked up at the pale blue sky and sent up a short prayer. *You could send me a friend today, Lord. I could sure use one.*

*   *   *

Tag was on his way back to the ranch from Bowie with a trailer loaded with fence posts and rolls of barbed wire. They'd run out of both in the middle of the afternoon, and he'd been sent to get more while the other three guys began to clean out the barn. In a couple of weeks, the east pasture would be ready to cut and bale, and Tag would sure like to have new fences up on one side of the ranch by then.

The radio was blaring and he was keeping time to the music on the steering wheel with his thumbs and singing along to Clay Hollis's song "Can't Let a Good Thing Get Away." Listening to the words, he wondered how many good things he'd let get away from him somewhere along the bumpy road his life had been on for more than a decade.

He grinned and didn't even wince when it hurt. The next song was "Live Like You Were Dying." That told him that no matter how many good women might have slipped through his fingers, he'd sown lots of wild oats for both him and his friend Duke Fields, who'd died in a motorcycle crash when they were both only seventeen.

He was singing along with the lyrics about riding a bull named Fumanchu when his phone rang. He turned the volume down and answered, "Hey, Billy Tom, what's up?"

"Lots of good things. Want in on some fun and make some money at the same time?" Billy Tom slurred his words.

Tag glanced at the clock on the dashboard. "Little early to be hittin' the bottle on a weekday, ain't it, Billy Tom?"

"Man, I ain't drunk. I'm high," Billy Tom said. "And me and the old boys are back in town, ready to romp and stomp. You with us?"

"Sorry, man, I've left the panhandle. I'm out here in"—

Tag hesitated—"another part of the state tryin' to turn a ragged-ass ranch into something profitable."

Billy Tom chuckled. "The boys will be real sad if you don't join us. We're ready to ride again. Meet us at the old stompin' grounds on Saturday night. Surely you can take a weekend off and hear our proposition. It'll only cost you a thousand dollars. We just need to rent a truck. It'll be a..." He paused so long that Tag thought he'd lost the connection.

"You still there or did that weed knock you on your ass?" Tag asked.

"Nah, man, where was I? Oh, we need a little investment. We got a new guy who can turn a thousand into ten thousand," Billy Tom said.

"No thanks. That buys a lot of fence posts and barbed wire. I'll pass. Y'all go on and have a good time," Tag said.

"Your loss, man, but just in case you change your mind, I'm going to tell the gang that you're with us. Just think of what a rush it'd be to have some fun like the old days when Duke was still with us."

Tag heard the roar of a motorcycle coming to life and then the call ended. He'd cut ties with Billy Tom and those guys more than five years ago. Tag lived close to the edge, but those guys went beyond that. They'd ride their motorcycles off a virtual cliff into the water thinking they could go so fast that they'd never sink. They were downright crazy and sometimes even illegal in their stunts, and Tag was glad he hadn't told Billy Tom exactly where he'd moved.

He turned up the radio to an old song from Vince Gill, "Go Rest High on That Mountain." He took the next right and found himself in a small parking lot at the city park. He pulled into a space, turned off the engine, removed his sunglasses, put his head on the steering wheel, and let the tears flow. What he was feeling was as fresh and raw as what he'd felt the day they'd lowered his best friend's casket into that deep hole while that same song echoed through the flat country of West Texas.

In spite of being named for John Wayne, Duke had been a small kid until they were juniors in high school. At the beginning of the school year, he'd barely reached Tag's shoulder. By the end of that same year, he'd outweighed Tag by thirty pounds and was an inch taller. That summer, the two of them used a big chunk of their savings from hauling hay to buy motorcycles. And that's when they got tangled up with Billy Tom and his posse of four other guys who all owned motorcycles.

Tag finally raised his head, dried his eyes, and put his sunglasses back on. That's when he realized that Nikki was sitting out there on a park bench eating a snow cone. He picked up his hat from the passenger seat, settled it on his head, and started the engine. But another song on the radio caught his attention and he stopped to listen to Vince Gill sing "Whenever You Come Around."

"I get it, Duke, I get it," he whispered as he shut off the engine, got out of the truck, and headed toward Nikki. She waved at him and smiled. That was a good sign, wasn't it?

*   *   *

Lord, this was not who I was thinkin' about, Nikki thought as Tag made his way across the playground toward her. *But, hey, if this is all you can do on short notice, I'll try not to bitch.*

Tag sat down beside her on the bench and she offered her snow cone. "Not much left, but it's cold and tastes pretty good on a hot day like this."

He took it and ate several bites before handing it back to

her. "I left a little so you could have the last of it. What're you doin' out here?"

"I might ask you the same thing." She finished off the last bite and tossed the empty cup at a nearby trash can.

"Missed that shot," he said as he stood and picked up the cup and trashed it.

"Thank you," she said.

"It wasn't a three-pointer, but at least I made the basket." He sat back down.

A full foot of space separated them, but the temperature rose by ten degrees. She wiped sweat from her forehead with the back of her hand. "Hot, ain't it?"

"It's Texas. We have four seasons. Hot, Hotter, Hottest, and Hot as Hell. We're just now to Hotter, but Hot as Hell is comin'," he chuckled.

"What in the world are you doing here, Tag?"

"It's a long story, but the truth is that a song on the radio brought back some tough memories. I couldn't drive with tears in my eyes," he said.

Nikki reached up and removed his sunglasses. His eyes were red and faint streaks were still visible down his cheeks. "Did the tears burn when they hit the stitches?"

"Little bit." He took his glasses from her fingers and put them back on.

"What was the song?" she asked.

"Vince was singing 'Go Rest High on That Mountain.' It gets me every time," he answered.

A lump the size of a grapefruit formed in her throat. They'd played that song at Quint's funeral, and even the guitar and piano lead-in made her cry. She quickly wiped at her eyes.

"Gets you, too, does it?" Tag asked.

She tried to swallow down the lump, but it wouldn't

budge. A vision of her precious little brother lying in that blue casket flashed before her eyes as the song played in her head. "Yes, it does," she whispered.

"My best friend and I bought our first motorcycles between our junior and senior years of high school. It wasn't a gang, but it was a rough bunch that we got tangled up with. They'd robbed a convenience store and were speeding out of town on their cycles. I learned later that they were going to an old cabin that Billy Tom's great-grandpa had used to run moonshine out of years before."

Another tear ran down his cheek, but he didn't even flinch when it pooled up in the stitches. "I've never told anyone this before. Don't know why I'm doin' it now. Guess after all these years, I just need to get it off my chest. You won't tell Emily, will you?"

"Not if you ask me not to." Nikki's mind flashed on another picture of her brother the first time he had gotten a nosebleed at the park.

"Don't tell Mama," he'd begged. "She won't let us come back if you do. She'll think I've got something horrible that she'll catch."

He was only seven that year, and yet the two of them already knew their mother's problems too well. At that age, kids shouldn't have even been at the park alone, much less worried about their mother's reaction to a bloody nose. But Wilma hadn't cared where they went or how long they were gone.

"I'm asking you not to, then." Tag's voice caught in his throat. "My friend Duke and I were riding our cycles out on the dirt road and being reckless when we saw the other guys. They came down the road five abreast, riding so fast that they were a blur with a cloud of dust behind them. We pulled off to the side to let them pass."

"Did the cops catch you?"

He shook his head. "Evidently the guys had lost them when they turned off on the dirt road, but we'd been wild and crazy with those guys all summer, so we wanted to see what they were into that night. Billy Tom motioned for us to follow, so we did. We didn't know about the big tree limb that had fallen over the road to the old cabin since the last time we were there. The first five split and went around it, but Duke never even saw it coming."

"Oh. My. God!" Nikki's hand shot up to cover her mouth.

Tag removed his sunglasses and leaned his head back against the bench. "My tire was about six inches from that tree when I came to a stop. Billy Tom and the others didn't even know Duke was hurt. I called 911 and held him in my arms until they got there, but he breathed his last on the way to the hospital. They played Vince Gill's song at his funeral, and every time I hear it, it tears my heart out."

She laid her hand on his shoulder. "I'm so sorry, Tag."

"Me too, Nikki. I got even wilder after that. I'm pretty sure Hud got his first motorcycle just to keep me out of trouble." He covered her hand with his. "Thanks for listening."

"That explains one of the stickers on your truck. What about the other one? The one with Tim McGraw's song on it?" She slipped her hand free.

"First time I heard 'Live Like You Were Dying' it seemed like Duke was speakin' to me right from the grave," he answered. "So I've lived every day with that in mind."

"Ever get any other messages from him, like it's time to put that song in your past and move on?" she asked.

"If I do, I don't pay much attention to them," Tag answered. "I still haven't ridden a bull named Fumanchu, and I haven't been skydiving."

Neither have you. Quint's voice was real in her head.

And I don't intend to do either one, she argued.

"Well, darlin'." Tag's blue eyes scanned her body from her toes to the top of her head. "Now you know my darkest secret. Will you go out with me now?"

"Not until you ride that bull and go skydiving. If you live through those two, then we might talk about it," she answered.

He picked up her hand and kissed the knuckles. "I'll have to get that done in the near future."

"I'll be waiting in the ER when you do." She smiled up at him.

Chapter Five

Tag glared at his reflection in the bathroom mirror. The stitches were still there, a blatant reminder that he wasn't going to ride a bull or a bronc that night at the rodeo. If Emily hadn't been going, he might have paid the fee for a late entry and ignored what Dr. Richards said. But the whole family had plans to attend, and besides, she'd insisted on going with him for his appointment.

"You goin' to stay in there all evenin' primpin' like a little girl?" Maverick yelled through the door.

Tag unlocked the door, picked up his toiletry kit, and stepped out into the hallway. "All yours," he said, vowing to himself that he wouldn't complain one time about the tiny bathroom in the cabin. At least he wouldn't have to share it with three other smart-mouthed cowboys.

When Tag reached the living room, Hud looked up from the shabby sofa and grinned. "All dressed up and no bull to ride. I can't remember the last time you had to sit in the stands at a rodeo."

"Me neither, and I don't like it," Tag growled.

"Then don't get hit in the face with a beer bottle," Hud said. "Too bad Nikki is working tonight so you won't even have anyone to flirt with."

"There are other women in this part of the state." Tag moved Hud's gear bag from the old wooden rocking chair in the corner and sat down.

"We've been here a whole month, and you haven't gone home with one of those 'other women.'" Hud made finger quotes around the last two words. "Or brought them home with you either."

"My mojo's in a slump," Tag said.

Paxton came through the front door. "You girls gonna sit here discussin' your feelin's all day, or are we goin' to go hang on to a bronc for eight seconds?"

Maverick joined them from the hallway. "Hey, I might want to talk about my feelin's, too, if I had the chance at a girl like Nikki Grady."

Tag whipped around and shot an accusatory glare at his brother.

Hud held up both palms defensively. "I didn't say a word."

"But Emily did," Maverick said. "When we were over there last night helping her move a few boxes, she told us you've been flirtin' up a storm with her friend Nikki."

Hud grinned. "Just think, if Tag got serious about her, he'd have his own personal nurse to put him back together when he gets into his crazy rebel mode."

"Sounds like a win-win to me."

Tag rolled his eyes. "We've got a rodeo waiting for us. Let's get this show on the road."

Paxton led the way outside, and Tag broke away from the group and headed toward his truck. "I'll be rootin' for all y'all, but don't wait up for me. I might not be home tonight."

*   *   *

Nikki hadn't planned on going to the rodeo, but Emily had begged her to be there for moral support to help handle Justin's mom, Gloria. Even though she'd have to go from the rodeo to the hospital for her shift, she couldn't say no to a friend in need.

The parking lot was full when Nikki arrived, but she finally nosed into a spot not too far from the stands. She adjusted the rearview mirror so she could see her reflection and reapplied bright red lipstick. Then she picked up her hat from the passenger seat, got out of the car, and settled it on her head. Wearing skinny jeans with rhinestones on the hip pockets, a Western shirt that hugged her body, and a big blinged-out belt, she pretty much blended in with the crowd.

It wasn't difficult to find Emily, not when the last of the day's sunrays lit up her red hair like a beacon. Then she waved, stood up, and pointed to the spot she'd saved beside her. Nikki held up a hand and started in that direction, but she almost came to a screeching halt when she got close enough to see that she'd be sitting between Emily and Tag.

"Well, hello." She tried to keep her voice cheerful as she sat down. "I thought you'd be riding some bull named Fumanchu tonight."

"Dr. Richards said no," Emily answered for Tag.

"Poor baby." Nikki patted him on the knee that was pressed against hers.

"Higher, darlin'." He winked.

"Poor baby," she said in a high, squeaky voice.

"Looks like you've met your match," Emily laughed. "I hope you can cheer him up, Nikki. He's been in a pout all day."

"I don't pout," he protested. "I'm just disappointed. I haven't got to ride a bull since we got here."

Justin's brother and sister-in-law, Cade and Retta, were sitting right behind Tag. Cade patted him on the shoulder and said, "There'll be ranch rodeos all summer. You'll get your chance. What's this about Fumanchu? Don't think I've ever heard of that bull."

"Two point seven seconds on a bull named Fumanchu," Retta reminded him of the line in the song. "It's part of that song from years ago that Tim McGraw sang about living like you were dying."

"You got it," Tag said.

"Y'all've come a long way this week," Cade said. "The fence is sure lookin' good over at your place."

"Thanks," Tag said.

"I knew he'd feel better once he got here. He's been an old bear because he can't ride tonight," Emily whispered in Nikki's right ear. "And thank you so much for coming. Gloria has been nice since she got here, but I can tell she's not happy about the carpet."

"It's your house," Nikki said out the side of her mouth.

"Amen," Emily agreed.

Retta leaned over her very pregnant stomach and whispered, "It'll get better, but you have to stand your ground."

"Oh. My. Lord," Emily gasped. "Did you hear what we…"

Retta shook her head. "But I can sure imagine what you

were talking about. Claire and I both had to come to terms with her."

"Claire too?" Emily frowned.

"Levi might not be a blood brother to Justin and Cade, but Gloria tried to put her two cents in on everything they were doin' with their house too," Retta said. "I'm glad Cade and I got the ranch house and didn't have to start from scratch. Shhh..."

Justin and Cade's parents, Gloria and Vernon, joined them, sitting down at the end of the row. Then Levi and Claire took the seats that had been reserved for them right in front of Tag and Nikki. Claire wasn't any taller than Nikki, and she owned a little quilt shop in Sunset. Levi, the foreman at the Longhorn Canyon Ranch, kept her hand in his when they sat down.

"Hey, son." Gloria smiled up at Justin. "Is the carpet all in now? Is it time to move in?"

"Got it done today," he answered. "Surprised me and Emily. We figured it'd take a week or more, but they had it in stock and they didn't have a big job starting until Monday, so they sent a crew over this morning. We've put some boxes in the kitchen already. Tomorrow we'll get the big stuff in."

"We thought we'd have Sunday dinner at our place," Emily said. "Everyone is invited."

"That sounds great. I'll bring the dessert," Gloria offered.

"Thank you," Emily said.

"Are y'all ready to get this rodeo going?" the announcer asked from the press box above them. The whole area reverberated when the crowd clapped, whistled, rang cow bells, and stomped their feet on the wooden stands.

"Lively bunch tonight, aren't they?" Tag asked.

"I'd say so." She nodded.

"First bull rider tonight is Maverick Callahan. He's a newcomer to this area, but he's got ten years under his belt from around the Tulia and Happy, Texas, area. Let's give Maverick a big hand as he gets into position on Blue Devil, one of the meanest bulls in the business," the announcer said.

The chute opened and the bull came out bucking. Maverick managed to hang on for five seconds before he landed in the dirt. He got up, brushed off the seat of his pants, removed his cowboy hat, and bowed to the crowd. Women threw kisses at him and the applause was deafening.

"Guess he's got a fan base up there in the stands," the announcer said. "Watch the number two chute for our next contestant, Riley Tate."

"You sure look pretty tonight." Tag leaned toward Nikki until their shoulders were touching. "I'd ask you to dance if we were at a bar."

"This is not my first rodeo, Tag, and I'm not a virgin to the Rusty Spur either," she said.

"So you'd dance with me?"

She shrugged. "It would depend on how many other sexy cowboys were lined up askin' me to dance."

"So you think I'm sexy?" He smiled, showing off perfect white teeth.

"Of course. I'm not blind," she told him.

"And yet, you won't go out with me?"

"That's right," she answered. "Most sexy cowboys are only interested in the sprint and not the marathon."

"Oh, honey, I like to take my time and do the job right no matter what I'm doing." His eyelid slid shut in a slow, sexy wink.

"You are impossible," Nikki said.

"Yes, he is," Emily agreed from her other side. "And he

loves to argue. The only way to get him to shut up is to ignore him. Want to change places with me?"

"No, I can handle him."

"Be gentle with me. My heart is fragile." Tag picked up her hand and laid it on his chest.

Nikki quickly pulled her hand free, but she couldn't stop the blush creeping up to her cheeks or the image of her hand on other parts of his body.

"And now we have another newcomer to our area. This young man and his brother, Tag, bought a ranch over around Sunset. Give it up for Hud Baker, folks. If he stays on Mister Salty for eight seconds, he'll be tonight's winner," the announcer said.

Glad to have something to focus on, Nikki kept her eyes on Hud when he came out of the chute. Mister Salty's hind legs pointed at the moon, and his nose smelled the dirt. At three seconds people jumped to their feet and started screaming Hud's name. At six, they were stomping the wooden bleachers again. At eight, the noise could've been heard all the way to the hospital. A rescue rider rode out and helped him get loose from the bull. When Hud's feet were firmly on the ground, he removed his straw hat and threw it like a Frisbee into the crowd. A teenage girl grabbed it and shoved it down on her head.

Emily leaned around Nikki and poked Tag on the arm. "Hud just stole your hat move."

"He deserves it. That rascal was a mean critter," Tag said. "I hope that girl gets him to sign the hat for her when the rodeo is over."

"Or sooner." Nikki motioned to the arena.

Hud jumped over the fence and the girl tried to give him back the hat, but he shook his head, pulled a pen from his pocket, and signed the brim. She and all her teenage friends blew kisses at him, and the crowd roared as he made his way back across the dirt toward the chutes.

"Nice move," Nikki said. "Have you given away many hats?"

"Quite a few over the years," Tag answered. "When I throw the next one, I'll make sure I sling it your way."

"Honey, I could never use your hat. Your head is way bigger than mine."

"You could just hang it above your bed and dream about me," he suggested.

I don't need a hat to do that, she thought.

When it was time for her to leave, she gave Emily a quick hug and stood up. "I have to work on Sunday, but I'll see you on Tuesday. If you don't have everything moved in and arranged by then, I'll be glad to help."

She was easing past Tag when he stood up. In the crowded stands, that put them chest to chest.

"Don't I get a hug too?" he asked.

"I don't think so. Nearly everyone in these stands knows me, Tag. And as much as the ladies have been salivating over you all evening, they'd never move in on what they thought was my territory. So if you ever want to get lucky again, then you better just shake my hand," she said.

His blue eyes were twinkling when he tipped up her chin and kissed her right on the mouth. The sweet kiss rocked her all the way to her toes and made her knees weak. She was surprised that she was still standing when it ended.

"That's all the gettin' lucky I need," he whispered so close to her ear that his warm breath caressed that sensitive spot on her neck. "Good night, Nikki. I'm sure I'll see you around."

"Good night, Tag," she said. "I hope it's not in the ER this weekend."

Her legs were still shaky when she reached the hospital a few minutes later. Rosemary met her in the waiting room and whistled through her teeth. "Where have you been?"

"That ranch rodeo." Nikki kept walking through the doors and down the hall to the tiny on-call room. She locked the door, slid down the back of it, and put her head on her knees. If a relatively chaste kiss could affect her this way, she couldn't help but wonder what a night in bed with Tag would be like.

She got her bearings enough to rise up, get changed into her scrubs, and grab her tablet from her locker. When she opened the door, Rosemary was standing right beside it. "Was that good-lookin' cowboy from last weekend riding tonight?"

"No, he wasn't." Nikki headed toward the break room for the briefing.

Rosemary followed behind her. "Was he there?"

"Yep," Nikki said.

Rosemary dug deep into the pocket of her scrub pants when her phone rang. "Hello," she answered as she kept pace with Nikki. "Is that so? Not half an hour ago?"

"Everything okay?" Nikki held the break room door open for Rosemary to enter first.

"Just fine," Rosemary said. "But after we get done with our briefing, I want to know all about that kiss you got right out there in public from that cowboy. Have you been holding something back from me?"

*   *   *

Tag glanced over at Nikki's cowgirl hat, which was sitting beside him in the truck. He should've just let Emily take it home with her, but truth was that he wanted to see Nikki again that night. Her lips on his had stirred something inside him that he thought had died years ago—a feeling of hope in life.

It was well past midnight when he marched into the ER waiting room. The place was as quiet as a tomb. Evidently no fights had broken out, no kid had shoved a bean up his nose, and no poor old cowboy had taken a blow to his jaw-bone. Surprisingly enough, there wasn't even a cowboy with a sprained ankle or a busted-up wrist from the rodeo that night. Hat with a feather stuck in a pink band in his hand, he went straight to the desk where folks checked in.

"Fill out this form, and I'll get someone to take a look at you as quick as possible," the lady said.

"I'm not here because I'm sick. I just need to see Nikki Grady. I'm returning something of hers." Tag held up the hat.

The lady looked up at him and her eyes widened in surprise. "You're that cowboy who came in last week with lots of blood."

"That would be me," he said.

"Wait right here, and I'll get Nikki. We're not very busy, so she should be right here soon," she said as she hurried through a door.

Nikki's expression was one of pure shock when she ran into the waiting room. She stopped so quickly that the soles of her shoes made a squeaking noise. "Where are you hurt this time?"

He held up the hat. "Not hurt. Just bringing your hat to you. You left it behind."

"Thanks. You didn't have to do that." She took it from him.

"It only meant driving a couple more blocks. Little quieter here tonight than it was last week at this time." He didn't want to just turn and walk away.

"Give it a couple of hours. The place gets to hoppin' about the time the bars close down." She smiled up at him.

He had to either get out of there or else he was going to kiss her again, and unless he was dead wrong, all those faces peering through the window in front of him were her coworkers. He might not mind the gossip that would spread like wildfire, but he didn't want to put her job at risk in any way.

"Okay, then, see you around," he said bluntly, and left without looking back.

When he reached his truck, he started the engine and turned on the radio. Leaning his head back, he thought about the night his best friend Duke had died. The two of them had been badass—and look where it had gotten them both. Duke was dead and here he was about to turn thirty before long.

"Give me something," he said to the DJ who was talking about the weather. "I don't care if it's going to rain or storm. I want a song to help me like Tim McGraw's has all these years."

Grow up and move on. Duke's high voice popped into his head. For a big guy, he sounded like a girl most of the time. But then his tone did have advantages—he could mimic Vince Gill so well that it was downright uncanny.

"And now we've got an hour of slow country classics comin' your way," the DJ said. "And we'll be playing five for five. Keep track and be the fifth caller. Tell me the song and the artist, and you'll win two tickets to Six Flags Over Texas."

The music started and Tag sighed. "That's Vince Gill and Patty Loveless singin' 'My Kind of Woman, My Kind of Man.' I'm not sure I'd ever be the kind of man any woman could trust, not with my past."

His phone rang just as that song ended. Hoping it was Nikki, his hands trembled as he dragged it out of his hip pocket. But it was Billy Tom.

"What's up?" he asked.

"You out on some old dirt road listenin' to country music with a woman?" Billy Tom chuckled.

"I'm in the emergency room parking lot listenin' to music all by myself," Tag answered. "Was there something you wanted?"

"Well, the boys and I have a little plan."

"I don't want any part of your little plans anymore," Tag answered coldly.

"Aw, c'mon. You used to be fun. Besides, all we're asking is to borrow your truck for a little bit. Hell, you should come too—for old times' sake."

"Is what you're about to do one hundred percent, guaran-damn-teed legal?" Tag asked.

"Hell no!" Billy Tom answered.

"Then my answer is hell no. I've got too much tied up in my ranch to be gettin' in trouble with the law again."

"You've gotten soft and old," Billy Tom complained. "When I come to see you on a brand-spankin'-new Harley, you'll be sorry you didn't buy into our venture."

"Maybe so, but when I come to see you in jail, you'll be sorry you didn't grow up," Tag told him.

Billy Tom ended the call without another word.

Tag turned the radio louder, put the pickup in gear, and backed out of the parking lot. His thumbs kept time on the steering wheel as he listened to Bebe Rexha singing "Meant to Be." When the song ended, he shut off the engine, got out of the truck, and walked across the yard. He wasn't ready to go inside yet, so he sat down on the porch. A redbone coonhound puppy settled in beside him.

"Where'd you come from?" Tag scratched the pup's ears and it crawled right up into his lap.

"Are you lost or did someone dump you?"

The dog whimpered and looked up at him with begging eyes.

"Hungry?"

"I thought I heard someone talking out here." Hud came out of the house and joined him. "Guess you didn't get lucky since you're home before daylight. See you've met our new hired hand. He's promised to protect the cattle if we feed him and scratch his ears every now and then."

"Where'd he come from?" Tag asked.

"Lady at the rodeo brought a litter in the back of her truck. She was giving them away. This was the last one and we felt sorry for him. We haven't named him yet. Thought we'd make that decision together." Hud sat down in a lawn chair on the porch. "Tomorrow evening we're going to decide for sure that we're going to name the ranch Canyon Creek or something else and we'll name this dog."

"Guess we're really puttin' down roots, aren't we?"

"It's time," Hud said.

"What's meant to be will be, and what's not meant to be might be anyway," he muttered.

"Granny says that all the time. What made you think of that when we're talkin' about roots?" Hud asked.

"Just a song I heard on the radio." Tag wondered if that statement his grandmother said about "what's not meant to be might be" could ever involve someone like Nikki.

Chapter Six

Nikki yawned as she got into her vehicle Monday morning at 1:00 a.m. Stars twinkled around the quarter moon, which looked like it was hanging right in the middle of her windshield. It had been the worst kind of weekend—slow and steady. The cubicles were never filled to capacity, and yet there was at least one patient all the time. The shifts went by faster when she was hopping busy and tired to the bone when she dropped to sleep.

She rolled the kinks from her neck and stuck the key in the ignition. Just as she put the car in reverse, her phone rang and startled her into hitting the brakes so hard that she flew backward against the seat with a thud. Her heart was thumping around in her chest like a bass drum when she finally found her phone in the bottom of her purse.

"Hello," she said.

"Someone is trying to break into my house," her mother whispered.

"Did you call the police?" Nikki whipped the car around and headed toward her mother's house on the other side of town.

"No, I called you," Wilma answered. "They're cutting the screen door. I can hear them."

"Is it locked?"

"Of course. Both locks on the screen door and four on the big door," she answered.

"Where are you?"

"Hiding in the bedroom closet. I've got a quilt over my head so whoever it is can't find me."

Nikki jacked it up another five miles per hour. "I'm on my way. Stay where you are. You call the police. They should be there by the time I am."

"If I'd wanted the police, I would've called them, not you. And turn off your lights and kind of coast into the driveway. If Mrs. Thomas sees or hears you, she'll come runnin' over here. She stays up all hours of the night and watches television. She's really fat, so you know she's eating the whole time," Wilma whispered.

"Hang up, Mama, and call 911," Nikki almost shouted.

"I will not!" Wilma yelled right back at her.

Nikki called the number herself, and the patrol car must've been in the area because a policeman was already there when she parked her car. She met him halfway between her car and the house. Her phone rang, but she ignored it.

"It was just a raccoon. He ran when I started up on the porch," the policeman said. "I walked all around the house but didn't see any signs. I think everything is all right."

"Thank you," Nikki told him as her phone rang again.

"Call if you need us. Better to be safe than sorry." He headed back to the patrol car.

"Yes, sir," Nikki said as she answered the phone.

"I told you not to call the police," Wilma said. "Thank God Mrs. Thomas didn't see the police car."

Nikki rolled her eyes and plopped down on the ladder-back chair beside the door. Why it was there had always been a mystery because Wilma never went outside to sit in it. "It was a raccoon scratching at the door, not a person. He's gone now. Open the door and let me in."

"I'd have to undo all the locks and put my dentures back in and my hair is a mess. I can't let you in or Mrs. Thomas might still see the lights and come over here. Weren't you listening when I told you that she's up all night watching television? You just go on home and get some sleep. We'll talk tonight at seven like we always do," Wilma said. "I'll get this quilt folded and put back on the shelf, and take one of my anxiety pills before I go back to bed. Now go away before Mrs. Thomas realizes you're here."

Nikki shook her head slowly and added paranoia to the list of her mother's disorders. "Four locks on the door. If she dies in that house, we'll have to break the door down."

She made her way from the house to her car and tried to close the door as quietly as possible so Mrs. Thomas wouldn't come rushing out of her house. Then she drove straight to her apartment. Once she was inside, she left a trail of clothing across the living room floor and was naked by the time she reached the bathroom. A three-minute shower took the smell of the hospital off her body. She dried off and didn't even bother with underpants or a nightshirt, just curled up between the cool sheets naked and was asleep the second her head hit the pillow.

The digital clock beside her bed rolled over to six-fifteen just as she opened her eyes, but she wasn't sure if it was a.m. or p.m. Surely she hadn't slept over fourteen hours!

Light peeking through the mini-blinds made her realize she'd done just that. Her mother would call in less than an hour, and there was no way she could talk to Wilma without a cup or two of coffee. She pulled on some pajama pants and a tank top, plodded barefoot to the kitchen, and put a pot on the stove. While the water dripped through the grounds, she gathered up her dirty scrubs from last night, shoved them into the washing machine with two other sets from her suitcase, started the cycle, and then checked her phone.

There were two messages from Emily: Got tied up. Moving in Monday night.

The second one read: Please come after you talk to your mama.

The third one was from Rosemary: Can you take an eight-hour on Wednesday? Four to midnight?

She hurriedly sent one to Emily: Be there at eight.

Then one to Rosemary: Of course.

She ate an energy bar and a banana while she waited on the coffee and was on her second cup when the phone rang. "Hello, Mama. Did you sleep well after we got rid of the intruder last night?"

"Don't you make light of that, young lady," Wilma scolded. "My heart was racin' worse than it does when I mop the kitchen. I swear if that woman you hired would do a better job of cleanin' this place, it would be nice. You should fire her and hire someone else. I liked that first lady. She did things right."

Nikki bit her tongue to keep from reminding Wilma that she'd hated the first lady and complained about her constantly. "Mama, I'm not firing Sharon. She does a fine job. Besides, what would Mrs. Thomas say if Sharon didn't show up every Friday? You want gossip going all over your neighborhood about you?" Nikki put the phone on speaker and brushed her teeth while her mother ranted about Mrs. Thomas being so nosy.

"When did you have four locks put on your door?" Nikki asked when she could get a word in edgewise.

"If you'd come over here to see me more often, then you'd know when. An old woman like me livin' alone needs to be protected."

Nikki got fully dressed and pulled her hair up in a ponytail while Wilma went on and on about a newspaper article she'd read where a ninety-year-old woman's house was broken into.

"She shot the man right in the leg and held him at gunpoint until the police came," Wilma said.

"You want a gun?" Nikki asked.

"Good Lord, no. I believe in Jesus and He'll protect me."

So why all the locks? Nikki thought.

"Speakin' of Jesus," her mother was saying. "You missed a good sermon at church yesterday. I just wish our new pastor would get married. Folks are goin' to talk about the way he's so friendly with the single women," Wilma said. "And those brothers of Emily's were there too. That one they call Tag is pure trouble. You can tell by his eyes, and I heard that he kissed you at a rodeo. I hope that's all he's done. You stay away from that boy, Nikki. You set your cap on the preacher. If I was a healthier woman, I'd invite him and you to lunch so you could meet him. I wouldn't mind you marryin' a preacher."

Yeah, right, Nikki thought. *I might not be ready for a rebel like Tag Baker, but I'll never be preacher's wife material—and there's another line that goes right behind it that says I don't want to be, either.*

"Mama, you are only sixty-one years old, and Dr. Richards told you that you're very healthy for someone your age," Nikki said.

"What does he know? He's not even a real doctor. He just works in the emergency room like you do, and he only runs the clinic two days a week. It takes forever to get an appointment, and I need him to check my blood again. I've been taking calcium and a whole bunch of other supplements, but I think I might need something to keep my hair from falling out."

So let's see, Nikki thought, *we've covered the preacher and Mama's hair. We still have the phone service and her newspaper not arriving on time, and then I'll try to set up a supper and she will give me some absurd reason why she can't go.*

Nikki picked up her purse and phone, made sure she had her keys, and locked the door behind her.

"Have you called the news office about my paper?" her mother asked, but she didn't wait for an answer. "It's gettin' here later and later, and that boy who delivers it *knows* he's supposed to lay it on the chair, but he just throws it from the road and hits my door." She stopped for a breath. "I want it laid on the chair at three thirty so I have an hour to go through it before I have supper."

"You call and tell them. I've got a job, too, Mama," Nikki said.

"I never thought a child of mine would talk to me the way you do," Wilma pouted. "I don't ask that much of you, and you won't even call the newspaper for me."

No guilt trips today, Mama, Nikki thought. *I've been on too many as it is.*

"How about I pick you up for supper tomorrow night? We'll go to the Mexican place." She got into the car and hurriedly started the engine so she could turn on the air conditioner.

"I hear a car motor. Are you coming over here? You

know the last show I watch comes on at eight. This is a bad time for you to visit." Wilma's voice was so high-pitched that it was squeaky.

"Then tomorrow evening?" Nikki backed up and headed toward the ranch.

"You know very well I can't eat that kind of food. My stomach is too delicate, and besides, you always want to eat later than four thirty, and if I don't take my meds on time, then I don't feel good the next day. We'll have to do it another day. It's eight o'clock. Good night, Nikki," Wilma said.

"Good night, Mama." The only way Nikki could actually visit her mother was to drop in unexpectedly somewhere between one and four, and even then it upset Wilma's schedule. It had been a while since she'd seen her mother in person so she made a mental note to go see her that week.

She turned on the radio and scanned through the stations until she found the one out of Dallas that she liked. "Here's an old one for y'all this evening," the DJ said. "Trent Tomlinson singing 'One Wing in the Fire.'"

Nikki smiled as she drove through Sunset and turned to head east. The lyrics talked about a man's father being an angel with no halo and one wing in the fire. That made her think of Tag and hope that he was at Emily's that evening. He certainly didn't have a halo, and there was no doubt that one of his wings smelled a lot like smoke, but still she liked the way easy banter between them lifted her spirits. After listening to her mother, for what seemed like eternity, she needed it, or maybe a shot of Jack Daniel's— or better yet, both.

*   *   *

The prickly feeling on the back of Tag's neck told him that Nikki had arrived. No other woman had ever affected him like that, but all his senses heightened whenever she was near. He and Hud were moving an old upright piano into Justin and Emily's place that had come all the way from Tulia when the movers brought Emily's things. It was the last big piece of furniture, and it weighed as much as a baby elephant.

"You're going to owe me"—Tag stopped to catch his breath—"a chocolate cake when this is done." He and Hud set the piano down where Emily wanted it. He glanced around the room, and he couldn't locate Nikki, but she had to be somewhere. His neck hairs did not lie.

"And Granny said to tell you that it will definitely need to be tuned after it's been hauled around like this." Hud pulled a bandana from his hip pocket and wiped sweat from his brow.

"There's a chocolate cake already made and on the kitchen counter," Emily said. "And I've got a piano man coming this week to tune it. I thought we'd have way too much stuff, but I was wrong. This is one big house."

Justin wrapped his arms around her waist from behind and buried his face in her hair. "We'll pick out one antique a year on our anniversary. How's that sound?"

She turned around and hugged him tightly. "That's so romantic. I love it."

A streak of pure jealousy shot through Tag, something he'd never felt before, not even as a child when he had to share everything with a twin brother. But right then, he wanted someone to look at him the way Emily looked at Justin.

Holy crap! What's happening to me? He raised his hand to his forehead. *There must be something in the water that's causing my brain to deteriorate.*

Then there was Nikki. She came out of the bathroom at the end of the hall. Wearing jeans, a cute little off-the-shoulder cotton top, and flip-flops, she looked fantastic.

"Looks like you big strong men have been workin' hard today." She smiled.

Dammit! Why did the clouds part when she grinned? She wasn't the most beautiful woman he'd ever set his eyes on, so what was it about her that jacked his pulse up several notches?

How many women have ever turned you down? His granny's voice was clear in his head. *Go on, count them.*

He dropped his hand and thought about the question, but he couldn't hold up a single finger. So what to do about this sudden attraction? Maybe do his best to get her to spend a night in his bed? Surely that would get her out of his system, and then he could go back to being his normal self.

Jackass! His grandmother's voice was very plain. *If you treat that girl like one of your one-night stands, I'm going to kick your ass myself. She deserves better than that.*

When he turned back around, Nikki was nowhere to be seen.

"She's in the kitchen," Hud whispered. "She's helpin' Emily put things in the cabinets."

"What makes you think I was lookin' for her?" Tag asked.

"I'm your twin, remember. I know what you're thinkin' all the time." Hud fell back on the sofa. "I'm worn out. Bring me a piece of chocolate cake. That'll give you a good reason to be in there with the women folks. Oh, and I'd like a cold beer too."

Tag sat down beside him. "I was thinkin' you might bring me cake and beer since I lifted more than you did today."

"Hey, now," Maverick said from across the room. "I believe I outdid you both, and me and Paxton ain't even family, so maybe y'all ought to tote beers to us."

"I'll settle this argument." Nikki brought in a tray laden with four thick wedges of double-layer fudge cake on plates and four bottles of beer. She put it in the middle of the coffee table. "You'll have to feed yourselves, no matter how tired you are."

"Be a sport and at least feed me the first bite so I can get enough energy to lift the fork," Tag teased.

"I don't think so, cowboy. That would be eating your cake and having it too—now, wouldn't it?"

"I tell you, Tag, this place has sucked the mojo right out of you." Maverick leaned forward and picked up a piece of cake and a fork. "Do you want a full-fledged funeral when you die or just a graveside service?"

"Darlin', please don't die. I'd be obligated to go to the funeral to console Emily and my black suit is too small," Nikki teased.

Tag shivered at the thought of death and then reached for the last piece of cake. "With friends like y'all, who needs enemies?" For some insane and unknown reason, Billy Tom's smiling face came to mind. Had he always been an enemy or at one point had he been the friend that Tag thought he was?

"Praise the Lord!" Nikki raised a hand as high as it would go. "He's eaten two bites. I think he's goin' to live. I'll let Emily know so she won't ruin her makeup with tears." She disappeared out of the room.

"You should marry that woman," Maverick said.

"The M-word scares me worse than that smartass remark about death." Tag grabbed a beer and tipped it up.

"Amen, brother." Paxton nodded. "We're all still young."

"And we've got wild oats to sow," Maverick agreed.

"You're preachin' to the choir," Tag chuckled.

"He's lyin' to us, guys," Hud said. "He's been thinkin' about settlin' down ever since we got here. I can see it in his eyes."

"For being my twin, you don't know me at all." Tag was tempted to call Billy Tom and ask him exactly what kind of trouble he and the boys were about to get into, just to prove his point.

*   *   *

The kitchen was put together by nine thirty, and the guys had all left except for Justin. He'd fallen asleep in a recliner in the living room. Emily poured two glasses of white wine and handed one to Nikki, and motioned to the two stools shoved up under the bar.

"Thank you for coming tonight. Gloria was here this afternoon and thought she could arrange everything. I gave her a hug and told her that I wanted to do things my way since this was my dream house. She decided that she needed to make a trip to town to get her nails done if she couldn't 'help.'" Emily put finger quotes around the last word. "I am too tired to put up with the guilt trip that she'd send me on if she came back tonight, so I'm glad she didn't. I just want to go to bed with Justin this first night in our own home and have him hold me until we both fall asleep."

"Talk about a guilt trip." Nikki told Emily about talking on the phone with her mother. "I tell myself every week that I won't let her affect me like this, but I always do."

"Yep." Emily took a sip of wine. "I'll fight a forest fire with only a cup of water most of the time, so why do I let Gloria get my goat?"

"You want her to like you since she's Justin's mama. I want my mama to love me, and maybe she does as much as she's capable to love anyone other than herself. You and I make quite the pair, don't we?" Nikki downed her wine and put a hand over the top of her glass when Emily started to refill it.

"That's enough for me. I've got to drive home," she said. "And I should be going just in case you and Justin have enough energy to christen this first night in your new home." She slid off the barstool and gave Emily a sideways hug. "I love the house. Someday I hope to have what you've got here."

"I want that for you too." Emily pushed her stool back and followed Nikki to the door. "Call me. Tomorrow is going to be like the day after Christmas. We were busy with the wedding, and the house, and now it's all done. Until the kids come out to the ranch for summer camp in a few weeks, I'll have free time."

"Will do. And if you get bored, just come on over to my place. We'll break out the ice cream." Nikki waved over her shoulder on her way to her car.

She sensed that someone was behind her and noticed that black Lincoln she'd seen a few days ago. She whipped around to confront whoever it might be and ran right into Tag's chest.

"Hey, I didn't mean to spook you." He caught her in his arms to keep them both from falling. "I forgot to get the key to the cabin from Emily. I'm moving in there tomorrow."

Her first instinct was to take a step backward, but his hold felt almost comforting. She looked up to find his gaze glued to her face.

His forefinger traced her cheek, then cupped her jaw, and then he bent enough that his lips covered hers in a scalding hot kiss. He picked her up and set her on the hood of her car. The tip of his tongue touched her lips, and she opened enough to let him inside, and she discovered that the taste of chocolate and beer together was pretty damned amazing.

"I've wanted to do that since the wedding," he whispered when the kiss ended, and their foreheads were pressed together as they both tried to catch their breath.

If she were to be perfectly honest, she had wanted him to kiss her, too, but she couldn't make herself say the words. Then of all the crazy things to come out of her mouth, she heard herself ask, "Want some help moving in tomorrow? I don't have to work again until Wednesday at four."

Did I really say that out loud?

The expression on Tag's face told her that she had, and she couldn't very well take them back.

"That would be great. I've got to work until dusk. We've got to get the fences bull tight so we can turn our cattle out of the corral. We've got good grass," he said. "And I'm talking too much. If you'll give me your address, I'll pick you up at your place at seven, and maybe we can start with some grocery shopping."

"I'll be ready," she said.

He brushed a sweet kiss across her forehead and disappeared into the darkness. With trembling legs, she slid off the hood and got into her car. When she turned the key to start the engine, the radio was on and the Pistol Annies were singing "I Feel a Sin Comin' On." It seemed like every single word had been written just for her that evening, especially when Miranda Lambert said that she had a shiver all the way down to the bone.

Chapter Seven

Tag stood in the middle of the cabin floor and did a slow 360-degree turn. For the first time in his life, he wouldn't be living in the same house with his twin brother. Had he made the right decision volunteering to take the cabin?

"Hey," Emily yelled as she entered the cabin. "I had half an hour, so thought I'd stop by and see how things are going."

Her red ponytail stuck out the hole in the back of a baseball hat and her face was bright red from heat and sweat. Hay stuck to her long-sleeved chambray shirt and her faded jeans.

"Glad to see you, sis. Can I get you a glass of sweet tea or a root beer? That and water is all you left for me in the fridge."

"Water is good," she said as she sat down on the sofa. "We're haulin' hay between this place and our new house. I really stopped by to talk to you more than anything."

He took two bottles of water from the small refrigerator, uncapped them, and handed one to her. "Am I in trouble?" Had she somehow found out about Billy Tom calling him?

"Should you be?" She gave him the evil sister eye.

The old wooden rocking chair groaned when he sat down. "Sounds like this thing needs some tightening up."

"Now that the house is built, I want to be part of the ranchin' business—outside of course. Retta can have that book work in the ranch house. I'm not sure Justin wants me to be in the field." She paused and tipped up the water bottle for a long drink. "I'm more than willing to go help Retta however I can if she needs me when the baby comes. But I want to do more than cook and be a housewife."

Tag chuckled.

"It's not funny. I'm confused."

"Justin has a new beautiful wife. If I were him, I'd have misgivings about you being in the field too. All those hired hands are lookin' at you. And you can bet they're layin' wagers as to who can throw more bales or stack them quicker than you. That makes you the person they're talkin' about," Tag said. "I'm surprised you're talkin' to me about this instead of Nikki."

"I need a man's viewpoint," she said. "Speakin' of Nikki, I hear that she's volunteered to help you do some shoppin' tonight. Tag, I know you and I know Nikki. She's my best friend. Promise me you won't have a fling with her and then break her heart."

"I promise," he agreed.

"That was quick. Where's my real brother, Tag? What have you done with him?"

He managed a weak smile. "I'm not sure, but I think I left him out in West Texas, and to be honest, I don't know what to do with this new critter inside me."

"I'm your sister. You can talk to me," Emily said.

"I'm twenty-nine years old, and I've sown so many wild oats that we'd have a silo full if we harvested them all. But I'm not ready to settle down or to live by myself. Do you realize that I've never lived away from Hud? That we've lived in the same house all of our lives, most of the time right across the hall from each other since the day we were born?"

"Of course I do," Emily said. "I think the old Tag is worrying about all these changes. He doesn't like them at all. He loved being the bad boy. But now the new Tag has the responsibilities of a ranch, two hired hands, and a dream to make it prosperous. The new one is fighting with the old one."

"Which one will win?" Tag asked.

"The one you feed. If you continue in your wild ways, then you're feedin' that one. The ranch will survive. Hud and the Callahan cowboys will see to that, so don't worry about being a failure there. If you feed this new responsible Tag, the old wild boy will gradually slink off to be nothing but a memory. It's up to you what you want to do with your life, little brother," she said.

"You sound like Granny. What if I don't know which one I want to feed?"

"I'll take that as a compliment, and, honey, another bit of her advice is that you can't ride two horses with one ass, especially across a raging river. When you go to sleep tonight, lie there in bed for ten minutes and think about going to the Rusty Spur this weekend, picking up a woman, and going home with her for a one-night stand. Then put that all away and think about settling down and coming home every night to a woman who will be there with you forever. Whichever one brings you peace, feed that one. Now, I've got to go. Enjoy the cabin." She stood up and tossed the empty water bottle across the room to the trash can.

"That was a three-pointer for sure." Tag hurled his bottle that way. It bounced off the wall, missed the mark, and rolled under the bed.

"Yep, and one more thing—if I find out you've brought one of your bar bunnies to this cabin, I'll kick you out, and that's a fact." Emily started for the door. "You can pony up the money for a hotel or go home with her."

When she was gone, Tag did another turn, taking in the whole one-room cabin again. A coffee table that had seen lots of boots propped on it sat in front of a well-worn sofa that faced a fireplace that wouldn't be used for many months. Behind the sofa was a table with four mismatched chairs. Two steps away in the back right corner there was a tiny kitchen area with an apartment-size stove and refrigerator, maybe five feet of cabinets, and a closet with a hot water tank. To the left was a nice king-size bed—he forgot to thank his sister for leaving the sheets and quilt—and a window air-conditioning unit. He'd always envisioned the first place he lived in on his own would look more like a bachelor pad and less like a home.

You've outgrown a damn bachelor pad, his granny's voice said sternly in his head. *It's time for you to grow up and settle down.*

*   *   *

Nikki didn't know whether she trusted herself enough to allow Tag to knock and invite him into her apartment, or if she should just wait on the steps for him to arrive. After the kiss from the night before, she finally decided that she'd better be sitting on the stairs when he drove up. She picked up her purse, locked the door behind her, and was halfway down when she heard a truck door slam. When she reached the bottom, he was opening the door for her.

"You're right on time," she said as she slid into the passenger seat.

"One of my many good qualities." His gaze held her spellbound.

"Well, I appreciate it." She blinked and looked away, but her heart was still racing. "Did you bring a list?" She took a deep breath and started down toward him.

He leaned on the door a moment. "I know for sure I need some towels and toilet paper."

"Have you ever lived on your own before? Not even in college?" she asked.

"Didn't go. All me and Hud wanted to be was ranchers, so we graduated high school and went on the full-time payroll the next Monday morning." When he started the truck, the radio was on the same country music station that she liked, but he quickly turned it off. "I love music. How about you?"

"Love country music and if I'm in a really funky mood, a little jazz, but only in small doses," she answered. "The cabin is really your first home away from home?"

"I guess the ranch house over on Canyon Creek is the first one, but Hud was with me there, and then Maverick and Paxton. The cabin is my first time to have a place all to myself."

"Do you even know how to do laundry, or cook or clean?" she asked.

"Oh, yes, ma'am. Mama lived by the goose and gander law. That meant that us boys had to learn all the stuff that Emily did, and she had to learn all the stuff we did on the ranch. I'm particular about laundry, and I can clean a house good enough to pass military inspection. And I can make the meanest ham and cheese sandwich and chili cheese nachos in the state," he said. "I'll be glad to make either one for you anytime you want to come by the cabin. Or if that doesn't sound good, I know how to nuke a bean burrito and open a bottle of beer."

"Sounds good to me," she said. "Take the next left."

"Thanks. I've never driven from this side of town before." He flipped on the turn signal.

"Canyon Creek? Is that what y'all decided to name the place?"

"Yep," he answered as he circled the parking lot in search of a spot. "Now we're trying to come up with a brand that we like. And we named the dog too."

"Dog?" She raised an eyebrow.

"Ranch has to have a dog. We're goin' to do our best to train him to be a cattle dog, but a redbone is really a coonhound. We named him Ol' Red, but we're just callin' him Red."

"For Blake Shelton's song, right?" she asked.

"You got it." Tag pulled into a parking space.

"Was he a stray?" Nikki asked as she got out of the truck and started toward the store.

"Nope. Some woman was giving them away at the rodeo. Hud snagged the last one." He fell in beside her. "You like dogs?"

"Love them and cats too. I'd get a cat, but I'm gone from Friday night at midnight until Sunday night for work. I'd feel guilty about leaving it alone that long," she said.

"Ever had pets when you were a kid?"

"Oh, no!"

"That was pretty definite." The store's automatic doors opened, and he pulled a cart out from the line. "You want to push?"

"Make it easier if I do. Then you can have both hands free to load it up. And it was definite. You'd have to know my mother to understand." She pushed the cart inside and made a right to go to the housewares side of the store to look at towels.

"Does she live in that apartment with you?" he asked.

"Good Lord no!"

"Another definite answer." He pointed up to a sign that said towels were down that aisle. "How long have you lived alone?"

"Since the day I was eighteen. That was right after high school graduation. I've lived in the same apartment for over ten years now," she answered.

A cart bumped into hers when she turned the corner. "I'm so sorry," she started.

"I've told you a million times to watch where you're going," her mother scolded.

"Mama, what are you doing here at this time of night?" Nikki was totally in shock.

Wilma wore a trench coat buttoned up the neck and white dress gloves. Her dark brown hair was shoved up under a plastic shower cap. Red and white polka dotted rain boots peeked out from under the hem of her coat.

"I'm tired of Mrs. Thomas coming over on Tuesdays, so I decided to get out and do some shopping. I was out of calcium and my morning stomach pills, and since you refuse to shop for me anymore, I have to do it myself." She sighed.

"We've been over this, Mama. If I keep doing everything for you, you'll never get off the recliner or out of the house," Nikki said.

Wilma held up a gloved hand. "Don't sass me, but you can tell me what you're doin' with this hoodlum. My preacher is never going to marry you if you get a reputation with this . . . " She eyed Tag up and down with an evil look.

"Mama, this is Tag Baker. Tag, my mother, Wilma Grady." Nikki made introductions in a tone so cold that it would have put a fresh layer of ice over the North Pole.

"Pleasure to meet you, ma'am." Tag tipped his hat toward her.

Wilma gave him another disgusted look and turned back to Nikki. "I've got things to do. I have to be home by eight to see my show."

Nikki reached out and laid a hand on Wilma's shoulder. "Mama, it's hot outside. Why are you dressed like this?"

"Germs." Wilma shrugged off her hand. "You never know what you'll catch in a place like this. I'll take a shower when I get home and use that bacteria-killin' soap to be sure. It'll get rid of anything that I might pick up in here. Woman in my condition don't need to take chances with germs. I'll talk to you on Monday." Her rubber boots made a squeaky sound on the tile as she hurried toward the checkout counter.

"I'm sorry," Nikki said to Tag.

"No need to apologize for something you have no control over," he said. "But now I see why you couldn't have pets."

"And that's just the tip of the iceberg," Nikki said. "Let's go buy towels and try to put what just happened behind us."

"Yes, ma'am." He began to study the colors, thickness, and size of each stack of towels.

She watched him and hoped that tomorrow morning she didn't find an email with a dozen new shots of people who go to Walmart in weird outfits with her mother among them. In some ways she felt sorry for Wilma. In other ways, she wished that she'd been born into a different family.

"Need a hamper?" she asked when he put a set of bath towels into the basket.

"Nope, brought that when we moved into the house, but

I do need soap of all kinds. Dish, laundry, and shower," he answered.

When they'd finished his shopping, they were lucky enough not to have to stand in line long and got everything loaded into his truck.

"You had supper?" he asked.

"I had a sandwich."

"I haven't eaten yet. Barely had time to get a shower after fencing and cutting hay all day. Want to join me for a burger or maybe a pizza?"

"I'd rather have some of those chili cheese nachos you were bragging about," she answered.

It might not be a good idea to be alone with Tag, but he'd met Wilma, and this was probably the last time he'd ever ask her out. After all, she had the same DNA and there was a possibility she could grow up to be just like her mother. Who was it that said if you wanted to know what a girl would look like when she got older, just take a look at her mother?

Besides, she'd been in the cabin many, many times in the past few months since Emily had moved into it with Justin. It had a homey feel to it, not a one-night-stand kind of aura.

"That can be arranged. Nachos and beer and ice cream afterwards," he said.

"Sounds good," she agreed. "But are you sure you want to be alone with me now that you've met my mother?"

"We all have skeletons in our closets, Nikki," he said. "In our part of the world, we don't hide our crazy relatives. We put them on the front porch with a glass of sweet tea and let them wave at all the cars that go by."

She giggled and then laughed and then snorted. "I'm picturing my mother on the porch with one of those beekeeper hats on her head."

His laughter was as deep as his drawl. "Why a bee bonnet?"

The laughter ended as quickly as it had started. "Because she's afraid to go out without protection for fear she'll get malaria."

"I understand." He gently laid a hand on her shoulder.

Was this Tag really the same playboy who'd tried to sweet-talk her into bed the night of Emily and Justin's wedding? Or was this just a new tactic with hopes that it would lead to a different result?

She was still pondering the questions when they reached the cabin, but not a single answer had fallen from the sky. "I'll help unload if you'll hand the sacks to me. I'm too short to reach over the truck bed."

A puppy barked a couple of times from the porch and then ran out to meet them. He found his way to Nikki first and wiggled all over. She stooped down to pet him and got a lick across her face for her efforts.

"You might as well go on and get a Catahoula now. This isn't ever going to be anything but a pet." She picked him up, and he fell over to lie in her arms like a baby.

"You pet him and I'll unload all this stuff," Tag said. "Might as well bring him on in the house and rock him. That'll keep him out from under my feet." He set two bags on the porch beside the door.

His phone rang, and he fished it out of his hip pocket and opened the door for her at the same time.

"He was waiting on the porch for us, and, no, I won't spoil him by letting him start staying in the house."

A long pause while he listened to whoever was on the other end of the line.

"It's not like that."

Another pause as she sat down in the rocking chair.

"I'll bring him back over in the morning. See y'all bright and early, and yes, I'll be there in time for breakfast," he said before he shoved the phone in his pocket.

He tossed the bags on the bed and went back outside, returning this time with three in each hand. They must've been heavier than the first ones because his biceps strained the fabric of the light blue knit shirt he wore. Nikki couldn't tear her eyes away from him and wondered how it would feel to wake up with Tag's strong arms around her.

"One more load," he said. "And then I'll make nachos while you take care of the baby."

"You got a deal," she told him.

He put away the groceries and then opened a can of chili and added several kinds of spices to it. Then he arranged chips on a platter that he'd bought that night and topped them with the chili and grated cheese. He nuked it all to melt the cheese and heat the chili, then added diced tomatoes and jalapeno pepper slices.

"Onions or not?" he asked.

"Not for me," she answered.

"Leaving the onions off," he said. "I'm not a big fan of them either." He put the platter in the middle of the table and opened two bottles of beer. "Dinner is ready, Your Highness. Red can nap on the sofa or go outside. His choice."

"But what about coyotes? Or hawks? Don't you worry that they'll kill him?" she asked.

"Not a redbone hound. He'll set up a howl and chase a coyote. That's his nature. And he's way too big for a hawk to carry off. I'd guess him at two to three months old," Tag said.

She set the dog on the floor, and he ran to the door. "That makes me feel better about him going outside. Give me time to wash my hands."

While Tag let the animal out, she went to the bathroom and washed the puppy smell from her hands and arms. She tiptoed to see her reflection in the mirror, and there was the same Nikki that she'd seen a month ago staring back at her. But this one had more questions in her eyes than the previous one—like even though the chemistry between her and Tag was undeniable, did she really want to take the next step with him? Was she setting herself up for heartbreak? And the biggest question of all was would it make things awkward with Emily?

She dried her hands and left the bathroom to find him holding a chair for her. "My first guest in my new home. Thank you for all your help and for coming over. It would be a sin to have to eat alone this first night."

"Well, when you get to the pearly gates, you be sure to let them know that I was the one who kept you from sinnin' tonight," she said.

"Well, dammit! I was hoping that since we broke bread—as in nachos together—it would wipe out the sin that will come after we get through supper." He grinned.

They were sure back on familiar ground now. "In your dreams, cowboy. Besides, Emily told me that she'd kick you out of your little piece of heaven here if you brought a woman home for the night. Last time I checked, I am a female."

"Yes, you definitely are, darlin'. I'll make a mental note to never attempt to date one of my sister's friends again, no matter how sexy and funny they are, because best friends share everything," he said. "Now, while we eat, tell me about yourself."

"Hasn't Emily already told you the Nikki Grady story? God, these nachos are fabulous. Better than any I've ever had at a Mexican restaurant," she said as she picked up another chip.

Tag shook his head. "All Emily's told me is that y'all worked together for a long time, and then you passed your RN test and went to work at the hospital. That was about the time that her Fab Five elderly buddies left the retirement center, right?"

The nachos were addictive. Like that commercial on television about potato chips, there was no way to eat just one. "Pretty much. That was when Emily decided to move to the ranch too. We all made a big change."

"I met those old folks at the wedding, and I've seen them at church the past couple of weeks, but I'd love to get to know them better. Emily says they're a hoot," he said.

She was sure that Bess, Patsy, and Sarah, the three elderly ladies from the retirement center, had already been swooning over him. That, and the fact that dogs loved him, too, had to be good signs, right?

"Have y'all adjusted to the change of not seeing those senior citizens every day?" he asked.

"Pretty much. Emily and I stop by the house the Fab Five bought together every couple of weeks and catch up on all their shenanigans. And, of course, she and I talk every day, except weekends when I'm working. How are you adapting to this big change in your life, Tag?"

"What did Emily tell you?"

"About?"

"Our talk this morning." He narrowed his eyes.

"Nothing except that you had one and that she forbade you to use this place as a brothel," she answered. "Let me tell you something, Tag Baker. Your sister would take a bullet to the head before she would betray a confidence. She told me what she said about you not bringing women here, but whatever else you told her is between y'all."

"Thank you." A smile covered his face. "And this cabin

is not a brothel. You have to pay for sex in those places. I've never charged."

She blushed at the idea of putting money on the bedside table as she left.

"As far as changes, darlin'." He leaned forward and his drawl got deeper. "Buying a ranch has been the biggest responsibility I've ever faced. I've never worked so hard or been as happy with the results or had dreams this big. Sometimes it overwhelms me."

She was almost as shocked by his admission as she'd been by her mother's appearance earlier that evening. "I thought you were ten feet tall and bulletproof, like Travis Tritt sings about. I didn't think anything would ever be an obstacle for you."

"Keep thinkin' that, darlin'."

It was after ten when he took her home and held her hand as they climbed the stairs side by side. She unlocked the door and turned to find him staring right into her eyes.

"I had a good time tonight, Tag," she said.

"Me too. When can I pick you up for a second date?"

"This wasn't a date," she told him. "It was a friend helping a friend move into his cabin and then having supper with him."

His hands cupped her face, thumbs brushing her cheeks. His palm felt like feathers dancing across the sensitive place on her neck. He leaned in for the kiss, and Nikki went up on her tiptoes.

She had been kissed before. She'd had long-term relationships. She'd had her heart broken more than once since she'd lived on her own. She'd made mistakes and learned from them. But nothing prepared her for the way she felt whenever Tag's lips met hers. The whole world disappeared in a flash, leaving only the two of them standing on a small upstairs porch with the moon and stars above them.

When the kiss ended, Tag took a step back and braced himself on the railing. "If that affected you the way it did me, then, darlin', this was definitely a date. Good night, Nikki."

He turned and walked away without looking back.

Normally she would have called Emily and confided in her about her evening, about the kiss and how it left her wanting more. But she couldn't tell Emily all that when she'd be talking about her brother. She threw herself on the sofa and finally called Patsy.

"Hello, Nikki. Are you all right? Do I need to get the other four up?" Patsy asked.

"I'm fine. I shouldn't be callin' this late, but I had to talk to someone," Nikki said.

"Darlin', I'm a night owl. You know that, and I'm here for you anytime you need me. So talk." Patsy was part of the Fab Five, as the five friends had dubbed themselves, and she was possibly the wildest one of the lot. She was a twin sister to Bess, and Sarah was their friend, right along with Otis and Larry. They were more like parents or grandparents to Nikki and Emily than just mere friends.

"I kissed Tag Baker tonight, and I liked it, and I can't talk to Emily about it. I can't like him, Patsy. I'm twenty-nine years old and ready to settle down. He's wild and never wants to be any other way, I'm afraid. Why am I attracted to the bad boys?"

Patsy giggled. "Because where's the fun in taming a sweet little preacher-type boy? You come on up here to Sunset and us girls will have a real face-to-face talk about this. And you're right, Emily would freak out, so don't tell her. Can you come tomorrow?"

"Have to work tomorrow. How about Thursday?" Nikki asked.

"That's even better. We'll send Otis and Larry to the store so we can have some time by ourselves. And, honey, if you liked that kiss, just imagine how he'd make you feel in the bedroom." She giggled again. "Or the hayloft."

"Patsy!" Nikki gasped.

"It's okay to dream, and thanks for callin'. It's been kind of dull around here since Emily and Justin got married. See you on Thursday at one o'clock. Don't eat a big lunch. We'll have snacks."

"Thanks, Patsy."

"Oh, no, baby girl. Thank you!"

The call ended and Nikki threw herself back on the sofa. Why couldn't Wilma invite her to have cookies and coffee or lemonade and treat her like a daughter instead of a liability?

*   *   *

When he got back to the cabin, Tag did what his sister had told him. He stretched out on the king-size bed and imagined always being that wild child he'd been since he and Duke got their first motorcycles. He closed his eyes and thought of the wind in his face, the dust boiling up behind him, and the thrill of going ninety miles an hour down a dirt road. He even thought about calling Billy Tom and asking if they could meet in Dallas some Saturday night so they could hit some biker bars.

Then he turned over in bed, pulled an extra pillow up next to his body, and put all those thoughts aside. He opened his eyes, looked at the ceiling; then he closed them again. He imagined that the pillow was someone he loved dearly, a woman like Nikki who'd be there waiting for him at the end of a long day on the ranch. Who would listen to his fears and share in his joys when the first new calf was born on the ranch, and at a later date when they could add more acreage to Canyon Creek. Who would cuddle with him before they went to sleep each night. The image was so real that his hand reached to stroke her long, dark hair before he remembered that what he was holding was just a pillow.

His eyes snapped open and he threw the pillow across the room. "Why is this so hard?" he asked himself.

No answer came.

Chapter Eight

By the time Nikki reached the ER waiting room that evening, she was wiping sweat from her forehead with the back of her hand. Once inside the cool room, she grabbed a fistful of tissues from the admitting clerk's desk and did a proper number on her face. Then she hit the hand sanitizer pump on her way back into the ER.

"Well, look at you," Rosemary said. "Is that twinkle in your eye because you've spent time with the sexy blue-eyed cowboy you were seen with last night at the store?"

"If anyone thinks they can hide anything in Bowie, Texas, they'd better think again. And what are you doin' here?"

"Same thing you are. The hospital is short staffed, so we both got called in. Let's hope we don't get it before we get our hours in," Rosemary said, and then whispered, "Is he as delicious as he looks?"

A deep crimson filled both of Nikki's cheeks. Good

Lord! She hadn't blushed this often in her whole life combined.

"Aha, he is, isn't he?"

"I wouldn't know, and we've got to get to reports." She whipped around and made a beeline for the break room.

The first name that popped up on her tablet was Sue Ann. Nikki covered her eyes and sighed. Talk about a buzzkill.

"She just got here a few minutes ago. I tried to assess her, but she told me to get the hell out and get you, Nikki. She's floating around and seeing spiders on the ceiling," the nurse who'd been on the eight-to-four shift said. "I hope you can do something with her."

"I'll do my best," Nikki said.

"There's a little boy from Nocona in number four. Leukemia in its last stages," the nurse said. "Dr. Richards said to give him whatever he needs to make him comfortable and ask his mother again if she wants to admit him. If she takes him home later tonight, then we should call hospice."

"I'll take that one," Rosemary said. "I can't do anything with Sue Ann."

Tears welled up in Nikki's eyes at the thought of a child dying. She knew this day would come someday, but she'd hoped that she'd have a harder heart when it did arrive.

"That's all we've got, ladies," the second nurse said. "Hopefully it'll be as slow for you as it has been for us. A heads-up—you'll probably be asked to pull a double, so get ready for it." They were both yawning when they left.

Rosemary touched Nikki on the shoulder. "You okay, kiddo?"

"Fine, just hurts me to hear about a child who's . . . well, you know," she said honestly.

"It's the job, darlin'. We do our best, especially with the

young ones. Now, let's get to it. You ready for a double and then the weekend too?"

Nikki nodded. "We'll have Thursday and Friday to catch up on sleep. Or at least I will. You've got kids and a husband."

"I won't bitch a single minute when I take my paycheck to the bank, though." Rosemary smiled. "Let me know if Sue Ann starts crawlin' the walls. I'll bring the restraints."

Nikki picked up her tablet, took a deep breath, and eased between the curtains into the cubicle with Sue Ann. "Hello, I'm kind of surprised to see you here so soon, and it's not even a weekend."

"It's devils," Sue Ann whispered. "I went to church Sunday after I was in here. I've got devils in me, and I took some pills to get rid of them."

"What did you take?" Nikki pulled up Sue Ann's chart.

"I don't know. Whatever was in the cabinet. Top shelf." She pointed to the ceiling. "That's where we kept Mama's pills."

"Sue Ann, your mama has been dead for ten years," Nikki said.

"Pills are still good, though, ain't they? Mama was a churchgoin' woman, so I figured her pills would get rid of the devils in my soul. Mama talks to me sometimes. I just have to be real quiet to hear her. She tells me to go to church and get right with the Lord," Sue Ann said.

Nikki stepped out of the cubicle and called the intern on duty. He was familiar with Sue Ann and told her to induce vomiting and call the psych ward. She went back into the cubicle with a dose of ipecac in her hand and thinking that compared to Sue Ann, her mother was the sanest person in the whole state of Texas.

"This is going to get the devil out of your soul, but you

have to drink it all," she told Sue Ann. "Don't sip it. Just throw it back like a tequila shot."

"You sure this will work? Don't you need to do one of the STI things where you put jelly on my stomach?" Sue Ann asked.

"No, Dr. Tillery said this is the very thing you need," Nikki assured her.

Sue Ann drew her eyebrows down into a solid line. "He's that good-lookin' new doctor, right? I like him. If Dr. Richards said to take it, then I'd throw it at the wall. I don't like that man. He don't believe I'm sick."

"Well, Dr. Tillery believes you. You take this to get rid of the devil and then we're going to admit you. How many of your mama's pills did you take?"

"Three bottles. Mama said that if I took them all that the devils would be gone and I'd be with her in heaven," Sue Ann whimpered.

"Well, honey, we're goin' to get rid of those mean things for you. Just take this," Nikki said.

Ten minutes later, Sue Ann had brought up dozens of undigested pills and was on her way up to the psych ward, where hopefully she would get some much-needed help. Unless, of course, history repeated itself and she checked herself out and went right back to the Rusty Spur. There was a very real possibility that she would be right back in the same cubicle with another devil or alien in her body come Saturday night or next Sunday morning.

Since they were short staffed, Nikki cleaned up the area and got it ready for the next patient. Then she slipped down the row and peeked into the room where the young boy was lying. His shaggy blond hair hung to his collar, and his eyes were sunken into his thin face. Frail hands held a computer game, but he finally dropped it and closed his eyes. She held her breath until his chest moved up and down a few times.

Other than the hair color, he reminded her so much of Quint those last days. If only she'd been a bone marrow donor, he'd be alive and well today. Or if they could have found a match for him before it was too late.

"We just got a call. Wreck out south of town and they're sending them here for first evaluations," Dr. Tillery said as he came out of his office. He peeked over Nikki's shoulder. "I hate it when they're kids."

"There's no way to find a bone marrow donor?" she asked.

"Too far along for that now. He's an only child, and from what I read in his charts, it would've taken a miracle to find a match," he said. "Better get ready for a rush. I understand there were six people hurt in the wreck, and I'm already going to ask you to work a double. You up for that?"

"Sure thing," she said.

* * *

Nikki was so bone tired when she left the hospital the next morning around eight thirty that all she wanted was a shower and a bed for at least twelve hours. Then she remembered that she'd told the ladies she would come to Sunset right after lunch.

"Oh well," she muttered. "That'll give me four hours of sleep."

She dragged her tired body up the steps and tried to wash away the smell of near death, blood, and tears in the shower. She forgot to turn off her phone when she fell facedown on her bed and wrapped the comforter around her. When she heard the ping, she glanced at it with bleary eyes. The text was from Patsy—she had forgotten that the Fab Five had promised to have dinner with Emily that day so they could see her new house. Could they postpone their time with Nikki until tomorrow? She sent a short message back that said: Sure thing. No problem.

While her eyes were semiopen, she read another one from Emily inviting her to the dinner. She sent one to her: Double shift. Need sleep. Rain check.

The last one was from Tag: Pick you up at eight on Thursday night. Have surprise for you.

I'll be ready, she replied.

Then she set her alarm clock for six, turned off her phone, and closed her eyes. The last thing she saw as she drifted off to sleep was Tag tipping his black hat toward her the first time she met him out in Tulia, Texas.

Chapter Nine

The apartment was straightened up, and Nikki was ready fifteen minutes early that evening. At first she thought she'd meet Tag on the steps like last time, but he said he had a surprise. If it was something that needed to be brought inside the apartment, then that would be awkward. After all, she'd been in his cabin—even shared nachos with him at his kitchen table, and talked about everything and nothing for a while. Not inviting him into her place would be downright rude.

She checked her reflection in the full-length mirror on the back of the bedroom door. She'd curled her hair, put on makeup, and chosen a brown-and-white-checkered sundress for the evening. Her brown cowboy boots matched it perfectly, but maybe she should have chosen sandals? Was she overdressed? Or worse, underdressed? Whatever, she didn't have time to change now.

After his comment about being on time, she expected

him to knock on the door at exactly eight o'clock. She was not disappointed, but the knock still startled her. She scanned the living room one more time to be sure everything was tidy before she opened the door.

Tag had a brown paper bag in his arms and a smile on his face. "You look gorgeous this evening. I'd thought we'd go for pizza, but since you're so dressed up, maybe we'll go somewhere nicer."

"Pizza sounds great." She couldn't keep her eyes off the bag. "I'm sorry. Please come in."

"Nice little place you got here." His eyes scanned the living room before he set the sack on the kitchen table. He removed a big round clear glass bowl first and carried it to the kitchen sink. Bright colored rocks were the first thing he added to the bowl before he filled it about halfway with water.

"I didn't know what your favorite color was, so I got the multicolored package," he said.

"What are you doing?" she asked.

"Fixin' up your surprise." He looked around again and set the bowl of water on an end table. Then he pulled out a small yellow container and set it beside the bowl.

"What is that?" she asked.

The last thing he brought out was a plastic bag with a goldfish in it. "This is your new pet. She can stay all by herself over the weekend. You only have to clean up after her about once a week and feed her every day. Maybe a little extra on Friday since she'll be all by herself all weekend. She told me that country music is her favorite, so you might want to leave the radio on while you're gone so it don't get lonesome."

For the first time in a very long while, Nikki was speechless.

"If you don't like it, I'll take it to the cabin." His eyes went to the floor, reminding her of her brother when their mother yelled at them about tracking dead leaves into the house or some other minor infraction that upset her perfect world.

"I love it. I'll tell her bedtime stories and let her listen to country music so she won't get lonely. Thank you, Tag." She took two steps forward and hugged him. "But how do you know it's a girl?"

He raised his head and his smile lit up the room. "It seemed like a good idea last night, but now it's kind of silly, isn't it? And it's a girl because she's so pretty."

"Tag, it's just about the sweetest thing anyone has ever done for me. Does she have a name?" she asked.

"You get to give her a name," he said. "And you get to welcome her home by dumping her out into the fishbowl. And there's a little booklet on how to clean the bowl in the bag too."

"I'll have to think about it for a few days to come up with the right name. Can I open the bag and set her free now?" She backed away from him.

"Yep, and then you can feed her. Look on the back of the can of fish food there to find out how much and how often," Tag said. "And once she's fed, we can go have our supper."

She picked up the can and read it, and then she opened the bag and set the goldfish free. Big bubble eyes stared at her through the side of the bowl, and then she made a couple of circles to check out the new housing. Nikki carefully pinched a little food between her finger and thumb and dropped it on top of the water. It floated for a few seconds and then began to sink. The fish gobbled down every sliver before it could hit the rocks.

"Is she still hungry?" she asked.

"The booklet says to just feed it twice a day, and the ideal thing is for it to eat all the food so that it doesn't pollute the water."

"Did you ever have one of these?" She popped the lid back on the food can.

"Nope. I thought about bringing you a turtle or maybe a lizard, but this seemed to be what would require the least upkeep. I'm glad you like it."

"I do. I really do," Nikki said. "Thank you one more time."

He pulled her back into his arms. "Nikki, I'm not good at this, so bear with me."

"Now that's a load of bull crap," she giggled.

"No, really, I'm not. I can sweet-talk someone I meet in a bar into bed in a heartbeat. I'm an expert at that, but anything more—well, I start to stutter and I'm all thumbs," he said honestly. "I don't know where this chemistry between us might lead, but I know for it to even take the first step outside this door, I have to be honest. So there it is."

He sounded sincere. There was definitely chemistry between them. But chemistry, vibes, sparks, electricity— whatever word was used for physical attraction—did not inspire trust, did it? She'd proven that when she'd given her heart to her last boyfriend, only to find out that he was married.

One date doesn't mean you're going to marry the man. Quint's voice was plain in her head.

"Surely you've had at least one long-term relationship," she said as she picked up her purse.

Tag shook his head. "I've lived like I was dying since I was seventeen. That doesn't leave room for anything except family."

"Didn't you ever want something more permanent?" She bent down and put a fingertip on the fishbowl. "You hold the place down, Goldie, until I get home."

"Nope." He opened the door for her and then waited on the porch while she locked it. "Truth is, I didn't think I'd ever want one."

"And now?" She started down the stairs ahead of him.

"Truthfully, I'm not sure what I want," he answered.

"Fair enough." She nodded. "Whatever it is that we're feelin'—let's take it real slow. And now changing the subject because I'm hungry. There's a Thursday night all-you-can-eat bar at the pizza place. Let's go get our money's worth."

The place was less than five minutes from her apartment. When they arrived, Tag escorted her inside with his hand on the small of her back. She was past being surprised at the electricity flowing through her body at his slightest touch. Like he'd said earlier, there was chemistry between them. To deny it would be lying.

He paid the lady at the counter for two buffet dinners. She handed them each a plate, bowl, and glass and said, "Silverware is over by the soft drink machine. Help your-selves. Place is a little crowded, but I see a booth in the back corner."

"If you'll take the plates and claim that table, I'll be the bartender." Tag handed her his plates and took her glass. "What're you drinkin' tonight, ma'am?"

"I'm not picky as long as it's diet," she answered.

She made her way to the back of the place, set the plates down, and slid into the booth to wait for him. Positioned just so she could see his every move, she got a full view of the way he filled out those jeans, and his swagger. Of course, nearly every woman in the place was watching him from the corner of their eyes as well.

He carefully carried two full glasses plus the silverware and napkins to the table. She took her glass from him, set it down, and together they went to the buffet to fill their bowls with salad and load up their plates with pizza.

She was back to the booth first, and a movement out the window caught her attention. Four motorcycles had parked, and the guys were wearing no helmets. The sleeves were gone from their denim jackets, leaving ragged edges. Evidently it was to show off the matching tattoos on their upper arms. Crossed swords with some kind of insignia in the middle. One of them had a gold chain from his earlobes to a ring in his nose. The swooping chains looked like they were holding up his bulldog cheeks. Didn't the fool know that in any fight someone could jerk on that and give him a world of pain?

Tag slid into the booth next to her and shook his head. "Girl, I thought you said you were hungry?"

"This is just the appetizer. I'll go for the main course after this and then finish up with a plate of dessert pizza," she said. "I might be small, but, honey, I love food."

"Well, damn it to hell," Tag muttered.

"You don't like women who enjoy their food?" Nikki asked.

"That *damn* wasn't for you," he whispered as the five bikers with dusty jeans headed straight for them.

"Well, well, lookit what we've found, boys. Pretty little lady with an ugly old cowboy. Let's whup his ass and show her what real men are." The one with the chains leered at her.

Nikki's blood ran cold as she slowly unzipped the side pocket of her purse and brought out a pink .38 pistol. She aimed it right at Mr. Chain's crotch and said, "Boys, I only got five shots, but I think I can take two of you out with one bullet so I don't waste ammunition. Now get your sorry asses back out there on those ratty bikes and leave before you get hurt."

Tag held up a hand. "It's okay. They're teasing. What are you doin' in Bowie, Texas, Billy Tom?"

"You know these people?" Nikki slid the safety back on the pistol and slipped it inside her purse, but she kept her hand on it—just in case.

Billy Tom slid into the booth and threw his big beefy arm around Tag's shoulders. He grabbed the top piece of pepperoni pizza from Tag's stack and took a bite. "We're on our way over to Tyler to do that little business I talked to you about. Thought we'd stop in here for some food and maybe call you to get directions to your ranch. Maybe talk you into changing your mind about the deal I offered you."

One of the other bikers reached for a piece of Nikki's pizza. She slapped his hand as hard as she could. "I don't share my food, and I'm not real good about sharing a date."

"Whoo-eee!" Billy Tom laughed with food in his mouth. "You done got yourself a piece of work there, Tag."

"She's a helluva bodyguard." Tag grinned. "Y'all best go on up to the counter and pay for your dinner. Sign over there says that sharin' ain't permitted."

"Bet she guards your body real good." Billy Tom gave her another lewd look.

She took her gun from her purse, again, and wondered if she could tangle those chains up in her fork. "What business are you talkin' about?"

"Just a little venture that we need Tag's help with," Billy Tom answered.

"No, thank you," Tag said. "I told you already, I'm done with that stuff. Now you've interrupted date night with me and my lady, and I'd appreciate it if you got on with your business and let us have a nice quiet meal."

"Sure thing, buddy, but remember, once a rebel, always a rebel. You can run but you can't hide from what's in your heart." Billy Tom stood up, grabbed another piece of pizza, and walked out with his posse behind him. The three of them got on their motorcycles and just sat there for a full five minutes waiting until Billy Tom came around the corner of the building and gave them a thumbs-up. When he had mounted his motorcycle, he and the others made a big show of revving them up. Through the window, Billy Tom flipped Tag off before he popped a wheelie and roared out of town.

"Guess they decided not to have pizza tonight." Nikki picked up the shaker with red pepper in it and shook it over a slice of sausage.

"I'm so, so sorry about that," Tag said.

"What're they into?"

"Who knows? It could be some get-rich-quick scheme or else some kind of crazy crap. How they stay out of jail is beyond me," he said.

"So that's the Billy Tom you told me about. Somehow I didn't picture him that big or that brazen," she said.

"Somehow I didn't picture you with a gun in your hand. Is that thing real?" he asked.

"Yes, and I have a license to carry it, both concealed and open. Last time I was at the range, I drilled five holes in a target that you could have covered with a half dollar. So as your bodyguard, I can take damn good care of you, Mr. Taggart Baker. Anything else you'd like to know about what's in my purse?" she asked.

"Hand grenades?" He wiggled his dark brows.

"I left those at home tonight, along with the sawed-off shotgun. I only bring them out when I carry my big purse," she answered. "Remember how I told you that I moved out on my own at eighteen? Well, honey, it didn't take me long to realize that a woman of my size needs a little backup companion sometimes. So now you've met my mama and my backup, and I've met your past. Guess we're even," she said.

"I think we just might be. Now let's talk about us. I started to buy you flowers tonight, but I didn't know your favorite color or if you like roses or orchids or what. Then I remembered that you'd never had a pet." He picked up a slice of pizza and bit into it.

"I like gerbera daisies in all colors. My favorite color is sunshine yellow, and I've never been fancy enough for roses or orchids. And I like Goldie better than flowers," she said. "Now my turn. What's your favorite color?"

"Blue, but I could stare into your brown eyes all night and never get bored," he said.

"That's a pretty good pickup line," she teased.

"It's the truth, not a line, but since we're bein' honest, I have used that one before. Would you fall for it?"

She shook her head and glanced out the window in time to see a black Lincoln parking not ten feet away. "I wouldn't fall for that one. Give me another one."

"Is it hot in here, or is it just you?" he said.

"Nope, not that one either. Do you know who's in that black car out there?"

Tag turned and cocked his head to one side and then the other, studying the vehicle. "Have no idea. Why are you asking?"

"For one thing, I've seen it several times and even felt like it was following me. For another, whoever it is isn't getting out of the car. Why go to the pizza place and just sit there?"

"I'll take care of this." Tag eased out of the booth and started that way with Nikki right behind him. But only the taillights of the vehicle were visible when they got outside.

"Did you get a look at whoever it was?" she asked.

He shook his head. "But this has surely been one crazy date. Next time we go out, I'm taking you out of town. Let's go back in and finish our dinner."

"Got to admit it hasn't been boring." She looped her arm in his and together they went inside and to their booth.

*   *   *

After sleeping all day and then the adrenaline rush of the evening, there was no way Nikki was going to bed when Tag walked her to the door and left her there a little before eleven. She kicked off her boots and slouched down on the end of the sofa.

"Well, Goldie, this has been a helluva night," she said.

The fish wiggled her big fan tail and did a couple of laps around the bowl. Nikki started to ask her if she was hungry, but her phone pinged. She dragged it out of her purse to find a text from Emily: Call me.

She hit Emily's number on speed dial and the phone scarcely finished the first ring before she heard, "We need to talk. What's this about you calling Patsy because you thought it would upset me that you kissed Tag? You should know none of them can keep a secret, especially when they're worried about you."

"I'm sorry, but if you want the whole story—"

"I already know y'all were together at the pizza place tonight and that he bought you a goldfish," Emily said. "I can't believe that my little brother is going out with my best friend."

"Are you going to yell at me and tell me that I have horrible taste in men? Especially after the last boyfriend?"

"No, but I might yell at *him* and tell him not to break

your heart or I'll break his neck," Emily said. "A goldfish? Why?"

"Because I told him that I'd never had a pet. She's a beauty. I named her Goldie. Did whoever tattled on us tell you about Billy Tom and his gang of wannabe thugs showing up?"

"Good God! I thought when he bought the ranch out here that he'd finally grown up and left that part of his life behind. What did they want?" Emily sighed.

"Something about a business deal that they needed Tag for," she said. "That's all I know except that he turned them down."

"Well, thank God for that," Emily said. "I hear you're going to visit the Fab Five tomorrow afternoon. I'll be there, too, so we can talk more then. My sexy husband and I are about to take a long shower together."

"Don't let me hold up that kind of thing," Nikki laughed. "See you tomorrow."

She ended the call and tossed her phone on the end of the sofa. "Well, Goldie, it's just you and me and late-night television. What do you want to watch, girl?"

She picked up the remote and surfed through the channels until she landed on reruns of *Justified*. The main character, Raylan Givens, didn't look a thing like Tag Baker, but they'd be a close match if attitudes could be measured by DNA. She fluffed up a throw pillow and stretched out on the sofa.

"I agree, Miz Goldie, this is just what we need tonight," she said.

Sometime near the fourth episode of the all-night marathon, she fell asleep only to dream of Tag. They were riding down a dirty road on his motorcycle. Her arms were around his chest, and his heart beat fast against her palms.

Her ponytail flew out behind her like a victory flag, and the wind rushed past her face. Then red and blue lights flashed behind them, and sirens started to scream. She yelled at him to pull over, but he just went faster and faster, until they hit a hole in the road. They were floating in slow motion from somewhere up high down to the ground when she awoke with a start.

"It was just a dream," she told herself as she went to get a glass of water. But she imagined that she could still taste the dust from the dream, and her heart thumped so loud that it hurt her ears. Was fate telling her that Billy Tom was right: once a rebel, always a rebel?

Chapter Ten

Nikki hadn't been to church since she'd taken the job at the hospital, but she considered going when she got off work that Sunday morning at eight. There was still plenty of time for her to get dressed and get there before service started. When she got home, she flipped through the hangers in her closet and chose a pink cotton dress with buttons down the front and a thin white belt. She slipped her feet into a pair of white sandals, picked up her purse, and told Goldie that she'd be back in a little while.

The congregation was standing, singing "Put Your Hand in the Hand" when she slipped in the back door. That definitely had to be an omen. She saw Wilma sitting on the pew behind Emily, but there wasn't room for another person there, so Nikki took a place in a pew right beside Emily and picked up a hymnal. Emily smiled and pointed at the page number in the book that she and Justin shared.

They were beginning the second verse when Tag tapped

her on the shoulder and stepped in beside her. She held her hymn book over toward him, and he took hold of one side. His deep voice sounded like it was made for Gospel hymns, but then she imagined it would sound pretty danged good singing something like "Your Man" by Josh Turner. When they'd finished singing and everyone had sat down, she and Tag were shoulder to shoulder, thigh to thigh, and the temperature in the church felt like it had risen twenty degrees.

The preacher, a young man probably in his midtwenties, took the pulpit, opened his Bible, and read some verses about Jesus being the light of the world. That's as much as Nikki heard before her mind started to wander. She knew that Tag had been a daredevil, but if he'd ever been like Billy Tom and that group of crazy bikers, then he'd already changed a lot. Emily nudged her on the elbow and tilted her head slightly toward the pew behind them.

Nikki glanced back to see her mother's eyes boring holes into her. There wasn't a drop of Jesus' light in that condemning look. Hoping that maybe she'd turn Wilma's negativity to something positive, she decided that she'd take her mother out to eat. She tried to focus on that idea, but it was impossible with Tag sitting that close to her. Finally, after what seemed like two hours instead of thirty minutes, the preacher asked Otis to deliver the benediction.

The moment the last amen was said and folks began to get to their feet, Wilma tapped Nikki on the shoulder. "What are you doing here?"

"I thought you'd be happy to see me in church," Nikki answered.

Wilma was wearing white gloves, but she wasn't dressed in her boots and a trench coat today.

"I am," she said. "But you should be at work."

"Got the day off since I worked Wednesday. Want to go to dinner with me down at the café?" Nikki asked.

"You know very well my delicate stomach won't take that kind of food. Besides, I'm already fifteen minutes late for taking my midday medicine. I left my sandwich ready to eat. We can talk tomorrow night," Wilma answered.

"How about I get a sandwich and bring it to your house?" Nikki asked.

"Sunday afternoons are when I have my weekly nap." Wilma glanced down at her daughter's legs. "And you really should wear hose to church, Nikki."

"I see you aren't wearing your Walmart garb," Nikki said.

"The blood of Jesus cleanses us in the Lord's house," Wilma said through clenched teeth.

There was no way Tag couldn't have heard the whole conversation. He was close enough behind Nikki that she could feel his breath on her neck. But it shocked her when he draped an arm around her shoulders. "Well, since you've got the day off and nowhere to go for dinner, you can come to Emily's for pot roast. Afterwards, I was thinking about going down to the creek and doing some fishing. Want to go with me?"

Emily turned around and smiled. "And we've got blackberry cobbler and ice cream for dessert. It's a pretty small group today. Just Claire and Levi, Retta and Cade and us. If you come, Tag won't be a third wheel."

"More like a seventh wheel," Nikki said. "But thank you, and yes, I'd love to join y'all. Do you need me to stop and pick up anything on the way?"

"Not a thing. We've got it covered," Emily answered. "But if you're going fishin' you might want to make a stop by your apartment and grab some different clothes and shoes."

Nikki gave her a thumbs-up and then glanced down to

see Wilma giving her a dirty look. "Want to skip that nap and go fishin' with us, Mama?"

"I hate fish and mosquitoes and being outside where God knows what infection I might get." Wilma stuck her nose in the air and blended in with the crowd heading for the front door.

"You can't fix it," Emily whispered.

"I know, but I keep hoping for a miracle." Nikki managed a weak smile.

"Fix what?" Tag asked.

"Mothers," Nikki answered.

*   *   *

The area just outside the yard fence looked like a used car lot when Tag nosed his truck into the line right beside Hud's. He frowned as he got out of his vehicle, shook the legs of his jeans down over his boots, and headed into the house. Hud, Paxton, and Maverick were already in the dining room setting the table.

"Emily, darlin', these three lazy bums didn't go to church this morning, so they don't deserve a good Sunday dinner," Tag said as he hung his hat on the rack in the foyer beside six others.

"We'll pray for their souls," Emily told him. "We can't deny our brethren bread on a Sunday."

"Then give them a slice of store-bought bread and send them home." Tag nudged Hud on the shoulder. "Move over. You're not doin' it right. Knife and spoon on the right. Fork on the left. Mama would kick your butt."

"So will I," Emily said from the kitchen.

"Get out of here. It don't take a fourth man to set a table." Hud pushed him toward the kitchen.

"And we can use some help in here," Emily said. "You can fill the glasses with ice, Tag."

Retta was sitting at the table tearing lettuce for a salad. She looked up and grinned at him. "They, and I mean the whole bunch of them, think I don't need to be on my feet."

"And I agree." Tag washed his hands at the kitchen sink and then lined up eleven tea glasses on the cabinet. As he filled them with ice cubes, a picture of Nikki wearing a maternity dress came to his mind. He shook his head to get it out—he wasn't even ready to think about the M-word. Children were a thing of the far distant future. "Have you come up with a name for the baby yet?"

Retta laid a hand on her stomach and shook her head. "We've narrowed it down to about a dozen. I told Cade that when we see her, we'll know immediately which name fits her."

"Hey, hey, everyone." Nikki came through the kitchen door. She stopped in the mudroom and kicked off a pair of grungy cowboy boots. She'd changed from that cute little dress into a pair of denim shorts and a loose-fitting chambray shirt that buttoned down the front. "I thought this was going to be a small group. What can I do to help?"

"It grew on the way home. Hud called and said he was starving. I can't let my brother go hungry," Emily said with a sideways glance at Tag. "And we'll take all the help we can get. You can fill the glasses with tea, and then you and Tag can take them to the table."

They'd just gotten the last of the tea on the table when Cade, Levi, and Justin began to bring in bowls and platters of food. A feeling of homesickness hit Tag right in the heart—so many Sundays at the Rocking B Ranch where he'd grown up, Sunday dinners were just like this. Everyone pitching in to help, and then family gathering around the table. He was glad that his sister lived close so they could continue the traditions.

"Next Sunday is at our place," Claire said as they all took seats. "If you're off work then, too, Nikki, you're welcome to join us."

"Thanks, but I doubt that will happen again for a while," Nikki answered.

"Justin, please say grace for us," Emily said.

Tag's hand closed around Nikki's. That's what married and dating couples did at the dinner table in his world, and he was glad that she didn't pull it away.

Justin said a short prayer of thanks and then everyone started talking at once. Paxton and Maverick thanked Emily for including them in the invitation for dinner. Justin picked up the meat platter and started it around the table. Emily did the same with the bread basket.

"You ever made Sunday dinner for this many?" Tag asked Nikki.

"Nope," she said. "When I was growing up, we usually had hot dogs, boxed macaroni and cheese, and pork and beans right out of the can for dinner after church. It's what I could fix. Mama always said that she had to have a nap because getting dressed and sitting through church exhausted her, so I fixed dinner for me and Quint and Daddy. Then Quint died and Daddy left, but I always fixed the same thing, kind of in their memory until I moved into my own apartment."

"If you had to make a family dinner, what would you make?" Tag passed the green beans to her.

"A family dinner would mean two people in my world." Nikki helped herself to two spoonfuls of beans and passed the bowl on to Hud, who was sitting on the other side of her. "And Mama has a strict schedule for what and when she eats, so that's a tough question."

"What if someday you have a big family of kids?" Tag asked.

Nikki's smile lit up the whole room. "Now that would be a miracle, wouldn't it?"

"Why's that?" Tag frowned.

"It takes two people to make babies. You've met my mother. Who would ever want that for a mother-in-law?" she said. "And besides, you know what my crazy hospital schedule is like. That makes it even tougher for a relationship."

"Hey, what are y'all whispering about over there?" Emily asked.

"Our favorite Sunday dinners," Tag said. "I love pot roast. What's y'all's?"

That sparked conversations all around the table. Tag lifted a forkful of corn casserole to his mouth and listened with only one ear. He had a bad reputation. Nikki had a crazy mother and an even more demanding work schedule. He could sure look past her issues if she could see past his.

Chapter Eleven

The bubbling sound of water flowing over a few scattered rocks reached Nikki's ears before they were in sight of the creek that hot Sunday afternoon. She carried a quilt. Tag had the rods and reels in one hand and a cooler with water and beer in the other. Although it had been years since she'd been to the clearing, she wasn't surprised to see that it was still free of willow and mesquite saplings.

Many years had passed since she'd gone fishing, but it had been at this very place, and it was only a couple of weeks before Quint died. Even though Wilma had thrown a hissy about her son going outside when he was so sick, her dad, Don Grady, had stood up to her. If Quint and Nikki wanted to go fishing, then that's what they would do. Quint had slept on a quilt they had brought along for most of the time. She remembered the sun rays coming through the trees and putting a halo around his bald head. Looking back, she knew that was the day she had finally given up hope and realized her brother wouldn't be with them much longer.

"Evidently Mr. Johnson liked to fish," Tag said. "I found this place a couple of weeks ago when I was walking the fence line to see if there was even one stretch that was worth saving."

"We used to have parties over on the other side of this creek when I was in high school." She flipped the quilt and it fell in front of a fallen tree.

"Why on that side?" Tag removed a plastic container of worms from the cooler. "From the looks of this old log, Mr. Johnson spent a lot of time down here, time he could have used to put up a decent fence and repair the barn roof."

Nikki sat down with her back to the log, took a worm from the container, and baited her hook. "We stayed over there because we knew Eli Johnson wouldn't come across the water to fuss at us. And if he did, it's only about a hundred yards from the creek to the road back there, so we could outrun him."

"Why'd you come here?"

"The water is spring fed, so it's always cold. We'd cross the Red River to Terral, Oklahoma, where they grow lots of watermelons. We'd steal three or four, bring them here, and put them in the water to chill. Then we would split them open and have a feast." She tossed the line out into the water.

"I can't believe you stole watermelons," he chuckled.

"Don't tell my mama, but I drank beer on those nights too." She wiggled around until she was comfortable but kept a firm hold on the rod. "Some of us actually fished and if anyone caught anything, we'd build a fire up next to the edge of the water and cook it."

"I should've known you'd fished before, the way you baited that hook."

Nikki's red and white bobber danced out there on top of the water. She took a deep breath. "My dad knew Eli Johnson, and I used to come here with Daddy to fish when I was a little girl, back before Quint got sick. Last time we were here was just before my brother died. Guess it kind of brings back memories."

"I'm sorry, maybe we could load up and go up to the Red River," he said.

"No, they're good memories. It's just that when we were in high school, I was still struggling with everything," she said. "I'm pretty much past that now."

"Want to talk about it?" Tag laced his hook with two worms and tossed it out a few feet from hers.

"Nothing to talk about, really. Mama was always sick with something, supposedly, and Daddy was gone much of the time. He drove a truck out of Dallas through the week, but he got to come home every Friday night. Saturday, he'd try to do something with me and Quint. Fishing when the weather was good. Hiking sometimes in the fall, but it was always away from the house and Mama's constant nagging. Then Sunday morning we'd go to church, and afterwards I'd make our dinner and he'd have to go back to Dallas for his next run."

Tag sat down beside her. "I think Eli used the log for a bench, but it makes a better backrest. I can't imagine not having a dad around all the time."

"It was a way of life for us. We couldn't wait until Friday nights. When he left on Sunday, Quint and I cried. But not where he or Mama could see it. It would make him sad, and Mama would think we were sick and want to give us some kind of awful medicine. So we'd go to my room and cry together."

Tag leaned over slightly and touched her shoulder with his. "Anyone ever tell you that you had a dysfunctional family?"

"Oh, yeah, I knew that the first time I brought a friend home with me after school and Mama told me we'd have to stay outside until her mama came to get her."

"That's harsh," Tag said.

"I didn't ever do it again." Watching the bobber was mesmerizing.

They were silent for a while and then she said, "Daddy came home for a whole week when Quint got bad and died. Then he left on Friday, as usual, and never came back. Mama got divorce papers in the mail the next month, and I haven't seen him since the funeral. But I got to give him a little credit. He set up an account for her, and money goes into it every month. She lives as comfortably as when he used to come home every weekend."

"Wow, that must've been a lot for you to process—losing your brother and dad at the same time."

She turned to answer him and could see genuine care in his blue eyes. Just that much was a comfort. "I've never told anyone that before, not even Emily."

"Why?"

She couldn't tear her eyes from his. "It sounds like I'm a victim, and I don't want to be like my mother. Even though he'd had all he could probably stand and left me to fend for myself with her, I wanted to be like him. That sounds crazy, doesn't it?"

"Not to me," Tag answered.

"She told me I was like him when I moved out of the house right after graduation. I thanked her and then closed the door behind me as I took out the last load of my things," Nikki said. "I took her words to mean I was strong enough to leave and if I had that much strength, I could make it on my own."

Tag scooted toward her, laid his fishing pole down, and cupped her face in his hands. His lips found hers in a sweet kiss of understanding and appreciation. When it ended, he picked up the rod again and stared out into the water.

If all that didn't run him off, Nikki thought, then he was one determined cowboy.

*   *   *

After hearing her story, Tag realized what a safe and love-filled environment he'd had the privilege of growing up in. No wonder Nikki was so independent and untrusting. He suddenly felt the need to call his mama and dad and thank them for all they'd done for him. He had been such a wild child, and he regretted all the nights when his mother probably lay awake wondering where he was.

"I guess I'll have to pay for my raising someday," he muttered.

"What was that?" Nikki asked.

"Just thinking of my own family and how I can't expect to have an easy life of parenthood. Everyone has to pay for their raising," he said.

"Your poor babies," she giggled. "Speaking of which. How's the jaw since the stitches came out?"

"Little tender yet. Dr. Richards said it'll still take a while to heal since the cut was so deep. And I do get to ride again. 'Course, the next ranch rodeo isn't for two weeks. Last day of this month to be exact. You going to be there to see me ride?"

"Probably, unless Emily needs me over at Longhorn Canyon. That's the day before the kids come in for the summer. I told her I'd help out with whatever she needs since it's her first time to be a bunkhouse supervisor," Nikki answered. "I don't think there's a fish in this creek anymore. We haven't even had a nibble since we got here."

"We need a beer. Can't expect to catch anything if you aren't drinking a beer. Fish come around when they catch the wonderful smell of cold beer," he teased as he opened the cooler and brought out two bottles. He twisted the lid off both of them and handed one to her. He took a sip, then set it to the side and reeled in his line.

"Givin' up?" she asked.

"Nope, just sharin'." He held the top of the hook with one hand and poured beer over the worms with the other. "Give the fish a little taste of something good instead of plain old worms."

"You're crazy," Nikki laughed.

There'd been so much sadness in her eyes when she talked about her family, and now one silly stunt with a few drops of beer made her eyes glitter again. Tag was suddenly floating on air for doing that for her.

"Been told that lots of times," he chuckled. "Can't deny it. Won't admit it."

"That old Fifth Amendment thing, huh?"

"Yep." He tossed the line back into the water, and immediately the bobber sank. "See, crazy works." He got so excited that he knocked his bottle of beer over.

She grabbed it before it spilled even a single drop. "Don't waste beer just because you've got Moby Dick on the line."

"Thanks," he said as he brought in a nice-size catfish. "A couple more of these and we'll have us a fish fry. You're invited even if you don't catch anything."

"Well, thank you for that, but my bobber is doing a cute little two-step out there." She motioned out to the creek with her bottle and then took a long draw. "That'll give me the strength to get it in. Want to bet who's got the biggest fish?"

"Sure. Loser has to kiss the winner."

She hauled in a bass about half the size of his catfish. Tag removed the fish from her hook and put it on the stringer with his. Then he took it to the edge of the creek and staked it in the soft mud and rinsed his hands. When he returned, she was in the process of baiting a hook and pouring a little of his beer on it.

"Hey, now, you got to use your own beer." He plopped down on the quilt beside her. "It don't work if you use someone else's."

"Bull crap," she said.

"Before you throw that line in the water, you owe me a kiss. Mine was bigger."

She laid the rod and reel down, threw a leg over his body so that she was sitting in his lap, and removed his old straw hat. Then she drew his face to hers and kissed him—long, hard, and with so much passion that he was panting when it ended.

"Damn, lady, I hope that all my fish are bigger than yours today," he said between short breaths.

"After that kiss, you're calling me a lady. What constitutes a lady?" She shifted her body until she was back at her original spot. She tossed her line out in the water and took a sip of beer.

"You do, Nikki," he said. "If you look up the word 'lady' in the dictionary, I'm sure you'll find your picture beside it."

"And where would I find your picture?" she asked.

"Beside the word 'rebel,' but I think it's beginning to fade." He smiled.

"And how does that affect you?"

"Some days I'm good with it. Some days not so much. Guess I'm still on the fence."

She watched her bobber go down and reeled in a catfish, not as big as his, but a good size. "A barbed-wire fence can get pretty uncomfortable."

He took the fish off and put it on the stringer. "I know it all too well. The barbed wire is biting into my butt pretty good."

"You deserve it," she told him as she put another worm on her hook and slung it out to the middle of the creek.

"You are a tough lady," he said as he poured some of his beer over the worms on his hook and then finished it off.

"Had to be to survive. Don't know how to be any other way now."

He watched both bobbers as they moved down the creek in the current, not touching but close to each other. Remembering what his granny had told him when he was making a difficult decision about not being able to ride two horses with one ass, he began to imagine himself crawling off the barbed-wire fence.

"But which side am I on?" he muttered.

"You're talkin' to yourself again," she said. "Look at that. It's like there's a magnet in our bobbers drawing them close together."

"I know the feelin'," he said, giving her a meaningful look. "How about you?"

"Little bit, but to be honest, I had a bad experience with a relationship last spring. It was getting pretty serious when I found out he was married, and his wife was pregnant," she said.

"And he's still alive?" Tag chuckled. "Did you have that pistol back then?"

"Oh, yeah, but I couldn't take a daddy from a baby, even if he was a sorry daddy," she said. "Just thought you should know before we take this any further. I'm not sure why I feel like I can talk to you like this, Tag. It doesn't have anything to do with chemistry, but more friendship."

"It's because we're both troubled souls," he whispered.

"Maybe so. I need closure, and you do too," she said.

"You got it, darlin'. I've never talked to anyone about serious things like I have you, so thank you for that," he said. "And anytime you need to talk about anything, my door is open."

"Thank you. Mine too," she said.

*   *   *

Later that night, Nikki sat on the end of the sofa next to Goldie and replayed the whole afternoon in her head. That song about living like you were dying came to her mind.

"Well, Goldie, he's been fishin'. Now all he has to do is stay on a bull named Fumanchu for at least three seconds and go skydiving, then maybe he'll have the rebelliousness out of his blood," she said.

Telling Tag about her early years and about Quint brought back the emotions of those last hours with him there in the hospital. Quint knew he wasn't going to get better, and he accepted it. But not Nikki—she had held out hope for a miracle right up until the moment when he breathed his last. She was holding his frail hand when that happened, and she sobbed into her father's shoulder. When the undertaker came for his body, the two of them had gone home to tell Wilma that Quint's race was finished.

Nikki closed her eyes at the painful memory. Wilma had yelled at them for letting the undertaker take him to be embalmed. She'd wanted him cremated so that all those germs would be destroyed forever, and she wouldn't get leukemia.

Why do you trust that cowboy enough to talk to him about our family? The past should be buried and forgotten, not hung out on the line like underpants for the whole world to see. Wilma's voice was very real in her head.

Exactly what was it in the past that her mother wanted to bury? The whole town knew that she had problems. Simply seeing her in the Walmart store in her outlandish garb was proof of that. A heavy feeling settled in Nikki's chest, and she knew that she had to talk to her mother, face-to-face.

Well, are you going to answer me or just sit there like your father and ignore me when I talk to you? Wilma had said that many, many times to both her children.

"Tag might be a renegade like you say, but he listens to me and tries to make me feel better," she said out loud. She wiped a tear from her cheek and put a finger on the gold-fish bowl. The fish swam right to it as if she understood that Nikki was having a tough time. "Goldie, I'm going to Mama's tomorrow evening. It's time we had a serious talk that has nothing to do with her medicine or her schedule."

She could have sworn that the goldfish smiled at her.

Chapter Twelve

Nikki awoke on Monday to a text from Tag: Want to get a burger tonight?

She sent one back: Have plans. When's the fish fry?

The next one said: Friday night. Interested?

She sent back a smiley face, crawled out of bed, and spent the day doing housework, laundry, and grocery shopping—and worrying about how her mother would react when she showed up at her house just before seven o'clock.

By late afternoon, her stomach was in knots, so she only had a bowl of chicken noodle soup for supper. She picked up her purse and locked the door before she lost her nerve. When she got to her mother's place, she sat in the car for a full five minutes. Maybe she should just take Wilma's call like usual. She could sit right there in her car and say what she was supposed to, couldn't she? For real closure, she had to have some real answers. She needed to know things that had never been talked about before.

She inhaled deeply, got out of the car, and marched up to the house with determination. The sound of her phone ringing in her purse came right before she hit the doorbell with her thumb. She heard the sound of all the locks clicking and then the door opened.

"What are you doing here?" Wilma asked through the storm door. "We're supposed to be talking on the phone right now."

"We're going to be talking face-to-face tonight. Are you going to let me in?"

"I suppose." Wilma's expression said that she wasn't happy. "Why did you come?" She went back to her recliner and took a sip of her seven o'clock glass of sweet tea.

"Are you going to invite me to sit or offer me something to drink?" Nikki asked.

"I didn't plan on you being here, and there's only enough tea to last me until I go shopping, and if you want to sit, then sit. I'm not keeping you from it," Wilma said.

Nikki kicked off her flip-flops, sat down on the sofa, and drew her legs up under her, which got her a dirty look from her mother. People did not put their feet on the furniture, and if they did, then it had to be sprayed with disinfectant.

"I want to know about when you and Daddy got married," Nikki said.

"That's old news," Wilma said. "I don't want to talk about it."

"I'm not leaving until I get some answers," Nikki said. "I can sit here all night if I need to."

Wilma gave her the old stink eye. "I was working at a café downtown. He drove a truck through here on Friday nights on his way to Dallas. He'd stop by for a piece of pie and we got to talking. I was almost thirty and had no intentions of getting married. After all, I've never been healthy, and I didn't want children."

"So why did you marry him?" Nikki asked.

"I was tired of working at the café, and he said he loved me. No one had ever told me that before. So we got married and before we could even discuss kids, I was pregnant with you. It was horrible. I was sick the whole time, and when you were born, you had the colic, and Don was gone all week on the truck. I thought I was getting a good man who'd take care of me. All I got was two squalling kids I didn't want."

Nikki's blood ran cold in her veins. What if she turned out to be like her mother when she had children? Would she feel like they were a burden too?

No, I will not. Her kind of problems are not inherited, and besides, I'd refuse to be like that, she thought.

What if you're like your father and get tired of a bad marriage and just walk out? asked that pesky voice in her head.

"Hush," she muttered.

"Don't tell me to shut up," Wilma said. "You asked, so I'm telling you."

"I'm sorry," Nikki said. "I wasn't talking to you. Go on."

"Then Quint got sick and I had to take care of him. I did my duty by y'all as best I could, but you got to realize just how sick I've always been. I should never have married or had children," Wilma whined.

"Did Daddy ever get in touch with you after he left?"

Wilma looked past Nikki at the picture of Jesus on the far wall. "Not with me," she answered. "He sent those divorce papers, and it said right there in them that he'd put money in my bank account every month, so I signed them. It was a relief. We hadn't..." She blushed.

Nikki had never seen her mother's cheeks turn that red and could count on the fingers of one hand the times she'd seen her smile. "Hadn't what?" she pressed for more.

"You know." Wilma blinked several times. "My mama was past forty when I was born and Daddy was fifty. Daddy was gone before I got married. Mama had the same problems I do. She didn't come from healthy stock either. She didn't want me to get married, told me how awful things would be...you know, in the bedroom. She was right, so after Quint was born, I told Don he'd have to sleep in a different room."

"You mean for twelve years y'all didn't have sex?" Nikki gasped.

"I didn't. I don't know what he did when he wasn't home, and I didn't care." Wilma's cheeks went scarlet again. "I was glad when he would come to Celeste so he could help with you kids. I loved you as much as I could, but taking care of you was just too much of a burden for me. Don was five years younger than me and his health was good."

Nikki understood more of her mother's background right then than ever before, and she felt so sorry that Wilma had never known what a real, loving relationship should be. She wanted to hug her mother and tell her that life didn't have to be like hers had been, but that would be going too far. The last time she'd even put her arm around her mother's shoulders was at Quint's funeral, and then she'd shrugged it off.

It's not her fault. Her dad's words came back to her mind. They'd been fishing out at Canyon Creek when she complained about her mother's coldness. *You have to understand why she is the way she is. I thought I could fix her, baby girl, but some things you just can't fix.*

There were no more questions. She could understand now why her father left and a little bit about why Wilma was the way she was. Knowing left an empty hole in her heart, and she wanted so badly to fix her mother, to help her know joy and happiness. But she knew her father had been right. Some things can't be fixed.

Wilma glanced at the clock sitting on the end table and got that blank stare in her eyes again as she gazed over Nikki's shoulder. "I guess Jesus is telling me to give you what's rightfully yours. It's in Quint's room. I used to hide it in my bedroom, but when you left, I didn't want to look at it."

She hurried to her brother's room, but it took several minutes for her to build up the courage to open the door. All of his things had been given away before his funeral because Wilma was convinced that the germs from his ailment were hiding in his toys, his pillow, even his furniture. Nikki had salvaged a teddy bear and kept it hidden in her closet until she moved out. It was part of that last load of things she had taken out of the house.

She finally eased the door open and peeked inside. The room was empty. Over there against the wall, she imagined Quint's bed. He was curled up on it with a book in his hands. Her eyes traveled around the room to imagine his dresser with a globe on it. They'd spin it and put a finger on the places where they wanted to travel someday, and then he'd check out books at the library and study about the places.

She didn't see anything that would be called hers in the empty room until she opened the door all the way. Just inside, so that Wilma wouldn't have to go inside to reach it, was a box with all kinds of mail in it. She picked it up and carried it to the living room.

"What is this?" she asked.

"Stuff that's been comin' for you for the last fifteen years. I'd like for you to get it out of here," she said. "And it's almost eight o'clock. You should be going now."

"Do you tell Mrs. Thomas to leave when she comes to visit?" Nikki asked.

"That would be rude, but I do sometimes pretend to fall asleep," she said.

"Good night, Mama," Nikki said.

"You stay on the porch until I get all the locks done up. I'll flash the porch light when I'm done." Wilma followed her across the floor.

Nikki did what she was told and then carried the box to the car. She drove home trying to figure out whether she was angry or sad for her mother, and glad that she'd broken the curse that must've run through the family for more than a generation.

She parked the car, picked the box up from the passenger seat, slung her purse over her shoulder, and headed for the Dumpster. A brisk wind whipped her dark hair into her face, and she set the box on the bottom step to tuck the strands behind her ears. The hot breeze had blown one of the envelopes back toward the car. She chased it down and realized that it had never been opened.

"Now that's downright rude," she said as she returned it to the box. About to toss it along with the others, she noticed that the handwriting wasn't hers. A cold chill chased down her back, and she stood there in the fading sunlight and recognized her name on the card written in her father's hand. She flipped several more pieces over and they were all the same.

She dug her phone from her purse and called her mother.

"Hello, Nikki."

"Why didn't you give me these when they came? Why did you hold them back from me?"

"Because your dad should have taken you with him, not left me with a teenage girl to raise. It wasn't fair," Wilma said. "You can do whatever you want with them. Good night, Nikki."

The call ended. Nikki picked up the box and took it upstairs. She set the box on the bed and began to sort the envelopes by the dates they were mailed. The first one had come the week after Quint had died. It took two hours to read through more than twenty letters, fifteen birthday cards, Christmas cards that had at least a hundred dollars in each one with a note telling her to buy herself something nice, a graduation from high school card with money in it, and one for when she'd graduated from nursing school only a few months ago.

When she finished, the front of her shirt was tear stained. "Oh, Daddy," she said as she picked up the first letter and scanned it again. He tried to explain that he couldn't live with Wilma any longer, and he should have never married her. She'd seemed like a shy, sweet woman when he met her and fell in love with her, he said. It wasn't until they were married that he realized what he'd gotten himself into. If she ever couldn't stand living there, she was welcome in his new home. It was the same address that was written in the upper left hand corner of every single piece of mail.

She paced the floor from one end of her living room to the other and looked up at the clock. She couldn't call Emily at ten o'clock at night, but Tag had said his door was open if she ever needed to talk.

She fed Goldie and walked out of the apartment.

Chapter Thirteen

Tag had just left the ranch house not thirty minutes ago, so the sound of an approaching truck wouldn't be one of the guys. Emily wouldn't be out at that time of night unless it was an emergency, and then she'd probably call on her way. The hair on his neck prickled—his sister wouldn't use the phone if his granny had died or if his parents or older brother was injured. She'd bring the news to him in person, but then he realized that in that case, someone would probably call him first. He'd be the one on the way to comfort her.

He stood up and focused on the noise. Two headlights shone through the darkness, but they weren't high enough to be from a pickup or low enough to be on the front of Emily's Mustang. When it got close enough, he recognized the little silver car as Nikki's. Before she turned off the engine, he'd crossed the yard and opened the door for her. From the dim light in the car, he could see that she'd been crying.

"What's wrong?" he asked.

"You said your door was open. I need to talk." Her words came out one at a time, as if she had trouble getting them past a lump in her throat.

He held out a hand. "Come right in. I'll put on a pot of coffee."

She put her hand in his. "Got anything stronger?"

"Part of a jar of apple pie moonshine and half a bottle of what's probably stale blackberry wine that Emily left in the refrigerator." He closed the car door and led her into the cabin with Red at his heels.

"Moonshine will be great."

She sank onto the sofa and kicked off her flip-flops. Red hopped up beside her and laid his head in her lap. Tag went to the cabinet and took down a quart jar of apple pie moonshine and a glass. He carried it to the coffee table and set them down.

"Double shot," she said as he twisted the cap off the jar. "No, make that a triple."

"It's pretty strong, Nikki. You sure?" Tag started to pour.

"Positive." She waited until the glass he held looked like three fingers before she reached out and picked it up. "I've never had this before, but it smells wonderful."

"How well do you hold your liquor?" He was genuinely worried, a new feeling for him. Before he met Nikki, he didn't care how much a woman drank.

"Not so well, but tonight I don't care. I want to be numb." She took the first sip. "Now this is some good stuff."

He sat down on the other end of the sofa. "You said you wanted to talk?"

"No, I said I needed to talk. There's a difference. If I was just lonely and wanted to talk, I'd call you. But I need to get a lot of crap off my mind, and to tell the truth I don't even know where to begin."

"Then give me a minute." He went back to the cabinet and got down another glass. "If it's going to be a long story, then I'll join you in a drink. But only one for me in case I have to drive you home."

Something about this budding friendship seemed comfortable and right. No, it was more than that. After the kisses they'd shared, it was definitely a relationship. With his past, it might be at a standstill for a very long time and then fizzle and he could accept that. He deserved it. But right now it was nice to be needed, not just wanted, in any capacity.

He sat back down and said, "Okay, shoot."

"It all started with me thinking back over our fishing trip yesterday and how I opened up to you. Don't know why I did that since..." She took another sip.

"I'm a damn good listener," he said.

"Probably gets more women in your bed than all those pickup lines you've got up your sleeve." She finally smiled.

"Hey, now. I've worked hard on those lines for a long time and sometimes they work, so don't go knockin' 'em," he argued.

"But not as well as when you look deep into a woman's soul with those sexy blue eyes and listen to what she has to say," Nikki told him.

"What does your soul want to say to me?" Tag asked.

She set the empty glass on the table. "I'm comfortable with you, Tag. The only other person I've ever been able to talk to is Emily. Don't know if I like you because you're like a brother, but no, that can't be it, because I wouldn't dream of kissing my brother. Anyway, to get on with it. After we talked, I was thinking about it, and Mama's voice got in my head... You ever have that happen to you?"

He nodded. "All the time. Most of the time it's my granny's voice. What did your mama say?"

"She asked me why I'd tell family secrets to a cowboy," she answered honestly.

"Why not?" he asked.

"She thinks you are too wild for me, but I'm not listening to her, not even when she gets in my head." She went on to tell him everything her mother had said.

Red jumped off the sofa, scooted across the floor, and stopped at the door. Tag let him outside and returned to sit close enough to Nikki to hug her. "I'm so sorry. That had to be tough, to know that you weren't ever wanted by one parent and to have the other one desert you."

"Oh, darlin', the story isn't finished yet." Tears streamed down her cheeks.

Tag jerked a blue bandana from his hip pocket and wiped them away. "It breaks my heart to see you weep like this."

Between sobs, she told him about the letters and cards and all the money. "He must think that I didn't want to live with him, and I did, Tag. I would have."

And if you had, I would have never met you, he thought.

"Where does he live?"

"Just outside Dallas in McKinney, not far from here."

"Let's go see him," Tag said.

"It's been fifteen years, more than half my life. What would I even say to him?"

"'Hello, Daddy' would be a good start," Tag suggested.

"I work weekends and he works through the week." She yawned.

Poor girl was mentally exhausted and probably just as tired physically since she'd worked a forty-eight-hour shift.

"If you really want to see him, you'll make it happen." Tag went to the bed and got a pillow. "You should stay here tonight. You can have the bed. I'll take the sofa."

"No!" she protested. "That moonshine is hitting me hard.

I'll just stretch out here until it all metabolizes." She took the pillow from him and laid her head on it and was asleep in seconds.

He covered her with the quilt that was draped over the back of the sofa and pulled the rocking chair up close to the coffee table so he could stare as long as he wanted. She looked lighter now that she'd shed that burden she brought with her that evening. And what a load it was. His heart went out to her, and he was amazed at how strong she was, given everything she'd had to deal with in her family.

Dark lashes rested on her cheeks. Equally dark hair fell over one side of her face. One hand rested under the pillow. The other was tucked under the quilt. She looked so damned vulnerable that he wanted to wake her with a kiss and carry her to his bed. Not to have sex but to simply hold her and melt away all that pain.

And that isn't a bit like you, Taggart Baker, his grandmother said.

He nodded in agreement.

*   *   *

Nikki woke with a start the next morning and saw a note lying next to the jar of moonshine. She reached for it and read: *There's milk in the fridge and cereal in the cabinet. Coffee is already made.* It was simply signed with a *T.*

She sat up and stretched, then padded across the floor in her bare feet to the cabinets. After she'd poured a bowl of Cheerios and added milk, she sat down at the table to eat. She'd just finished when someone knocked on the door. Figuring it was Tag since she hadn't heard a vehicle approaching, she hurried across the floor and swung the door open.

Cold fear ran through her veins when she looked up into Billy Tom's menacing eyes. "What are you doing here? Where's your motorcycle?" She hoped she sounded a lot meaner than she felt.

"Where's Tag?"

"He's taking a shower," she lied. "How did you find this place?"

"I talked to a guy in town, asked where Tag and Hud Baker's ranch was, and he gave me the directions, then told me that Tag was staying in this place." He pushed his way into the house, scanned the whole cabin with one look, and then pushed open the bathroom door. His eyes drew down until his dark brows were one solid line, and then he jerked a pistol from his belt and leered at her. "I hate liars. Can't trust 'em."

She glared at him, determined not to show fear.

"Not so mouthy now that I'm the one with the gun, are you? Since Tag ain't here to do what I tell him, I'll just take his woman. Is that your car out there?"

"No, it's my mama's," she said.

"Well, it'll do anyway. You've got the keys, don't you?"

She shook her head and he pressed the end of the gun to her temple. "Remember I hate liars."

"The keys are in the car. Take it." She stared him right in the eyes without blinking.

"Oh, no, darlin', me and you, we're going for a little ride in your mama's car. If you make a sound or try to warn someone, you are dead. Understand?"

She nodded. Her purse and her pistol were in the passenger seat. If she could get to it, she'd show the big overgrown smartass just how mouthy she could get.

His left hand shot out and he grabbed her arm so tight that it hurt. "A hostage will come in real handy. Besides, it's been a while since I had a woman to keep my bed warm at night." He pulled her out the door, leaving it wide open.

"Can't I at least get my shoes?" she asked. "If I get caught driving barefoot, the police will ask questions."

"Get them," Billy Tom said through gritted teeth. "You can get behind that wheel and drive us out of here. And, darlin', I'll be right behind you. I can't miss your heart if I shoot through the backseat."

"Where are we going?" Nikki reached for her purse the second she was in the car, but Billy Tom grabbed it from her and flung it out the window. "No driver's license. You're askin' for trouble."

"Don't get stopped. Not one mile above or below the speed limit. Drive north to Nocona and catch Highway 82 going west," he said. "We'll have us a nice little road trip. Maybe if you do what I say, I'll even tell you stories about Tag and the good old days."

There was a very good possibility that she'd never see her father if she didn't do what he said. Life wasn't fair. She should at least get a chance to explain what had happened to his mail. She started the engine, turned the car around, and then braked. "The gas tank is nearly empty. If you don't let me get my debit card from my purse, we won't be going very far. I've got less than a quarter tank of gas."

"Get out and get it." He stepped out of the car and pointed the gun at her. "If you run, I'll put a bullet in your back. I can always drive myself if I have to."

She slowly walked back to where her purse was located, picked it up, and started to unzip the end pocket that held her pistol, but he grabbed it from her. "I'm not stupid, woman. I remember that you keep a gun in your purse."

He fumbled inside with one hand, brought out her wallet,

and then threw the purse on the ground. "Now go back to the car."

"Can I take my phone?"

"Nope," he said.

"Can I move my purse so I don't run over it when we drive off?"

"I'm watching you," he said.

She picked it up by the strap and carried it off to the side, where she deliberately pretended to stumble and fall over a rock. While she was setting her purse out of the way, she reached inside, grabbed her phone, and since Tag was the last person she'd called, she hit redial. Then she stood up and marched back to the car, yelling the whole way. "Thanks so much for being a jackass, Billy Tom. Where are we going?"

"Don't you scream at me, woman, or I'll put you in the trunk and drive myself," he threatened her again.

"I'd rather ride in there than smell you the whole way," she shot back.

He chuckled as he got into the backseat again. "I'll tell you when to make turns. You just obey me like a good little woman until we get there; then maybe I'll show you what a real rebel is, and it ain't Tag Baker, honey."

Nikki gritted her teeth and turned toward Sunset when she left the ranch. Hopefully Tag would get the call and know when she didn't answer that she was in trouble. It was a crazy world when her first thought in the face of danger was to reach out to Tag rather than hitting her mother's number.

"Not one mile over the speed limit." Billy Tom reached around the seat and pulled back her hair with the barrel of the gun. "Tag must've meant it when he said he was through with our way of life, fallin' for your type like he's done. So I bet he'll do exactly what we tell him to get you back."

Nikki held on to the steering wheel with a death grip to keep her hands from shaking. If she got out of this alive and unhurt, she would enroll in a self-defense class as soon as she got home to Bowie. When she reached Nocona, she turned west on Highway 82, just like he said.

She pointed to the left. "We should get some gas if we're going more than twenty miles. All right if we stop at that station right there?"

"That's fine, but don't you try anything funny. I'm hungry. We'll get some road food while we're here too."

She pulled up to the gas pump, picked up her wallet, and slipped her debit card into the slot. When she had filled the tank, Billy Tom got out, slung an arm around her shoulders, and walked her into the station. Either Billy Tom was stupid and didn't realize that the police could track her payments with the card, or the whole ordeal would be over before they even knew she was gone.

Her skin crawled at his touch and her nose twitched at the rancid odor coming from him. She wanted to kick him in the shins and run, but she could feel the barrel of the gun against her ribs.

"We'll go to the bathroom while we're here. If you crawl out a window or run while I'm in the men's room, when I come out I'll shoot everyone in the place. That's a promise, not a threat," he whispered as he pushed the door open.

"Can I help you?" the young pregnant clerk asked.

"Just need to use the restrooms and get some food," Nikki said sweetly.

"That's good," Billy Tom said from the side of his mouth. "Real good. Be a shame for a mama and baby both to die today."

She went to the ladies' room and used the facilities. Then she removed her library card and a pen from her wallet. She wrote *West on 82* on the back of the card and stuck it in the corner of the mirror. When she went back out into the store, Billy Tom was covering the counter with potato chips, cookies, fried pies, and a six-pack of beer.

"Y'all must be taking quite a road trip," the lady said.

"Yep, our very first one together," Nikki said.

Billy Tom gave her a dirty look. "We'll have half a dozen of them burritos in your hot food case, too, and half a dozen of them sausage biscuits."

"Yes, sir." She got it all out and bagged up. "Anything else?"

"What do you think, darlin'? You want some milk?" Billy Tom kissed her on the cheek.

She fought the desire to wipe her face. "Root beer, please. Bottles not cans. If you'll get it for me, all this should be rung up by the time you get back."

"You go get it," Billy Tom said. "I'll wait right here for you."

That squashed the idea that she might get a word with the clerk, but there were ways to slow the trip down. She picked up two six-packs of root beer and set them on top of a case of water.

"My little woman is sure strong." Billy Tom beamed to the clerk. "And looks like she's real thirsty too."

"That apple pie moonshine from last night makes a girl want water." Nikki set everything on the counter and took out her credit card.

"I'll need to see your ID if you're paying for the beer," the clerk said.

"That's sweet but I'm twenty-nine years old," Nikki told her, and flipped her wallet around so the lady could see her ID.

"Nikita Colleen. What a pretty name. Irish?" the woman asked.

"That's what my mama Wilma tells me." Nikki nodded. "As far as I know, we don't have any Irish in us. Go figure why people name their kids what they do."

"My mama got my name Jenny from a character in a book," she said. "If you'll sign this, you can be on your way, Miz Nikita."

Nikki signed her name with a flourish on the receipt. Billy Tom had picked up the water, so she wrote HELP below her name and nodded at Jenny as she picked up the two bags he'd left behind.

Of all the times for the convenience store's phone to ring—Jenny shoved the sales slip into the cash register without even looking at it. Nikki couldn't catch a break.

In her car and back on the road, Billy Tom kept the gun in one hand and twisted the cap off a bottle of beer with his teeth. When he spit it on the floor of her car, she grimaced. She was proud of her car. She'd worked hard to save up to buy a decent vehicle and she kept it in pristine condition. She was tempted to slam on the brakes when he tipped up the beer, gulped down half of it, and then burped loudly.

"Want one?" he asked.

"Want me to get drunk and pulled over for speeding? I'm sure the cops would love to get their hands on you, so, yes, hand me a beer," she answered. "What'd you do anyway?"

"I stole a white pickup and put the license plate I pinched from Tag's truck on it. Y'all were so much in love you didn't even suspect that I switched it at the pizzeria. That was a stroke of luck for sure, finding y'all in there like that. I used the truck to steal a load of ephedrine headed for a little meth lab over in East Texas. Then I sold the goods to another meth cooker. Now everyone is going to be looking for your precious Tag. He wouldn't join us, so we figured he could take the blame for driving the getaway truck." Billy Tom tossed four bottles of water over into the passenger seat.

"How'd you get to the cabin?" she asked.

His phone rang and he put it on speaker. "Hello, y'all at the hideout?"

"We're here. Where are you? You should've beat us here," a man answered.

"Stole me another car. Damn one I was driving ran out of gas a mile from the ranch, so I had to walk. All I wanted was for Tag to give me a ride to Mesquite to get my bike and maybe a hundred dollars to get me to my little hideout, but he wasn't there."

"Is this damn phone on speaker? I hear road noise."

Billy Tom burped loudly. "Hell, yeah. I've got a gun in one hand and a bottle of beer in the other. Tag's woman is driving. I figure he'll buy her back from us."

"We don't need that shit. We can divvy up the money we already stole and then lie low for a few months."

"Tag needs to pay for not goin' with us," Billy Tom said.

"You're crazy." A different voice laughed. "But I like it. Reckon he'll cough up five grand?"

"I'm thinkin' ten might get me a good used motorcycle, and I'll just leave mine out in Mesquite where I stole the car. Y'all get that money counted out. We'll be there in a few hours."

"We already got it in stacks. Damn driver of that ephedrine haul didn't even know what hit him," a third guy said. "We'll see you soon."

He ended the call, patted her on the shoulder, and then dug into the bag for the sausage biscuits. "Want a biscuit?"

"No, thank you. I'll just drink water," she answered. "And, Billy Tom, just so you know, I'm not Tag's woman."

"Then what the hell were you doin' in his cabin this mornin' or out on a date with him the other night?" He burped again.

Chapter Fourteen

Tag had just flipped two large pancakes on his plate when someone knocked on the door. Hud raised an eyebrow and started across the kitchen when they heard Maverick say, "Good mornin', Officer. What can we do for you?"

Tag set his plate on the table and followed Hud to the living room.

"May I come inside? I'm Deputy Davis. I'm looking for Taggart Baker."

Tag stepped around his brother and nodded. "Yes, come on in. I'm Tag."

"I'm here about your white pickup truck. Where were you last night between eight and midnight?" the officer asked.

"I was here until ten with these guys, and then I walked about a quarter mile over to Longhorn Canyon Ranch, where I stay in a cabin," Tag said.

"So how did your truck come to be in a robbery over

around Mesquite? I got a note this morning from the sheriff over there saying the plates match that truck out there in the driveway. One that was reported stolen."

"I have no idea," Tag said, and then groaned. "Billy Tom."

"You're runnin' with him again?!" Hud's voice bounced off the walls.

"No, I'm not." Tag wiped a hand across his forehead. "You'd better sit down, Deputy, sir. Billy Tom, that would be William Thomas if you want to look up his rap sheet, has been after me to give him money for some deal he had going. I wouldn't do it and he was in the pizza place in Bowie the other night when I was there." Tag went on to tell the whole story. "I've seen him switch plates on vehicles lots of times."

"So you do know him? How do I know that you didn't switch the plates yourself after you helped with the robbery? If you're his friend, you might do that, right?"

"I didn't do it." He didn't want to get Nikki involved in this or smear her reputation, but there didn't seem to be another way out. "A lady I've been seeing, Nikki Grady, can vouch for me." He slipped his phone from his hip pocket, just as it started to vibrate. "This is Nikki right now. Let me put it on speaker and you can ask her yourself."

"Hello?" he said. "Would you..."

"I'll tell you when to make turns. You just obey me like a good little woman until we get there. Then maybe I'll show you what a real rebel is, and it ain't Tag Baker, honey."

There was the sound of a car engine that faded as it got farther and farther away.

Tag tensed and balled his hands into fists. "That's Billy Tom's voice. He's got Nikki. I can almost guarantee it, and I know where they're headed."

"It's Billy Tom's voice, sir," Hud agreed as he got up to let in the dog scratching at the door.

Red came trotting in, dragging a handbag behind him. Tag took it from the puppy. "This is Nikki's purse. Red must've been there when they left. They don't have a very long lead. We might catch them if we head out now."

Davis headed for the door. "If you really want to help, tell me where they're going."

"They usually hole up at an old run-down cabin over near Tulia in Swisher County. I can draw you a map if it'll help. It's about five hours from here. The place belonged to his grandpa, but the old guy's been gone for years."

"Okay, son, I'll alert the local authorities, and they can check it out."

"Make sure you talk to Sheriff Lester Roberts," Tag advised as he followed Davis out of the house.

"You know him?" Davis asked.

"My parents own the Rocking B Ranch," he said. "And my brother Matthew is a volunteer deputy out there."

"With a family like that, how in the hell did you get in with someone like Billy Tom?"

"Bad decisions."

"Well, I hope you learned that every choice has consequences," Deputy Davis admonished.

"I have, sir, and I'm doin' my best to get past the bad choices," Tag said.

Davis nodded and got back into his patrol car. Tag was watching him leave when Hud yelled at him from the porch. "If you take your motorcycle, you might be able to catch them. I packed you some clothes and other things just in case," Hud said. "You go get it while I pack a bag, and then I'll call Matthew and give him the scoop while you're on your way."

He started out the back door toward the barn where his cycle was stored.

"Call when you get there and give Mama a hug for me," Hud yelled.

Tag held up a hand in acknowledgment. Choices, bad decisions, consequences, fate, and karma—he had a good thing started with Nikki and now he'd lost it for sure.

* * *

Nikki had drunk all four bottles of water by the time they reached Wichita Falls. "We're going to have to make a pit stop. I can't go much farther."

"Once you're on Highway 287, you can stop at the next station you see. I'll go in with you and the same rules apply. You run or turn me in and I start shooting everyone I see," he said.

"I understand," she said.

She whipped into a service station and hurried inside, glad that she had on flip flops, because the sign said NO SHIRT, NO SHOES, NO SERVICE. She pushed into the bathroom, praying there would be another woman in there, but no luck, so she removed a grocery store rewards card from her wallet and wrote *Help me. I've been kidnapped.* She wrote Tag's phone number on the back and laid the card on the vanity.

Once she'd finished, she slowly washed her hands and checked her reflection in the mirror above the sink. Lord have mercy! She looked horrible. Her hair was a tangled mess since she hadn't had time to brush it before Billy Tom knocked on the door. There were black mascara streaks down her face from all the tears she'd shed, and bags under her eyes. She took time to wash her face and then pulled her hair up into a ponytail with a rubber band she took from her wallet.

When she opened the door, Billy Tom was right there blocking her way with a hand on each side. "What took you so damn long?" he hissed.

"If you'll notice, I washed my face and tried to do something with my hair," she said.

"Gettin' pretty for me, were you?" He grinned.

"No, just trying to look less like someone you kidnapped so you won't cause a scene. Can we go now?"

"I want another six-pack," he told her. "Get it and pay for it."

She saluted smartly and walked under his arm. "Anything else?"

"Nah, we got enough food to last until we get to the hideout," he said. "We've wasted enough time. The guys are waiting for us."

"When are you calling Tag to ask for ransom money? It'll take him five or six hours to bring it to you. You willing to sit still that long and wait?"

Billy Tom glared at her. "He's got rich relatives. His brother Matthew can get it to us in less than thirty minutes, and after the money is in my hands, I'll tell him where he can find you."

"Am I going to be dead or alive? You've been letting me use my debit card everywhere. You do know they can track me with that?" she asked.

"I don't give a shit. This'll be over before they find you anyway. And dead or alive depends on whether you make me mad..."

She shot him the evilest look she could muster and marched straight up to the beer cooler, got out a six-pack, and went to the counter to pay for it. The old gray-haired fellow asked for her ID, and she gladly gave it to him, hoping that when someone came to find them, he'd remember the name Nikita Grady.

"Good girl," Billy Tom said. "You even remembered the brand I like."

"If I hadn't been afraid you'd shoot some kid's grandpa, I'd have bought you arsenic," she said as she started the engine. "I need more water."

He flipped four more bottles up on the passenger seat. "Sure you don't want something to eat? I've got burritos and one sausage biscuit left."

"You ate five biscuits?" She wrinkled her nose at the sight of him in the rearview.

"Didn't eat all day yesterday," he sneered back at her.

"Tag is going to kill you," she muttered.

"Tag is probably trying to talk his way out of a jail cell right now," Billy Tom laughed.

"Well, genius, did you remember to get the tag off that truck in Mesquite and put it back on his truck, or were you in such a hurry to kidnap me that you forgot?" she asked. "I don't remember us taking a detour by the ranch for you to take care of that."

He slapped himself on the head with the gun. "Don't you worry, darlin'. By the time the cops figure out my tag-switchin' business, it'll be too late. I'll just wait and call Tag when we get to the hideout. It won't take Matthew long to get the money."

Billy Tom's attempts at intimidation weren't working. For the last three hours, his tactics just made her that much more determined to go against the oath she'd taken as a nurse to help heal people. At some point, she'd take that gun away from him and enjoy giving him a reason to beg her to call an ambulance.

"Ain't got nothing to say to that, do you?" Billy Tom talked with food in his mouth.

There was so much tension in the car she thought for

a minute that Billy Tom would tell her to pull over to the side of the road, shoot her, and take her car on to wherever his hideout was located. But a glance in the rearview let her know real quick why he had slumped down in the seat. There was a police car coming up on them pretty fast from the rear.

She sent up a silent prayer asking that the lights would begin to flash and the sirens would blare.

"You better hope we don't get stopped, or I'll shoot the cop the minute he walks up to the car," Billy Tom threatened.

"I'm sure someone has missed me and put out my tag number," she said.

"Honey, your tag changed while you were in the bathroom at that first gas station. I switched it with a car the same color as yours in the parking lot of that convenience store." Billy Tom slouched down farther.

As if in answer to her prayer, the lights on the police car came on and the noise of the siren filled the air. Then the police car whipped around them and sped down the road until it was nothing but a dot in the distance.

"Now ain't this that policeman's lucky day?" Billy Tom sat up straight and took a bean burrito from the sack. "Riding makes me hungry. Want one?"

Nikki's stomach knotted up at even the thought of food. "No, I don't want food, but I need to go to the bathroom."

"Good God, woman, you got a bladder the size of a thimble. It ain't been thirty minutes since we stopped. Stop up here at Estelline, but this is the last time. Once you get done, we'll get on Highway 86 and in an hour and a half, we'll be at the end of the road," he said. "Remember the rules when we're in the gas station. You might as well fill up with gas while we're there. Once me and the guys divide up the money, I'm going to use this car to go back to Mesquite to get my motorcycle."

"I thought you were going to use the ransom money for a new bike." She pulled up next to one of the two gas pumps.

"We'll all split five ways and won't see each other for a month until this all dies down. Ten thousand dollars will go a long way in Mexico, and I like my motorcycle just fine, so I've changed my mind," he said.

"What about all that money y'all got by robbing an ephedrine truck?" She looked up into the rearview mirror.

"That won't last a long time, and besides, me and the boys like adventure, so we'll get back together after a few months, just like always," he answered.

Billy Tom had probably been a fairly good-looking kid as a teenager, Nikki thought. He had a square jaw and nice green eyes, but the life he'd chosen had made him hard and downright mean. Now he made her skin crawl. One thing for absolute sure, she would not be spending an hour with him, much less a month. Someone would come get her before that happened. Emily checked on her every day, and Tag would know something was wrong when he found her purse lying on the ground outside the cabin.

"You going to call your thug friends and tell them we're close?" she asked as she turned off the engine, undid her seat belt, and opened the car door. "Do I go to the bathroom first or pump gas?"

"No, I'm not calling my buddies. They know I'm on the way," he told her. "Pump the gas and then we'll go inside."

That meant she had no way to leave a message on the gas pump for the folks in the car who waited behind her. After she'd filled the tank, Billy Tom got out of the back-seat, threw half a dozen empty beer bottles into a nearby trash can, and followed her into the small convenience store.

"Bathrooms?" Nikki asked.

The young lady behind the counter pointed toward the far corner of the store. Nikki felt as if she'd never had a shower or washed her hair as she entered the two-stall ladies' room. When she left the restroom, an older woman with gray hair passed her in the doorway, but Billy Tom was standing not three feet away with his hand inside his nasty vest.

"Thought I might have to wait in line, judgin' by all the cars out there, but looks like it's empty," the lady said.

"It's all yours." Nikki smiled.

"You done good," Billy Tom growled as he grabbed her arm. "I was ready to pull the trigger and drop that old bag where she stood."

When they got close to the beer cooler, Billy Tom grabbed a case. "We'll take the boys a little something. They're probably spittin' dust since they can't go to a store."

Paying for the beer aggravated Nikki so badly that she almost refused, but then the lady from the bathroom set a candy bar and a root beer on the counter and leaned over the counter to hug the cashier, who didn't look a day older than eighteen. "How's things goin' today, darlin'?"

She stretched over the top of the counter and hugged her back. "Slow, Granny, but it's a job. The money will help with my college fees this fall. Then it's on to grad school."

Nikki paid for the beer with her debit card, hoping all the time that the police were already tracing the places she'd used it. Without incident, they got back on the highway and she made the next turn Billy Tom demanded. He yawned several times, but he kept his eyes wide open for the next hour and a half.

*   *   *

Tag cursed every single one of the 250 miles to Tulia.

"She's never goin' to speak to me again," he muttered to himself. Tag couldn't blame her if she didn't. He'd brought all this crap down on her head—Billy Tom might have been the actual culprit, but if Tag hadn't ever been associated with him, then it wouldn't have happened.

Guilt lay on his shoulders like a heavy wool blanket every time he even thought her name, and yet he couldn't stop thinking about her. Had Billy Tom hurt her? Why had he even taken her? He could have demanded her car keys and left her alone. He should have thought of all this at the pizza place. He knew Billy Tom and the guys he rode with—that they were ruthless and wild. He should have protected Nikki better.

When he went through Vernon, Texas, it hit him that he'd never told Billy Tom where his ranch was or that he was staying in a nearby cabin, so how did he know where to go?

"Small town living," he muttered. All he'd had to do was ask someone in Sunset about the Baker boys who'd recently settled there. Everyone probably even knew that he was now staying at the cabin.

He wanted to stop the motorcycle and kick something—a tree, a cactus, even one of those "Don't Mess with Texas" trash cans along the side of the road would do just fine. But he didn't have the time to give in to his anger. He had to keep riding until he got to the hideout—and he just hoped he could beat Billy Tom there.

But what if he doesn't go there? It's been years since you rode with him. He could've changed places.

If that was the case, then Tag couldn't rescue Nikki. He couldn't apologize to her, beg her forgiveness, and own up to the fact that this horrible kidnapping was all his fault. One for being such a stupid teenager, the other for getting her into the mess with Billy Tom to begin with.

He was a ball of nerves, anger, and guilt when he finally reached the turnoff to the cabin. He parked his motorcycle under a big scrub oak tree and dismounted, looked around and caught a movement to his right. Matthew came out from behind a big scrub oak tree and gave him a quick hug. "He's not showed up yet, so you've beat him."

"Thank God," Tag said. "Are you the only one here?"

"No, there are others, but they're well hidden. We didn't want to spook him since he's got the hostage," Matthew said quietly. "I've got to get in position up on that rise over there. You wait until they're parked."

"Y'all goin' to let me go in first?" Tag asked.

"You armed?" Matthew asked.

"No. I didn't even think to bring a gun," Tag answered.

"Good." Matthew laid a hand on his shoulder and squeezed gently. "You don't need one. We've got your back, but if you want to try to talk him into surrendering, you can have the job. But don't worry, we will get her back. Just talk calmly so he don't hurt Nikki." Matthew touched the phone on his shoulder.

"Baker here," he said.

"He's been spotted turning off to the main road," a voice said.

"Thank you, Darrin," Matthew said and then looked at Tag. "That's my cue to get up on that little rise behind an old log. See you when it's over."

"Thanks for letting me be a part of this," Tag said.

Matthew nodded and disappeared across the clearing and into the trees that led up to a high spot.

Tag took a deep breath and leaned on the old log blocking the path to the cabin, his heart pounding, guilt still filling his heart and soul, and hoping with everything in him that Billy Tom hadn't hurt Nikki. If he had, Tag wouldn't need a gun to take care of him.

*　　　　*　　　　*

Billy Tom sat straight up in the backseat and growled, "Make a right at the next gravel road. We'll go about a mile and then turn into a lane. I'll tell you where, and, honey, no cuttin' and runnin'. I'm a damn good shot, and you can't run as fast as a bullet."

Nikki drove slowly, hoping that at any minute she'd see police cars behind her, but there were none. A mile of dust boiled up behind them, and then he motioned with the gun for her to make another right turn. There was nothing more than a rutted path from that point on. She'd only driven a couple of minutes when she saw the old tree lying across the road and remembered the story of how Duke died. She braked and brought the car to a stop.

"We'll walk from here. It ain't far." Billy Tom picked up a case of beer in one hand and held the gun in the other.

Nikki got out of her car and caught a movement in her peripheral vision. Then Tag walked out from behind a fallen down log right in front of her. At first she thought she was seeing things, or dreaming, or maybe Billy Tom put a silencer on the gun and she was dead.

No, she couldn't be dead because Tag had come all that way to rescue her. She had to be alive so she could thank him. Things began to blur around the edges, but she refused to give in to it and faint. She stiffened her back and took several deep breaths so that Billy Tom wouldn't have the satisfaction of winning.

"I think you have something that's mine." Tag didn't

even look her way but locked gazes with Billy Tom. "I want it back."

What was Tag talking about? A few kisses didn't make her his.

"You can have her for ten thousand dollars." Billy Tom leveled the gun at Tag's chest.

"I don't think so." Tag folded his arms over his chest and finally looked Nikki in the eye.

Fear and anger all rolled into one was the message she got, not that she wasn't important enough for the ransom.

"So she's not worth that to you? She's just another one of your bar bimbos after all," Billy Tom taunted. "If she's worthless to both of us, I can just kill her right here."

"I'd give everything I've got for her, but that's not the issue here." Tag's gaze went back to Billy Tom. "You are surrounded by men from the Swisher County Sheriff's Department and the Tulia police. Did I ever tell you that my brother Matthew is a volunteer deputy? He can take the eyes out of a rattlesnake at a hundred yards. If you'll look to your left, you'll see the glint from his gun."

Billy Tom cut his eyes around toward the shiny dot among the trees on the slight hill. His face went gray as the blood drained out of it. "Nobody can make a shot that good."

"Maybe. Maybe not. You willing to take that chance?" Tag asked.

"You think his bullet can get here faster than mine can get to her?" Billy Tom moved the gun to point at Nikki's forehead.

"I wouldn't want to see if Matthew's can, but maybe one of these other fellers' will." Tag held up a hand and motioned.

Uniformed policemen began to circle around him. The one with the sheriff's badge said, "We have already got your buddies from the old shack back there in custody. We've confiscated the money, and you've got nowhere to run, Billy Tom. It's taken us twenty years but this time, boy, you're on your way to prison for a long time. The Montague County police called me a few hours ago and said you were on the way. We've been waiting for you."

Billy Tom glared at Tag and then at Nikki, his eyes shifting from one pistol to another—all aimed right at him. He must've realized he was out of options because he dropped the pistol on the ground, fell to his knees, and put his hands behind his head.

Nikki picked up the gun and, using the butt, hit him square between the eyes. He tumbled backward, squalling like a little girl as he tried to catch the blood flowing from his nose. She dropped the gun in the dirt and turned to see Tag coming toward her, his arms outstretched. She couldn't let him touch her, not when she still had the stench of Billy Tom in her nose. She shook her head. "Don't touch me, not until I get this filth off me. Where's the nearest motel?"

"You can stay at my folks' ranch," he offered.

"No, thank you. I'd rather stay in a motel." Her hands shook so badly that she had to clasp them together.

"I need to talk to you, and we've got showers at the jail," the sheriff said. "I can even get you a set of scrubs if you don't mind orange."

"Then I'll follow you." She started for her car.

"You shouldn't be driving alone," Tag said.

"You're going with this deputy right here," the sheriff said. "I'll take Billy Tom with me."

"I'll drive her car," Matthew offered. "Keys still in it?"

It wasn't easy to let them make decisions for her, but the adrenaline rush was crashing. She nodded toward Matthew. "It stinks of him and beer."

"I'll take care of it, Nikki. You just go with the deputy," Tag assured her. "I'll be right behind you, and thanks, Sheriff, for letting me be part of this."

"Matthew had a lot to do with that. I called him the minute the sheriff from over in Montague County got in touch with me."

"I need a doctor," Billy Tom whined.

"Shut up or I'll tell everyone in the jail that a woman half your size took you down," a deputy told him as he put him into the back of a police car.

Chapter Fifteen

Tag followed Nikki and the deputy to the squad car and opened the passenger door for her. "I can go with you and send someone for my motorcycle."

"I'm fine," she said, but her voice shook.

"Just follow us," the officer said.

"I'll be right behind you, Nikki. Did he hurt you?"

She shook her head. *Define hurt,* she thought as he closed the door. It didn't always mean bruises or cuts. Sometimes it went way deeper than that and couldn't be put into words.

"I didn't hear you answer Tag," said the gray-haired deputy as he took the same route back to town that Nikki had driven. It seemed like hours instead of only minutes.

"He didn't physically hurt me, but he kept a gun pointed at me for the last five hours," she said in a thin voice that she hardly recognized as her own.

"I'm sure that was scary," he said.

Nikki was glad that he didn't have any more questions

because she didn't want to answer them. Tears welled up, but she refused to let the dam loose. She'd been strong right up to the end, and now she might get fired for having a record. That stunt with the gun might get her charged with assault with intent to do bodily harm—which was the God's honest truth.

The deputy pulled into a parking spot and got out of the car. Nikki reached for the door handle, but before her hand even touched it, Tag opened it and said, "I'm going with you."

With Tag on one side of her and the deputy leading the way, they went inside the police station. Nikki took a deep breath, sucking in the smell of cleansers. After inhaling beer and nasty burps all day, she wanted to sit down on the tile and enjoy the scent for hours.

The deputy led the way into an office with his name on the door. "The sheriff is on the way. Can I get you something to drink, Miz Grady?"

She shook her head. "I just want a shower."

"All in due time. Tag, you can wait outside now. This won't take long."

"I'd rather stay," he said.

"There's a chair out there." The deputy pointed.

"I'll be waiting, Nikki," he said.

The sheriff entered the room and motioned for Nikki to take a seat across the desk from him. "Can you answer some questions for me?"

She nodded.

"I will record your interview." He set a recording device on the edge of the desk. "You still look pale. Do you need a few minutes to collect yourself?"

"I'm fine. Let's just get this over with," she answered.

"You are a strong woman, Miz Grady. I admire your strength," the sheriff told her, and then pushed a button on the tiny recorder. "This is Sheriff Lester Roberts taking Nikki Grady's statement. Now tell me what happened today. Don't leave out any details."

His comment about her strength gave her the courage to start talking. "I was kidnapped at gunpoint."

*   *   *

Matthew carried a second folding chair down the hallway and set it up beside his brother. "You okay?"

"Another thirty minutes and I wouldn't have been there," Tag said. "I caused this mess. I needed to be there for her when she got out of that car."

That the two cowboys were related was evident by their clear blue eyes and dark hair, but that's where the resemblance ended. Matthew wasn't as tall as Tag, and he'd always been the serious one of the three Baker boys. Tag was the rebel. Hud was the quiet twin. Matthew was the responsible son. Right then Tag wished he had a helluva lot more Matthew in him.

"Is she going to be all right?" Matthew asked.

"She's tough. Had to be coming from the family she did. It wasn't like ours." Tag removed his hat and laid it on the floor beside him. "Crazy mother. Father who left her after her brother died. She was fourteen when all that happened, and she's made her own way since she was eighteen."

"Then I expect she'll be fine. Did he..." Matthew paused.

"I hope to hell not." Tag took a bandana from his pocket and wiped sweat and dirt from his face. "I really like her, Matthew, but now I've got to back away from her for her own safety. Dammit!" He slapped his knee.

"What?" Matthew asked.

"I need to call Emily. She's been worried sick." Tag jerked his phone from his pocket.

"I talked to her on the way here. Also talked to Mama and Dad. Now all you've got on your plate is her," Matthew told him. "Never saw you like this over a woman."

Tag shrugged. "And now I've ruined it with my past mistakes."

"You need to leave the past in the past and move on to the future," Matthew said.

Tag shook his head. "I'm trying but it keeps coming back to bite me on the ass."

"Give it a chance. Things will take on a new light when you get back to your ranch." Matthew patted him on the shoulder.

Tag drew in a long breath and let it out in a whoosh. "I've got to talk to her."

"I've got a solution. Ride home with her and leave that damned motorcycle here," Matthew said.

"If she'll let me, you can do whatever you want with the cycle. If I ever got on it again, all I'd be able to think about is the fear and anger that had a hold on me the whole way from the ranch," Tag said.

"Aww." Mathew grinned. "My baby brother is growing up."

"Go ahead and say it. I deserve it," Tag said.

"About damn time." Matthew chuckled.

"I'd say it's past time."

"Looks like Lester is finished talkin' to her," Matthew said, and pushed up out of his chair.

Tag settled his hat on his head and got to his feet.

Sheriff Roberts came through the door and extended his hand to Matthew. "Thanks for your help today. We didn't know what we might get into out there. Didn't expect to find them all asleep or for it to be so easy. I sure felt better knowin' you was up there on that little hill with your rifle. Thought for a minute there we might have a killin' on our hands." He turned to face Tag and shook hands with him as well. "I hope you're makin' better friends over in Montague County."

"I assure you I am," Tag said. "Can I talk to Nikki now?"

"Yes, but right now she's in my bathroom getting cleaned up. Here are her car keys and wallet. I gave her a set of orange scrubs to change into."

"Was she"—Tag swallowed hard—"hurt?"

"She said Billy Tom threatened her in all kinds of ways but that's all," the sheriff said. "You wait right here. She'll be out in a few minutes."

"Thank you." Tag sat back down.

"Matt, I think I owe you a cup of coffee," Sheriff Roberts said. "And maybe a piece of apple pie."

"With ice cream?" Matt asked.

"Only way to eat it is with two scoops of ice cream. See you later, Tag, and I sure hope it's never like this again," he said as he and Matt started down the hallway.

Then Matt turned and came back. "Here, brother, trade keys with me. I'll take that cycle out to the ranch. You drive my truck to the motel. I'll make arrangements with the detailer to have Nikki's car fumigated and cleaned up for her by tomorrow morning. Just call me and tell me what motel she's in so we can deliver it to her."

"Thank you," Tag whispered.

"Hey, family takes care of family."

*   *   *

Nikki threw her clothing into the trash can as she undressed, including her flip-flops. She adjusted the water to the right temperature and then stepped into the sheriff's shower. First she let the hot water run through her hair and down her back. Then she picked up the soap and a white washcloth. She soaped her whole body down three times and still didn't feel clean, so she gave it one more lathering. After that she picked up a small bottle of shampoo and squeezed the whole thing into her hair. It didn't matter if it wasn't her usual special volume-building product. It could have been pure lye soap and she wouldn't have complained.

When she finished, she dried herself off with one of the two towels that the sheriff had given her. Her skin was red when she got through, but the well-worn scrubs were soft. She didn't have a bra or underpants, but there was no way she would ever touch those things in the trash can again. She wasn't sure she could even get into her car until all that stuff from the backseat was gone and it had been scrubbed.

With her hair still damp, she went back out into the sheriff's office to find it empty, but the door leading out into the hallway was open and there was Tag. His hat was in his hands and her wallet was on the chair beside him. He stood up when he saw her, but he didn't open his arms like before.

She walked, barefoot, right up to him, went on her tip-toes, and put her arms around his neck. Tears began to flow down her cheeks. "I was mad and afraid, but I kept telling myself you'd find me."

His arms encircled her, drawing her so close that their hearts beat as one. "I was terrified I wouldn't get there in time."

"I can't get in my car," she whispered.

"You don't have to. I'm taking us to a motel in my brother's truck." He kissed her on the forehead. "You ready?"

"As I'll ever be." She picked up her wallet, took out all

the cards and cash, and stuffed them into the deep pocket of her scrubs. Then she tossed her wallet in a nearby trash can.

They walked out of the building, hand in hand. Once they were on the hot sidewalk, Tag scooped her up like a bride. She laid her head on his shoulder, and for the first time since Billy Tom showed up at the cabin, she felt safe. He put her into the big black truck and buckled her in. She closed her eyes, and Billy Tom's leering face appeared. She snapped them open and in that second decided she wouldn't be a victim. She was strong like her daddy. She'd survived having a gun in her back for hours, and she hadn't let Billy Tom intimidate her. The sheriff had said the bloody nose she'd given him was self-defense, as far as he was concerned. She wouldn't have a record.

It wouldn't be easy, but she'd get past the trauma—with Tag's help.

"We don't have a lot to offer in the way of hotels here in Tulia. You'd be more comfortable at my parents' ranch," Tag said as he fastened his seat belt.

"I'm not fit to be around people yet, Tag. You can drop me off at a motel and go on home," she said.

"I'm not leaving you. First we'll pick up some clothes for you and then some food. When did you last eat?"

"Not since breakfast." She was grateful that he was taking charge because her brain was still in a fog, even if the sheriff had assured her that she was a strong woman.

He whipped the truck into the parking lot of a Family Dollar, the only place in town to buy clothing, and snagged a place right in front. "Look, that's an omen if there ever was one." He pointed to a cart filled with rubber flip-flops. "What size do you wear?"

"Ladies size five to six will do fine," she answered.

"Color?"

"I'm not picky," she said. "Anything just so that I don't get thrown out." She nodded toward the sign on the door that said NO SHIRT, NO SHOES, NO SERVICE.

He dug around in the cart, took a pair inside the store, and returned to open her door. "Stick your feet out here, darlin'. You can be Cinderella."

"Does that mean you're Prince Charming?"

"I'll be anything or anyone you want me to be," he told her.

That was guilt talking, and she knew it, but it sounded good to her ears right then. She was surprised that no one stared at her when she entered the store. Then she saw another lady in there in orange scrubs.

"The nurses who work in the local nursing home wear orange," Tag said.

She nodded and threw a package of panties into the cart. Then she sorted through a rack of jeans and tossed in two pairs. Tag stayed right beside her, and finding a couple of bras in her size was more than a little embarrassing. After that, they found T-shirts and a nightshirt and headed toward the shampoo and toothpaste aisle. When she'd gotten everything she needed and they were at the counter, Tag whipped out a credit card.

"You're not buying my underwear," she protested.

"Yes, I am. This is my fault and there's no telling how much of your money you spent today. Your backseat looked like a trash bin and that suitcase of beer wasn't cheap," Tag said.

"Tulia's not a big place," she said softly. "Tomorrow, the fact that you were here with me and bought me clothes will be all over town."

"Good." He accepted the total, swiped his card, and put his signature on the screen. Then he carried the bags out to the truck and tossed them in the backseat with his duffel.

"Where'd that come from?" she asked.

"Hud packed it for me. Matthew put it in the truck when he took my motorcycle back out to the ranch. If you'll give me a ride home tomorrow or whenever you're ready to go, I'll leave my bike here."

That was a huge step for him to take, but she didn't want that burden on her conscience. In six weeks or maybe in six days, he'd resent her for his decision.

"You sure about that? Don't do it out of guilt, Tag," she said. "If I'd gone home last night instead of drinkin' moonshine, I wouldn't have been in the cabin this morning. If I'd brought my purse in, I'd have had my gun. This isn't your fault."

"Yes, it is." He drove away from the store and straight to a small motel. "Wait right here." He ran inside and came back with a key. "It's my fault because of decisions I made as a teenager. Duke might have approved of the crazy stunts that we pulled when I was a stupid kid, but my heart tells me it's time to grow up."

"You should always listen to your heart." She didn't even have to wonder if she was talking to him or to herself.

"We can get something pretty quick at Sonic. That okay with you?"

Food suddenly sounded wonderful. "Burgers and a chocolate shake, and the biggest root beer they make. I'm sick of water," she said.

"Fries?" he asked.

"Tater tots, double order, burger with mustard and no onions."

He nosed the truck into a slot, rolled down the window, and pushed the call button. A lady's voice asked if she could

help him. He looked over at Nikki and said, "Are you serious about wanting that much?"

"If I don't eat it now, I will before bedtime," she said.
"Want my credit card?"

He waved her away, ordered four burgers, two chocolate
shakes, two Route 44 root beers, and a double order of tater
tots and a double of fries. "And add two chicken strip dinners to that," he finished.

"How long are we staying in that motel? You've ordered
enough food for a week," she said.

He turned to face her. "I paid for two nights, but we can
leave earlier than that, or we can extend it as long as you
want. This is going to hit you in a little while. I just hope
you don't hate me when it does."

"This is still Tuesday, isn't it?" In some ways, it seemed
like the incident with Billy Tom had happened a year ago
instead of only that morning. In other ways she felt like if
she looked in the rearview mirror, she would see him sitting
in the backseat grinning with food in his mouth.

"It is," he said.

"Less than twenty-four hours ago, I faced off with my
mother, and I thought that was the hardest thing I'd ever
have to do," she said. "I was wrong, Tag, but I refuse to be
a victim in either case. That gives Mama and Billy Tom—
Seems strange to say their names in the same sentence.
Anyway, that gives them power over me, and I won't let
them make me a victim."

"You have the strength of an elephant, Nikki." Tag
reached out and tucked a strand of damp hair behind her ear.

A young girl brought his order and he paid with cash,
adding a couple of dollars for a tip.

"Now let's get you to the hotel so you can eat and call
Emily. She's frantic to hear your voice." He drove them all

the way to the end of the motel and parked at the last room in the row.

"Food, then talk." Nikki felt faint as she got out of the truck, grabbed the paper bags from the backseat, and followed Tag into the room.

Two queen-size beds with standard blue and green bedspreads took up one wall. A microwave sat on top of a small dorm-size refrigerator. The four-drawer dresser held a television, and there was a small green upholstered chair over in one corner. In the other was a tiny round table with two chairs. The bathroom had a shower above a tub. Looking at it, Nikki decided that she'd take a long, soaking bath before she went to sleep that evening. Maybe that would help her truly get the day out of her mind.

Tag set the paper bags of food on the table, left the door open, and went back out to the truck. He returned with his duffel bag. Kicking the door shut with his boot heel, he said, "Soon as we eat, I'd like to have a shower to get the dust off me."

"Tag, you don't have to stay with me," she told him. "I'm a big girl. I might go to pieces, but if I do, I'll get over it, just like I have in the past."

"I'm not going anywhere. I'll take the bed closest to the door," he said.

She crossed the room and wrapped her arms around him. "Thank you."

His phone rang and she stepped back.

"Hello," he said cautiously.

"I'm calling because I just found your number along with the words HELP ME on a card in a convenience store bathroom," a lady said. "Do you know what that means?"

The woman on the other end was practically yelling and Nikki was close enough to hear every word.

"Yes, ma'am, I do and it's all taken care of now. My girlfriend is safe," he said.

"Well, thank God for that. Y'all have a great day."

"Girlfriend?" Nikki smiled.

"If you'll have an old cowboy renegade like me," Tag answered.

"You came to rescue me. I think that forgives the rebel part," she said.

"If you'd disarmed him, we might have been rescuing him." Tag took her by the hand and led her to the table.

"If I could've figured out a way to get that gun away from him, you'd have been burying him, not saving his sorry ass."

Chapter Sixteen

The adrenaline rush for Tag crashed after he'd eaten a couple of burgers and drank half a milk shake. The whole day had been surreal, from the time the policeman knocked on the door until that moment.

"Are you ready to talk about the day?" he asked.

"I can't remember ever being this tired." She yawned. "Can we take a short nap before we talk?"

"Yes, ma'am. Just promise me if you wake before I do that you won't leave?"

"You've got my word," she said.

"I'm calling Emily and then I'm getting between the sheets—that is, if you'll loan me your phone," she said.

He kicked off his boots and headed to the bathroom with his duffel bag in hand. "I'm taking a shower. I'm too dirty to stretch out for a nap." He kissed her on the cheek, on his way across the floor. His reflection in the mirror above the vanity didn't show much of a change in him. A few flecks of dust hanging to the scruff on his face, but that was all. He had expected to see that he'd aged ten years in one day, maybe even see a few gray hairs.

He dropped all of his dirty, sweaty clothing on the floor and adjusted the water in the shower. He stepped into the tub and let the warm water beat down on his back for several minutes before he even lathered up the washcloth with soap. He and Hud had made the trip to Bowie on motorcycles last spring. That trip hadn't tired him out like this one had. Must've been the tension and worry the whole five hours, he thought. Or maybe he really was getting old, and it was time to reassess this business of living like he was dying and just live—period.

He got out of the shower and wrapped a towel around his waist. He had a change of clothing plus a pair of pajama pants and a tank top in his duffel bag. Digging deeper, he discovered underwear and Hud's go kit that held a new toothbrush and travel-size containers of toothpaste, mouthwash, and deodorant, as well as a disposable razor. Tag smiled. He didn't need the razor that day, but he appreciated all the other items.

He found a plastic laundry bag in the closet and stuffed all his dirty things into it. Then he stopped at the side of Nikki's bed and watched her sleep for a few minutes. She'd gotten between the sheets and was curled up in a ball, covers pulled all the way to her chin, hair flowing out on the pillow like a halo. But she wasn't an angel. She was a fighter. And he loved that about her.

He'd looked his fill of her, and then made sure the safety lock was engaged on the door and turned back the bedspread and top sheet on the other bed. He bit back a groan when he stretched out. The warm water had helped, but every muscle in his body was still tense. He closed his eyes and thought about the decisions he had made throughout the day. He was sure he'd made the right one in giving up his motorcycle—but there was no way he'd give up the rush of riding a bull or a bronc.

The room was dark when he awoke. The clock on the nightstand told him that it was ten thirty. Nikki was curled up against his back with one arm thrown around him and a leg hooked over his thighs. For a minute he thought he was dreaming; then she moved.

"I had a nightmare," she whispered.

He laced his fingers in hers but didn't move. "Tell me about it."

"You weren't there at that old tree across the road, and Billy Tom dragged me into that cabin. His friends were all leering at me, and Billy Tom was flashing that gun around and telling me that he'd kill me if y'all didn't pay him ten thousand dollars. That's when I woke up. I...needed to...," she stammered.

"I told you I'm here for you." He flipped over and drew her close to his body. "I might have been a scoundrel, but my word is as good as gold. If you need me to hold you every night, I'll do it."

"Out of duty?" she asked.

"Out of whatever this is between us," he answered.

*   *   *

At first light the next morning, Nikki sat up in bed and wrapped her arms around her knees. "What is this with us?"

"I'm not sure," Tag answered. "But I kind of like it." He propped two pillows against the headboard and leaned back. "Now let's talk about what happened yesterday. Tell me the whole thing, Nikki. I need to know."

"I woke up and found your note," she said. "Had a bowl of cereal. Heard a knock on the door. I thought maybe it was you, that you'd locked it behind you and couldn't get in. I opened it to find Billy Tom right there in front of me. My purse with my gun was out in my car."

"Were you scared?" Tag asked.

"More pissed than afraid—did you even hear anything on the phone when I called you?"

"Loud and clear, and then Red dragged your purse into the front yard. I think that's what really convinced the Montague County sheriff to believe me," he said.

"I drank eight bottles of water on the trip so I'd have to keep stopping to go to the bathroom, and I stayed as long as I could," she said.

"You were very brave and resourceful. Don't blame yourself for any of this, Nikki. I'm the one you should hate," he said.

"It's not your fault that Billy Tom found out where the cabin was and kidnapped me," she said. "I'd have crawled out a bathroom window or screamed for help, but he said he'd shoot everyone in the store if I did. You think he would have? After the way he curled up and bawled like a baby when I hit him with that gun, I'm not sure he'd have the balls to actually kill someone." She stretched her legs out and scooted back to share the pillows with him.

"Billy Tom has always been a loose cannon, so I don't know about killing, but I wouldn't put anything past him." Tag's tone was dead serious. "I stopped right after my twenty-first birthday. I hadn't seen or heard from him in eight years; then a couple of weeks ago, he called me out of the blue, wanting me to go in with them on this big deal."

"Were you even tempted?" she asked.

"No, not a bit. I might still be a rebel, but I'm not stupid."

He held her close and stroked her hair until she fell asleep again.

Sun rays flowed through the split in the window curtains later the next morning when Nikki awoke for the second time. The last thing she remembered was telling Tag about all the emotions that had run through her body on that horrible trip. Her back was against his chest and her stomach was telling her that it was time to eat.

"Hungry?" he whispered.

"Little bit," she answered. "Let's heat up some leftovers. Have you heard from your brother? When are they bringing my car?"

"Turned off the phone after you talked to Emily. I didn't want it to ring and wake you." He threw back the covers. "But we don't have to eat leftovers. They serve breakfast here."

"Give me a few minutes to shower and get into some clothes." She hopped out of bed and went straight to the bathroom, then remembered that she hadn't taken her things with her. He was talking on the phone when she returned, and from the look on his face, it was pretty serious.

She retrieved her new clothing and hung them on the hooks on the back side of the bathroom door. Then she stripped out of the orange scrubs, tossed them on the floor with no intentions of ever wearing them again, and ran a bath. She sank down into the warm water and wondered if she went under, would it be kind of like a baptism? Would she wash away all the fear and anger from the day before, like getting rid of sins and being reborn a new woman?

Sliding even farther down until only her nose was above water, she took a deep breath and lay on the bottom of the tub for a few seconds before she came back up. Water sluiced down her face and neck, but she still felt like Nikki

Grady. There was no washing away the sin of wanting to shoot Billy Tom—because she would still do it in a heartbeat if she had a gun and he threatened her again.

She finally pulled the plug on the tub, got out and dried her hair, and dressed in new clothing right off the rack that she'd have washed before putting on if she'd been home. She wiped the fog from the mirror and brushed her teeth. Tag was still on the phone, but the smile on his face said this call wasn't as serious.

"Talk to you later, Granny, and I'll ask Nikki about supper," he said.

"Supper?" she asked.

"I want to see my folks while I'm here, and Hud sent hugs for Mama. I understand if you don't want to go out to the ranch, though," he said.

"Supper at the ranch sounds fine. I owe Matthew a thank-you for helping rescue me," she said. "But I'm more comfortable staying here. That doesn't mean you have to spend another night protecting me."

"Billy Tom escaped," he said bluntly. "They think he's headed back to Mesquite for his cycle and they've got authorities on the lookout between here and there."

"Then would you please stay with me?" she asked. "And if you've got access to a pistol out at the ranch, would you please bring it with you after supper? But tomorrow morning, Tag, whether Billy Tom is back in custody or not, I'm going home. I have to work Friday night, and I refuse to let that son of a bitch make me afraid or upset my life."

"Deal, but just in case they don't catch him, will you let me sleep on your sofa or stay with me at the cabin or even at Emily's?"

"I'll think about it. Now let's go get some breakfast. What are we doing until supper?"

He wiggled his eyebrows. "Well, we've got this room, and the sheriff did say that you were my girlfriend."

They were back on solid ground one more time. She air slapped his arm and said, "But I don't go to bed with my boyfriend after only one date."

"You did last night—twice," he teased.

"With clothes on," she reminded him. "Know what I'd like to do today?"

"Name it and I'll do my best to make it happen," he said.

"We're close to the Palo Duro Canyon, aren't we? Emily's talked about it and I'd love to see it. The only state I've ever been to, outside of Texas, of course, is Oklahoma. I crossed the Red River a few times when I went to the Watermelon Festival in Terral," she said.

"You want to sightsee?" Tag looked genuinely shocked.

"Unless you need to be at the ranch all day," she said.

"No, ma'am." He grinned. "We'll leave right after we eat. Long as we're at the ranch for cocktails at five o'clock, we'll be fine."

"Cocktails?" She frowned.

"Very informal," he said. "We just like to gather up for a beer or a shot of whiskey before supper. It's not dress-up. You've been there before?"

"Not for cocktails. I went with Emily once, but we weren't there at supper time. Then at the wedding everyone was going every which way to get things done," she said. "Truth is, it scares me just a little to be there in the middle of your family."

He looped her arm into his. "Honey, you faced down Billy Tom. I'm surprised that anything scares you."

She slipped her feet into pink flip-flops at the door. "He's a wicked piece of trash. Your folks know we spent the night together. I can only imagine what they probably think of me."

"I talked to them this morning. They know this room has two beds, and they're happy that you let me stay with you." He locked the door behind them. "You really want to eat buffet, or would you rather go to a little café for breakfast?"

"I'm with you. You make the decision," she said.

"Then good hot food brought to the table, it is." He led her to the pickup.

It was only a short drive to the café. When they were inside, it kind of reminded her of the one in Bowie where she liked to treat herself some Monday mornings after forty-eight hours of ER duty.

They chose a booth in the back corner beside a window, and the waitress brought two coffee mugs and then filled them. "Hey, did you hear Sheriff Roberts has locked up that crazy crew you used to run with? I heard they robbed some big-shot drug dealer's shipment of ephedrine and sold it to someone else. Then the fools came back here to Tulia to that old shack they used to hang out in."

"That's what I heard," Tag said.

"Did you hear that Billy Tom escaped? That piece of slime could worm his way out of hell. Now what can I get y'all this mornin', and are you goin' to introduce me to your lady friend, or not?"

"I'm sorry, Charlene." Tag smiled. "This is Nikki Grady, my girlfriend. Nikki, this is Charlene. She cooked at the ranch for a while when I was a little boy, then opened this café."

"Pleased to meet you. I was at Emily's weddin'. You was the maid of honor, right?" Charlene said. "Y'all don't bother with orderin'. I'll bring you my big country breakfast, and it's on the house."

"Thank you, and it's a pleasure to meet you, Miz Charlene." Nikki smiled.

"You're welcome." Charlene headed back to the kitchen.

"Does she always give you free meals?" Nikki whispered across the table.

"No, ma'am. This is the first time. She must like you." He took her hands in his and brought her knuckles to his lips. "I liked waking up with you all curled up around me."

"The nightmare was so real that I woke up crying," Nikki admitted. "If you hadn't been there, I wouldn't have been able to close my eyes again all night."

"It's kind of nice to be needed and not just wanted." Tag gently squeezed her hands and took a sip of his coffee. "I liked it when you let me comfort you last night, even though I don't deserve it."

"I keep telling you that it's not your fault," she said.

"I'm glad that you believe that, but I'm not sure I'll ever forgive myself."

Chapter Seventeen

The landscape in the western part of the state was very different from back where Nikki had grown up. Here the land was flat, almost treeless and reached all the way out to the sky. By stretching the imagination a little, she could almost see the place where the earth actually rounded off a little. Back around Bowie, rolling hills were covered with scrub oak and mesquite trees and lots of cow tongue cactus.

But then a few miles out of Silverton, a town not much bigger than Montague, Tag suddenly cut the speed and they were going straight down into a big canyon. It was eerily beautiful that morning. Burnt umber and ochre, the two colors that she'd used in art class back in high school, came to her mind as she tried to take the whole scene all in with one glance.

The narrow road took them around curves, up hills, and down the other side. On every side of her were amazing rock formations, some reaching so high that she had to strain her neck to see the tops, and others looking like sand castles a child would build on the beach.

"This is awesome," she said. "No cafés, nothing commercial, just a big hole in the ground with all kinds of gorgeous sights. This must be the best kept secret in the whole state," she whispered.

*   *   *

Tag had grown up around Palo Duro, but seeing the canyon through Nikki's eyes opened it up in a whole new light for him. He hadn't thought of her travel being limited because of the disruptions in her family and then her decision to move out and live on her own at such a young age. Suddenly, he wanted to take her every place he'd ever been. Granted, most of them had been family vacations to wherever a rodeo was held, and the majority of them had been in the United States. But they had gone on a couple of cruises. He'd been bored out of his mind most of the time and had even considered jumping overboard and seeing if he could swim back to Texas. Now he wondered what it would be like to see the Mayan ruins and go snorkeling in the Gulf with Nikki.

"Look at that." She pointed.

"That's called the chimney," he said. "I've seen bald eagles sitting up there a few times. This was one of my favorite places to ride my motorcycle."

"Tag, you don't have to give it up. If you love riding, then you should keep it."

He shook his head slowly. "I don't think I can ever ride one again without flashbacks of worrying about you. When I talked to Mama this morning, I told her to donate it to the police department. Seemed fitting since they're the ones who really saved you."

"They couldn't have done it if you hadn't known where to send them."

Tag didn't know how to answer that comment, so they rode in silence for more than half an hour. He drove slowly all the way through the canyon. When they came up on the other side and reached the small town of Claude, he finally asked, "Do you want to go back the same way we came or go through Amarillo?"

"Let's hit that little convenience store right there for a bathroom break and maybe something cold to drink, and then go right back the way we came. The light will be coming from a different angle that way. And could we stop at that place at the top and take a couple of pictures?" she asked. "We'd have to use your phone. Mine is still in my purse at your ranch."

"Sure thing," he said. "Want to pick up some snacks and have a picnic? There's a table for that at the lookout over the canyon."

"Sounds great. Let's have junk food and root beer," she suggested.

He held her hand on the way into the store. She headed off to the bathroom and he gathered up candy bars, chips, and a six-pack of root beer, set it on the counter, and handed the young man a twenty-dollar bill. The guy dropped his change and had to bend down to pick it up, then fumbled when he was putting the food into a bag.

"Sweet Jesus! You're like a bad case of the itch that just keeps showing up." Tag heard Nikki raise her voice at the back of the store.

"He's got a gun," the clerk whispered.

Tag dropped his wallet on the counter and headed toward Nikki but didn't get there before she had kicked off her flip-flops and landed a square kick in Billy Tom's crotch. He rolled forward, and she picked up a gallon of motor oil from a display and swung it like a Louisville Slugger. When it made contact with the side of his head, he fell backward, taking out a stand of Twinkies on the way down.

"Tell that kid I need some duct tape and call Sheriff Roberts," she hollered at Tag. "I believe we've got something that belongs to him. And he doesn't have a gun. If he did, he'd be brandishing it like he was a badass. He was bluffing."

"Did you kill him?" Tag caught the roll of duct tape the kid threw toward him.

"I wouldn't be so lucky." She took the tape from Tag's hand and peeled off a length wide enough to tape Billy Tom's mouth shut. "He'll wake up in a minute. It'd take more than that tap on the head to keep him down. He's high as a kite on something. I can tell by his eyes." She stuck the tape firmly across his mouth, then made two wraps around his legs. "You can work on his wrists. Do a good job or he'll break free. I'll be waiting in the truck. I've seen more of this sumbitch than I want to for the rest of my life."

"She's one badass woman," the kid said. "I was terrified of him, but she scares me more. He got out of a semi that was filling up on gas. Guess he was hitchhiking. He told me that I would give him the keys to my motorcycle when he came out of the restroom and if I called anyone, he'd go to the school and shoot all the kids on the playground. I got a niece in kindergarten."

"He was bluffing. Get on your phone and call the Claude police. Tell them to come get Billy Tom, the guy who escaped from the Swisher County jail last night." Tag wrapped the tape from Billy Tom's wrists to his elbows and did the same from ankles to knees, then trussed the man's hands and feet together like a calf at a roping.

Billy Tom groaned and his eyes fluttered open. He tried to sit up, but Tag had roped him down really well. If it had been possible, he would have shot fire from his eyes at both Tag and the kid.

Tag leaned down and whispered right in Billy Tom's ear. "If you ever, ever come after Nikki or any member of my family again, I will go on the stand and testify to all your past sins. Some of those will put you so far back in jail you'll never see daylight."

Billy Tom's eyes popped out and all the color drained from his face. He struggled against the tape, but it wouldn't budge.

Tag kept talking. "You know that I don't make idle threats. But if that don't work, they will never find your body. Nod if you understand what I'm saying."

Billy Tom shot him a dirty look, but his chin bobbed up and down.

"That's good, and you might pass it on to your buddies. The same goes for them."

Another nod.

The kid made the call and turned to Tag. "He'll be here in five minutes. Could you stick around?"

"Sure thing, but I already hear the sirens. They'll be here right soon," Tag said.

"Thanks," the kid said. "I'd just feel better if..."

Tag nodded and pointed out the window. "They're here now and will be coming in soon. My lady is waiting. I think you can handle this until they get in here. Just go on back to the cash register. He can't get loose." Tag picked up his purchases and wallet as he passed the counter and walked out.

On his way out, he passed two police cars, and four officers were running toward the store with guns drawn. Tag recognized one of them from the bar down in Palo Duro that he used to frequent on Saturday nights. "Hey, Kyle. That's Billy Tom in there and you might want to keep part of that tape on him. He's high on something and slippery as a slug."

"Thanks for the heads-up." Deputy Kyle Robertson kept running. "We might be callin' you about this later."

"You got my number," Tag hollered back.

He was more than a little surprised to see his own hands shaking when he put the bag of snacks in the backseat of the truck. When he got behind the wheel, he leaned over the console, took Nikki's face in his hands, and kissed her—long and lingering and then passionate. When the kiss ended, his nerves were as steady as a rock.

"What was that for?" she asked.

"For just bein' you," he answered.

"Well, I got to admit I was trembling from head to toe when I got out here, but your kiss settled me right down. If that sorry sucker escapes again, I vote that we put out an order to shoot first and ask questions later," she said.

A surge of pure happiness swept through Tag. She had acknowledged that his kiss had affected her the same way it had him. He turned the key to start the engine and Elizabeth Cook was singing "Sometimes It Takes Balls to Be a Woman."

Nikki shot a sideways glance toward him and giggled. He chuckled and before he could put the truck in gear, they were both laughing so hard they could hardly breathe.

Tag finally wiped his eyes. "Talk about perfect timing and something taking all the tension out. You sure you're all right?"

The laughter stopped as suddenly as it had begun, and Nikki looked like she might start crying any minute. Tag had never been good with weeping women, not even his sister or mother, who seldom shed tears. He followed her gaze, and there was Billy Tom, his hands now cuffed behind his back and all the duct tape gone, and he was looking straight at Nikki. The noise from the radio blocked the evil words spewing from his mouth, but Tag could read his lips. Nikki was right. If he escaped again, they should put out a shoot-on-sight order.

Tag laid a hand on her arm. "Are you okay?"

"I am strong. I can do this. I will not be intimidated." She recited the words like a mantra.

"Okaay." Tag dragged the word out.

"I'm not losing my mind." She covered his hand with hers. "'I am strong and I can do this' is what I would say to myself after my brother died and my dad left, and I had to deal with my mother's problems. That last part I've added since I moved out on my own," she said. "Sometimes I have to say it a dozen times before I begin to believe it. I refuse to let the likes of Billy Tom or his evil looks put fear in my heart, even if I have to stand in front of a mirror and repeat it for a whole hour." She inhaled deeply and removed her hand.

"You are strong, and you can do this. I believe in you," Tag said as he drove west out of Claude toward the highway that would take them south and back through the canyon.

*   *   *

Nikki was glad for Tag's faith in her, but her stomach was still twisted up like a pretzel. Kicking Billy Tom like that had been pure impulse. Thank God for that display of motor oil at her fingertips, because even on his knees and groaning, he looked like he could break her in half like a twig.

They started descending into the canyon, and Tag handed

her his phone. "Snap away. Just tell me if you want me to pull off to the side of the road so you can get a better view of something."

"That sounds great. I'm already thinking about a collage to go above my sofa." She started taking pictures, one after the other.

"We'll stop and get copies made of whatever you want on the way home tomorrow," he offered.

"Or we can wait and let me study them before we do that." She took several more out the car window.

When they reached the turnout to the picnic area, two hours had passed and she'd snapped more than a hundred pictures. The tiny place had a couple of big empty trash cans, one picnic table, and an awesome view of several formations. Tag got the snack bag from the backseat and set it on the table. Nikki headed straight for a fenced walkway that overlooked miles and miles of the canyon. She'd snapped a dozen more pictures when she turned around to see Tag sitting on the concrete table with his feet on the bench. She motioned for him to join her.

Without asking why, he meandered that way. "I've seen this place dozens of times. Even donated a few empty beer cans to those trash bins over there."

"But I haven't. And I want a picture of you right there." She pointed to the end of the fenced area. Tag propped one arm on the fence and looked right at her with those clear eyes that matched the cloudless sky behind him and the blue of his Western shirt. He'd rolled the sleeves up to his elbows, showing off arms that had seen lots of hard work. His black cowboy hat against the sky set off the whole picture. In the distance to the right was a huge ochre-colored formation.

"Should I smile?" he asked.

"Not in this one," she said. "Just look at me and follow me with your eyes."

"No problem there. You look pretty damn cute today."

She took a couple dozen pictures. "That should do it."

"No sexy come-hither grin?" he asked.

"Give me the best you've got." She focused on him one more time.

"This works better than a grin anytime." He slid an eyelid shut in a sexy wink. She caught the picture perfectly and decided that would probably be the one in the center of her collage.

"Now it's time to reverse the situation. Give me the phone and you come out here right where I'm standing and let me take a few pictures of you."

"Are you sure? The wind is blowing my hair every which way. I don't have makeup on."

He took the phone from her hand and nodded. "Very sure. Face me and the wind will blow your hair out of your face."

When he'd taken half a dozen shots, he shoved the phone in his pocket and held out his hand. The sparks that danced around like dandelion blossoms in the wind didn't surprise her at all. The place where they were standing wasn't roses and champagne, but it was magical to her. It erased all the fears of that morning and left behind only peace. Tag had rescued her and then hadn't said a word when she'd taken care of matters. This man was worth a chance, no matter what his past had been.

Chapter Eighteen

Tag's mother, Anne, poured three glasses of white wine and handed one to Nikki. "Glad to have you with us this evening. You've surely been through a lot the past couple of days. I understand that Billy Tom is back in the Swisher County jail now, thanks to you." She lowered her voice to a whisper. "He's been bad news his whole life."

Anne stood a full head taller than Nikki and had flaming red hair that she wore in a ponytail at the nape of her neck. That she was Emily's mother wasn't a surprise, but Anne was slim built and Emily was a curvy woman.

"I can believe that," Nikki said.

Tag's grandmother Opal, a gray-haired lady not nearly as tall as Anne, touched her wineglass to Nikki's and smiled. "Would you like a sawed-off shotgun, just in case that sorry sucker shows up in your neck of the woods again? I've got a couple of extras."

"Thank you, but I have a gun."

"Pistol?" Opal asked.

"Yes, ma'am. And I practice often," Nikki answered.

"They're fine, but up close, nothing brings about fear like the sound of racking a shell in a sawed off," Opal said.

"A little red dot does pretty good." Nikki smiled and then took a sip of the wine. "Especially if you move it slowly from their heart to the zipper in their jeans."

"Girl after my own heart," Opal chuckled.

Why in the name of all that was good and right in the world couldn't God have given her to Anne instead of Wilma Grady so that Opal could be her grandmother?

Because that would make you Tag's sister, a pesky voice in the back of her head said loudly.

She glanced across the room to find Tag staring right at her. She held up her glass, and he gave her a long, slow wink as he raised his beer bottle.

Supper was served family style—fried chicken, mashed potatoes, gravy, and all the trimmings. Proper manners, according to Wilma, said a lady ate like a bird when in polite company. Nikki figured she was adhering to her upbringing when she had a second helping just like Opal and Anne did. Wilma hadn't said a sparrow. She'd said a bird and ostriches were classified as birds.

"I like a woman who enjoys good food," Tag whispered.

"I don't get a supper like this very often," she said.

"I hear there's a ranch rodeo this weekend over in your neck of the woods," Matthew said. "And you're not going to believe this, but there's a bull named Fumanchu they say is meaner than Devil Dog."

Tag's eyes glittered. "Oh, yeah, when exactly?"

"Friday night. I heard that no one will sign up to ride him. After that song you play all the time, I figured you'd want to give it a try," Matthew said.

"Dammit!" Opal hit the table hard enough to rattle the dishes. "Why'd you have to tell him that?"

"There's a few things he's got to get out of his system." Matthew grinned. "But now that he's had two run-ins with Billy Tom, maybe he's given up on that song."

"Not hardly," Tag said. "I been waitin' more than ten years for this. I'll check into it soon as supper is over."

Nikki's breath caught in her chest. That pink line of scar under the scruff on his face would be nothing compared to what it would look like if a mean bull trampled him. Maybe all this with Billy Tom had only slowed him down, not ended his rebel days. But then would she care as much for him if he didn't have just a little bit of wild in him?

That's a question that needs an answer. This time it was Emily's voice in her head.

A visual of Tag being carried into the emergency room on a stretcher with a broken leg—or worse, with a broken neck—flashed into her mind. Tears welled up in her eyes, but she refused to let even one fall down her cheek. Could she ever commit one hundred percent to a man who was constantly living on the edge?

Opal nudged her with an elbow. "You ever listen to Miranda Lambert?"

Nikki nodded.

"I like her stuff and the Pistol Annies too. Ever heard her do 'Storms Never Last'?"

Another nod.

"Don't give up on him, Nikki. Storms don't last forever. He's fightin' his way out of a web of guilt, and we see a lot of progress," Opal whispered.

*   *   *

Tag was so excited about the bull that he called the ranch rodeo number on the website as soon as supper was over. With adrenaline climbing almost as high as it had the day before when he faced off with Billy Tom, he gave the lady his information and told her he'd bring the entry fee with him on Friday.

"Want to enter in the bronc as well?" she asked. "We're having it before the bull ride, and we're saving Fumanchu for the last ride of the night, because he's one mean son of a gun."

"Can I bring my own saddle?" he asked. "I'm kind of partial to it."

"We encourage that," she answered.

"Then yes, ma'am. I'll come prepared to ride a bronc and the bull," he told her.

"You should be here by seven thirty, then," she said.

"You can count on it." He ended the call, picked up Nikki, and swung her around until they were both dizzy.

"You're crazy." She wobbled when he finally set her firmly on the floor.

"I might be. I wish you could be there to see me," he said.

"She'll be waiting at the hospital to fix you up afterwards," Matthew teased.

"I'll make sure there's a cubicle ready. He's in luck. Dr. Richards is on duty again, and he's the best at stitchin' and mendin' broken bones," Nikki said.

"Y'all goin' to come watch me?" Tag asked.

Opal shook her head. "I'm not drivin' five hours to watch an eight-second ride."

"Eight seconds?" Nikki chuckled. "The song says that he just has to stay on the bull for two point seven seconds, don't it? And then he has to go skydiving to finish up the list, right?"

"I thought there was something about fishin' in there," Anne said.

"He's done that." Nikki nodded. "I'll sign the affidavit for that part."

"And on that note, I think Nikki and I'd better be going. I've got a couple of places I want to show her before the sun goes completely down. Mama, Hud sent a hug from him, so you better hug me twice," Tag said.

"Long as you promise you won't swing me around like you did Nikki, I'll take both those hugs." Anne walked into his open arms. "You take one back to Hud and the other boys for me. I bet Maverick and Paxton are missing their folks."

"Truth is, we've been so busy tryin' to get fences up that we drag in at dark, ready for sleep," he answered. "We're hopin' to get things in shape before winter sets in. They tell me there's not as much snow out in that part of Texas, but it can still get bitter cold and there's the occasional ice storm."

Matthew clamped a hand on his younger brother's shoulder. "After this little vacation, you should really work by the light of the moon until about midnight to make up for your lost time."

"Coming from the Baker boy who stays in an office ninety percent of the time?" Tag teased.

"Hey, now, I've offered to show you the ropes when it comes to the paper end of a ranch. Which brings me to the question—who's doin' that at your place? Have you roped Nikki into it? Which also reminds me." Matthew dug into his pocket and brought out a set of keys. "Nikki's car's been delivered to the motel. I told the guys to leave it in the parking lot. I'll send one of the hired hands to get my truck tomorrow. Just give the keys to Clarissa at the front desk."

Nikki shook her head. "Thank you, Matthew. You can't

begin to know how much I appreciate this. And about the book work at the ranch, Tag has not talked me into doing it. I can get around my tablet at work, but all that ranchin' lingo isn't up my alley. I barely know a cow from a goat. I'm a nurse, not a ranchin' woman."

Frank Baker had been quiet most of the evening, but his eyes, so much like Tag's, held a double dose of humor. "What this boy of mine needs worse than someone who can pull a calf or put a roof on a barn is a nurse to take care of all his injuries."

"I'll do my best," Nikki said as serious as she could. "But I don't do miracles."

By the time they said their goodbyes and left the Rocking B Ranch that evening, the sun was just a sliver out on the far horizon, past miles and miles of flat land. "One Wing in the Fire" by Trent Tomlinson was playing on the radio when Tag parked the truck in front of the motel door.

"I'm not sure I want my kids to ever think that I had one wing in the fire," he said seriously. "I want to be there to fix their cars and their hearts like the song says, but I want my kids to think that I have a halo like I thought my grandpa had."

"You think that about your dad too?" she asked.

"Pretty much," he said.

"Must be nice. My dad probably had one wing in the fire and no halo at all," she said.

"But he could have turned into a preacher in a little church over around Dallas," Tag suggested. "Don't judge until you know."

Her temper flared for a split second until she realized that he was right. The letters, the cards, the money, they all said that he hadn't stopped caring for her. And before Quint died, they'd gone to church every Sunday. Now, wouldn't it be a twist if she was dating a rebel and her father was a preacher?

"I thought we were going to see some stuff in town before the sun went down," she said as she reached for the door handle. "Look, there's my car. I'm going to go drive it up close to the motel door."

"You want to go sightseeing or grab a shower and throw back on the bed and watch reruns of whatever's on television? I made up that story because I hate goodbyes, and I wanted to get away from the ranch rather than put it off," he said.

"I've really seen enough for one day. I don't even want to talk to Emily tonight. I can call her on the way home tomorrow." She yawned.

"I'm sure she'll be tied up with Mama and Granny all evening anyway. They were probably lightin' up the cell phone towers between here and there before we even got into the truck. I'll open the door while you get your car. You aren't goin' to take off and leave me stranded, are you?" he asked.

She reached across the console and pinched his cheek. "I wouldn't leave my knight in shining armor behind. I might need rescuing again."

He grabbed her hand and brushed sweet kisses across the palm. "I hope not, darlin'."

Her hand was still tingling when she reached her car, and she fumbled the keys. They landed on the ground by her toes, and when she reached down to get them, a cold chill found its way down her spine. What if Billy Tom had a friend on the outside who'd done something to her car?

She was crawling around on the pavement looking for flashing red lights when she noticed a man's boots on the other side. Her heart leapt right up into her throat. She plastered herself against the driver's door and wished that she'd taken Opal up on that sawed-off shotgun. She could hear whoever it was walking around the car and then a hand shot out and touched her shoulder.

"What are you doing? Did your keys scoot under the car?" Tag asked.

"I guess I don't have balls after all. I'm as paranoid as my mother." She was honest when she told him about being afraid there was a bomb under her car.

"You never know with Billy Tom." He extended a hand and pulled her up to a standing position. "Billy Tom isn't smart enough to make a bomb, and besides, he's never going to bother you again. He and I had a little visit after I got the duct tape on him. I'll drive the car up to the motel. Door is open."

She tossed him the keys and stood perfectly still until her vehicle was parked in front of their room. When she started walking, he met her halfway and they walked to the door together.

"What did you tell him to make you so sure that he'll never bother me again?" she asked.

"Just that I knew a lot of stuff about him and his past that could get him a long time in the county jail or maybe even some prison time. I did say that if he threatened you again, they wouldn't find his body."

"That's pretty strong," she said.

"It wasn't a threat. It was a promise."

"Thank you for being honest with me," she said. "It means a lot, but I do wish I'd taken your grandmother up on her offer to let me have one of her sawed-off shotguns."

Tag closed the door behind them and locked it. "I've got one at the ranch back home that I'll let you have if you really want it." He sat down on the end of the bed and removed his boots, then threw himself backward. "I'd feel better if you'd let me sleep on your sofa, or if you'd stay at the cabin for a while. From now on there'll be protection at your fingertips, I promise."

She giggled nervously.

"Why's that funny?"

"I'm on the pill." She kicked off her flip-flops and headed to the bathroom. "I don't need your protection."

He popped up to a sitting position. "You are a lesson in confusion, woman. One minute you're thinking bombs and the next condoms."

"One can blow you to an up-close-and-personal visit with St. Peter. The other can change everything on this earth for the rest of your natural life. And the confusing thing—well, darlin', that keeps you on your toes." She shut the bathroom door, but it didn't keep out his laughter.

She took a short shower and washed her hair and then stepped out and wrapped a towel around her body and one around her hair. After she was dry and dressed she towel dried her hair and thought about what her mother would say if she were to move in with Tag. Wilma Grady might even curl up and die at the very idea of her daughter living in sin.

That brought up a picture of a long black hearse, which looped around and made her think of the black Lincoln she'd seen several times in and around Bowie. Could that be her father? Holy hell! Had he been keeping tabs on her all this time?

She slung open the door and announced, "Tag, I want to find my father. I think maybe he's been looking for me." She told him about the black Lincoln and the glimpses of the guy in sunglasses and a cap.

"Only way to find out for sure is to ask him." Tag unbuttoned his shirt and took it off on his way to the bathroom. "You sure you're ready for that? Want to let this all settle before you take that on?"

"Nope, I want to know. I'm going to that address on the envelopes and cards this week." She couldn't take her eyes off his ripped abdomen or the little patch that was just the right amount of hair on his chest. Her fingers itched to see if it was as soft as it looked, so she sat on the bed and tucked her hands under her thighs. He undid his belt, laid it on the dresser, and emptied his pockets. Thinking about him taking off his jeans put a crimson blush on her cheeks.

He stopped at the bathroom door. "So what evening do you want to do this?"

"Monday I have to talk to Mama or the world will come to an end. Tuesday or Wednesday probably," she said. "Why?"

"I'll go with you. Pick you up at seven on Wednesday?"

"You don't have to do that, Tag."

In a couple of long strides he crossed the room, bent so their eyes were on the same level, and gave her a quick kiss on the lips. "I want to go. I can stay in the truck or go up to the door with you. Your choice, but I'll be there for support."

"Thank you," she said softly. "And you don't have to sit in the truck."

Chapter Nineteen

Tag went to sleep alone on Wednesday night, but when he awoke on Thursday, Nikki was curled up against his back again. Before he could turn over, she slipped out of bed and went to the bathroom. When she returned, she was fully dressed.

"Nightmares again?" he asked.

"Oh, yeah," she said. "But they say the third time is the charm, so after tonight they won't be there anymore."

"I'd still feel better if you'd either let me stay at your place or you'd sleep at the cabin or with Emily." He sat up in the bed and stretched.

"I wouldn't put Emily at risk. He knows where the cabin is, and he doesn't know where I live," she said. "But he does know my car, and I just remembered, I have to get my real license plate back."

"Why?" He stood up and headed for the bathroom.

"Billy Tom switched plates at one of the service stations.

Or at least he said he did. God, I hope the nightmares end soon."

"If we get to Bowie before they close, we can stop on the way. Nikki, I apologize again for everything, but most of all for the horrible dreams that bring it all back to you."

"I'm just glad that you've been there the past two nights to comfort me." She sat down on the edge of the bed.

She'd never know how much it meant to him that she accepted his apologies and let him stay with her. The whole way to Tulia, he'd figured that she would never speak to him again, and then when she wouldn't even let him touch her after Billy Tom was handcuffed, it seemed like he'd been right.

He heard her humming when he'd finished brushing his teeth and was getting dressed, but he couldn't figure out what the song was. At least she was happy. He scanned the bathroom one more time to make sure he'd remembered everything and then went on out to talk to Nikki.

Her things were all in plastic bags and waiting with the snack sack from yesterday on the end of her bed. She was organized and neat, which was another plus in his book.

"Want to eat breakfast in the hotel dining room before we leave or get something on the way?" he asked.

"Food here is free, so we might as well eat." She picked up the bags on her bed. "We should be home by early afternoon, right?"

"You anxious to get there, are you?"

"I imagine Goldie is getting pretty hungry. She may decide to run away from home if I treat her like this very often," Nikki answered.

"I'm picturing a goldfish holding a stick tucked up under her arm. There's a little sack of food at the end, and she's bouncing down the stairs on her fat little belly," he chuckled.

"Well, what can you expect? You gave her to me, so she's probably a renegade just like you." Nikki threw her bags into the backseat of her car. "Man, this looks and smells new, like it did the first day I bought it."

"We've got a real good detail guy. He even takes care of Granny's vintage '59 Chevy pickup."

"You're kiddin'. She's got a sixty-year-old truck?" Nikki asked as they started toward the motel.

"Yep, Grandpa was driving it when they went on their first date. She wouldn't let him trade it in or sell it. She gets it out at least once a week to 'blow the cobwebs out of the engine.'" He put air quotes around the last phrase.

"What color is it?"

He held the door open for her to enter the lobby first. "Two tone. Gold on top. White on bottom. It has a special stall in the barn and stays covered except for her weekly trip to town or once a year when she has it detailed. But when Grandpa was alive, they used it every year on their anniversary. They'd usually leave the ranch for a week."

"Where'd they go?" Nikki asked as she scanned the small dining area with its buffet laid out on one side.

"Road trips. No reservations. No plans. Grandpa said they went where the wind took them. They ate when they got hungry and stayed in hotels whenever they were tired. Granny looked forward to the trips all year. I'll get two cups of coffee and set them on that table." He nodded toward one at the back of the room where he could watch the door. He'd feel a lot better when Billy Tom was in a more secure place than the county jail.

"That kind of travel sounds amazing." She picked up a paper plate and started down the line.

Tag was thinking about a week on the road with Nikki and overflowed the first coffee cup. He dumped enough to get the lid on the cup and then wiped down the outside. His thoughts went back to where he'd like to take Nikki, and he did the same thing with the second cup.

"A little distracted?" She was already seated when he set the coffee on the table.

"Little bit." He spun around and headed toward the buffet. The beach at Florida would be a nice stop for a couple of days, he thought. When he realized what he was doing, his plate had a mound of scrambled eggs on it big enough for three lumberjacks. He couldn't scrape them back, so he covered them with sausage gravy and added a couple of biscuits to the side.

Nikki's eyes popped out at the sight when he set it on the table. "You need sideboards for that."

"Distracted again," he muttered.

"Billy Tom?"

He took a sip of the coffee. "No, I was thinking about a road trip with you."

"Oh, really, and where are we going?"

"East to Shreveport, south to New Orleans, then over to a little secluded beach in the panhandle of Florida, maybe back up through Montgomery, Alabama, and Nashville, Tennessee," he said.

"Do we get to take Opal's truck?" She spread cream cheese on a bagel and then added strawberry jam.

"She doesn't even let Emily drive that truck, and Emily is her favorite," Tag chuckled. "If you could do a weeklong road trip, where would you want to go?"

"That one you said would be pretty nice for a starter. I've always wanted to see the ocean," she said.

"The beach I had in mind is in the panhandle, so it would be the Gulf of Mexico, not the ocean," he said between bites.

"Is the water salty?" she asked.

He nodded.

"Then it's the ocean to me, but as much fun as it is to think about that kind of trip, I don't see it happening," she said.

"Me neither. At least not for two or three years until we get the ranch going good. If things were to work out on a long-term basis for us, maybe we'll never sell my truck."

"So you've got hope that this chemistry between us could be more than a flash in the pan?" She finished off her bagel and sipped at the black coffee.

"Oh, my hopes are mighty high." He polished off the last of his breakfast. "How about a coffee refill for the road?"

"No, thanks." She covered a yawn with her hand. "Am I driving or are you?"

"I'll be glad to," he offered. "Looks like you're still sleepy. I'm wide awake."

"Thank you. It was a rough night. I'd love to catch a little more sleep," she said as she got into the passenger seat and leaned it back as far as it would go.

For the first hundred miles, he constantly kept an eye on the rearview mirror. He wouldn't have been surprised at any minute to see a motorcycle coming up fast, but it never did. He settled down to listen to the radio and let his thoughts wander back to the conversation about a road trip. They'd just passed the city limits sign to Childress when Nikki roused.

"Where are we?"

"You've slept a little less than two hours. We're on Highway 287. It will take us all the way to Bowie," he answered.

"Can we stop at that Pilot station up ahead for something cold to drink and a bathroom break?" she asked.

"Of course. No nightmares?" He flipped on the turn signal to get off at the next exit.

"Nope. Slept like a baby," she answered.

The parking lot was crowded, but he snagged a place right in front of the store. Nikki was out of the vehicle and practically jogging to the store before he could be a gentleman and open the door for her. Once he stepped outside the car, he understood her rush. The heat was downright oppressive, and it was only midmorning. He hurried after her, pressing the button on his key fob and listening for the click to tell him the doors were locked. As much as he'd loved his motorcycle, he was glad that he wasn't riding it that day.

He made a sweep through the place before he went to the men's room. There was no one who even resembled one of Billy Tom's gang in the store or in the restroom. When he came back out, Nikki was standing in front of the glass doors where the cold soda pop was displayed.

"Root beer is over there." He pointed.

"I'm trying to decide if I want something in a bottle or a fountain drink with ice," she said.

"I'm getting a big sweet tea with ice. It'll stay cold for at least another hundred miles and then we'll stop for lunch," Tag said.

"That sounds really good." She headed toward the drink machine at the front of the store.

They didn't have to stand in line, so they were back in the car and on the way in a few minutes. Tag groaned when he slid behind the steering wheel. "I miss my truck."

"I guess my car is a little small for you, isn't it?" she said. "What about your motorcycle? Do you miss it?"

"Not in this heat." He took a long drink of the tea and then put it in the cup holder in the console.

"Y'all rode out to Bowie and back when you came to visit Emily last spring," she reminded him.

"And the weather was fairly cool. Come to think of it, where were you while we were there?"

"Working and studying to take my test to be a registered nurse. If anyone had told you what would be happening this past couple of months back then, would you have believed them?"

He pulled out of the parking lot and merged with the traffic on the highway. "I could have believed that we'd own the ranch. Hud and I have been looking for something we could afford for the past couple of years. I wouldn't have believed that we could talk Maverick and Paxton into moving with us so we'd have some help. Or that you'd finally agree to go out with me."

"Maverick and Paxton seem more like brothers to you and Hud than distant cousins. I'd think they'd be happy to join you," she said.

"They've been with the Rocking B since they got out of high school, and we've been through a lot together even before that. It's complicated. Granny's cousin went to Ireland when he was in the military and brought home an Irish wife. She and Granny became fast friends and have remained so all through the years."

Tag watched the landscape change from flat as a pancake to rolling hills. Sometimes he missed what he'd grown up around, too, and a day didn't go by that he didn't miss his family. "How'd you handle it when your dad left?"

"I was mourning for my brother, so I guess I kind of clumped it all together and grieved for him like he was dead too. I don't know where I got it, but since Mama was so..." Nikki frowned like she was searching for the right word, then finally threw up her hands in defeat. "Well, you've met her and I told you what she said when Quint died, so you can guess how she was. I felt like I owed it to both of them to grieve for a whole year. It sounds insane, but a year passed before I had the first little bit of closure."

"When did you have it all, the closure, I mean?" he asked.

"I still don't, not any more than you do for Duke," she answered.

"Giving up the motorcycle has helped," he said.

"Seeing my father in person might do it for me." She reached into the backseat and brought up the snack bag, dug around until she found a package of chocolate doughnuts and a bag of peanuts. "Can I open something for you?"

"Maybe a candy bar if there's one left," he said. "Something about riding makes a person hungry."

"Why did you decide to give up your motorcycle?" she said.

"I haven't ridden it since we bought the ranch. But more importantly, I thought about it all the way to Tulia. Granny told me once that if I was arguing with myself, then I should go somewhere quiet and take five minutes to imagine not doing whatever it was. And then spend another five minutes imagining doing it. Whichever vision delivered peace at the end was the way I should go."

"So you did that?" Nikki bit off half a miniature doughnut.

"I was going down this very stretch of highway. I didn't have a clock, so for twenty miles from this spot I tried to remember all the really good times I'd had on the bike. There was only one that I could really say was fun and not dangerous. That was last spring when Hud and I rode our cycles to Bowie. Then I thought about the fun times I'd had in my truck and on the ranch, especially Canyon Creek with the guys and with you. It wasn't a tough decision after that."

"You think if I think about not seeing my father and then seeing him, it will do the same for me?" she asked.

"I thought you were already resigned to going to see him on Wednesday evening," Tag answered.

"Give me ten minutes. Don't talk to me, but you can turn on the radio. Sometimes songs help me more than words," she said.

He found a country music station and set the volume low. He looked at the digital clock on the dashboard and got ready for ten minutes of nothing but soft music and no talking. Three songs later, Nikki turned to him and said, "I'm going to see him on Wednesday. The last card he sent was dated three months ago, so I hope he still lives there."

"Then I guess we've both made the right decision," Tag added. "Any of those songs help you?"

"Not a single one." She finished off the doughnuts and picked up her tea. "How much farther is it to Bowie?"

"If we only take thirty minutes to eat dinner, we'll be there by one," he answered.

"After that breakfast and our road food, we don't really need to stop, do we?"

"I'm game if you are," he answered.

"And now a classic from 1996," the DJ said. "Let's give it up for Deana Carter."

"1996," Nikki said. "I was just a little girl back then."

"Me too. Born in August 1990."

"July," she said.

"I always did like older women." He grinned.

*   *   *

Nikki stayed just long enough at the ranch to drop off Tag and retrieve her purse and phone. Of course, the phone's battery was dead, so she couldn't call Emily on the way to her apartment. It seemed like a year since she'd seen her friend, but she wanted to get home, collect her thoughts, and feed Goldie.

She parked in her usual spot and climbed the stairs. She was about to unlock the door when she heard the crunch of tires on gravel. She whipped around to see Emily getting out of her van. She unlocked the door and held it open while Emily took the steps two at a time and almost bowled Nikki over when she wrapped her up in a hug. Then she stepped back and eyed Nikki from her toes to the top of her head. "He didn't hurt you, did he?"

"No, just made a lot of threats," Nikki answered.

"I'll get out the ice cream and two spoons and then you're going to tell me every single detail." Emily headed straight to the freezer while Nikki fed Goldie a double amount of food.

Emily carried the container of ice cream and two spoons to the sofa, kicked off her shoes, and sat with her legs drawn up under her. Nikki took the spoon Emily handed her, sat down on the other end, and dipped deep, bringing up lots of chocolate bits.

"Talk," Emily said.

"How much do you already know? What did Tag tell you?" Nikki asked.

"I haven't seen Tag. Mama called and said that she'd talked to him, that y'all were home and he was going out to help the guys for the rest of the afternoon. I knew you would come straight home. This is your nest, like my apartment used to be mine. So start from the beginning and tell me the whole story. I hear you and my brother shared a hotel room. Did you?" She raised an eyebrow.

"We did *not*." Nikki put emphasis on the last word.

"I'm sure you know the basics. Kidnapped. Threatened. Rescued."

"Just start talking or I'm not sharing this ice cream," Emily said.

"It's my ice cream," Nikki reminded her.

"But I'm bigger than you are, so I can keep it away from you," Emily laughed. "I want to hear, so please start talking before my head explodes. I've been so worried. Here's your phone and your purse."

Nikki had told the story twice already—once to the sheriff and then to Tag—but there were certain details she'd left out. The sheriff didn't need to know how bad Billy Tom smelled or the way he made her skin crawl when he leered at her, and neither did Tag.

"Okay, it all actually started Monday night when I went to see Mama." Tears streamed down her face as she told Emily what her mother had said about never wanting her and wishing her father had taken her with him rather than leaving her behind.

"Oh. My. God!" Emily gasped. "I knew Wilma had mental issues but that's downright cruel."

Nikki pulled a tissue from a box on the end table and blew her nose. "Then I read everything in that box of letters and cards from my father." She pointed. "There's probably three or four thousand dollars in those cards. Every birthday, Valentine's Day, Christmas, graduation for the past fifteen years, he sent me a hundred-dollar bill. I'm going to see him on Wednesday, and Tag is going with me."

"Good." Emily took the ice cream back to the freezer and put on a pot of coffee. "Go on."

"I couldn't sleep, and I wouldn't call you because it was way late at night, so I went to the cabin and wound up sleeping on the sofa." Nikki went on with the story from there.

Little by little, word by word, from friend to friend, it all came out, and when she had finished the telling, Nikki felt something like closure. Not the kind that she needed where her dad was concerned, but hopefully that would come later.

"After all that, you've got to come home with me, or at least stay at the cabin with Tag," Emily said.

"If I beg, will you let Tag sleep on the sofa here in your apartment for a while?"

"I'll be fine right here," Nikki insisted. "And no, you can't stay either. You belong in bed with your husband."

"Okay, okay!" Emily put up both hands. "You're mean and tough and you don't take no shit off nobody."

"Just like John Wayne," Nikki giggled.

"I should be getting home. Oh, I almost forgot," Emily said. "We're having brunch tomorrow morning at ten for you and the Fab Five. They've been every bit as worried as I have. And you'll have to tell the whole story one more time. Claire is going to close up shop for a couple hours so she can be there too, and Retta is coming."

"Want me to come early and help get things ready?" Nikki asked.

"That would be great." Emily gave her a kiss on the cheek and disappeared outside.

"It's just you and me now, Goldie. Did you miss me?" Nikki asked as she plugged her phone into the charger. "Of course you did. I'm the one with the fish food."

She sat down on the sofa and called her mother.

"Why are you calling me? This isn't Monday," Wilma said.

"Did you hear that I was kidnapped?" Nikki asked.

"They had a prayer circle at church. Guess God heard them because you're home, right?" Wilma asked.

"Yes, I am."

"Then we'll talk Monday like we always do." Wilma ended the call.

Nikki sighed and bit back tears, reminding herself that her mother was ill, and nothing Nikki did or said would change that.

Her phone rang, and thinking it might be her mother with an explanation for hanging up on her, she didn't even look at the caller ID.

"Nikki, we're calling it a day," Tag said. "We ran out of fence posts and the place we get them is closed until tomorrow. Are you sure I can't stay with you?"

"I'm fine. Really, I am. If I don't see you again, good luck on that bull tomorrow night," she said.

"Thanks, but you'll see me before that. Good night," Tag said.

"Night, Tag," she said.

She was truly now in her nest as Emily called it. Her phone was working. Her pistol was on the counter just in case. And she felt almost as safe as she did when she snuggled up to Tag in the bed at the hotel.

Chapter Twenty

The Fab Five—Otis, Larry, Sarah, Bess, and Patsy—came into Emily's new house that morning like a whirlwind.

"Are you okay? I don't mind spending the rest of my years in jail if you want me to kill that sumbitch." Otis was the first one to reach Nikki and hug her.

Otis and Larry had always reminded her of the two old cartoon characters Mutt and Jeff. Otis was short with a round face and a mischievous look in his eyes, and Larry was the opposite—tall and lanky.

"Me neither," Larry declared. "And I'm meaner'n Otis. I'll make him suffer." He bent to hug Nikki.

"Thank you, both, but he's locked up and far away." She peeked around Larry. "Where're the ladies?"

"Right here, darlin'." Sarah patted her gray hair as she entered the dining room. "Damn wind. I just got my hair done yesterday. I didn't know them two could move so fast. At home they can barely get up and down off the kitchen chairs." Like Larry, she was tall and thin and had to bend to give Nikki a hug.

"We had to hurry," Otis said. "Once y'all get in here, we wouldn't have a chance."

"Or to get a word in." Larry nodded.

"You've had your time. It's mine now." Patsy wiggled her round body between Sarah and Nikki. Not any taller than Nikki, she was the firecracker of the Five. Her short, kinky hair was dyed red, and trouble followed her around like a puppy.

Patsy and Bess were twins, but they were as different as night and day. Bess wore her gray hair in two long braids twisted around her head, but she and Patsy were built alike and had the same eyes. Attitude was what made them different.

A lot like Hud and Tag, Nikki thought as Bess finally got her turn to give her a hug. *Tag is the rebellious one like Patsy. Hud is the grounded one like Bess.*

"Honey, they're all a bunch of hot wind. You want something done, you leave it to me. I won't go to jail because I won't get caught," Bess told her.

"I appreciate y'all so much." If only her mother could be as supportive as these folks.

None of them have the mental issues your mother has. Was that her father's voice she was hearing? *It would have been better if you'd had a different childhood, but her example was a lesson in how to not live your life.*

She stood very still, but evidently that was all that her father had to say for now.

"Brunch is on the bar. It's buffet style," Emily said. "We have champagne and orange juice for mimosas, but no more than one for each of you."

"This is a celebration," Otis said. "Nikki lived through a life-threatening ordeal. We should get at least two."

"One." Emily held up a forefinger. "Besides, by the time we each have one, the champagne will be all gone."

"Then I'll take Bess's," Patsy said. "When I hear this story, I'm sure I'll need it."

"Over my dead body," Bess declared.

"Someone can have mine," Retta said as she and Claire arrived through the back door. "I'll be glad when this little girl gets here so I can have a beer again."

"It'll be a year past her birth before you can do that if you breastfeed," Sarah said. "I've been readin' up on birthin' and breastfeedin' and all that, just in case we have to help you. Never know when a tornado will come blastin' through the state, blow a tree down over the road to the hospital, and we'll need to deliver the baby."

"I did that once," Bess said. "Our neighbor's wife went into labor during a blizzard and they couldn't get to the doctor. Wound up at our place and I helped Mama deliver the baby. Patsy fainted."

"It wasn't because of that. The room was too hot, and I hadn't eaten supper. That's what made me get weak in the knees," Patsy protested as she loaded her plate and headed for the table. "We're not here to talk about the one weak moment in my life. We need to hear the whole story about what Nikki had to live through."

Nikki carried the chilled champagne and the carafe of orange juice to the table and filled the fluted glasses. "It was hair-raising at the time, but looking back, I think Billy Tom wanted me to believe he was a tornado, but the truth is that he's just a big bag of wind."

Patsy giggled and gave her another hug. "That's the spirit, darlin'."

They all took their places and she went on to tell the story for what seemed like the hundredth time. When she finished with the part about hitting him with a gallon jug of motor oil, Otis clapped his hands and said, "That's my girl. I wish it would've broken open and gotten all over him."

"Would've been poetic justice to have a slime ball like that all slick with oil," Larry agreed.

"I wish you'd have had on your cowboy boots. That would have put his balls all the way to his throat," Patsy said.

"Are you sure you're all right?" Claire asked. "I remember when Levi came through the cabin door and scared the bejesus out of me and my niece last winter. I can't imagine how I'd have reacted if he'd been like Billy Tom."

"You'd have shot him," Nikki said. "You had a gun trained right on his chest if I heard the story right. If I'd had my gun, Billy Tom would be dead instead of sobering up in a jail cell."

"Have you had any nightmares?" Retta asked as she poured herself a second glass of orange juice and passed it off to Nikki.

"First two nights I did." Nikki set the carafe on the table, and opted for a second cup of coffee. "But last night I was in my own nest, as Emily calls my apartment, and I slept fine."

"I bet your mama was worried out of her mind," Bess said.

"My mama"—Nikki took a deep breath—"has severe mental problems. She's OCD and she's a hypochondriac. Lately, she's even gotten paranoid and she's pretty negative. I never said anything about it before, because I don't want anyone to think I might be like that too."

"Wouldn't that make her even more worried?" Sarah asked.

Nikki's smile was forced. "Mama is too self-centered to worry about anyone other than herself and her schedule."

"Well, honey, you got three mamas right here," Patsy said. "And we were all worried plumb crazy."

"And us two old grandpas here, we wanted to load our shotguns and come after you, but Emily wouldn't let us. She said Tag and her cop brother would take care of it, and she was right," Otis said. "And you old hens need to look at the clock. If you're going to get to the beauty shop on time, we should be going."

Patsy poked Otis on the arm. "Don't you call me an old hen."

"That's better than callin' you a sow or a heifer, ain't it," Larry chuckled.

"You try that and I'll poison you," Bess told him. "But Otis is right. We need to get going. I feel bad that we don't have time to help with cleanup."

Retta patted her on the shoulder. "Honey, we'll have this put to order in no time with four of us working at it. Y'all go get beautified. You might be called upon if a tornado knocks down a tree, and I need some help delivering this baby."

"You just call and we'll be here if we have to ride the tornado's tail wind to get here," Sarah said. "Y'all are the kids we never got to have, and we love you all."

Nikki passed Retta a napkin when she got all misty eyed. She dabbed at her eyes and said, "I appreciate that so much. My baby girl is going to have lots of sweet grandparents."

Emily followed the Five out to the porch. When she returned, the other three women had the table cleared and were busy loading the dishwasher. "We've got to put them on the list to call as soon as you go into labor, Retta. They want to be there when the baby is born."

"Good Lord!" Retta gasped. "The waiting room will be overflowing."

"What waiting room?" Tag poked his head in the door

and then led the other three guys into the house. "I'm not planning on getting hurt tonight, so y'all don't have to reserve a waiting room."

"I hate to burst your bubble, Taggart Baker, but the world does not revolve around you," Emily said.

"Ouch! That had to sting." Maverick grinned.

"Don't tell him there's no Santa Claus too," Hud teased. "He couldn't take that much heavy news all in one day."

"And be very, very quiet about the Easter Bunny," Paxton whispered.

Tag removed his hat and held it over his chest. "Y'all are breakin' my poor little heart, talkin' like that. But if you'll feed us the leftovers from your party this mornin', I'll forgive you, sis."

Emily pointed to the bar. "You're welcome to what's left. The mimosas are all gone, but there's a gallon of sweet tea in the fridge. Help yourselves."

"Okay if we wash up here in the kitchen?" Maverick asked.

"Sure." Emily nodded.

Hud rolled up his sleeves. "I'll go first."

"I'm not above stealing food off your plate if you don't leave anything for us," Maverick said, getting in line behind Hud. "I haven't had a good quiche since we left the panhandle."

Paxton elbowed his brother in the ribs. "Real men don't eat quiche."

"That's an old wives' tale," Maverick told him. "Real men eat whatever they want, and if anyone says anything about it, they beat the shhh...crap out of them."

Tag got in line at the very end, which put him right next to where Nikki was standing. "Did you sleep all right last night?"

"Yes, I did," she said. "You?"

"Not worth a damn. Kept waking up and worrying about you. You could let me stay at your place or you could stay in the cabin, just to help me out," he said.

"We heard there was a party here." Justin came through the door and joined the crowd.

"So did we," Levi said right behind him.

Cade brought up the rear. "And we thought we'd help get rid of leftovers."

Nikki looked at what food was left: part of a pan of quiche, half a pan of cinnamon rolls, and very little fruit in a bowl. The bacon platter was empty and the biscuits were all gone. There wasn't nearly enough to feed that many hungry cowboys.

"Good thing I'm prepared for emergencies," Emily said. "Justin, be a darlin', and help me bring out the second round for these late comers."

"Yes, ma'am." He stopped to give her a kiss on the forehead. "And since we crashed the party, we'll do cleanup afterwards."

"What can I do to help?" Hud asked.

"Follow me," Justin said.

"Please let me stay with you, for my own peace of mind," Tag whispered in Nikki's ear.

"I go to work at midnight tonight and don't get off until my last shift ends at midnight on Sunday. I'll be fine," Nikki said. "But you are still plannin' to go with me on Wednesday, right?"

"Yes, ma'am, and is it all right if I come over at eight on Monday? That's after you talk to your mama, right?"

"Of course. I'll make supper for us," she said.

"I'll be there on the dot." He grinned. "Looks like it's my turn to wash up. I wanted to hug you or kiss you or both when I came into the kitchen, but I've been working outside all morning, and I'm not fit."

Nikki started to hug him, but he turned away too quickly and headed for the sink. Emily and Justin brought out four more quiches from the pantry, and Hud carried in a large pan of biscuits.

"How'd you keep that warm?" Nikki asked.

"There's a warming oven in there. I had all this finished and warming when you got here this morning. I knew the guys were all coming around to eat," Emily answered. "Justin, honey, if you'll bring out the crockpot of sausage gravy, I'll get the platter of bacon, and we'll see just how hungry seven old cowboys really are."

"You are amazing," Nikki said.

"She grew up on a ranch," Hud said.

"But I'm still amazing," Emily teased.

"Yes, you are." Tag slung an arm around her shoulders. "And we love you best when you make us food."

Nikki slipped back into the corner so she could enjoy the huge family and all the banter between them. This was exactly what she'd want if she could be absolutely certain that once she had children, she wouldn't feel about them what her mother felt about her.

*   *   *

Tag came in fourth place with the bronc riding that evening. That didn't get him a prize, but it wasn't too shabby. When he finished his ride, he spent the better part of the rest of the evening sitting on a sawhorse right outside Fumanchu's pen, trying to getting to know the big bull. The beast glared at Tag as if he were trying to get a feel for his next challenge, but Tag stared right back at him without blinking.

"I don't care if you throw me halfway to the stars and I land on my head coming back down," Tag told him. "I don't even care if I can't hang on for eight seconds. If I can make it for two point seven seconds like the song says, I'll have accomplished something."

The bull pawed the ground and snorted, and they continued to stare at each other for the next hour.

It was near eleven o'clock when the announcer finally said, "And the last event of the evening is coming up. Y'all remember this?" He played "Live Like You Were Dying," and the crowd went wild, stomping and singing along, screaming even louder when Fumanchu was mentioned in the song.

"I'm sure that's where this bull got his name, but few cowboys have had the nerve to crawl on his back, and he's never been ridden for the full eight seconds," the guy said. "So let's give it up for Taggart Baker, who's agreed to give it a shot."

"You don't have to do this." Hud stepped onto the first board of the corral. "That's one mean sumbitch."

"I can't let the crowd down." Tag shoved his hands down into his gloves, settled his hat on his head, and eased down from the top board onto the bull's back. Fumanchu snorted and pawed at the ground, but his big body practically filled the chute, and there was nowhere for him to wiggle and very little room for Tag's legs.

"It's gonna hurt." Hud tried to dissuade him.

"Well, yeah, but it's Fumanchu," Tag said. "This ain't a kitty cat, brother. He weighs more'n a ton."

"And he ain't that buckin' barrel Daddy built us when we were kids, or like any other bull you've ever ridden," Hud said.

"Don't expect him to be." Tag tucked his hand under the

rope around the bull's massive body, raised the other one, and nodded toward the guys to open the gate. "Be nice to me, boy. Give the folks a little something to brag about."

The gate opened and Fumanchu came out with his head practically on the ground and his hind feet doing their damnedest to reach the stars. Tag moved with the bull, keeping his balance and waving his fist in the air. His butt hurt like hell when the bull came down with a thud and then twisted his hindquarters to one side as they shot for the moon again.

"Three seconds," the guy in the press box yelled.

Tag had made it past his goal, but now he wanted more. He concentrated on the ride and managed to stay on through the bull's next twist. The crowd was on their feet chanting his name.

"Five seconds!"

He thought he'd figured out the old boy's next move, but he had misjudged it, and suddenly he was flying through the air. The breath was knocked out of him when he landed square on his back. Fumanchu must not have appreciated someone sticking to him that long because he decided to do a victory kick. Hind legs up, front legs firmly on the ground, and then one of the animal's hooves came down—right on the end of Tag's cowboy boots. The clowns rushed out to draw the bull away, and Tag managed to stand up and wave at the crowd.

"Six point seven seconds!" the announcer yelled into the microphone. "It's the longest anyone has ever stayed on this bull. Congratulations to Taggart Baker."

Tag took a bow and threw his hat into the noisy crowd, and then did his best not to limp on his way back to the chute where Hud, Maverick, and Paxton waited.

"How bad is it?" Hud asked.

Maverick patted a wooden box. "Hand or foot?"

Tag sat down and held up a foot. "Hand will be bruised and sore, but a ton of bull on toes doesn't work."

Paxton pulled off his boot and jerked off his sock. "Big one looks good, but we'd better take you to the hospital and get the others X-rayed."

"Hell of a thing to go through to see your woman," Maverick said.

"But I stayed on more'n two point seven seconds." Tag tried to smile but it came out a grimace.

"You're not going to lay up on the sofa because of this," Hud told him. "You already took three days off to go rescue your woman, so you can work with a busted foot."

"Just get me to the hospital," Tag said.

Maverick pulled on his arm. "Stand up. Me and Paxton will be your crutches. Don't put any weight on it until we see what's goin' on. Looks like we might get there at the same time as Nikki checks in for her shift. Don't she go on at midnight?"

"Yep." Hud threw his brother's saddle up onto his shoulder. "The things my brother does for a date."

"Rejection is tough." Paxton grinned.

"He's proven her right, hasn't he?" Maverick said. "She told him she'd be waiting for him in the ER."

"Didn't want to disappoint her. I'm sure she had her heart set on seeing me tonight." Tag's toes throbbed with every beat of his heart. Who'd have thought that toes could hurt even worse than his jaw did when it was laid open with a broken beer bottle? And as much as he wanted to see Nikki, he wished he could stroll into the hospital with the news that he'd stayed on the bull's back for the full eight seconds, then pick her up and twirl her around like he had in Tulia.

It was only ten minutes to the hospital, but it seemed to

Tag like it took an hour. Maverick and Paxton helped him inside while Hud parked the truck, and the first face he saw was Nikki's. She looked so damn cute in her scrubs and her dark hair pulled up in a ponytail that he almost forgot the pain in his foot.

"Where's the blood?" She grabbed the nearest wheelchair and rolled it toward the three guys.

"Bull trampled his foot," Paxton said.

"But I stayed on for more'n six seconds," Tag told her. "Almost went to the full eight."

"Almost only counts in hand grenades and horseshoes," she said as she pushed him toward the doors. "Y'all can come on back if you want. It's startin' off to be a slow night, so there's no one else here."

*   *   *

"Nikki, I'm dyin'." Sue Ann's voice cut through the air.

"I'll get the pretty cowboy." Rosemary took the wheelchair from her. "Don't worry. I'll be gentle with him. You're the only one who can talk Sue Ann down. Thank God you're here."

Nikki turned around and barely caught Sue Ann as she ran past the check-in desk and fell into her arms. The woman reeked of booze, and her eyes were completely glazed over.

"I tried to be good for Mama, but I got bored," she whined.

"Okay, let's get you back to a bed and talk about this." Nikki kept one arm around her so she wouldn't collapse and took her to the second cubicle, right next to where Rosemary was examining Tag's foot.

Sue Ann stretched out on the bed and crossed her arms

over her chest. "Tell them to bury me in a dress and granny panties. Mama will be really mad if she sees these." She pulled down the waist of the fake black leather leggings to show a bright red lace thong. "But if they can, they could put a pint of tequila in the edge of the coffin just in case Mama don't let me into heaven. I might as well have a drink or two if I got to go to the other place."

"I thought you were in rehab getting some help," Nikki said.

"I was, darlin'." Sue Ann pushed her hair back out of her eyes. "But that place wasn't no fun. So me and Gilbert, we escaped."

"Who's Gilbert?" Nikki asked. "And can you tell me what you've drank tonight and did you take pills with it?"

"Gilbert is my buddy. He's been my friend since I was a little girl. Mama says he's not real, but he is. And I had a lot to drink, but I didn't take any pills. No, ma'am, I did not." She giggled. "But me and Gilbert smoked some stuff. He wouldn't eat the worm but I did. You got to get it out of me."

"We can fix you right up." Nikki patted her bony arm. If she had to compare Wilma to someone, it should be Sue Ann, not the Fab Five, she thought. Then her mother didn't look bad at all. "I'll get in touch with the on-call doctor, and we'll get you a bed."

"I knew you'd know what to do. When I die, promise you'll tell them about the panties?" Sue Ann whispered. "And don't call Darla June. Mama said she's dead."

"You got my word," Nikki said as she picked up her tablet and stepped out into the hall. When she found Dr. Richards, he told her to do exactly what she thought he would. Send Sue Ann back to the psych ward and tell them to watch her closer this time.

She poked her head back into the room to find Sue Ann

curled up in the fetal position and snoring like a hibernating bear. She made the phone call to the right people and sat with Sue Ann until two orderlies arrived. They released the brakes on the bed, and she awoke with a start.

"Nikki, where are they taking me? Am I dead like Darla June?" Sue Ann asked.

Nikki held up a hand for the orderlies to stop. "No, you're not dead, and who is Darla June?"

"Shhh…" Sue Ann put a finger over her mouth. "Don't tell Mama I said her name. Darla June is dead to us. Mama said so when she got pregnant and she wasn't married. We can't say her name."

"Do you have a sister, Sue Ann?" Nikki asked.

"I did have, but Mama says she's dead now." Sue Ann pulled the sheet up over her and closed her eyes. She was snoring before they were out of the exam room.

Nikki stepped out of the cubicle to find Dr. Richards coming straight at her. "Guess our cowboy has had a run-in with a bull this time rather than a beer bottle. I heard he rescued you from a kidnapper this past week. Reckon you might talk some sense into him."

"Don't think I'm that much of an influence on him," Nikki answered.

"Honey, if he rode a motorcycle all the way to the panhandle in this unbearable heat to get you, surely you have some kind of influence on him. Let's go see what he's done now."

"Rosemary is taking care of him this time," she said.

"She was. You are now. She can have the next one," Dr. Richards said.

"Why?"

"Because I said so." Dr. Richards pulled back the curtain. "Rosemary, there's a little guy coming in with a bean up his nose. You take that one since it's your son. The rest of you cowboys can go to the waiting room."

"Good God." Rosemary rushed out with Maverick, Paxton, and Hud behind her.

"I always thought God was pretty good myself." Dr. Richards examined Tag's foot. "The two smallest toes are broken. We'll get an X-ray to see how badly and to prove I'm right. Also to be sure none of the other small bones in your foot are fractured."

"What happens then?" Tag asked. "A cast?"

"I'll tape them to the toe next to them, and you'll have to wear something other than boots for about a month until they heal. Takes four to six weeks. Ice packs help and elevation does wonders," Dr. Richards said. "What's it going to take for you to stop punishing your body like this?"

Tag shot a look toward Nikki.

"Maybe he will stop once he's gone skydiving." Nikki frowned.

Chapter Twenty-One

"What's the verdict?" Hud asked when Nikki pushed Tag out in a wheelchair.

"Ice, elevate, and stay off it as much as possible for four weeks," she answered. "He's got a follow-up appointment with the doctor in a month, and he can't wear a cowboy boot on that foot until it's healed."

"Well, that'll keep your ornery ass in the house." Hud grinned. "You can use the time to get acquainted with the bookkeeping program Matthew set up for us. This settles the argument about who's going to do the paperwork for the ranch."

"It's my left foot, so I can still drive," Tag protested.

"Good." Maverick nodded. "When we need posts or wire or stuff to work with, you can go get it, and we'll keep working."

"I'll bring that shoebox full of receipts and the laptop over to your cabin in the morning," Hud told him.

Tag groaned. "I hate computers. You know anything about them, Nikki?"

"Not me." She shook her head. "I'm lucky just to run the little patient tablet that I use."

The doors swung open, and a nurse pushed a wheelchair with Retta in it down the hall. Nikki stopped in her tracks and asked, "Is it time?"

Retta grimaced and laid a hand on her bulging stomach. "I thought it was false labor all day, but I was wrong."

"Has everyone been called? Does Emily know? Have you talked to the doctor?" Nikki was so excited that she forgot all about Tag for a minute.

"No one has been called yet. Would you please..." Retta moaned. "The pains are less than a minute apart now."

"I'll get a hold of Emily and the rest of the family," Nikki said.

"Might as well turn around and take me back to the baby waiting room," Tag said. "Where's Cade?"

"Parking the truck. He'll be here real soon," Retta panted.

The hall was wide enough that Nikki and a nurse's aide pushed the wheelchairs side by side toward the maternity area.

"You ready to have this baby?" Hud asked. "I bet Cade is a nervous wreck."

"I'm so ready," Retta said. "And you're right about Cade. Knowing y'all are here for him means the world to me."

"I can't believe that we're going to have a new baby in the family. This is beyond exciting, Retta. She's going to be here before long," Nikki said.

Retta brushed away a tear. "But she's a little early."

"Not enough to hurt her," Nikki assured her. "She'll be fine."

"This is where we part company." The nurse pushed the button to open the doors into the maternity part of the hospital. "Nikki will show the rest of you to the waiting room."

Nikki rolled Tag into a large room with sofas and chairs grouped into several seating areas. "I have to get back to the emergency room, but I'll run by and check on things every chance I get." She pulled a chair over and propped his leg on it. "I'll send an ice pack up with Cade."

"Thanks for everything," Tag said.

"Hey, I'm not anywhere near even with you for rescuing me," she told him.

"Then you'll come over through the week and do all that book work for me?" He looked up at her with those mesmerizing blue eyes.

"I don't owe you that much." She blew a kiss as she left the room.

On her way back to the ER, she met Claire and Emily almost jogging down the hall. "Are we too late?" Emily asked.

"I was just fixin' to call you," Nikki said. "How did—"

"Cade called Justin about a minute ago. We were all on our way home after the ranch rodeo, so we just whupped a U-turn in the middle of the road and came right back. Can you believe it? We're getting the first Maguire grandbaby tonight," Emily said.

"It could be tomorrow if she decides to make an entrance and hold out until after midnight," Nikki told them, and then gave them directions to the waiting room. They rushed off in that direction, and Nikki turned to find Cade, Justin, and Levi coming around the corner.

"How is she?" Cade looked like he might faint any minute.

Nikki laid a hand on his arm. "She's fine, but I bet she'll be glad to have you in the room to hold her hand." She pointed to the signs on the wall leading to the maternity section and returned to her post in the ER.

Rosemary jerked the curtains back on a cubicle and startled Nikki so badly that she jumped. "Didn't mean to scare you. We just now got that bean out of my kid's nose. Damned thing had swollen up and filled his whole nostril. It's a wonder he didn't have to have surgery. How's your cowboy?"

"He's got two broken toes that's going to keep him off bulls and out of boots for a month or more. Retta Maguire just checked in to have her baby, so the maternity waiting room is going to be full all night." Nikki helped Rosemary straighten up the room.

Through the week, nurses' aides did that kind of work, but weekends were a whole different matter. Not that Nikki minded. She liked staying busy.

"And Sue Ann?"

"Was high and drunk, and Doc sent her right back to the psych ward. Trouble is that she signs herself in, so she has the authority to sign herself out. She said that she had a sister. I wonder where she is. I feel so sorry for her, but I realized something tonight. Mama has plenty of problems, but at least she's not as bad as Sue Ann," Nikki said.

"I've known Wilma my whole life, and you're right. But, honey, that don't make it any easier on you to deal with, just easier to accept. You know it seems like I remember Sue Ann's older sister. She was maybe sixteen when Sue Ann was born, so she was quite a bit older than me. I wonder if she's on any of the social media sites." Rosemary piled the dirty linens into a bin and pushed it out into the hallway. "Now tell me more about this cowboy and the kidnapping.

We haven't had a free minute since we got here. Let's get a cup of coffee and wait until the next round hits. Bars close at two, so you know we'll have some business then."

"It'll be a miracle if we don't." Nikki followed Rosemary to the break room. They'd each poured a cup of coffee when Rosemary's phone rang.

"I told Steven to call me when they got home. Be right back." She stepped out into the hallway to take the call from her husband.

Nikki's thoughts went to the real miracle that was going on in the maternity section of the hospital that night, not in the ER. A baby was coming into the world. One who would be so loved that the waiting room was packed with people who could hardly wait to see her for the first time. Nikki wondered if there'd be that many people supporting her if and when she had a child.

"Hey, that lady out there said I'd find you here." Tag rolled his wheelchair through the door. "Cade just came to tell us that Retta is ready to push. I don't know how he's keeping his cool. If my wife was having a baby, I'd be spinnin' around on my head."

"Holy smoke! She must've been in labor all afternoon and didn't tell anyone until the last minute." Nikki set her cup down. "I figured y'all would be here until morning."

"Emily swears that Retta knew exactly what she was doin'. If they'd called her mother-in-law this afternoon, she'd be here already and she would be tryin' to take over the whole show. I saw how bossy that woman can be when we were moving Emily into her new house, so I don't blame her a bit." Tag maneuvered the chair around and started back out the door. "I'll come back and let you know when the baby arrives."

"I'm not busy right now. I'll push you." Nikki grabbed

the wheelchair handles. "So you'd be spinnin' on your head, huh? That brings up a pretty funny picture in my mind."

"How about you? What if you were the one in Retta's shoes?"

She slowly shook her head. "I don't let myself go there."

"You ever go down to the nursery and look at the newborns?" Tag asked.

"Yep. Especially if it's been a hectic night and I can't settle the adrenaline rush of running from one patient to another. Sometimes I even volunteer to rock a baby if there's more of them than the pediatric nurse can take care of," she said.

"How does that make you feel?" he asked.

"All warm and cuddly," she answered.

He reached over his shoulder and covered her hand with his. "You've got so much kindness in your heart, Nikki, that you'll make a great mother."

"How can you know that—not just say it, but know it?"

He removed his hand and tapped his chest. "This right here tells me so."

Could he possibly be right? She thought again about the way she felt with a baby in her arms. She often sang a simple lullaby that her father had sung to her when she was a little girl and couldn't sleep. For her thirteenth birthday he'd given her a music box that played the song. It sat on her dresser and had become part of her birthday ritual. She was about to turn the wheelchair into the room when she caught sight of Cade coming down the hall.

"She's here and she's perfect, and I'm a father," he said loudly.

Nikki pushed Tag's chair, and they followed Cade to the waiting room.

"And we're the first to know," Tag said. "Is that the same as catchin' the bouquet at a wedding? Are we next?"

"Not unless we have another case of immaculate conception," Nikki said.

Tag chuckled. "I reckon we could have a normal wild child."

"Tag Baker, are you askin' me to be your baby mama?" she teased.

"No, ma'am, I want more than a baby mama when I have children," he answered.

"Our baby girl is here," Cade announced to everyone in the waiting room.

"What's her name?" Emily asked.

"How much does she weigh?" Otis wanted to know.

"Is Retta okay?" Justin asked.

"When can we see her?" Patsy clapped her hands.

Poor old Cade had trouble answering them.

"Right now I'd give up all my rebel ways to be in his shoes," Tag whispered.

"Now that's a line you should put in your little black book," Nikki, leaning down, whispered in his ear.

"Didn't think I'd ever say that or feel this way," Tag said.

Nikki's phone pinged. She pulled it out of her pocket to find a text from Rosemary. Two ambulances had been dispatched to a wreck north of town. They'd be bringing in six injured patients in a few minutes.

"Got to go," Nikki said. "Keep that foot up and don't be too macho to take the pain pills Dr. Richards prescribed."

Tag stood up, balanced on one foot, and pulled her close to his chest. "It's going to be a long weekend, but the light at the end of the tunnel is that I'll get to see you Monday evening." Then he tipped up her chin and kissed her, right there in front of everyone.

Chapter Twenty-Two

Any other morning, Tag would have simply crawled through the barbed-wire fence or hopped over it and walked from the cabin to the ranch house, but on Saturday he drove. He hopped on one foot from the truck to the porch and used the railing to help him maneuver the steps. Hud threw open the door and handed him a set of crutches before he reached the top step.

"Guess Granny was right to insist that we bring these with us," he said.

"I never knew how much two toes could hurt," Tag admitted. "When I busted my arm in two places, it didn't hurt like this."

"That's because you were young. Kids heal faster than adults. It was Maverick's turn to make breakfast. He's still flippin' pancakes if you're interested." Hud led the way to the kitchen.

"I thought maybe I could at least string barbed wire on

one foot." Tag sat down at the table and propped his foot on an empty chair. Maverick stacked four huge pancakes onto a plate and set them in front of him.

"You'd do it in a wheelchair to get out of all the paperwork, wouldn't you?"

"Thank you. And you're right. I hate to paint, too, but I'd do the whole barn to get out of what y'all are making me take on." Tag slipped pats of butter between the layers and then covered the top with warm maple syrup.

"Too bad." Paxton set a cup of coffee by Tag's place.

"Thanks for waiting on me," Tag said.

"We'll drop in when we break for noon each day, and maybe if you go to church tomorrow, we'll let you take time off if you talk Emily into inviting all of us to Sunday dinner," Hud said. "Other than that, you're going to spend an eight-hour day in front of the computer learning what Matthew does. Everything has to be input from cows to bulls to fence posts, and how much winter wheat seed we bought. After the initial input, the job shouldn't take but a day a week, according to what Matthew told me this morning."

"And I'll be the only one, other than Matthew, who knows how to do it, right?" Tag groaned.

"You can always take care of that part of the business on Saturday when Nikki's at work." Hud refilled his coffee cup and sat down at the table.

"What's she got to do with this?" Tag asked between bites.

"You're in love with her. You might not know it yet, but you are, and in another year, two at the most, you'll be the one coming to tell us about your new baby." Maverick set a plate full of pancakes in the middle of the table. "You can fight it, but when a good woman grabs you by the heart, you're a goner."

"I'm not in love," Tag protested. "I like Nikki a lot, and for the first time in my life, I'm calling someone my girl-friend, but we've only made out a few times, and gone out together twice. How does that mean the L-word, much less talk about babies?"

"It was obvious to some of us at Emily's wedding. You looked across the room at her in that pretty blue dress and it was all over," Paxton told him. "Just mark our words. And that idea of doing all the drudge work when she's at the hospital is a good thing. Besides, it'll keep you out of the bars, off bulls, and hopefully away from the hospital."

Tag shot a dirty look his way but had to acknowledge, albeit silently, that Paxton was right. And it would give him something to do over the weekends when he couldn't see Nikki. But that stuff about being in love—that might happen on down the road, like in a couple of years—but not now.

*   *   *

When things slowed down in the ER that morning, Nikki slipped into Retta's room to find her sleeping. Annie was in a little portable crib beside her. Her eyes were wide open, but she wasn't fussing. Nikki gently picked her up and held her close to her chest as she sat down in a rocking chair and began to sing to her.

They'd named her Annabelle and planned to call her Annie. Nice and simple. Nikki loved it and thought the name fit the little angel who had a full head of dark hair. She breathed in the clean baby-fresh scent and wished that she was holding her own child.

Cade slipped into the room and smiled down at Retta with so much love in his face that Nikki felt guilty for even sharing space in such an intimate moment. "Want to hold Annie?"

He sat down on a sofa and held out his arms. "I'm a little afraid of her, Nikki. She's so little, and I'm such a big man. I'm terrified that I'll hurt her. I've never been around a baby this small."

Nikki settled Annie into the crook of his arm. "Just support her head and hold her close. She's listened to her mama's heartbeat the whole time, and hearing yours will bring her comfort. The fear is natural. All new daddies feel that way with their first child."

"So you've been around lots of babies?" he asked as he gently touched Annie's tiny hand with a forefinger. "She's so beautiful that it almost makes this rough old cowboy cry."

"I was never around babies until I had pediatric clinical training for my nursing degree. Sometimes I go down to the nursery here and help out. It calms me," she admitted.

Annie wrapped her hand around his finger.

"Look!" Cade whispered. "How can someone so small make me feel like a king?"

"It's called the miracle of life," Nikki whispered.

"You are going to be a great mother," Cade said, but he didn't take his eyes off his little girl.

She was thinking about what Cade said as she climbed the stairs to her apartment that night. She didn't notice the black Lincoln parked across the street until she heard a noise and turned to see it pulling away from the curb. If that was her father, she sure wished he'd just get out and talk to her. But then why would he if he thought that she'd ignored him all these years? And if it wasn't her father? A shiver went up her spine at the thought.

She stopped long enough to feed Goldie and then stripped out of her scrubs, put them into the washer with other laundry, and started the cycle. The load would wash while she slept most of the day. She took a shower and slid beneath the sheets. Her eyes were closed when her head hit the pillow. The last thing she remembered thinking was that she should have set the alarm.

When she awoke and glanced at the clock, it said three thirty-five. She'd been asleep more than twelve hours, but that wasn't unusual for Monday. She threw back the covers, slipped on a robe, and was on the way to the kitchen when her phone pinged.

She dug through her purse and found three messages from Emily and one from Tag. The ones from Emily included pictures of Annie and Retta from Sunday morning when they had brought the baby home. Looking at them set Nikki's biological clock to ticking loudly. Tag sent a selfie of him holding a whole sheaf of papers and a message that said: Save me!

She sent one back that said: Hang on until 8. I'll bring supper.

He sent back an emoji blowing kisses to her.

She sang as she cleaned Goldie's bowl and then fed her, hummed as she stripped the bed, tossed her scrubs into the dryer, and threw the sheets into the washer. Then she cleaned her little place. Never would she let herself get into a habit of doing anything by the clock or the day of the week like her mother did.

She was starving by the time she finished her chores, so she made herself a peanut butter and jelly sandwich. That would have to do until she picked up some tacos to take out to the cabin for supper. She watched a rerun of *Law & Order* while she waited on her mother's call. The show ended and she did a countdown from ten. When she got to number one, the phone rang.

"Hello, Mother," she said.

"Why are you callin' me that? You've always called me Mama before. You wanted me to be honest with you and I was, so why are you acting like this? You know it raises my blood pressure when you are ugly," Wilma said.

"Let's start all over," Nikki said. "Hello, Mama. How's your week been?"

"Well, for starters, Mrs. Thomas got a cat and it's been walkin' on my porch and leaving footprints. I have to go out there every day and shoo it away, and then take a dust mop to the porch. If she has to have a pet, she should keep it in her own house," Wilma said. "And I'm down to seventeen nerve pills, so you need to call the pharmacy because they said they can't refill it until they're all gone. What if I'm short one on a day when things are going bad for me like that rotten cat traipsing across my porch?"

"How many do you take each day?" Nikki rolled her eyes and thought about the difference in cat prints and getting kidnapped.

"I take three a day. I can't be without them. You should call the pharmacy tomorrow and demand that they bring me a new bottle."

"I'm sure they'll bring your medicine as soon as they can," she said. "What else has been going on?"

"That man you hired to mow my yard left a whole lot of grass on the sidewalk again. You just can't get good help anymore," Wilma said.

"Were you worried when I was kidnapped?" Nikki asked.

"Did you flirt with that man? Is that why he stole your car and made you drive him way out there to West Texas? You must've done something to encourage him," Wilma said. "You're like your daddy that way. He flirted with every woman he saw."

"Oh, yeah? What did he do that made you think that?"

"He used to smile at every single woman who checked us out in the stores and chat with them. And he always smiled at all the women in church like he wanted to get to know them better. He said he was just being cordial. I told him I hated it when he did that, but did he listen to me? Oh, no! Not your daddy! I bet you smiled at that man, didn't you?" Ice dripped from Wilma's words.

Nikki closed her eyes tightly and reminded herself: *Think about Sue Ann. Don't let her negativity get to you.*

"Are you still there?" Wilma yelled.

"I'm here, Mama. Did you go out today? It's been up in the nineties." Nikki changed the subject. Surely the weather wouldn't be something that would get her in trouble.

"Lord, no! I don't go out on Monday." Wilma went into her normal tirade about everything, and all Nikki had to do was murmur now and then.

Her mother finally brought their conversation to an abrupt end. "It's eight o'clock and I have things to do. Good night, Nikki. We'll talk again next week."

"Love you, Mama," Nikki said.

"Okay, goodbye." Her phone screen went dark.

You tried, her brother Quint's voice whispered in her head. *That's all anyone can do.* He'd told her the same thing so many times when they were kids that his words were burned into her brain.

Tears welled up in her eyes. She tossed the phone into her purse and headed for the door. "Hold the fort down, Goldie. Don't wait up for me. I might be late." She swiped at her tears with the heel of her hand. A swing by the drive-through netted a bag full of tacos and burritos. She made another stop at a convenience store for a six-pack of beer and one of root beer. Then she drove out of town straight for the cabin.

When she arrived, she carried the bag and beer up to the door and started to knock with the edge of the six-pack. Tag startled her when he swung the door open before her knuckles even hit it.

"I heard you drive up. That stuff smells wonderful." He stood back and let her enter the cabin; then using one crutch, he followed her to the table. "But seeing you beats all the food in the world. You are gorgeous."

She turned around to find that he'd laid the crutch down and opened his arms.

"I missed you," he said.

She took two steps and his arms wrapped around her. Rolling up on her toes, she cupped his face in her hands and brought his lips to hers. One kiss and it didn't matter what Wilma had said or what she was afflicted with. Nikki was at peace for the first time in her life right there in Tag's arms.

He hopped over to the sofa and pulled her down onto his lap. One kiss led to another, going from a sweet brush of the lips to something deeper and deeper, until they were both panting. His hand slipped under her shirt up to her bra, and in one swift motion, it was undone, and he began to massage her back. She unbuttoned his shirt and slid it from his shoulders.

"Honey," he nibbled on her ear, "we either need to stop this or take it to the bed."

"Bed." In one swift motion, she pulled her shirt and bra off and tossed them toward the end of the sofa. His soft hair against her breasts felt just like she thought it would, and the touch of it sent tingles from her scalp to her toes.

"I'd carry you, but I'm afraid I can't hop that far," he said.

Nikki pulled him up and draped his arm around her shoulders. "I'll be your crutch. You sure you . . ."

Together they made it to the bed, where he pulled her down and the make-out session started all over again. "I don't need my toes to make love to you."

She wasn't sure when her jeans and underpants came off or even her shoes. But they were both naked and his blue eyes were staring into hers as he stretched out on top of her. Wrapping her legs around his waist, she reached between them and gasped when she realized how ready he was. She drew him into her and began to rock with him. On that miraculous night, he brought her to heights she'd never known, taking her right to the edge of a climax and then backing off until finally he said her name in a growl and together they reached the mind-blowing end.

"There are no words," he panted as he collapsed on top of her.

"Yeah, right. As many notches as you've got on your bedpost, you can't say..." Her breath came out in short bursts.

"Honey, what we just had deletes all those notches."

"Are you serious?" she asked.

"More than I've ever been in my whole life," he said.

"Ready for round two." She rolled over on top of him.

"Kiss me, darlin'. One kiss and I will be," he said.

The next morning, Nikki awoke to the smell of coffee and bacon. Sun rays flowed through the window and onto the quilt that covered her. That meant it had to be at least seven o'clock. "Good mornin'," she said.

"Awww, I meant to wake you with a kiss and breakfast in bed. I was trying to figure out how to hop over there with a tray." He smiled.

She sat up, wrapped the quilt around her body, and eased her feet to the floor. "If you'll share it with me, I'll do the carrying."

"And then we might see if morning sex is as good as it was at midnight, right?" he asked.

"I've got a feeling that whenever we have it, it'll be fabulous." She tiptoed for a kiss.

"Me too, darlin', me too," he said.

Chapter Twenty-Three

I spent the last two nights with Tag." Nikki held Annie close to her chest and rocked the baby in an antique chair.

"You've done that before," Retta said as she sipped from a cup of hot chocolate. "The way you are with babies, you should have a dozen."

"I would love that." Nikki's thoughts went back to the short conversation that she and Cade had in the hospital. She'd been on her own for so long that somehow she'd thought she'd have to raise a child without help if she ever had one. But seeing Cade and Retta together, both so eager to help with little Annie, had changed her mind. Even with her tough schedule, with help, she could have a career and a family both—just like her friend Rosemary.

"Time isn't our friend to have that many." Emily brought a plate of cookies to the living room and set them on the table. "And you've got to have sex to have a baby—at least in the normal way."

"Tag and I had sex the past two nights. I think it was a little better than plain old normal." Nikki bent to kiss Annie on the top of her head.

Retta spewed hot chocolate on her shirt. "You mean you didn't before?"

"Holy smoke!" Emily gasped. "Tag's reputation is ruined for sure. He spent at least three nights with you and didn't sweet-talk you into bed?"

"Didn't even try." Nikki's frown told them she was being honest.

Retta wiped the brown spots from her paisley shirt. "Get out the brides' magazines, Emily. We've got a friend on the way to the altar."

"Not just yet. Annie is chewing her fists. I think she may be hungry." Nikki kissed the baby again and handed her to Retta. "Neither of us are ready for that step. He's still getting over the death of his friend Duke, and I've got this thing with my father tonight. We both have to close the door to the past before we can open the one to the future."

Retta lifted her shirt and held the baby to her breast. "It's hard to believe that less than a week ago, this little darlin' wasn't even born. She's stolen my heart and got her big old cowboy daddy wrapped around her finger. Cade and I are living proof that sometimes the future slips up on you real fast, Nikki."

"I can believe it." Emily nodded. "Your little angel has inspired Justin and me to have a baby of our own. I stopped taking the pill this morning."

"Hello, everyone. Is it my turn to hold the baby?" Claire made her way into the living room. "Did I hear right about you and Justin?"

"It's your turn when she finishes eating," Retta said.

"And yep, you heard right. When are you and Levi going to do the same?" Emily answered.

"Already did. We're announcing it at Sunday dinner this next week. I went to the doctor this morning and the due date is Christmas."

"Oh!!" Retta squealed. "Annie will have a playmate. How has Levi ever kept this a secret? You must be two months along."

"It hasn't been easy," Claire laughed. "I've had to figure out ways to dump mimosas and wine so y'all wouldn't suspect. But we wanted to see the doctor and be certain before we told anyone. My jeans are already tight around the middle, so you would've figured it out soon anyway."

"The ranch is growing." Emily shot a look at Nikki. "The Canyon Creek needs a baby too. You and Tag need to get that crap about his past settled and move on to the future."

"One step at a time," Nikki said. "And baby steps for us. But I will admit that I'm bullfrog green with jealousy right now."

"Good!" Emily said. "You know I'd love to have you for a sister and an aunt to our kids."

"Oh, honey, I'll be their aunt no matter what. It don't take blood to make folks kin to each other, and sometimes blood don't mean jack squat," Nikki said. "I should be going. Tag is picking me up in an hour. I'm still torn about what to even wear, and after the last two nights, I can't imagine what I'll say to my father."

"Keep it simple," Emily suggested.

"That's what Tag advised."

"That's exactly what I'd tell you too," Claire offered. "We'll all be thinkin' about you this evening."

"Thanks. That means more than you'll ever know."

Nikki felt that the three women might never know the extent of her sincerity, but what she said came from her heart. It had taken her a while to understand that family didn't always share DNA.

*   *   *

When Nikki got back to her apartment, she changed clothes three times before she decided on a simple black and white sundress and a pair of sandals. She whipped her long, dark hair up into a ponytail, applied a little makeup, and was about to change her mind about her choice of clothes when she heard a vehicle. She picked up her purse, rushed outside, and hurried down the stairs.

"I was hoping you'd have pity on a poor cripple and not make him climb those steps," Tag joked as he held the truck door open for her.

"Cripple, my butt," she sassed as she got inside.

"Your butt is much too pretty for anybody to cripple it, and if I may say so, darlin', you look amazing tonight."

"Yes, you may say so and thank you. You clean up really nice yourself, for an old cowboy with only one boot," she said.

"Had to give the other guys a fightin' chance. It wouldn't be fair to them for me to have two boots," he teased as he shut the door and crutched his way around the front of the truck.

"Nervous?" he asked when he'd settled into the driver's seat.

"Yep."

"How much?"

"More than I was when Billy Tom was in the backseat.

Almost as much as I was when he had a gun pointed at you. And a little more than I was when I knocked on your cabin door that first night," she answered.

"Don't be. If it goes well, you will have a father in your life. If it doesn't, then you've still got your friends, the Fab Five, and me," he reassured her.

"That's what I've been tellin' myself all afternoon," she sighed. "And I appreciate every one of you." She stopped short of saying that she loved all of them, but she did. Maybe in different ways, but the love was there.

He reached across the console and took her hand in his. "I miss the trucks that had a bench seat. Our old ranch work truck doesn't have a console. Someday I'm going to get one like that so you can sit all snuggled up beside me."

She let go of his hand, flipped the console up and slid over to the narrow seat. "Like this?" she asked.

"Exactly." He slipped an arm around her shoulders and drove with one hand. "You've got such a big personality that sometimes I forget how small you are."

"I'll take that as a compliment." She laid a hand on his thigh. "I used to envy the big, tall girls. Don't tell Emily, but I've been jealous of her too. She's curvy and looks so cute in her clothes, and now she's so damned sugary happy that it makes my teeth ache."

Tag chuckled. "I have to admit that her honeymoon glow makes me jealous too."

"Is that what's going on with us?" Nikki asked. "Are we caught up in their happiness, and we want what they've got?"

"Maybe, but then it could be that what we see in them is waking us up to what we might have if we want to work at it. They didn't just sit down on a quilt under a shade tree and fall in love. They had to jump through fire hoops and go through obstacle courses too," he answered. "When she came home last spring after one of their arguments, we figured it was all over between them, but they got through it."

"What if six months down the road one of us decides we're tired of all the work it takes? I've got a lot of baggage for you to contend with," she said.

He drew her even closer. "What you've got is nothing compared to the burdens I'm bringing into this relationship."

She looked up at him and raised a dark brow. "This is a relationship?"

"I think it just might be." He kissed her on the forehead. "I've never slept with the same woman two nights in a row, so it must be special."

A little streak of jealousy shot through Nikki when she thought of all those other one-night stands, but then she reminded herself that she had by no means been a virgin. And she realized that what each of them had done in the past shouldn't affect the future they might have. What happened going forward was the important issue.

Looking back from Emily's wedding to now, she tried to figure out the exact time when their easy banter turned into something more than mild flirtation. It had happened gradually, she realized, and she couldn't narrow it down to a date or an incident.

They rode in comfortable silence for the first thirty minutes of their two-hour trip toward Dallas. But when Tag made a turn onto Highway 380 and headed east, butterflies started flitting around in her stomach. She wanted to tell him to turn around at the next exit and take her home, but after that comment about her being such a strong person, she couldn't do it.

"You're fretting," he said. "You've gone all tense."

"Walk a mile in my shoes right now," she said.

"Okay, but since my toes are hurt, it'll take me a little longer than normal. Let me just imagine I'm doing it. Give me ten minutes. I can usually do a mile quicker than that, though, just for the record," he said.

"Sounds fair to me," she said.

They passed an exit for Denton before he spoke again. "My feet hurt from walking in your shoes. Even at my worst, my mama would fight a forest fire for me. And even when my dad was dealin' out the discipline, and that was often in my case, I knew it was because he loved me. So you have every right to fret. What can I do to help?"

"I'm not sure anyone can actually help, but I appreciate the concern and the understanding. How much farther is it?" she asked.

"Less than half an hour. Would you turn on the radio? I've only got two hands, and they're both doing something pretty important."

She turned the dial and found a country music station in that area. Catching the middle of Blake Shelton's song "I Lived It," she hummed along with it. When that one ended, Miranda started singing "The House That Built Me." The irony that those two songs played back-to-back didn't escape either of them.

After some thought, Tag spoke. "Kind of poetic, ain't it?"

"How's that?" she asked.

"You've lived it. Maybe not like what Blake talks about. And your mama's house built you. It taught you what you don't want to be, and sometimes that's as important as learning what you should be. I know because you're teaching me that same thing. I don't want to live like I'm dying anymore."

Alison Krauss started "When You Say Nothing at All."

"This is my song to you," she said.

"She's right. I would catch you if you fall," he said. "And thank you for the song, and for everything that it means."

She looked up to see a sign welcoming them to the city of McKinney. "I can do this," she whispered.

"Yes, you can," he reassured her. "Plug the address into your phone and navigate for me."

They found the house on the south side of McKinney. She stared at the small brick home that was set back on a large lot. Two huge pecan trees shaded the wide lawn, and the front porch had a swing on one end and a rocking chair on the other. A sliver of light flowed out from between the drapes covering the living room window.

The driveway was empty, but there were two black Lincolns parked across the street. Was one of them her father's? She slid across the seat, took a deep breath, and wrapped her hand around the door handle, but she couldn't force herself to open it.

"You sure about this? We've made progress. We know where he lives," Tag said. "If you're not comfortable, we can go back home and meet him another day."

She shook her head. "We've made the trip. It won't be a bit easier in a week or a month than it is right now."

"Okay, then." He opened his door, got his crutches out of the backseat, and rounded the rear of the truck. When he opened the door for her, she leaned out and kissed him.

"Thank you," she whispered.

"You are very welcome."

They walked up the sidewalk side by side. She rang the doorbell and waited. The guy who opened the door was as tall as Tag, but he was slim built, rather than muscular. His dark hair needed to be cut even worse than Tag's did, and his brown eyes reminded her of someone, but she couldn't figure out who.

"We're looking for Don Grady," she said. "Is this his address?"

"It was, but he moved last week over to Alvord. I'm just here to give the new owners the keys," he answered. "Can I ask you why you're looking for him?"

"I'm his daughter, Nikki Grady," she answered.

"I can believe that. You have his eyes. He's out of town on business right now, but he'll be home tomorrow evening if you'd like to stop by his place then."

"Yes, I would," Nikki said. "Alvord is just south from where I live in Bowie."

"How about that? And you drove all the way here to find him. Should I tell him that you'll be coming to see him tomorrow evening?"

"Sure," Tag answered for her. "How do you know him?"

"It's a long story and he'll want to tell you himself. I'm Lucas, by the way, and I'm sure Don will be glad to see you." He smiled.

The hair on Nikki's neck prickled. "Does my dad drive a Lincoln?"

"No, ma'am. He's got a Dodge Ram truck, kind of a chocolate brown color," Lucas said. "I'm sorry. Where are my manners? Would you like to come inside? There's nothing in here, and all I've got is a couple of bottles of water in the refrigerator, but you're welcome."

"No, that's all right," Nikki said. "If you give me his address, we'll be going."

"Sure thing." Lucas rattled it off.

She typed it into her phone. "Thank you."

"Well, those are the new owners coming up the sidewalk. I guess it's time for me to give them the keys and be on my way," Lucas said.

"Thank you again," Tag said.

He nodded at the property's new owners as they passed and said, "Good evening."

"Is this a sign for me to forget this?" Nikki asked when they were back in the truck.

"Or is the fact that he lives close to you a sign that you need to at least ask him a few questions?" Tag asked. "You reckon Lucas is an employee of his? He sure didn't want to answer questions, did he?"

"Or maybe he's a driving buddy of my dad's. He was a trucker for years and might still be doing that," Nikki said.

"Guess we'll find out tomorrow evening. What time do you want me to pick you up?"

"Seven, but don't climb the stairs."

"You are goin' home with me tonight, aren't you?" he asked.

"I should stop by the apartment to feed Goldie first, and maybe pack a bag."

"Pack for two days," Tag urged. "After tomorrow night, you should stay with me, no matter which way the chips fall." He glanced over at her. "Are you terribly disappointed?"

"That I'm staying the night with you again or that I didn't get to meet my dad?"

"Both." He started the engine.

"Never on spending time in your arms. Yes on seeing my dad. Now my stomach will have to get tied in knots again, but I'm determined to do this. He needs to know that I never got his letters."

Tag traced her jawline with his forefinger. "It would be so easy to fall in love with you, Nikki."

"But you never take the easy way out of anything, do you?" She pulled his face to hers for a long, lingering hot kiss.

Chapter Twenty-Four

Nikki arrived at the café a few minutes before noon the next day and was waiting to be seated when Emily joined her. They were escorted to a booth and a waitress appeared immediately with menus.

"What can I get y'all to drink?" she asked.

"Sweet tea," Emily said.

"Same." Nikki nodded.

"Be right back with some chips and salsa and your drinks." She started to walk away and then turned. "Lemon?"

"Lime," Emily and Nikki answered at the same time.

"I'm sorry you didn't get to meet your dad last night. Are you more nervous or less now that you know he's not that far away?" Emily turned her focus back to Nikki.

"Even worse than yesterday," Nikki answered. "I've thought of a thousand questions I should have asked Lucas since last night."

The waitress returned with a tray bearing chips and

drinks. Emily squeezed the slice of lime into her tea and took a drink. "Like what?"

Nikki did the same thing with the lime. "Like how did he know my dad? Does he work for him? Is he kin to him? Daddy never mentioned that we might have cousins somewhere. Relatives never came to visit us, but lookin' back I can understand why. If anyone came before I was born or when I was a toddler, Mama's attitude would have sent them runnin' for the hills. And maybe Daddy didn't tell us because he knew we'd want to get to know them."

"Well, you'll find out tonight," Emily said. "You ever worry that this can of worms you're opening might be as bad as what your mama said last week?"

"Yep, I have." Nikki loaded a chip with salsa and popped it in her mouth.

"I'm glad Tag is going with you. I can't believe how much he's settled down since he moved here and you two started seeing each other. I've thought that he and Hud would figure out real quick that being boss of their own place was tougher than they'd imagined. But they've surprised me." Emily used a chip to dip deep into the salsa.

"Me too. He's so"—Nikki searched for the right word—"different from how he was at your wedding."

"It's amazing. Mama and Daddy are over the moon with the way he's taking on responsibilities now. Matthew says it won't last if the guys make him keep doing the book work, but I think it just might," Emily said. "But enough about Tag. We're here to talk about your visit this evening. I have faith in you. If you don't like where this journey takes you, you can slam the door on it. But good Lord, girl. Think about all those letters and cards and all that money. He didn't forsake you even when he thought you'd turned your back on him."

"It would have been easier if he'd been in McKinney last night. Now that he's less than thirty miles away, it'll be harder on us both if things don't go right," Nikki said.

The door opened and Nikki looked up to see Tag maneuvering his way inside on his crutches. She waved and he smiled as he made his way around tables and chairs. "Mind if I join y'all?"

Nikki scooted over. "Not at all. We haven't ordered yet."

"What are you doing in town?" Emily asked.

"Had to make a run in to get some lumber and corrugated sheet metal for the guys. The barn roof is leaking and we're planning to start cuttin' hay next week. We'll need a dry place to put it, so they're working on that today." Tag laid a hand on Nikki's thigh. "Thought I'd get some lunch and some takeout for the guys before I go back home. What's on your agenda for the rest of the afternoon?"

"I'm driving a hay wagon for Justin," Emily said.

"I'm going to buy groceries for the next couple of weeks. Want me to pick up anything for you?" It seemed only natural that Nikki would ask, but then she wondered if that was too much and got a little flustered.

His hand moved a little bit higher. "We're out of everything at the cabin. Just buy whatever you think we need, and keep the receipt so I can reimburse you."

"Are y'all living together?" Emily asked.

"No!" Nikki put a hand on his to stop it.

"Well, that was pretty definite," Tag chuckled.

"My mama would put out a hit on me if…Wait a minute." Nikki frowned. "I'm almost thirty. If I want to live with someone, that's my business."

Tag gently squeezed her leg. "That's my girl."

"Does that mean you might live together sometime in the future?" Emily asked.

"Mind your own business, sis." Tag removed his hand, picked up a chip, and dipped it into the salsa.

"Nikki?" Emily asked.

"Let's just get through tonight, but the question is kind of moot since I haven't been asked. I don't think, at this point in our relationship, it's time for that anyway."

Before they could continue with the conversation, the waitress came with another menu and asked Tag what he'd like to drink.

"Coke with a wedge of lime, please," he said. "And some more chips and salsa. If the ladies are ready to order, I know what I want."

The waitress whipped a pad from her pocket. "Yes, sir?"

"The taco plate with refried beans and rice and an order of guacamole on the side. And while we're eating, would you fix up three more of those for me to take with me?"

"You got it." She turned to Emily.

"That sounds good. I'll have the same."

"And you, ma'am?" she asked Nikki.

"Two chicken taco plates, no beans on the side, double the rice." Nikki glanced out the window in time to see a black Lincoln pull up to the curb. "Tag, let me out, please."

He slid out of the booth and stood to one side. "The bathrooms are at the back."

"Not going that way." She made her way through the tables and stepped out on the sidewalk in time to see the vehicle back out onto the road. Lucky devil didn't even catch a red traffic light at the next corner but sped right through a green light and made a left-hand turn before she could read the license plate.

It wouldn't be her father because Lucas said he drove a pickup truck, so who in the hell was stalking her?

"Did you get a look at him?" Tag asked so close behind her that she jumped.

"Nope, but I could swear it's the same car that was parked across the street from my dad's old place last night," she said. "Next time I'm going to get his license number and call the police."

"Billy Tom?" Emily gasped right behind Tag.

"Nope, can't be. This has been going on since before Billy Tom even showed up at the pizza place. We might as well go on back inside. Let me get the door for you."

"A gentleman opens the door for his lady," Tag muttered. "I hate these crutches."

"So I'm your lady? Is that the same as your girlfriend?" Nikki raised an eyebrow.

"I hope so." Tag finally smiled.

*   *   *

Nikki had a full cart of food by the time she'd finished shopping. She divided it as she set it on the conveyor belt. What she planned to take to her apartment would be in separate sacks from what she'd bought to go to the cabin. She paid the bill, shoved it into her purse, and piled all of it into the trunk of her car. It took two trips up the steps to get all of her things into her place. Once it was put away, she fed Goldie and told her not to wait up for her because she might not be home until morning again.

Face it. You are practically living with Tag, and you've only known him a month. Quint's voice in her head put a smile on her face.

"But I feel like I've known him forever," she muttered as she locked the door and went down to her car.

When she got to the cabin, Tag was sitting on the porch,

his crutches lying next to him on one side and Red sprawled out on the other. He waved and started to get up when she parked. She shook her head at him.

"Just sit still. I can get this. Thought I'd make some supper before we leave. It'll give me something to do until it's time to go," she said.

He got up, hopped over to the door without his crutches, and held it open for her. "I can think of something better to do than cooking."

"Oh, yeah, well, let me get this stuff put away, and you can show me what you've got in mind." She lined grocery bags on her arm and carried them into the house.

"It's got something to do with giving you a massage for doing all this for me, and then we'll see where that takes us," he said. "But first you have to get naked."

"I've never had a massage from a sexy cowboy. This could be interesting." She set the bags on the kitchen table and put away the food as she unloaded it.

"Well, today is your lucky day," he told her as he went back for his crutches.

Red dashed into the cabin ahead of him and went straight to Nikki.

"Look at those big old sad eyes," she crooned as she ripped open a package of doggy treats. "He knows who loves him the most."

"If I get a sad look in my eyes, will you treat me?" Tag asked.

"You can have as many bacon-flavored little bites as you want," she told him. "But first you'll have to sit up and beg for them."

"Red don't have to beg," Tag protested.

"Red is a puppy. You're a big sexy cowboy." Nikki put the last of the groceries away and kicked off her shoes and socks.

"I'll get the oil. You just get naked and stretch out on the bed," Tag said.

"Oil? How many women have you..." She stopped. The past was the past and was none of her business.

"None, but while I was in Walmart this morning, I saw this stuff and thought it would be fun," he said. "I also bought the shower gel to go with it. It smells like coconut, and it reminded me of the beach. You said you'd love to see the ocean, so you can pretend that you've got your toes in the water."

"I shouldn't have asked." She pulled her T-shirt over her head, and then her bra came off. She laid both over the back of a kitchen chair.

Red curled up on the end of the sofa and put his paw over his eyes.

"He's pouting because it's my turn to spend time with you." Tag's eyes went all dreamy as he watched her undress. "You are stunning, in and out of clothes."

"I've always felt like I'm too small." She took off her underpants and threw them on the pile.

"You are perfect," he told her. "Now stretch out on your stomach and let me take your mind off all your worries." He leaned the crutches against the wall and picked up the oil from the nightstand.

She tossed the pillow that she used at night to the side and stretched out. "Did you plan this?"

"I cannot lie to you, darlin'. Yes, ma'am, I did, and I've been pretty aroused just thinking about it since you agreed to get groceries for me," he said.

He applied oil to her back and began to gently rub it in. Then he got serious. He started at her neck and slowly worked his way to the bigger shoulder muscles.

"Where did you learn to do this?" she asked.

"YouTube," he chuckled. "I watched several videos while I waited on you."

"You were supposed to be doing ranch paperwork," she reminded him.

He stopped long enough to nibble on her ear. "It's all done and caught up. Besides, the videos were way more interesting."

"I bet they were." Nikki sighed in contentment as he worked out a particularly large knot in her shoulder. "What are you going to do all weekend if you've caught up on work?"

"I'm going to another ranch rodeo to watch the guys ride bulls. But don't worry, I'm going to be a spectator, not a rider. And I've been thinking that when I get around to the skydiving thing, we just might do it together," he said.

"Honey, I go skydiving every time you make love to me." She relaxed and he worked his way down her entire body.

Every part of her was tingling when he reached her toes and then worked his way back up. It wasn't until he reached her shoulders and flipped her over that she realized he was as naked as she was.

"Oh, when did that happen?" she asked.

"What? The fact that just touching you aroused me or that I took off my clothes?"

"All of the above," she gasped.

He stretched out beside her and ran a hand down her ribs, causing even more fire to build up in her insides. "You had your eyes closed, enjoying the massage. I took off a piece at a time. Your skin is so soft. It's like wrapping these old rough hands in silk."

"We've had enough foreplay, cowboy." She moaned as she rolled over on top of him. "Do we need a YouTube video for what comes next?"

He flipped her over onto her back and his lips found hers in a string of kisses that left them both panting. "Honey, I think we can manage this part just fine."

Afterwards, they curled up together in a quilt cocoon and fell asleep. Nikki's breasts were pressed against his chest, and his arms were around her. Then like a bolt of lightning hit him, he jumped out of bed and spit out a long string of swear words. It startled her so bad that she bounced to her feet in the middle of the bed and looked around for a mouse or a spider or even a snake.

"What's wrong?" she asked.

"God, my toes hurt." He fell backward on the bed.

His weight caused her to bounce and fall flat on her butt. "You aren't supposed to put weight on them. What happened?"

"Damn Red cold nosed my bare leg. I thought it was something crawling on me," he answered breathlessly.

She giggled. "Looks like you scared the poor pup half to death. He's cowering under the table."

"Well, he did the same to me." Tag laughed with her. "Next time, he's going outside."

"Oh, there's going to be a next time?" she asked.

"You bet there is, and according to the clock, it can be right now," he said as he pushed her back on the bed and strung kisses from her neck to her lips. "We've got lots of time before we go to Alvord to see your father."

Chapter Twenty-Five

For the second night in a row, Nikki sat in Tag's truck in front of a house. This one was a two-story frame house set back at the end of a lane lined with pecan trees. Half a dozen rocking chairs were lined up behind the railing of the wide front porch.

"I remember this house," she said.

"You've been here before?" Tag asked.

"No, but I saw something like this in a magazine when I was a little girl. I told Daddy when I got big, I wanted a two-story house," she said.

Lights poured out of several windows, both upstairs and down. A brown pickup truck was parked at the curve of a circular driveway. Tonight there was definitely someone at home, but there wasn't a black car anywhere in sight. That meant Nikki's stalker wasn't her father.

"Whoa!" Nikki said. "I just assumed that whoever is driving that black Lincoln is tracking me. But what if they were following me because of you? What if you have some baby-mama out there somewhere and they want to know exactly what's going on between us," she said.

"Whoa there, darlin'," Tag said with a laugh. "I think your nerves have made your imagination run wild. Relax and take a deep breath. Let's just get through tonight, okay?"

"You didn't answer my question." She folded her arms over her chest.

"I would always do right by a child if it's mine, but I wouldn't marry for that reason," he said. "Now let's go talk to your dad. This isn't something that we need to discuss tonight."

She didn't wait for him like she usually did, but got out of the truck and headed up the sidewalk. He'd answered honestly, but it made her think what percentage of the time the pill failed. There was a slim chance that she was pregnant.

Tag caught up to her just as she rang the doorbell. "Why are you mad at me?"

"I'm not," she said.

"And pigs can sprout wings and fly," he said.

The door opened and her dad said, "Hello, Nikki."

"Daddy, I'd like you to meet my boyfriend, Tag Baker."

"Please come in." Don stood to the side and motioned them inside. "It's a pleasure to meet you, Tag. I'd shake your hand, but it looks like you've got both of them pretty tied up. This is Lucas, but then y'all met him last night. I'm so glad you're here, Nikki."

"He always talks too fast when he's excited." Lucas came out of a doorway. "But I really can't say much, because I do too. Y'all come on in the living room. We aren't totally unpacked yet, but this room is done, and we've laid out a little snack on the coffee table. Can I get you a glass of wine? A drink? Maybe some coffee?"

The look on her father's face was like those times when she was a little girl and he didn't quite know what to do—whether to say he was sorry for the words that had just spewed from her mother's mouth or to give Nikki a hug. She wanted to comfort him, but the moment was awkward.

She took a deep breath and stepped forward. "It's been a long time, Daddy." She rose up on tiptoes and wrapped her arms around his neck. "I've missed you so much."

With tears rolling down his cheeks, Don hugged her tightly. "Oh, Nikki, I've waited for this moment for years. We've got so much catching up to do."

"Yes, we do." She took a step back and looped her arm in his.

Lucas led the way into the living room. Nikki looked around, and her head began to swirl. She thought for a minute that she would faint right there. A collection of framed photographs of her and Quint were lined up on the fireplace mantel. A collage of photographs above the sofa included one of her in her cap and gown at her high school graduation, one at her capping ceremony when she became an LPN, and another had been taken when she received her RN degree. Scattered among them were pictures of Lucas at various functions.

She turned toward her dad. "You were there?"

"At every single thing you ever did." He sat down on the end of the sofa and patted the cushion next to him. "Sit beside me and tell me all about yourself."

She eased down onto the buttery soft leather sofa. "I didn't get any of your letters until last week. Mama kept them in a shoebox. I had no idea that you'd offered to let me live with you."

"I'm so sorry. I came to the house several times, but I couldn't make myself go inside." He pulled a tissue from a nearby box and wiped away his tears. "So I wrote the letters and sent them to you. I had no idea that Wilma would keep my mail from you. Let's have a drink to settle our nerves. Lucas, will you pour for us? And forgive me, Tag. I'm so excited to see y'all that I'm being a bad host. Please sit in the recliner and prop up your foot. What happened to your leg? You want a beer?"

"A mean bull stepped on my foot at a rodeo. Guess he wanted to show me he was still the boss. And a beer sounds great." Tag eased down in the chair and nodded toward the pictures on the wall. "Quite a collection you've got there."

"Thank you," Don said.

Nikki slid long, sideways glances at her father. His hair was gray and wrinkles around his eyes and mouth testified that he was an older man now, but he could easily pass for much younger than the fifty-five or -six that he had to be.

"You've grown up." Don handed her a glass of white wine.

"Not much taller but a lot older." She smiled.

Lucas removed the cap from a bottle of beer and waited until Tag was comfortable in one of two recliners before he put it in his hand.

"I understand y'all met Lucas last night," Don said. "I should tell you about him before we get into catching up. Lucas is my son and your half brother. He's about seven years older than you, Nikki."

She almost shot wine out her nose. "You were married before?"

"No, ma'am. Your mama was my one and only wife. I swore I'd never make that mistake again, and I haven't. His mother was my high school sweetheart. We started college together, and we both dropped out after a year. She moved to California with her parents, and I got a job driving trucks.

She died about a year after Quint's death, but she told Lucas all about me before she passed away."

Lucas sat down in a rocking chair. "Mother married my stepfather before I was born, so I just figured he was my father. He died when I was sixteen and Mama died after a short fight with cancer when I was twenty-one. It was my last year of university up in Weatherford, Oklahoma. Academic scholarship," he answered her unasked question. "I finished up the year and got a job in Dallas. Figured I might as well see if I could locate Don Grady, who Mama said was my biological father. I found him in McKinney and we hit it off. I lived with him a couple of years before I 'fell in love.'" He put air quotes around the last three words. "I got married. It lasted about four years. And I moved back in with Dad. Last year I sold my company and retired. Now I'm writing books on running a business and retiring early in life. I'm probably making more with them than I did with a computer software company. So that's my story. I'm your half brother. I've always wanted to know you beyond those pictures up there."

"Why didn't your mama tell my dad she was pregnant?" Nikki asked.

"Mother told me that she wasn't sure she ever loved him, that what they had was a high school fling," Lucas answered.

Nikki glanced over at Tag. Would they grow apart like that?

He raised his beer bottle to her. "Can you believe you've got a brother?"

Have a brother? she wanted to scream. *I had a brother. His name was Quint. His pictures are on the mantel. I don't know this man.*

"I'm in shock." Nikki drank the rest of her wine and refilled the glass. "Are you retired, Dad?"

"Yes, as of six months ago. After your mother and I divorced, I worked hard, bought the trucking company I was driving for, built it up to be a fairly prosperous business, and then sold it last year. I stayed on for six months to help the new owners with the transition. I bought this place because it's secluded and quiet. I don't want to hear the noise of the city. You'll have to come sometime in the morning and see the deer. There's a big deck we can sit on and watch all kinds of wildlife. Remember when you used to sit still by Canyon Creek and watch for rabbits?"

"I remember." She smiled. "Over on Longhorn Canyon Ranch, there's a bunny that comes up all the time. His name is Hopalong, and he lets us pet him." This was all surreal. A father and a brother, all at once, and they both acted like they wanted her in their lives.

"Are you going to get bored here?" Tag looked over at Don.

"Haven't so far, but then we've had the move to think about," Don said. "I understand you own a ranch near Sunset."

"How..." Nikki started and remembered the black car. "You're the one who's been spying on me."

"Yes, I am." Lucas nodded. "I couldn't figure out why you didn't send him at least one letter all these years, so I'm the one in the black Lincoln that's been watching you. Besides, I've always wondered what it would be like to have a sister, so..." He shrugged.

Tag raised both eyebrows at her. "Never thought it would be a brother, did you?"

"Not in my wildest dreams," Nikki answered.

"I kept thinking that you might show up at my door after I sent that first letter to you, but months went by and then years. I thought maybe you blamed me for Quint's death and never wanted to see me again. I had no idea that Lucas was spying on you until about a month ago. That's when he found out the Baker boys had bought old man Johnson's ranch. And that they were your best friend, Emily's brothers. I was at the retirement home where you worked last year the night of your Valentine's party."

"No!" Nikki gasped. "I would have known you."

"I stayed in the shadows and I wore a baseball cap and glasses. Have to have them now when I read," he said. "You wore a pretty red dress and the residents there loved you. Especially five who sat together at a table with Emily's boyfriend."

"The Fab Five," she whispered. "Did you know that I moved out into my own place when I graduated from high school?"

"I did," Don said. "I wanted to help you, but I was afraid you'd spit in my face since you didn't acknowledge my letters and cards. But I couldn't stop sending them."

"We've sure wasted a lot of time, haven't we?" she said.

"Yes, we have," Lucas answered for him. "And to make up for it, we'd like for you and Tag to come down tomorrow night for a real meal with us. Dad is a fantastic cook."

"He wasn't when we were kids," Nikki said.

"I learned." Don grinned. "Try one of my homemade taquitos."

She picked one up from the plate on the coffee table and bit off half the tiny tortilla wrapped chicken and cheese mixture. "This is great. You've got to share your recipe."

"Gladly."

"And one of those little sugar cookies," Lucas said. "If he made those all the time, I'd weigh five hundred pounds."

Nikki ate one of the cookies and then put three of the spicy tidbits and an equal number of cookies on a napkin and passed them across the coffee table to Tag. "You've got to have these. They're fantastic."

Tag ate one and told her, "If you ever make this at the ranch, the guys will take you away from me. And Maverick has a terrible sweet tooth, so he'd love these cookies, but not as much as I do."

"You'll come tomorrow night?" Don asked. "I've got more pictures you might want to see. I couldn't put them all on the walls or the mantel."

"I have to work tomorrow night," Nikki told him. "Monday night I talk to Mama. So how about Tuesday night? You got anything planned, Tag?"

He shook his head. "Not until these toes heal and then I'm making a date with a skydiving company."

She shivered. "That comes from 'Live Like You Were Dying,' a song he's lived by since he was a teenager."

"Did you stay two point seven seconds on a bull named Fumanchu?" Lucas asked.

"Six point seven seconds," Tag answered.

"Been fishin'?"

"Yep, couple of times a year at least." Tag nodded.

"Then all that's left is skydiving. Sounds like fun. Want some company?" Lucas asked. "I've loved that song ever since it came out."

"Nikki is going with me, but you can tag along if you want," Tag said.

"The hell I am!" she said. "I'm not on a guilt ship with that song as my sails."

Don guffawed so hard that they all laughed with him. "I worried about you living with your mother for nothing, girl," he said between hiccups. Finally, he opened a bottle of beer and took several swallows. "You speak your mind like my mother did."

"Do I have any other family? Cousins? Grandparents still living?"

Don shook his head. "No, darlin', what you've got is right here in this room. You said you talk to your mother on Mondays. So she's still alive?"

"You should know. You send her money every month," Nikki said.

"I put that in my lawyer's hands when I bought the company. I told them when she died, not to even tell me. Other than having you and Quint, like I said, that marriage was a mistake. I mistook her neediness for love. But why do you talk to her on Monday? Don't you keep up with her all week?"

"Nope," Nikki said. "Mama only wants to talk on the phone on Mondays. When I was kidnapped, if she worried about anything, it was that I wouldn't be there on Monday so her schedule wouldn't be interrupted."

"Kidnapped?" Lucas asked.

Tag spoke up and told the shortest form of the story that he could, taking all the credit for the trouble.

"So that's why you were gone those days. I thought maybe you and Tag slipped off for a little midweek getaway," Lucas said. "I was afraid to ask too many questions in town for fear I'd get caught."

Don's face registered pure shock. "I'm so sorry. I had no idea. If I had known, I'd have helped in some way. I know people all over the country from my truck driving days."

"It's okay. It's all over now. Billy Tom is locked up," Nikki said. "And we should be going."

"So soon?" Don asked.

"Dad, it's after ten." She pointed at the clock on the far wall.

"We'll be back Tuesday." Tag put the footrest down,

popped another cookie into his mouth, and picked up his crutches. "What can we bring?"

"Not a thing but a healthy appetite." Don and Lucas both stood up and walked them to the door. "Nikki, this has been great. I just knew when I found this house that someday you'd visit me in it."

"That's not what he told me," Lucas laughed. "He said that someday he'd sit on the front porch in one of those rocking chairs and watch his grandchildren play on the lawn. I told him he'd better get in touch with you because I have the Grady curse. That means I don't do well with women."

"You sound like my friend Maverick, who works with me and my twin brother on the ranch. He says he has the Callahan curse," Tag said.

After hugs and handshakes, Nikki's father and brother waved at them from the porch until they were out of sight. She wrapped her arms around herself and wondered if it had all been a dream.

"Well, that went well," Tag said.

"Yes, but I'm mentally exhausted," she sighed.

"Then let's go home and fall into the bed."

"Tag, I need some time alone to process this. I think it's best if I go to my apartment tonight," she told him.

Tag was more than a little disappointed. "Whatever you want, darlin', but I'm here for you whenever you need me for anything."

Chapter Twenty-Six

Nikki was doing laundry the next morning trying to decide how she really felt about having a brother and whether she'd be dishonoring Quint if she decided that she liked Lucas. Lucas had stepped in to fill a void in her dad's heart not long after Quint had died, and Don had thought Nikki had forsaken him forever. She was jealous of that, even if it wasn't right. Lucas had had a mama and a stepdad who evidently loved him enough to see to it that he had an education and followed his dreams. She and Quint had had to pretty much fend for themselves.

It's not his fault, Quint said softly in her mind. *Don't ever blame Lucas for what we didn't have. And don't be afraid to let Tag into your life. Not just for a night or a week, or even for a year. Open up your heart and let love into it.*

"I made a mistake the last time I did that. The guy was married," she said as she made a round through the bedroom and back to the kitchen.

Don't judge Tag by his past or by some other bastard.

Nikki giggled. "You said a dirty word. Mama would have a fit. God, my head hurts." She cupped her cheeks with her hands and rubbed her temples with her fingertips. If she couldn't get these roller-coaster emotions settled before she went to work the next night, maybe Rosemary could give her some advice. Emily had met Wilma only once. Rosemary had known her all her life, so she'd understand what Nikki was facing. If she could just put one thing to bed forever that night, it would be the absolute fear that she'd become like Wilma and be a burden to Tag. Maybe she should make a trip to Sunset tomorrow before she went to work and talk to the ladies of the Fab Five. None of them had been married, but they were pretty sage in their advice.

While the wash cycle ran, she stretched out on the sofa and fell asleep. She dreamed that she and Tag were naked in the bed at the cabin when a tornado ripped through the county. They barely made it into the tiny bathroom and were huddled together in the shower that was so small it made one person feel crowded. Tag's arms were around her when the cabin's roof was suddenly ripped off, and she could feel the vacuum inside the vortex of the tornado sucking her away from him. She held on as tight as she could, but the force of nature finally pulled her away from him. She awoke flailing her arms and hanging on to a throw pillow.

Her hands hit Goldie's fishbowl and sent it flying across the room and upended against the wall. When she realized what she'd done, she ran across the room and chased the poor flopping fish all over the floor before she finally got her in her hands. She ran to the kitchen, put her in a bowl, and ran water straight from the tap, hoping that it was the right temperature and wouldn't kill the thing.

"There, there, now, you're going to be all right. It was

time to clean your bowl anyway. Just swim around in there until I can get my heart to settle down, gather the pieces, and clean up your bowl. Thank God it didn't break." Nikki talked to the fish in the same tone she used for Sue Ann and her other patients.

She could hear Wilma's voice in her head as she scraped up the rocks from the carpet and put them back into the bowl. *That's why you can't have a pet. You're not responsible enough to take care of one properly. Now look at this mess you've made. I'll probably step on those sharp rocks and get sepsis in my foot. When I'm dead and in my casket, you'll wish you'd have taken better care of me.*

Nikki had heard those words so many times that it wasn't even surprising that they came back to haunt her that morning. Would she ever say something like that, even in anger, at her child?

"Hell no!" she said aloud, answering her own question, just as the doorbell rang.

She peeked out the peephole to see her father standing there on the tiny landing. She opened the door and said, "Daddy?"

"Is it a bad time? After I rang the bell, I figured I should have called first. I shouldn't just drop in like this."

"Come on in. Watch your step. I just knocked over the fishbowl and haven't cleaned up the mess yet," she said.

"I'll help," Don said. "Where do you keep the vacuum?"

"In that closet." She pointed. "But you don't have to..."

"I want to," he said as he headed into the kitchen. "I see your faucet is dripping. I could fix that, too, while I'm here. I carry wrenches in the car."

"Did you come here to fix all my problems?" she asked.

"I wish I could do that, honey," he sighed. "I came so we could visit without Lucas and Tag. I wanted to talk to you, just the two of us. But I don't mind helping with whatever you need while I'm here." He pulled the vacuum out into the living room floor and quickly cleaned up all the rocks.

When the machine was back in the closet, he asked, "Mind if we both sit down for a visit?"

"I'm sorry, Daddy. Yes, please sit. Can I make you a cup of coffee? Get you a glass of sweet tea?"

"I'm good for now." He sat down on the sofa.

She took a place beside him. "Okay, I'll go first. It's going to be tough to accept Lucas. Quint wouldn't want me to be that way, but..."

He covered her hand with his. "It'll take time. It did for me. I'm having trouble accepting Tag. Sounds like he's kind of a daredevil, riding bulls and wanting to go skydiving. And to tell the truth, I'm having a terrible time thinking of you in a relationship. To me, you're still fourteen."

"And to me, it's just days after Quint died, and you're coming home for the weekend," she said.

Don patted her hand. "I guess time stood still at the same time it moved ahead with warp speed, didn't it? If you'll give Lucas a chance, I'll be more open-minded about Tag. Deal?"

"Deal," she said. "Now how about a beer? I could sure use one."

Don shook his head slowly. "I'd love one. It's still hard to see my little girl with a wineglass in her hands or think about her drinking a beer."

"Your little girl isn't so little anymore, Daddy." She leaned over and kissed him on the cheek. "I'll get those beers."

* * *

Tag reached for Nikki when he awoke on Friday morning, but all he got was a pillow. He threw it across the room, hit the end of the sofa, and woke Red. The dog jumped up and started barking.

"It's okay, boy," he said as he flipped the covers back and, holding on to furniture for balance, hopped to the door and let the dog outside. "You probably need to get out for a minute anyway, but I'll prop the door with my boot so you can come back to eat when you're done."

Red scampered out and back in before Tag could get dressed in pajama pants and pick up his crutches. "I hate this toe stuff worse than the stitches in my jaw," he muttered as he headed toward the kitchen area to make coffee.

The puppy came back into the house and jumped around in excitement wanting to be fed, and Tag almost tripped over him. "Okay, okay, give me a minute. This feller needs his coffee since his lady isn't here to brighten his morning."

Maverick came into the cabin without knocking. "Where's Nikki? Her car isn't out there. Did you ruin things with her?"

"Good morning," Tag said. "Nikki needed some time to sort out her feelings after seeing her father. I hope to hell I didn't ruin anything."

"I brought over a whole envelope full of papers that Hud found on the top of the refrigerator that needs to be put into the computer. Don't shoot the messenger, but you could give him a cup of coffee." Maverick put the envelope on the top of the microwave.

Tag motioned toward the kitchen table. "Have a seat. It'll be done in a few minutes, and I won't shoot you this morning. I'll get to those papers eventually, but today I'm going to straighten up the tack room in the barn. I can do that with one crutch, and I feel the need to do something physical."

"To keep your mind off Nikki, right?" Maverick pulled out two chairs and sat down in one. "What happened last night?"

Tag told him about what had happened when they went to see her father. "It had to be overwhelming for her because it was for me. It was the first time I'd met any girl's father. I've seen Nikki's mother at church, and we ran into her that time in Walmart, but that's not like actually meeting her."

"And what'd you think of her father and her brother?" Maverick pushed the chair back and poured two large mugs of coffee.

"Thank you." Tag blew on the top and took a sip. "I liked them both. They seemed honest and genuine."

"So you're wonderin' about your past? If you're really settling into this lifestyle? Or if you'll go back to being a rebel?"

"Yep, that's exactly it," Tag admitted.

"Are you missin' your old way of life?" Maverick asked.

Tag thought about it for a minute and then shook his head. "No, I like where I am now with Nikki, and I like sharing the ranch with y'all. I don't think I ever want to go back, but how can I convince Nikki of that?"

"You can't. You have to continue to keep living every day without doin' crazy stuff that will get you killed and show her, not tell her. All the talk in the world is worthless if you don't have the deeds to back it up," Maverick said.

"You speakin' from experience?" Tag asked.

"My heart was broken last year when Paxton and I went to Ireland with our Mam. It was love at first sight for me. Her name was Bridget. We had a month together, roaming the green hills of Ireland. I didn't ask her to come with me to America because I didn't feel like I was good enough for her. That was a big mistake not to let her choose. Now she's over there with my heart, so how could I ever give it to another woman?"

"You never told me that before," Tag said. "And you could call her or talk to her, even if she is over there and you're here."

"I tried that. It didn't work. Her phone number had been changed," he said. "We sound like a couple of old women talkin' like this." Maverick went back to the cabinet and brought the coffeepot to the table. "We'll have another cup and then you can give me a ride to the barn."

"I'm very serious. I'm getting cabin fever. I can clean it without a boot on my foot," he said.

"We've got a rodeo tonight and we're going to the Rusty Spur tomorrow night. You ain't much of a dancer right now, but you can sit at the bar and draw in the women like flies to a honey pot and then turn them over to us," Maverick teased.

"Y'all don't need my help, but I'll think about it," Tag said.

"Mam would say that you've done got moonstruck, my friend," Maverick said. "Never knew you to turn down a night in a bar, and this is not your first rodeo on crutches."

"Your grandma might be right." Tag hopped over and took his jeans and a work shirt from a dresser drawer.

"Mam also told me that if you can't tell a girl that you love her in six months, you should move on and not waste any time for either of you," Maverick said.

"Did you tell Bridget that you loved her?" Tag tugged a knit shirt over his head.

"No, I didn't and that was a mistake for sure. I thought it should be six months so I didn't say the words. But when we got home and I was moping around like a lovesick puppy, Mam told me that I hadn't showed my Irish blood one bit, and she was disappointed in me. She said when everything clicks with a woman, then there will be no doubt in your mind. It will overtake you like a web around a cocoon. It will calm you. And it will inspire you. I lost my Bridget. Don't you make the same mistake."

"It's only been a month for me and Nikki." Tag removed his pajama pants, tossed them on the bed, and pulled on his jeans.

"Ask yourself if it's clicking and if you are calm, and if she's inspired you to be a better man. I'm going to finish my coffee while you finish getting dressed, and then we'll go to work. Sometimes hard work is better than a therapy session. When you're working with your hands, your mind can figure things out," Maverick said.

"Amen." Tag shoved one foot into a cowboy boot and the other into a sneaker. "Let's go to work."

Chapter Twenty-Seven

The ER was full when Nikki checked in to work that Friday night. They spent a few minutes getting caught up, and then she and Rosemary hit the floor in a run. Another type of influenza had hit the area and every cubicle was full and folks were practically standing in line in the waiting room.

There was no letup until dawn, when everyone had been treated and either admitted or sent home. Nikki and Rosemary collapsed into chairs behind the nurses' desk, leaned back, and closed their eyes.

"I'm putting in for a day shift soon as summer is over," Rosemary said.

"Why'd you ever start working weekends?" Nikki asked.

"We don't have to hire a babysitter or pay for day care. I take care of them through the week while my husband works. He spends time with them on Saturday and Sunday while I work. But the youngest will be in preschool this fall, so I can go to days," she said. "I'll miss working with you."

"Me too," Nikki said.

"So how'd things go with the cowboy this week? I didn't hear of him having to get on his white horse and go rescue you," Rosemary said.

Nikki gave her a rundown of the week, ending with, "How do you know when you can fully trust someone? I've tried it a couple of times and got burned."

"First of all, you ask yourself if that person has ever given you a reason not to trust him. Has he lied to you? Cheated on you? That kind of thing. Then you ask yourself what it is that makes you distrust him. If it's that fool that you let into your life and then found out he was married, it's not fair to the cowboy. My granny used to call that judgin' one person by another's half bushel. Never did figure out what all that meant," Rosemary said.

"Makes sense to me." Nikki stood up.

"How do you know that?" Rosemary asked.

"I hear sirens."

The ambulance backed up to the ER doors, and EMTs brought in an older man who thought he was having a heart attack. His wife came with him, sat down behind the curtain with her purse in her lap, and watched every move Nikki made.

"I been with that man sixty years. We got married when we was sixteen and eighteen, and I ain't about to leave him, so don't tell me to," she said.

"Congratulations," Nikki said. "You don't hear of folks stayin' together like that so much anymore." She thought of her own parents and the horrible marriage they'd had.

The gray-haired lady smiled. "Thank you. He was a rounder, that one was. Took me a while to tame him."

"Really?" Nikki put in an IV, checked all his vital signs, and then hooked him up to an EKG machine. At that young age, surely he couldn't have gotten around that much. If they wanted to see a real rebel, she could introduce them to Taggart Baker.

"Honey, he was outrunnin' girls when he was thirteen, and kissin' them behind the barn at fourteen. Don't let them wrinkles and that bald head fool you. He was quite a handsome feller in his youth," she said.

"I'm layin' right here, Inez," her husband said. "And all that talk ain't goin' to keep me from dyin' if it's my time."

"Hush," Inez said. "I'll tell you when it's your time, and it ain't today."

"I'll take over here." Rosemary popped into the room. "You're needed down in cubicle one."

"Did Sue Ann escape again?"

"One of your cowboys is hurt. He's askin' for you," Rosemary said.

"I didn't have time to input information into the tablet. EKG is running. Blood pressure is good. IV is in place." Nikki pulled back the curtain and hurried down the hall. Trust, hell! Tag had promised he wouldn't ride tonight.

She slipped inside the room to find a worried Tag beside the bed where Hud was lying. Both of them looked pale and frightened.

"Bronc?" she asked.

"No, he fell off the barn roof," Tag said. "He said he was fine but his eyes looked dilated to me and he could have a concussion."

Nikki took her penlight from her pocket and checked. Tag was right. Pupils were bigger than Sue Ann's after she'd mixed booze and pills. "Are you hurting anywhere other than your head, Hud? Can you raise your arms and wiggle your toes?"

"Yes," he answered, and showed her. "I'm not broke, but my head hurts. Where's Grandpa? He was there when I fell."

From what Tag had told her, their grandfather had been dead for a long time. She picked up the phone and called Dr. Richards. "I think we've got a concussion in exam room two." When she hung up, she said, "We'll be taking him for a scan, but you're probably right, Tag. You had these before, I suppose."

"He's had everything before," Hud chuckled. "Broken bones and stitches. He's the bad twin. I'm the good one."

"Maybe you're switchin' places." Nikki took all his vital signs.

"What did he hit when he fell?" she asked.

"The last of a few broken bales of hay," Tag answered. "I was in the tack room. Maverick and Paxton were on the roof with him. His foot slipped and he fell through the rafters. If they'd had the last piece of sheet metal up there..."

Nikki touched his arm. "We'll take good care of him."

"I know you will. That's why I wouldn't let anyone else near him." Tag patted her hand.

"Hud, we're going to roll this bed out of here and take you down to radiology for a scan. Can you tell me your name?"

He gave her a dirty look. "I'm Hudson Baker and that is my twin brother, Taggart Baker. I'm fourteen years old. I live on the Rockin' B Ranch and Grandpa told us to stay off the old barn roof, so don't tell him."

"I won't tattle on you," she said. "Tag, you can go as far as the door and wait outside."

She pushed the bed out of the waiting room and met the

technician coming down the hall. "I hate to be on weekend call. Is this our heart attack patient?"

"No, he'll be in next. This is our concussion patient, Hud Baker," Nikki said.

"Well, wheel him in here," the technician said.

Tag sat down in one of the two folding chairs against the wall and laid his crutches on the floor. Nikki was a few minutes getting Hud situated in the right place. When she returned, Tag had his elbows on his knees and his head in his hands.

"They'd just gotten up on the roof when it happened. I'm the one who gets hurt, not Hud." His voice sounded hollow. "Now I know how he feels every time I've been carted off to the hospital."

"Still want to go skydiving?" she asked.

Tag raised his head. "No, I don't. I don't ever want to put anyone through this kind of pain again. Not my brother. Not my sister. Not my parents. And especially not you, Nikki. Are you disappointed?"

"About skydiving? Not in the least. I'm afraid of heights. It took me a while to get used to the landing outside my second-floor apartment. I still don't look down from there." She slipped her hand into his.

He brought her hand to his cheek. "I'm scared, Nikki. Really, really scared. What if he's like this the rest of his life?"

"Then we'll deal with it, but mostly people with concussions usually come out of it in a few hours. He might remember the fall, and maybe not the day before if it's a minor one. We'll hope for that." She scooted closer to him and laid her head on his shoulder.

"Thanks for being here for me," he said.

"It's my job."

"This part isn't. Just having you here beside me right now helps," he said.

"Tag, I'm always here for you. You're my knight in a shiny pickup truck." She kissed him on the cheek.

*   *   *

Lying on the bed with his eyes closed, Hud almost looked fourteen again. Tag removed his boot and sneaker and propped his feet on the extra chair in the room. Maverick peeked in and whispered, "Okay if we come in for a minute?"

"Sure it is," Tag said. "They're going to keep him for at least twenty-four hours for observation. If he comes out of it by tomorrow, he can go home. If not, they said they'd reevaluate the whole thing."

"We'll go on home, then," Paxton said. "No need in all of us missing a day's work and we need to get that hay cut soon as we nail down that last piece of sheet metal."

Tag nodded. "I should be there, but I can't leave him. He thinks he's fourteen. He's remembering the time Grandpa told us not to go up on the roof, but we did anyway and I fell. He thinks it was him."

"It's that twin thing," Paxton said. "You stay with him. We'll hold down the ranch until y'all get home. If you need anything, just give us a call and we'll have it here soon as we can."

"Thank you both. I'm learning it's different when you're at the side of the bed instead of in it," Tag said.

Maverick clamped a hand on his shoulder. "Kind of gives you something more to think about, don't it?"

Tag swallowed the lump in his throat and nodded. The Callahan brothers slipped out as quietly as possible and closed the door behind them.

Tag's job was to wake Hud every hour all night, ask him if he recognized him and if he knew his name. The sun was up when Hud roused on his own, looked at Tag with a frown, and said, "I'm Hudson Baker. You're my twin brother."

Tag had spent time in rooms almost just like this one with an IV in his arm like what Hud had. He'd had a couple or three concussions, and like Hud had said, broken bones and stitches. Who knew what kind of damage all that knocking his brain took might lead to in the future? When he got to be old and gray, arthritis would set in where the bones had snapped. And the scars wouldn't be nearly so sexy in sagging skin. Nikki deserved better than that.

As if she knew he was thinking about her, she pushed into the room with a tray in her hands. "I brought food. You need to eat. And there are two bottles of water for you to sip on this afternoon. How is he?"

"In and out. Sleeping, groaning a little. I've been where he is, so I know he's got a killer headache," Tag said. "I really hate this, Nikki."

She bent down and brushed a sweet kiss across his lips. "I remember when Quint was in the hospital and how much I hated feeling helpless, so I understand. I've got to get back to the on-call room and catch a few winks so I'll be ready for the next eight hours. Call me if he wakes up and is lucid or if you need me for anything."

He pulled her lips to his for a more passionate, lingering kiss. "I love you, Nikki."

She blinked several times but didn't say a word. Maybe he'd only thought the words and hadn't actually said them out loud. He'd never told a woman that before, so perhaps it was normal for them not to answer and leave the room immediately.

"I love you, too," Hud muttered. "I've always loved you, Cactus."

Tag jerked his head around to stare at his brother. "Oh, really? Cactus who?"

"Cactus Rose O'Malley. I've always been in love with her. Shh…Grandpa. Don't tell Tag. If she sees him, she'll like him better," Hud muttered.

"I don't remember anyone by that name. Have you been keeping secrets from me?"

Hud's eyes popped wide open. "Where are we? Where's Grandpa?"

"You're in the hospital. You've got a concussion," Tag said. "Do you know who I am?"

"Of course, Tag." Hud's brow drew down so tightly that his eyebrows almost touched. "What happened?"

"You tell me," Tag said. "Where's Grandpa?"

Hud continued to look totally confused then his expression changed as if a light bulb went off.

"He died years ago, didn't he? Am I dying, too?" Hud asked.

"No, you're not dying," Tag answered. "What's the last thing you remember?"

"Stayin' on the bronc for eight seconds. Did he throw me?" Hud tried to sit up.

"Be still and let me call a nurse." Tag pushed the button on the side of the rail to raise the bed. "You fell off the barn roof, not a bronc. They think the concussion is minor, but you've got to stay here for twenty-four hours."

"Bullshit! You fell off the barn, not me. You've made me trade places with you, haven't you?" Hud said.

"Not this time," Tag told him. "Hungry?"

"No. The thought of food makes my stomach turn over. Are you serious? This isn't a joke?"

Tag smiled. "No, it's not a joke and it's very serious. It's a good sign that you woke up so quickly and that you remember riding the bronc Friday night."

Hud stared at his brother. "I don't remember falling off the barn or coming here."

"Nikki says that's normal," Tag told him. "But you need to rest. I'll be right here with you until we can take you home."

"You don't need to stay here. I'm a big boy. I can sleep without you by my side."

"How many times have I said that to you, and you never left me for a minute?" Tag asked.

"I don't have enough fingers and toes to count that far," Hud answered as his eyes slowly closed and he began to snore.

Tag dug his phone out of his pocket and called Nikki.

"Hello," she said.

"He woke up and he remembers some things, but not the fall. He's asleep now," Tag said. "I hope I didn't wake you."

"You didn't, and, Tag, I love you too," she said.

"Say that again?" he whispered.

"I love you," she said. "I was about to call and tell you. I couldn't go to sleep without saying the words."

He was completely speechless for several seconds. "Will you tell me in person next time we're together?"

"Yes, I will. See you later, Tag."

"Sleep tight, my darlin'."

Chapter Twenty-Eight

In some ways, the weekend lasted forever; in others, it went by at warp speed. And then it was midnight on Sunday, and Nikki was free to go home. She and Rosemary walked out together into the sweltering night air, the concrete still hot from the boiling sun pounding on it all day.

"It was strange not seeing Sue Ann this weekend," Nikki said. "But I'm glad her sister from Oklahoma stepped in and offered to take her for some real help. With Sue Ann signing herself into the psych ward at the hospital and then either walking out or signing herself out, she wasn't getting the long-term help she needs."

"Me too. I'm glad you tracked her sister down and told her about Sue Ann," Rosemary said.

"Families can sure screw things up, can't they?" Nikki sighed.

"If you let them, they can. Maybe now Sue Ann can get clean and have a decent life. Darla June seemed to really want to help. The expression on Sue Ann's face when she saw her sister for the first time in years almost brought tears to my eyes," Rosemary answered.

"Mine too," Nikki agreed.

"I'm getting all misty eyed again just thinking about it, so let's talk about something else," Rosemary said. "How are things with the cowboy and his brother?"

"Hud went home today, and I told Tag that I love him," Nikki said.

"How'd it make you feel?" Rosemary stopped by Nikki's car.

"At peace," Nikki answered.

"Then it was the right thing to do. Girl, I sure hope this week is better for you than the past two have been. I'll be waiting to hear all about it next Friday." Rosemary gave her a hug and headed on down the row of vehicles to her own car.

Nikki drove to her apartment, fed Goldie, and shoved a couple of outfits into a bag. As she made her way down the stairs, she caught sight of a flash in the sky and saw her very first shooting star. A warm glow filled her from the inside out as she remembered her father telling her that when she saw a star falling from heaven that she got to make one wish.

"I wish for a lifetime with Tag," she said as she got into her car, tossed her bag into the backseat, and headed toward the cabin.

When she arrived, the lights were still on, so she rapped on the door lightly before she entered. Tag was sitting on the sofa, the laptop on the coffee table, and Red was curled up in front of the fireplace.

"I was hoping you'd come," he said.

"I'm glad you're still up." She sat down beside him and laid her head on his shoulder. "How's Hud?"

"No physical work for a week until the doctor sees him again, and then maybe not for a while after that. But Justin is sending us two of their hired hands to get the hay cut tomorrow and he's loaning us their big round baler so we can stack it outside instead of in the barn. And Emily is coming to help out too." Tag draped an arm around her shoulders.

"I'll help any way I can," she said.

He pushed a strand of hair behind her ear. "Darlin', you are helpin' just by bein' here beside me. But if you want to go with me to the tack room and help get it organized tomorrow, I'd love to spend the time with you."

"Done." She yawned.

"I'd carry you to bed, but..." He glanced down at his foot.

"I'd carry you, but..." She grinned.

"Let's just lean on each other and go get some sleep," he said.

"That sounds great." She stood up and got her bag from the end of the sofa where she'd dropped it. "And, Tag, I love you."

"Never thought I'd say those words or hear them either. They're pretty powerful, aren't they?" Tag stood and draped an arm around her shoulders.

"Me neither. And yes, they are. They can still a restless heart." She served as his crutch to the edge of the bed. He sat down, and she dug around in the bag for a nightshirt.

"I like it better when you come to bed naked," he said.

"Tonight we'd better sleep in clothing."

"Why?"

"Because we don't have the energy to make love all night and then work all day tomorrow." She yawned again. "I just want to fall asleep in your arms."

"I can be satisfied with that tonight." He slid between the sheets and waited, then gathered her close to his body when she joined him.

*   *   *

Tag awoke to the aroma of coffee and bacon. When he sat up in bed and opened his eyes, he saw Nikki in the kitchen area making breakfast. "Good morning. You sure look sexy in that outfit."

"What, this old thing?" She tugged at the bottom of her faded nightshirt. "I wore it to a White House dinner, and then to tea with the queen."

He laughed out loud. "And I bet you wore diamonds with it to one and pearls to the other."

"One can't meet the queen without her pearls. Pancakes are ready. Need your crutches or can you hop," she said.

"I can actually walk a little on the foot now, if I'm careful. Trouble is I look like an old man." He got out of bed and eased his way across the floor to the table.

"Honey, we all get old eventually." She waited until he was seated and gave him a kiss and then handed him a cup of coffee. "Eat up. We've got a tack room to clean this morning, and we need to check on Hud."

Tag would have liked to spend an hour in bed before they left, but Nikki rushed through breakfast, did the cleanup, and got dressed so fast that he didn't have time to seduce her. Oh, well, he'd make up for that later that evening, after she'd talked to her mother.

They passed Maverick and Paxton, each operating a John Deere tractor that morning. The smell of fresh-cut hay filled the cab of the truck. It reminded Nikki of Saturdays when her father mowed the grass. She always thought it was a big privilege when he let her push the lawn mower for a few rounds.

Tag's phone rang and he didn't even check the caller ID before answering it.

"Hello."

"Hud is in the tack room," Maverick said. "Paxton and I took four-hour shifts like you suggested all night, but we figured it'd be easier on you to take care of him in the barn. Just giving you a heads-up. He's an old bear."

"Thanks for everything. I'll take it from here, and I owe you," Tag said.

"It's just through today and then he should be fine," Maverick said. "And we volunteered. Did you tell her yet?"

"I did," Tag answered.

"Good for you," Maverick said. "Holler if you need us."

"Will do." He ended the call and turned to tell Nikki what was going on.

When he finished, she simply nodded. "I'll watch the time for you."

They found Hud stretched out on the worn-out sofa in the tack room. He was snoring loud enough to wake hibernating grizzly bears all the way up toward the northern part of the States.

Nikki checked her watch. "He can sleep until nine o'clock. Now, where do we start?" Her eyes scanned the messy room.

"We don't have to do it all today. I don't think Eli Johnson threw away anything." Tag picked up a jar filled with bent nails.

"I remember his wife. She and Mama could've been sisters. Not so much in looks but in their attitudes. The two of them were always comparing medicines and illnesses. I bet Eli spent hours out here." Nikki picked up a box of empty milk jugs. "We probably need a whole box of big trash bags to start with." She turned around slowly, taking in the whole room. "There's a bathroom right there. Has it got a shower?" She crossed the room and stepped inside. "Yep, it does, and you're not going to believe this, but it's above an old claw-foot tub. I bet this was his doghouse. When she was on a rampage, he probably lived out here. My dad's escape was the cab of a truck. Eli's was this tack room."

Tag slipped his arms around her waist and buried his face in her hair. "Am I going to need a doghouse?"

"No, but you do need a bunkhouse, and I'm seeing a possibility here. If you knock out that wall and claim the two stalls on the other side, throw up some drywall and insulation, you could have a really nice bunkhouse right here. Or you could just cut a door through right about here and make two bedrooms."

"You are a genius." He leaned his crutches against the work table and envisioned the area as a small apartment. "Or this could be a living area and the room beyond it could be a bedroom. With water already out here, we could even put in a small kitchen. I bet Justin could draw some plans pretty quick."

"We?" she asked.

"Darlin', I can't offer you dinner at the White House or tea with the queen, but this is doable real soon. Will you live with me in this five-star bunkhouse when it's finished?"

"Let's get it done and then we'll talk about it." She hopped up on the work table. "My rent is paid for June. Offer me a closet, and I might consider it."

"I think we can manage that." Tag turned to face her and his lips found hers in a long, hot kiss.

"Are we jumping into this too fast?" Her breath came out in short gasps.

"Hey, it's a whole month away. That's not fast enough in my book," Tag said.

"Well, before we can do anything, we need to get our future living room cleaned up," she said.

"Hey, what are y'all doin' in my bedroom?" Hud sat up and scratched his head. "Oh, I forgot. Maverick and Paxton made me come out here. Give me something to do. I'm going crazy with boredom, and they kept waking me up all night. Really, what are y'all doing?"

"We're going to make an apartment out of this room and a couple of stalls next door. We need plans drawn up, but first we have to get things in order," she answered.

"Do I get the apartment?" Hud asked. "I refuse to live with those Callahan cowboys if they're going to wake me up all the time. It's just a concussion."

"No, it's for me and Nikki," Tag said.

"Will you make one of them Callahan cousins move to the cabin so we have more room in the house?"

"You got it," Tag agreed.

Hud eyed the room. "A doorway over there and you could take it all the way to the end of the barn for a bedroom. This could be the living room. If you knock out the wall on the other side of the bathroom and close it on this side, it could be a private bathroom."

"I'd say he's doing much better," Nikki said.

Tag kissed her on the forehead. "He had an amazing nurse."

*   *   *

Nikki couldn't think of a single reason to put off telling her mother that she planned to move in with Tag as soon as their tiny barn apartment was finished. But she wasn't nearly as prepared for the Monday night conversation as she thought she would be. When the phone rang at exactly seven o'clock, she'd already had her shower and Tag was taking one.

"Hello, Mama, how are you tonight?" Nikki answered.

"My gout is acting up. I was drinking cherry juice twice a day, but it caused me to have colon problems."

In the Grady house, no one said diarrhea or constipation. "Colon problems" covered both maladies. Women didn't get pregnant. They were in the family way. The word *sex* was spoken in whispers when used at all.

"I'm sorry. Have you talked to your doctor?"

"He's a quack. I keep tellin' you that I want to change doctors, but you won't do a thing about it. He's going to let me die and it'll all be your fault."

Nikki inhaled deeply and let it out slowly. "I'm going to move in with Tag Baker at the end of June or before if we get our apartment finished. We're building a two-room apartment in the barn on his place."

"You've lost your mind! You never were real smart, but this takes the cake." Ice coated every word Wilma said. "Do you know what people will say about me?"

"Mama, this isn't about you. I love Tag. We want to spend time together, so we're going to do this. I've been spending most of my nights with him anyway, ever since I was kidnapped," she said.

"I'll never be able to hold my head up in town again," Wilma sighed. "You've ruined my reputation. I've just built it back from when your worthless father divorced me."

"If you don't want to talk to me, we can hang up now," Nikki suggested.

"It's not eight o'clock, yet," Wilma told her.

"Okay, then, I'll also tell you that I'm having dinner with

Daddy and he came to see me in my apartment." Might as well get it all out in the open.

Dead silence for several moments, and then Wilma said, "You've always been more like him than me. Quint took after me. He never was healthy, poor little darlin' boy. I still miss him."

Nikki rolled her brown eyes toward the ceiling. Add narcissism to the long list of her mother's mental problems. When it suited her purpose to be the victim, she rewrote reality. "So you aren't going to give me grief over visiting with Daddy and having dinner with him?"

"It's not time to hang up, but I need to go to the bathroom. I guess the cherry juice is affectin' me. Goodbye, Nikki. We'll talk again next week," Wilma said.

A click ended the call before Nikki could say another word.

Tag came out of the bathroom wearing nothing but a towel and a smile, and suddenly it didn't matter one bit what her mother, her father, or anyone else on the face of the earth thought. She wanted to be with Tag for the rest of her life.

"Let's go for a walk down to the creek," she said. "I need a breath of fresh air."

"Your mama upset you?" Tag dropped the towel and got a pair of jeans from the dresser.

"Nope, she reacted to the idea of me living with you just like I figured she would," Nikki said. "Everything always has been and always will be about her. Nothing is going to change. The thing I have to learn is to accept it and move on. It'll be interesting to see what Daddy says about us living together. Somehow I think he might be happy for us."

"Me too," Tag said. "Darlin', you're forgetting that I'm still on crutches, so how about we drive over to Canyon

Creek and sit on the banks of the creek for a while? Will that do?"

"Oh yeah," Nikki said.

The radio was playing Rascal Flatts's "Back to Life" when they got into the truck. "This is my song to you tonight," Tag said. "Listen to every word. Just like the song says, you really do bring me back to life."

"This is one of my favorite songs. It should be our song, because you pull me up every time I feel like I'm going under," she said. That's when the idea hit her and she smiled. She took her phone from her pocket and found the right karaoke music.

He parked as close to the creek as possible and got out of the truck. "I'll have to use the crutches on this uneven ground. I like it back here. Someday we'll build a house in this copse of pecan trees," he said.

"I'd like that, Tag, but I'll be content in our little corner of the barn until we can afford to build," she said as she let herself out of the truck. She walked down to the edge of the water and removed her boots and socks.

"Going to do some wading," he asked. "Reckon it would hurt my foot if I joined you, Nurse Nikki?"

"If it doesn't hurt them to take a shower, then this creek water shouldn't either," she said. "But I had something other than wading in mind," she answered. "I betcha I can get undressed faster than you can." She tugged her shirt over her head.

"You're on." He tossed the crutches to the side, sat down, and jerked the boot off his good foot, his sneaker off the other one, and then his socks. She tossed her clothing on the ground and would have beat him if he'd worn underwear. But while she was pulling off those cute little black lace panties, he was already on his feet.

"It's not deep enough to swim," he said.

"Who said anything about swimming?" Nikki pushed a button on her phone and tossed it on the ground with her clothing. The music to "Live Like You Were Dying" started playing. When it got to the chorus, she sang about going fishing and riding a bull named Fumanchu, but when it came to the part about skydiving, she substituted "skinny-dippin'."

Tag laughed out loud as he waded into the cool bubbling water. "I'd rather go skinny-dipping with you than skydiving any day. Have I told you today what a lucky cowboy I am?"

"No, but don't ever forget it," she said.

He bent at the waist and splashed water on her. "My rebel days are over."

She grabbed his hand and pulled him down into the water with her, then shifted her position so that she was sitting in his lap. The fast-moving current flowed around them at waist level. "I love my rebel cowboy in the bedroom, but outside of it, I'd sure breathe easier if he took those stickers off his truck."

"Anything for you, darlin'." He scooped water up into his hands and poured it down her back.

"Will you tell me if you begin to regret any of this or change your mind?"

"Yes, I will, but it ain't happening. I've finally got closure. How about you?"

"I do." Nikki nodded.

"Maybe someday in the not too distant future, you'll say those two words in a church."

Nikki cocked her head to one side. "Tag, are you proposing to me?"

He ran a hand down her naked sides. "If and when I do, do you reckon you'll say yes?"

"Probably."

"What do you mean, probably?"

"You'll have to ask me to find out. I'll tell you right now I want the whole nine yards—you down on one knee with a ring in a velvet box. I'm not real crazy about a wedding like Emily's. Can't you just see my mama and daddy in the same room? It would be a total nightmare. A trip to the court-house will be fine with me, but I want the big engagement so I'll have the memory to hold on to."

"Darlin', you will have everything you want, however you want it. And I'll always be your bedroom rebel." Tag pulled her face to his and sealed the promise with a kiss.

Keep reading for a preview of

CHRISTMAS WITH A COWBOY

Coming September 2019

Chapter One

Maverick Callahan was singing "Jingle Bells" when he opened the door to the bunkhouse, but the singing stopped the minute that he realized the lights were already on and the place was warm. The black hair on his neck stood straight up, giving testimony that there was someone there. Chills chased down his spine, and his feet were glued to the floor. For a moment everything was so quiet that it hurt his ears. Then he heard someone humming "Tulle Rose," an Irish lullaby his grandmother used to sing to him and Paxton.

"Hello?" His voice came out raspy and barely a whisper. In a few long strides, he crossed the floor and peeked around the corner to find a woman with long red hair sitting in a rocking chair with a baby in her arms.

"Bridget?" he whispered.

"Sweet Jesus. I wasn't expectin' to see you until tomorrow," she muttered when she turned. Her Irish lilt was even more pronounced than he remembered.

Her mossy green eyes looked up at him as if she wasn't even surprised to see him. Then she eased out of the chair and carried the baby to a crib across the room.

"What? How? Why?" His eyes darted back and forth from the crib to Bridget.

"I might be askin' you the same things." She popped her hands on her hips. "Like how could you break my heart like you did? Why did you leave without saying goodbye? And what were you thinking?"

He leaned against the doorjamb and tried to get his bearings. When he'd left Ireland a year ago, he thought he'd never see Bridget again. What in the world was she doing in Texas? He wanted to take a closer look at the baby, but his boots felt like they were filled with concrete.

"I tried to call when I got back to Texas," he said.

"I changed my number," she admitted.

He folded his arms over his chest. "Why didn't you call me?"

"I was angry with you, and I still am. I'm here to get over you, Maverick Callahan, and the sooner the better," she said. "My nana got very sick and her best friend, your grandmother, came to be with her those last days." She wiped a tear away with the back of her hand.

"They knew each other?" Maverick raised an eyebrow. He wanted to take her into his arms.

"It was a surprise to me, too." She sat down on the edge of the bed. "But I'm here, and I'm on a mission, so..." She shrugged. "And your grandmother is here, too."

"Mam is here? What's she doing here?" Maverick asked.

"She wanted to surprise you and Paxton." Bridget sat down on the edge of the bed.

Maverick's phone dinged, and he pulled it from his jacket pocket to find a message from his brother, telling him to put down his paintbrushes and come to the ranch house for a big surprise. Well, guess what? The bigger surprise was in the bunkhouse.

"How did..." he started.

She put up a palm. "We flew from Ireland together and she helped me with the baby on the trip."

His mind whirled in circles. He'd never stopped thinking about Bridget or the amazing romance that he knew from the beginning could only last the few weeks he was in Ireland. He'd thought that he could come home to Texas, go right back to his old ways and move on, but he couldn't. Every single moment he'd spent with her was like a chapter in a book that had already been written, could never be erased, and he kept reading it over and over again.

He couldn't blame her, not after the way he'd left without even telling her goodbye. "I'm sorry," he whispered. "But..." He glanced toward the crib where the baby slept. "Is that..." His heartbeats pounded in his ears. Had those glorious nights in Ireland produced that wee babe with dark hair, so much like his?

Bridget's eyes followed his. "I can see where you'd think she belonged to you. Her father was tall, dark and handsome, too. But I didn't give birth to her. Do you remember Diedre, my friend who worked at the pub with me?"

Maverick nodded.

"That's her daughter. She died when Laela was two months old. Automobile accident. Diedre didn't have any family so she named me as Laela's godmother at her christening. So, I became an instant mother." Bridget paused.

Maverick breathed a sigh of relief. "I'm sorry that you lost your friend and your grandmother both in such a short time." He took a deep breath before continuing. "Most of all, I'm sorry about what happened in Ireland."

"Sorry isn't enough, Maverick."

The words cut straight to his heart. "Maybe someday you can forgive me," he said. "You said you came here to get over me, so I'll try to stay out of your way." He picked up a plastic bag and shoved several little bottles of paint into it. Then he left through the back door and slammed it behind him.

About the Author

Carolyn Brown is a *New York Times* and *USA Today* bestselling romance author and RITA® Finalist who has sold more than 5 million books. She presently writes both women's fiction and cowboy romance. She has also written historical single title, historical series, contemporary single title, and contemporary series. She lives in southern Oklahoma with her husband, a former English teacher, who is not allowed to read her books until they are published. They have three children and enough grandchildren to keep them young. For a complete listing of her books (series in order) and to sign up for her newsletter, check out her website at www.carolynbrownbooks.com or catch her on Facebook/CarolynBrownBooks.

And if you love Carolyn Brown's small-town and sweet
stories, we think you'll like *USA Today* bestselling author
Annie Rains too.

Keep reading for the bonus novella:

A Wedding on Lavender Hill

FOREVER
New York   Boston

Chapter One

Claire Donovan had a bit of a reputation in Sweetwater Springs. She loved to shop.

As an event planner, she was always looking for a special item to make the *big day* just a touch more special. Last week she'd found a clown costume for a purse-sized Chihuahua to wear to its owner's eightieth birthday bash. It was a huge hit with the crowd; not so much with the little dog, who yapped, ran in circles, and tore at the shiny fabric.

The only shopping Claire would be doing this morning, however, was glancing in storefront windows on her way to meet with her newest client, Pearson Matthews. Claire's reputation extended beyond shopping. In Sweetwater Springs, she was also known for being professional and punctual, and for putting on the best parties in town.

She passed Sophie's Boutique and admired the window display, wishing she had more time to pop inside and say hello to the store owner—and try on one of those dresses that she absolutely didn't need. Then she opened the neighboring door to the Sweetwater Café and stepped inside to a cool blast of air on her face. She was instantly accosted by the heavy scent of coffee brewing. *Best aroma in the world!*

"Good morning," Emma St. James said from behind the counter. She had the smile of someone who'd been sniffing coffee and sugary treats since five a.m.

"Morning." Claire glanced around the room, looking for Pearson. The only people seated in the coffee shop though were two twentysomething-year-old women and a man with his back toward her. Judging by his build, he was in his twenties or thirties and liked to work out. He wore a ball cap that shielded his face. Not that Claire needed to get a good look at him. If his face matched his body, then he was yummier than Emma's honeybuns in the display case. Claire would do better to have one of those instead.

Pulling her gaze away from him, she walked up to the counter.

"Your usual?" Emma asked.

"You know me so well."

Emma turned and started preparing a tall café latte with heavy cream and two raw sugars. "Your mom was here the other day," she said a moment later as she slid the cup of coffee toward Claire.

Claire's good mood immediately took a dive. She loved her mom, but she didn't exactly *like* her. "Oh?" she said, her tone heavy with disinterest. "That's nice."

Emma tilted her head. "She asked about you."

"Well, I hope you told her that I'm fine as long as she stays far away."

"She said she's going to AA now," Emma told her as she rang up Claire's items at the register.

Drinking had always been Claire's father's problem though. Nancy Donovan had so many other, more pressing issues to deal with, none of which Claire wanted to concern herself with right now. She paid Emma in cash, took her coffee and bagged honeybun, then turned and looked around the shop once more.

"Are you meeting someone here?" Emma asked.

"Pearson Matthews. I guess he's running late," Claire said, turning back.

Emma shrugged. "Not sure, but his son is over there." She pointed at the man in the ball cap, and Claire nearly dropped her coffee.

What is Bo Matthews doing here? She didn't have anything against his father, but the youngest Matthews son ranked as one of her least favorite people in Sweetwater Springs. Or he would have if he hadn't left town last April.

Bo glanced over and offered a small wave.

"Maybe he knows where his father is," Emma suggested.

A new customer walked in so Claire had no choice but to step away from the counter. She could either walk back out of the Sweetwater Café and text Pearson on the sidewalk or she could ask his son.

You hate him, she reminded herself as attraction stormed in her belly. She forced her feet to walk forward until she was standing at his table.

Hate him, double-hate him, triple-hate him.

But *wow*, she loved those blue-gray eyes of his, the color of a faded pair of blue jeans. The kind you wanted to shimmy inside of and never take off.

"What are you doing back in town?" she asked, pleased with the controlled level of irritation lining her voice.

He looked up. "I live in Sweetwater Springs, in case you've forgotten."

"You left." And good riddance.

"I had a job to do in Wild Blossom Bluffs. But now I'm home."

Like two sides of a football stadium during a touchdown, half of her cheered while the other side booed and hissed. She was not on Team Bo anymore and never would be again. "Where is your father?"

"I'm afraid he couldn't make it. He asked me to meet with you instead."

Claire's gaze flitted to the exit. Pearson Matthews was her biggest client right now. He was a businessman with money and influence, and she'd promised to do a good job for him and his fiancée, Rebecca Long. Claire also had her reputation to maintain. She took her responsibilities seriously and prided herself on going above and beyond the call of duty. Every time for every client.

And right now, her duty was to sit down and make nice with Bo Matthews.

* * *

Bo reached for his cup of black coffee and took a long sip as he listened to Claire do her best to be civil. If he had to guess, the conversation she really wanted to be having with him right now was anything but.

"The wedding is two months away," she said, avoiding eye contact with him. "We're on a time crunch, yes, but your father could've called and rescheduled the initial planning session." Her gaze flicked to meet his. "It's not really something you can do."

Bo reached for his cup of coffee and took another

sip, taking his time in responding. He could tell by the twitch of her cheek that it irritated her. She couldn't wait to get out of that chair and create as much distance between them as possible. Regret festered up inside him. He couldn't blame her for being upset. He'd handled things with her all wrong last year. "There's a problem with the wedding."

Claire's stiff facial features twisted. "What? Pearson and Rebecca called the wedding off?"

"No, unfortunately," he said, although that would've made him happy. Bo had been certain his dad would eventually come to his senses about marrying a woman half his age. Then, a few months ago, the lovebirds had announced they were pregnant.

"If the wedding is still a go, then what's the problem?" Claire lifted her cup of coffee and took a sip.

Naturally that brought his focus to her heart-shaped lips. He'd kissed those lips once—okay, more than once—and he wouldn't mind doing it again. Clearing his throat, he looked down at the table. "Rebecca is in preterm labor. The doctor put her on hospital bed rest over the weekend. She's not leaving there until the baby is born. Not for long at least."

From his peripheral vision, he saw Claire lift her hand to cover that pretty pink mouth. "That's awful."

He nodded and looked back up. "She wants to be married before little Junior arrives, which could be a couple days to a couple of weeks from now, if we're lucky."

Women weren't supposed to be beautiful when they frowned, but Claire wore it well. "So the wedding is postponed?" she asked. "Is that why Pearson sent you here to talk to me?"

"Not exactly. Dad and Rebecca want to speed things up a

bit. Rebecca can get approval to leave the hospital, but only for a couple hours."

"Speed things up how much?"

Bo grimaced. This was a lot to ask, but his dad was used to getting things done his way. Pearson Matthews demanded excellence, which was one of the reasons Bo guessed he'd hired Claire in the first place. "They want the wedding to happen this weekend."

"What?" Claire nearly shouted.

"No expense spared. Dad's words, not mine."

She shook her head and started rattling off rapid-fire thoughts. "I don't even know what they like or what they want. I haven't met with Rebecca for planning yet. She's the bride; it's her wedding. Today is Thursday. That only gives me—"

"—three days," he said, cutting her off. "They want to marry on Saturday evening."

Claire's face was flushed against her strawberry locks. Her green eyes were wide like a woman going into complete panic mode. He'd seen her in this mode when she'd woken up beside him in bed last spring, and that had been his fault as well.

She pulled a small notebook and pen out of her purse and started writing. "I guess I could meet with Rebecca in her hospital room to discuss colors and themes."

Bo cleared his throat, signaling for Claire to look up. "About that. Dad doesn't want Rebecca involved. No stress, per doctor's orders. Dad wants you and me to plan it."

Claire's mouth pinched shut.

Yeah, he wasn't exactly thrilled with the idea either. He had other things to do than plan a shotgun wedding that he didn't even want to happen. For one, he had architectural plans to finish by Friday for a potential client. Having just returned to town, he knew it was important to reestablish his place as the preferred architect in Sweetwater Springs.

"You and me?" She folded her arms across her chest. "I don't think so."

He shrugged. "Dad said he'd double your fee for the trouble."

That pretty, heart-shaped mouth fell open. After a moment, she narrowed her eyes. "What's in it for you? Aren't you busy?"

"Very. But despite his poor sense in the love arena, Dad has always been there for me. He even bailed me out of jail once."

Her gaze flicked away for a moment. Claire had told him about her family history during their night together last spring. Not that he hadn't already heard the rumors. Her dad was a drunk, now serving time for a DWI. Claire's mom couldn't hold down a job and had a bad habit of sleeping with other women's husbands. Most notably was her mom's affair with the previous mayor of Sweetwater Springs. That had ensured that the Donovan family's dirty laundry was aired for everyone to talk about.

Claire was cut from a different cloth though, and she did her best to make sure everyone saw that.

"Why am I not surprised that you would've spent the night in jail?" she asked with a shake of her head. The subtle movement made her red hair scrape along her bare shoulders.

"I guess because you have low expectations for me."

She pinned him with a look that spoke volumes. "How about *no* expectations?"

Maybe that was another reason Bo had agreed to help with this farce of a wedding. Claire might never forgive him, but maybe she'd stop being angry at him one day. For a reason he didn't want to explore too deeply, he hoped that was true.

* * *

Saying yes to this request would be insane.

Claire lifted her coffee to her mouth, wishing it had a splash of something stronger in it right now. "Okay, I'll do it." She'd never bailed on a job, and she wasn't about to start now.

Even if the wedding was in three days. And she had to plan it with Bo Matthews. And..."Oh no."

"What?" he asked.

"There aren't going to be any venues available. You can't book a place three days out. Everywhere in town will be taken. I wouldn't even be able to empty out a McDonald's for them to get married in with this short a notice."

Claire's hands were shaking. *The best and nothing less* was her personal motto. But she wasn't going to be able to deliver this time. There was no way. Her eyes stung with the realization.

"What about the Mayflower?" Bo asked.

That was a popular restaurant that she sometimes reserved for less formal events. "It'll be booked."

"The community center?"

Claire rolled her eyes. "Such a male thing to say. No woman dreams of getting married at the local community center." Claire dropped her head into her hands. *Think, think, think.*

She listened as Bo rattled off some more options, and shot them all down without even looking up.

"A wedding should be about the people, not the place," he said a moment later.

She looked up now. "I wouldn't have pegged you as a romantic."

He smiled, and it went straight through her chest like a poisonous barb. "It's true. If two people are in love, it shouldn't matter where they are. Saying vows under the stars should be enough."

She swooned against her will, immediately imagining herself in his arms under said stars. She'd danced with him at Liz and Mike's wedding reception last year. And he'd smelled of evergreens and mint. She remembered that when he'd held her in his arms, she'd thought he was the perfect size for her. Men who were too large put her head level at their chests. Too small put them face-to-face, which was just awkward.

But in Bo's arms, her head was at the perfect height to rest on his shoulder. Close enough to where she had to tip her face back to look into those faded denim eyes behind the Clark Kent glasses.

Bo reached for his coffee. "I couldn't care less where they get married. They'll be divorced within the year if my dad maintains his track record."

Right. Rebecca would be the third Mrs. Matthews.

"Maybe Rebecca is *the one*," Claire said, feeling a wee bit of empathy for the man sitting across from her.

"Nah. But I am going to have a new brother. *That* I'm excited about."

"You'll lose your spot as the spoiled youngest," she pointed out.

"Trust me, I was never spoiled." He tipped his coffee cup against his lips and took a sip. "I started working at the family business as a teenager after school. Dad made me save every penny to put myself through college."

Claire already knew the history of Peak Designs

Architectural Firm and how it had grown from a one-man show to employing all three of Pearson's sons. Bo was the architect of the group. The middle son, Mark, was in construction management with the company. Cade did landscape design. The project he'd done that Claire liked best was Bo's own yard on Lavender Hill. The landscape, covered with purple wildflowers, was open and elevated over the water, with Bo's home—one of his own designs—seeming to touch the sky. She'd often looked out on that home while canoeing downriver and thought to herself that it was one of the most romantic places on earth.

"I've got it." She bolted upright. "Your place on Lavender Hill is the perfect place for a wedding!"

"My place?"

"I'm assuming your yard isn't taken for the weekend."

"It is. It's taken by me. No."

His expression was stiff, but she wasn't going to be deterred.

"Yes," she countered, leaning forward at the table. As she did, she caught a whiff of his evergreen scent, and her heart kicked at the memories it brought with it. Him and her, kissing and laughing. "It's your dad, your stepmom."

He groaned at the mention of Rebecca.

"And you owe me."

His eyes narrowed behind his glasses.

Yes, she knew she'd gone into his hotel room on her own volition last year. But he'd never called the following day, and she'd hoped he would. Instead, he'd taken a job in Wild Blossom Bluffs and promptly left town. She'd pined for his call even after the rumors had started popping up about them. Some people, more accurately, had compared her to her wanderlust mother. In reality, only a handful of people had talked, but even one comparison to Nancy Donovan stung. Claire wasn't like her mom and never would be.

Bo stared at her for a long moment behind those sexy glasses of his and then cursed under his breath. "Fine," he muttered. "You can have the wedding at my place."

Chapter Two

Bo was in over his head, and he'd barely waded into the water.

Helping Claire pick out colors or themes for his dad's wedding was harmless enough. Inviting her into his home on Lavender Hill, letting her rearrange things and set up for a wedding was another.

And even though he was convincing himself of how awful this new turn of events was, there was some part of him that was excited to spend time with her. The night they'd shared last spring had been amazing. Being best man at the wedding of his childhood buddy and the woman who'd left Bo at the altar a year earlier had promised to be akin to having his appendix removed sans anesthesia. Instead, as the night was ending, Bo found himself kissing Claire, who'd tasted like some exotic, forbidden fruit. They'd both been too drunk to drive home and had gone up to the hotel room he'd booked. Best night of his life without question, even with hindsight and the events that followed tainting it.

In the morning when he'd woken, he'd watched Claire climb out of bed, looking sexy as anything he'd ever laid eyes on. She'd had that sleepy, rumpled look he found so attractive. She'd smiled stiffly and had made some excuse about needing to go. Then he'd promised to call later, knowing good and well he wouldn't.

That was his main regret. What was he supposed to say though? *That was fun* or *Have a nice life*? Claire was the kind of woman who men fell in love with, and he wasn't a glutton for punishment. He'd gone that route once and had been publicly rejected by Liz. He didn't fancy doing it again.

He also hadn't looked forward to seeing Liz and Mike be newlyweds around town. So he'd taken a job opportunity outside of Sweetwater Springs to clear his head. Putting the lovely Claire out of his mind, however, hadn't proved as easy.

His cell phone buzzed in the center console of his car. He connected the call and put it on speakerphone. "Hello."

"Our new stepmom is in the hospital?" his older brother Cade asked.

"That's right. She's at Mount Pleasant Memorial on bed rest. And she's not our stepmom yet...not until Saturday," Bo corrected.

"So I hear. You're planning the wedding with the event planner? Isn't she the one you disappeared with after Liz and Mike's wedding?"

"Yes and yes," Bo said briskly. "I plan to give her free rein over all the details. Dad said money was no object, and I trust Claire's taste. I just hope she doesn't mess up my house in the process."

"Your house? That's where you're having it?"

"Outside." But guests had a way of finding themselves inside at events, either to use the bathroom or to lie down when they weren't feeling well. Bo wasn't naive enough to think that wouldn't happen. His cousins would likely want to put their small children to sleep in one of his guest rooms.

"Well, I'd say 'Let me know if I can help,' but..." Cade's voice trailed off.

"But you'd be lying."

"And I'm an honest guy," Cade said with a chuckle. "No, seriously. I'm designing some gardens behind the Sweetwater Bed and Breakfast right now. It's a big job, and Kaitlyn Russo wants it done before the Spring Festival and the influx of guests she has coming in for the event."

"It's okay. Claire will do most of the work. She's top-notch."

"You speaking from experience there, brother?" Cade teased.

Bo ground his back teeth. "I already told you what happened." And he took offense at people jumping to the worst conclusions about Claire just because of who her parents were. "Listen, I have to go," he said as he pulled into the driveway of his home. He'd taken years to design this house himself, working nights while creating the plan. He loved every curve and angle of the structure. He loved the rooms with their high ceilings. His bedroom even had a skylight that allowed him to stare up into the sky while lying in his bed at night. Set on a hill, the house overlooked the river and the mountains beyond. *This* was his idea of heaven. He'd missed it while he'd been licking his wounds in Wild Blossom Bluffs. But now that he was back, he didn't plan on leaving again.

He walked inside, went straight to the kitchen, and grabbed an apple. Taking it to his office, he started working on the proposal designs for Ken Martin. Landing this contract would be good for business.

An hour later, he let out a frustrated sigh. He couldn't concentrate. All he'd been able to think about was that night he'd shared with Claire last spring. And the next three days he'd get to spend with her.

* * *

Claire had briefly considered going to school to become a nurse. Then her grandmother had fallen sick during her senior year of high school, and Claire had spent quite a few months visiting her at Mount Pleasant Memorial. That experience had ended any nursing dreams. She didn't like hospitals. Didn't like the sounds, the smells, or the dull looks in the eyes of the people she passed.

Making her way down the second-floor hall, Claire avoided meeting anyone's gaze. She liked being an event planner because most of the time people were happy. They were excited and looking forward to the future.

Just like the patient she was here to see.

Stopping in front of the door to room 201, Claire adjusted the cheerful arrangement of daffodils she'd picked up at the Little Shop of Flowers on the way here and knocked.

"Come in," a woman's voice called.

Claire cracked the door and peered inside the dimly lit room. Rebecca was lying in bed wearing a diamond-print hospital gown. The TV was blasting a soap opera, and she had a magazine in her lap. "Hi. How are you feeling?" Claire asked, stepping inside.

"Like a beached whale," Rebecca said with a small smile. She was practically glowing with happiness.

"Well, you definitely don't look like one. Pregnancy looks great on you," Claire said. "I know you're not supposed to be doing work of any kind right now so I'm only here as a friend. I brought you flowers."

"Oh, they're so beautiful!... And that rule about no work of any kind is Pearson's," Rebecca added in a whisper, even though no one else was in the room. "He's so protective toward me. It's adorable, really."

Rebecca also had that look of love about her. Her brown eyes were lit up and dreamy. Bo might not think what his father and Rebecca had was real, but Claire always got a good feeling for her clients. She could tell who was legit and who was getting married for all the wrong reasons. Maybe the baby was speeding things along, but Rebecca loved Pearson. It was as clear as her creamy white skin.

"I agree with Mr. Matthews. You should be taking it easy. We don't want that baby of yours coming any sooner than he needs to."

Rebecca sighed. "It's just, I've been dreaming about getting married since I was a little girl," she confided. "I wanted more time to plan this out and do it right."

"Relax. If you and Pearson are there, it will be perfect," Claire said, remembering how Bo had told her something similar this morning. "All you'll remember by the time it's over is the look in his eyes when he says 'I do.' Assuming you can see through the blur of your own tears."

Rebecca's lips parted. "Wow. You're good."

"Thanks. And don't worry—your wedding day is going to be everything you ever dreamed."

"I hope so. The main thing I want now is to have it before the baby gets here."

"We'll make sure that happens," Claire promised. "Do you have any favorite colors?"

Rebecca drew her shoulders up to her ears excitedly. "I was thinking that soft purple and white would be pretty."

"That's a nice springtime combo." Claire pulled a little notebook out of her purse along with a pen and wrote down Rebecca's color preference. "I'll see if Halona at Little Shop of Flowers can do some arrangements in those colors. Maybe with a splash of yellows and pinks as well for the bouquets."

Rebecca's eyes sparkled under the bed's overhead light. "Perfect."

"What about food? Since it's such short notice, I was thinking we'd skip a full dinner and just have light hors d'oeuvres at the reception. And drinks too, of course, for everyone except you." Claire winked at the bride-to-be.

They sat and chatted for another ten minutes while Claire wrote down a few ideas. Then she stood up and shoved her little notebook back into her purse. "I promised I wouldn't stress you out so I better go. You need your rest. But I'm so glad we got a chance to talk. I'm clearing my schedule for the rest of the week to focus solely on your big day."

And not on Bo Matthews. Which would be easier said than done, since she would be spending the next several days at his house.

"Thank you so much," Rebecca said, bringing a hand to her swollen stomach.

"You're very welcome." With a final wave goodbye, Claire headed back down the hospital halls, keeping her gaze on the floor and not on passersby. She resisted a total body shudder as the smells and sounds accosted her. Once she was outside again, she sucked in a deep breath of fresh air. She walked to her car, got in, and then drove in the direction of Bo Matthews's home on Lavender Hill.

Butterflies fluttered up into her chest at the anticipation

of seeing him again. But this was just business, nothing more, she reminded herself. And that was the way it needed to stay.

* * *

After a walk to clear his head, Bo settled back at his desk and worked steadily, making good progress on his proposal. Somehow, he put Claire out of his mind until the doorbell rang. Just when he'd gotten into the zone. With a groan, he headed to the door and opened it to find Claire staring back at him for the second time today.

She looked away shyly and then pulled the strap of her handbag higher on her shoulder as if she needed something to do with her hands. Did he make her nervous?

What would've happened had he called her the morning after they'd spent the night together? Would they be a couple right now? Would she be stepping into his arms to greet him instead of looking anxious and agitated? Would she be pressing her lips to his in a kiss that promised to turn into more later?

Bo cleared his throat and then gestured for her to come inside.

"I thought I'd go ahead and get started," she said. "I want to walk around the yard and get a good feel for the size and layout so I know where we can set up chairs and a gazebo."

"Okay." He was working hard to keep his eyes level with hers and not to admire the pretty floral dress she was wearing and the curves that filled it out so nicely. She had shiny sandals strapped to her feet that glinted in the light of the room.

"I stopped by to see Rebecca on the way here and brought her flowers." Claire held up her hand. "Don't worry.

I didn't cause any stress. But she did give me her color preferences though."

"That's good," Bo said.

"I was thinking we should keep things simple. Even though your father said no expense spared, less is more depending on the venue. Your yard is the absolute perfect place for a wedding. The view is amazing, and as long as there's good music and food, it'll be as nice as some of the bigger events I plan in pricier spots."

Bo wasn't going to argue with her about saving money. Especially since his father was likely to have another wedding sometime in the next five years if history repeated itself.

"Feel free to walk around and do whatever you need to do," he said. As long as she kept her distance from him. He needed to work, and he had a feeling his brief streak of productivity was now broken for the rest of the afternoon. "There's a spare key on the kitchen counter for you to use over the weekend. You can come and go as you need." He gestured toward the back door. "That'll take you to the gardens. Let me know if you have any questions."

"Thanks." She turned and headed in the direction he pointed. His gaze unwillingly dropped as he watched her walk away. With a resigned sigh, he returned to his office to work.

This is going to be a very long three days.

An hour and a half later, he lifted his head to a soft knock on his open door. Then the door opened, and there was Claire, her cheeks rosy from her walk outside. The wind off the river was sometimes cool this time of year, and the humidity had left her hair with a slight wave to it. "Sorry to disturb you."

She'd been polite and civil toward him since their new

arrangement. Whatever resentment she harbored toward him, she'd locked it away for the time being. The same way he was doing his best to keep his attraction toward her under wraps. "What do you think?" he asked. "Will Lavender Hill work?"

She nodded. "You have quite a few acres of land. We'll need to set up a few Porta Potties somewhere out of sight so that guests don't come in and out of your house all night. I think three will be enough, and I know a company that can arrange that on short notice. I'll also be having wooden fold-out chairs delivered. We rent them, and the company typically picks them back up on the day after the ceremony. The ground is nice and firm, and I checked the weather for Saturday. Sweetwater Springs isn't expecting rain again until later next week."

"Sounds like everything is falling into place."

"There's still more to do, of course. There are so many things to consider when you're planning an event for nearly a hundred people. But first I was thinking about having some food delivered. I'm starving, and I can't think when my stomach is growling. Are there any pizza places around here that deliver?"

He thought for a moment. "Jessie's Pizza delivers. It's my favorite." Just thinking about it made his mouth water. "The number is on my fridge."

She gave him a strange look as if she was debating whether to say something else. With a soft eye roll that he suspected was at herself rather than him, she folded her arms across her chest and met his gaze. "Are you hungry? I certainly can't eat a whole pie."

This was where he should practice self-control and say no. "I haven't eaten all day, actually. But if we're sharing, I'm buying. It's the least I can do considering the pinch my dad has put you in."

"Great. What do you like on your pizza?"

"I like it all," he said, not intending for the sexual tone in his voice.

Claire's skin flushed. "Okay, well, um...I'll let you work until it gets here," she called over her shoulder as she headed back out of his office.

Work. Yeah, right. With the anticipation of eating his favorite pizza with Claire, his brain had no intention of focusing on architectural plans right now. The only curves he was envisioning were those underneath that floral sundress she was wearing.

Chapter Three

While Claire waited for the pizza to arrive, she sat at Bo's kitchen counter and made a to-do list. Priority number one was lining up all the services for Saturday's wedding. Years of planning events meant she had close contacts for everything. Most would drop whatever they were doing and work extended hours to meet her needs. She'd already spoken to Halona about the floral arrangements, and that was a go. *Thank goodness.* She jotted down several people she planned to call after lunch, and then she found her mind wandering while she drew little hearts on the side of her paper and thought about Bo.

Whoa! She wasn't going down that path again. It'd been a long hike back the last time. Being seen coming out of Bo's hotel room had been mortifying enough. Even worse, she'd left that morning so smitten with him that she couldn't see straight. He was charming and funny, and undeniably gorgeous. She'd always thought so. He had this Clark Kent sexy nerd look about him that just *did it* for her.

Bo also had muscles plastered in all the right places. Not too bulky. No, his were long and lean. They'd run their hands all over each other's bodies last spring. That night had been hotter than anything she'd ever experienced, even though their clothes had stayed on—mostly. She was drunk, and he'd said he didn't want to take advantage of her. So they'd spent the night driving each other crazy with their roaming hands. They'd also spent it talking and laughing. Then, after Claire had left the next morning, it was out of sight, out of mind for Bo. But not for her.

The doorbell rang. As she walked down the hall, she turned at the sound of heavy footsteps behind her.

"I told you I'd pay." Bo caught up to her and reached to open the door ahead of her.

A young, lanky, twentysomething guy held a box in his hand. "Someone ordered an extra-large pizza and chicken wings?"

Bo glanced over his shoulder. "Wings, huh?"

Her cheeks burned. "I'm going to be here awhile tonight so I thought it'd be a good idea to have plenty of fuel on hand." And pizza and wings were her biggest weaknesses, right after the clearance racks at Sophie's Boutique. And Bo, once upon a time.

Bo chuckled as he pulled out his wallet and paid the guy at the door. Taking the food, he closed the door with his foot and walked past her into the kitchen. "I'll get the plates. There's sweet tea and soda in the fridge. Help yourself."

She opened the fridge and peered inside. A man's fridge said a lot about him. If there was more alcohol than food, that might be a problem. Bo appeared to have only one bottle of brew, and a healthy selection of fresh fruit and vegetables was visible in the drawers. She reached for the pitcher of tea and brought it back to the counter, where Bo had put out two plates. The open box of pizza was at the center of the kitchen counter.

He placed a slice of pizza on each plate and carried them to the table. "I have two glasses over here," he said. "You can bring the pitcher over."

Apparently, they were eating together. She'd just assumed that he would take his food back to his office and work.

He glanced at her for a moment. "Everything okay?"

She softly bit the inside of her cheek. She'd already had breakfast with the man. Lunch too? Her stomach growled. "Yep. Just fine." She moved to the table and took a seat, where the delicious smell of Italian sauce and spices wafted under her nose. "Mmm. If that tastes as good as it smells, I'm going to be having seconds."

Bo laughed. It was a deep rumble that echoed through her. "It tastes even better than it smells," he promised. "Jessie's is the best."

Her eyes slid over as he brought the slice to his mouth and took a bite. A thin string of cheese connected his mouth to the pizza for a moment, reminding her of all the pizza commercials on TV. Bo could be the guy in those commercials. Watching him bite into a slice of pizza would have her craving it every time. Craving *him* every time.

She lifted a slice herself and took a bite, closing her eyes as her taste buds exploded with pleasure. "You're not kidding," she moaned. When she looked over, he was watching her.

She swallowed. "It's very good."

For the rest of the meal, she kept her eyes and moans

to herself as she filled Bo in on Rebecca's thoughts for the wedding. "She's really excited. She has the bride-to-be and the mother-to-be glows combined."

Bo grunted.

"I've known Rebecca ever since she moved to town two years ago. I don't think she's the type to marry someone for anything other than love."

Bo finished off his third slice and reached for his glass of tea. "It's just hard to fathom that a twenty-eight-year-old woman would want to marry a fifty-year-old man."

Claire laughed. "Love is crazy that way. It doesn't let you choose who you fall for."

"True enough. Maybe if you did, it would turn out a whole lot better."

She knew the whole ugly story about his ex-fiancée, who'd fallen in love with his best friend. Even after their betrayal, Bo had stood in as best man for the wedding that had led to him and Claire spending the night together.

"Have you ever been in love?" he asked, surprising her. They'd talked about a lot that night last spring, but that topic hadn't come up.

She nearly choked on her bite of pizza.

"Sorry. You know my history. It's only fair."

She reached for her glass of tea and washed down her bite. "I've been in what I thought was love in college. It was really just infatuation though."

"How do you know the difference?"

"Well," she said, chewing on her thoughts, "infatuation fades. Love survives even after you know about all the other person's faults. Sometimes knowing the faults makes you like them more…This is not personal experience talking, of course. I'm talking as an event planner who has worked with countless couples in love. I've seen couples crumble under the pressure of big events, and I've seen others come out stronger."

He wore an unreadable expression on his face. "I guess I could say I've seen the same in my line of work. Making plans for the house you want to grow old in can be as stressful as it is exciting. Couples have torn into each other in the process, right in front of me. At those times, I'm almost glad that my ex walked away from me." He sat back in his chair. "That just meant I got to plan the home of my dreams all by myself. No drama involved."

Claire shook her head. "Well, you did a great job. This could very well be my dream house," she said. "I haven't seen the upstairs, but I'm sure it's just as perfect as the downstairs."

"I'll have to give you a tour at some point."

She shifted restlessly. Was his bedroom upstairs? She didn't think stepping inside alone with him would be wise. Probably asking him the question that sat right at the tip of her tongue wasn't wise either. She asked anyway. "Why didn't you call?"

Bo shifted his body and his gaze uncomfortably. She needed to know though. Yes, he'd left town, but he hadn't gone far and not for good. "I needed some space from everything. It had nothing to do with you. It wasn't personal."

But it was to her. She hadn't felt so connected to anyone in a long time. They'd had such a great time, and he'd promised to call. Only he never did. He must have been hurt watching his ex marry his best friend, and he'd used her as a crutch to get through the night. That was all.

"I see," she said briskly. Then she started cleaning up her lunch, even though she could stomach another slice of pizza or a chicken wing. What she couldn't stomach was continuing to sit with Bo right now.

"I had a good time that night," Bo said, as if backtracking from his response. "A *very* good time."

"So good that you never spoke to me again."

"We didn't sleep together, Claire. Why are you so mad at me?"

She slammed her paper plate and napkin in the trash and then whipped around to look at him. "Is that what defines whether a guy calls the next morning? Sex? You know, forget I asked the question. Forget everything. I have work to do and so do you."

* * *

It was well after eight p.m. when Claire arrived home. Her slice of pizza and sweet tea had worn off midafternoon, and she'd been running on adrenaline and fury since then.

It wasn't personal.

Those three little words had burrowed under her skin and had been festering for the last several hours. How dare he? She'd shared intimate details of her life with him that night. Hopes and dreams. She'd told him about her dysfunctional childhood that she never spoke of with anyone. It was *very* personal to her.

Stepping into her bedroom, she shed her clothes and traded them for something comfy. Then she turned off the lights, climbed into bed, and reached for the book on her nightstand. She kept rereading the same line because her brain was still trained on Bo. It'd only been one night, but that night could've filled several years' worth for some couples. She always left a wedding feeling romantic and hopeful for her own happily ever after. Like a fool, she'd felt there was a potential for that with Bo.

A few days later, she swung by his house on Lavender

Hill. Instead of finding Bo, she'd run into his brother Cade, who'd informed her that Bo had taken a job out of town. He didn't know when Bo was coming back, but it wasn't anytime soon. With him, Bo had taken a little bit of her pride and a big piece of her foolish heart.

Well, not this time. In fact, she wasn't even going to waste any more energy being mad at him. Bo was right. This wasn't personal; it was work.

* * *

Bo startled at the sound of his front door opening and closing early the next morning. He jolted upright, realizing he'd fallen asleep at his desk, which wasn't uncommon. His muscles cried out as he moved. Even though he was only thirty years old, he was too old to be grabbing shut-eye in an upright office chair.

"Bo?" Claire's voice called out from the front entrance hall.

How had she even gotten in? Oh, right. He'd given her a key.

"Bo?"

He stood and met her in the hallway. Unlike him, she appeared to be well rested. Her hair was soft and shiny— perfect for running his fingers through. Today she was wearing pink cropped pants along with a short-sleeved top featuring a neckline that gave him ample view of her breastbone—the sexiest nonprivate part of a woman, if you asked him. Claire's was delicate with a splash of freckles over her fair skin. He'd spent time sprinkling kisses there once.

And if he didn't stop thinking about it, he was going to have a problem springing up real soon.

"I brought you a cappuccino and a cream cheese bagel." She lifted a cup holder tray and a bag from the Sweetwater Café. "And you look like you could use it." She laughed softly. She'd been royally ticked off the last time he'd seen her. What had changed since then?

"I fell asleep working on my latest design," he told her.

"And you have the facial creases to prove it." She smiled and breezed past him, leaving a delicious floral scent in her wake. He followed her into the kitchen and lifted the coffee from its tray.

"To what do I owe this act of mercy?" he asked suspiciously.

Claire lifted her own cup of coffee. "I'm calling a truce. What happened last spring is done and over. We won't think or talk about it ever again."

He sipped the bittersweet brew. The only problem with that suggestion was that he'd been thinking about that night for the past twelve months.

"I can put it behind me. It wasn't personal for you so I'm assuming you can as well." She notched up her chin, projecting confidence and strength even though something wavered in her eyes as she waited for him to reply.

"I can do the same," he lied.

"Great." She smiled stiffly. "Then I need your assistance this morning. If you're available."

"I got a lot done workwise last night so I guess I have some time. What do you need?"

"I brought some fairy lights to hang outside. You have some great gardens. Your brother Cade is so talented." She shifted her gaze, almost as if looking at him directly made her uncomfortable. "Since the ceremony will be at night," she continued, her voice becoming brisk, "I thought fairy lights in your garden

beyond the arbor will add to the romantic feel. Do you
have a ladder?"

"Of course."

"Great. I'm just going to take a walk around out there
while you finish your cappuccino and bagel. I usually walk
in the mornings down my street, but when I woke this morning, I just couldn't wait to go for a stroll behind your house.
If that's okay?"

"Sure. I need to shower. I'll meet you out there with a
ladder in about twenty minutes." Showers and coffee were
his usual morning ritual. Perhaps he should start adding in
a morning walk as well. Especially if it included a gorgeous
redhead with dazzling green eyes.

He grabbed his cappuccino and went upstairs to prepare
for the day ahead. It was Friday. Last night, he'd made a lot
of progress on the Martin proposal. Tonight, he was meeting the couple over dinner to discuss his plans. He hated the
social aspect of his job. Going to the Tipsy Tavern downtown with his buddies was fine, but having a nice dinner
and wooing potential clients made his skin itch. It was a
necessary evil though. He'd just have to suffer through it
and hopefully come out of the night with a contract.

* * *

The gardens were a feast for Claire's eyes, but watching Bo
string those fairy lights over the last hour was even yummier. His arms flexed and stretched while he hammered
nails into the wooden posts that weaved in and around his
garden. And the tool belt he'd looped around his waist was
a visual aphrodisiac.

"You okay back there?" Bo asked, glancing over his
shoulder.

She jolted as if she'd been caught with her hand in the proverbial cookie jar. Nope, she'd just been checking out the way he filled out the backside of those jeans. Her gaze flicked to his eyes, which were now twinkling with humor. *Yeah*, he knew exactly what she'd been doing. "Fine."

"Fine, huh? A woman who says she's fine never is. Am I hanging these things to your satisfaction?"

"You are. I might have to contract you for all my jobs."

"As much as I'd love to be at your beck and call, I'm afraid I already have a job that keeps me pretty busy." He climbed down the ladder and folded it, then carried it out of the garden and toward the arbor that had been delivered yesterday evening. He set the ladder back up and climbed to the top.

Claire handed him another string of fairy lights. "I'm meeting with the caterer in an hour and then swinging by the Little Shop of Flowers after that. Since your father asked you to help, I thought you might be interested in coming along."

Bo looped the lights around the arbor with an eye for spacing them out perfectly. "I'm not sure I'm the best person to ask for opinions on catering or flowers. Can't you get one of the women in that ladies group you go to?"

The group in question was a dozen or so Sweetwater Springs residents who regularly made a habit of having a Ladies Day (or Night) Out. They went to movies, had dinner, volunteered for community functions, anything and everything. It was girl power at its finest.

"I spoke to Rebecca, but you know your dad's tastes. I always like to represent the groom as much as the bride. Going to a wedding or anniversary function that is one-sided is a pet peeve of mine."

She watched him shove his hammer into the loop on his

tool belt. Part of her physical attraction to Bo was his intellectual look, complete with glasses and a ready ballpoint pen always in his pocket. He had those thoughtful eyes too, always seeming to be thinking about something.

But this handyman look was really appealing as well. She'd created an online dating profile on one of those popular websites a couple of months back with the ladies group, but she hadn't activated it. She was a bit chicken, and the spring and summer were her busy months for planning events. Maybe she'd make it active in the fall and expand her search for bookish professionals to include muscle-clad guys who did hard labor. Bo was a perfect blend of both, except he wasn't available. After the way his ex betrayed him with his best friend, he might never be again.

He climbed back down the ladder and faced her. "I've got a proposition for you. I'll go with you to meet the caterer and look at flowers if you have dinner with me tonight."

She blinked him into focus. "You mean a date?"

"No."

She swallowed and looked up at the work he'd done with the lights, pretending to assess the job. Why had her mind immediately jumped to the conclusion that he was asking her on a date? If he was going to do that, he would have last spring. "Why do you want me to have dinner with you?"

"I'm meeting a potential client and his wife. It's social as much as it is business, and I hate doing these things alone. So yes, I guess they'd see you as my date, but—"

"It isn't personal," she said with a nod. "Fair enough." She jutted out her hand.

As his hand slid against hers, her body betrayed her iron-clad decision not to want him. Those hands were

magic, she recalled. The stuff that her fantasies would forever be made of.

She quickly yanked her hand away. "Deal."

* * *

Two hours later, Claire was standing beside Bo and
sampling finger foods and hors d'oeuvres at Taste of
Heaven Catering. Claire usually came to her friend Brenna
Myer's business with the prospective brides and grooms. It
was usually them sampling the cheese, crackers, and little
finger sandwiches.

"This is divine," Claire said with a sigh. She turned to
Bo. "What do you think?"

"It's good," he said with a nod.

Claire punched him softly. "It's better than good. Are
you kidding me?"

He chuckled softly. "Okay, it's the best thing I've put into
my mouth in a long time."

Those words sliced right through her like a knife on that
soft cheese spread in front of them. *Get it together, Claire.*

Brenna was watching them the way she usually did with
the clients that Claire brought in. Claire guessed that her
friend, who was also a member of the Ladies Day Out
group, was scrutinizing every facial reaction and weighing
whether her potential clients were satisfied.

Speaking of clients... "Do you think Pearson would like
it?" Claire asked Bo.

"My dad is a carnivore. Put any meat in front of him, and
he's a happy man."

"Especially with Rebecca at his side," Claire said, throwing in two cents for her currently bedridden client. If Rebecca made Pearson happy, then Bo should be happy too.

"Great. We'll definitely have a spread of various meats then," Brenna said, pulling a pen from behind her ear and writing something down on her clipboard.

"And the cheese," Claire said. "What pregnant woman doesn't love cheese?"

"I don't know any," Brenna said on a laugh. "You'll probably want something sweet as well."

"That's what I'm looking forward to sampling." Bo rubbed his hands together as a sexy smile curved his mouth.

"You have a sweet tooth, huh?" Claire asked.

"I do."

"Me too," she confessed. "Brenna's cheesecake squares are my favorite. I swear that's what she named this business after. They are the epitome of what heaven would taste like if it was food."

Brenna laugh-snorted.

Bo was also grinning. "Then we need to add them to the menu," he said, turning to Brenna.

"Oh no. This event is not about me and what I like," Claire protested. "It's about your dad and future stepmom."

The word *stepmom* drew a grunt from him. "We're the ones planning this wedding, and if cheesecake squares are your favorite, then cheesecake squares it will be."

Claire melted just a little bit at his insistence. "Let's add some chocolate macarons and white-chocolate-dipped strawberries as well," Claire said, with a decisive nod in Brenna's direction. Those were also one of her favorites, but Rebecca had also mentioned how much she enjoyed those.

By the time they left Taste of Heaven, their bellies were full, and there was no need for lunch.

"That was actually a lot of fun." Bo walked on the traffic side of the sidewalk as they strolled down Main Street to their cars. They'd driven there separately so that she could go home and prepare for tonight.

"It was. Thanks for coming."

"Well, as you pointed out, it's my dad and his soon-to-be wife. Coming along with you is the least I can do. Plus, now I get you tonight." He raised his brows as he looked at her.

It wasn't a date. He'd said so himself. But her heart hadn't received that message, because it stopped for a brief second every time he looked at her.

He opened her driver's side door and then stared at her for a long, breathless second.

There went her heart skipping like a rock over Silver Lake. He leaned forward, and she forgot to breathe as his face lowered to hers and kissed the side of her cheek. Part of her had thought maybe he was targeting her mouth. Would she have turned away? Probably not.

"See you tonight." He straightened, holding her captive with his gaze.

Maybe she should've held on to her anger at him. At least that would have buffered this bone-deep attraction that she couldn't seem to kick.

"Yes. Tonight." She offered a wave, got into her car, and watched him head to his own vehicle. She could still feel the weight of his kiss on her cheek. His skin on hers. She touched the area softly and closed her eyes for a moment. When she opened her eyes again, she saw a familiar face crossing the parking lot.

Everything inside her contracted in an attempt to hide. Luckily, her mom didn't seem to notice her as she walked to her minivan and got in. Seeing Nancy Donovan was just a reminder of everything Claire wanted and didn't want.

She wanted respect, success, and a man who wanted her as much as she wanted him.

She didn't want to lose her heart or her pride to an unavailable man. No, Bo wasn't married, which was the kind of guy her mom preferred. But he was no more on the market. Being with him tonight would have to be more like window shopping. Claire could look, but there was no way she was taking him home.

Chapter Four

Bo wasn't sure if he was more nervous about meeting with the Martins tonight or about spending the evening with Claire.

He pulled up to her house, parked, and headed up the steps. As he rang the doorbell, he felt empty-handed somehow. Maybe he should've stopped and gotten flowers. That would've been stupid though. This wasn't a real date. But the tight, hard-to-breathe feeling in his chest begged to differ. It was a blend of anticipation and nerves with a healthy dose of desire for this woman.

The door opened, and Claire smiled back at him. She had on just a touch of makeup that brought out the green of her eyes. She'd swiped some blush across her cheeks as well, or maybe she really was flushed. With her strawberry tones and fair skin, she seemed to do that a lot.

There was something between them. There always had been. Their chemistry was off the charts, but it was more than that. Claire was funny and smart, and he admired the heck out of her. She would've had a right to view the world with bitterness and skepticism as much as anyone. Instead, she seemed to have unlimited optimism, and she romanticized everything. Bo could learn a lot from this woman, if he chose to spend more than three days with her.

"You're staring at me," Claire said. She looked at what she was wearing and back up at him with a frown. "Do I look okay? I wasn't sure what to wear for a business dinner, and there was no time to go shopping for something new. I can go back upstairs and change if you think this isn't good enough."

"It's perfect. You look beautiful." And heaven help him, it was all he could do not to move closer and taste those sweet lips of hers.

"Great," she said. "Let me just grab my purse. You can come on in."

Bo stepped inside her living room and looked around. It had been her granddad's place before he'd moved south to Florida and left it to her. Bo had never renovated a historic home before, but his mind was already swimming with ideas on how to modernize it just a touch by adding more windows for natural lighting.

As he waited for her to return, he walked over to the mantel and looked at the pictures encased in a variety of frames. There was a photo of Claire with her grandparents, who'd done a good bit of raising her while her parents shirked their duties. He thought he remembered that her grandmother had died several years back. There was one of Claire and her brother, Peter, whom Bo hadn't seen in quite some time. He wasn't even sure what Peter had been up to in the last decade since high school graduation.

Claire breezed back into the room. "Okay, got my purse, and I'm ready to go."

Bo turned to face her, and his breath caught. He wasn't dreading tonight's dinner like he had been this morning before inviting her along. On the contrary, now he was starting to look forward to it.

When they got to the restaurant, Ken and Evelyn Martin were already seated and waiting for them.

"Oh, you brought a date," Evelyn said, looking between them with a delighted smile. "This is such a nice surprise."

Bo wondered if he should clarify that Claire was just a friend. Evelyn didn't give him time to say anything, though, before launching into friendly chitchat.

"I'm Evelyn, and this is my husband, Ken," she said, reaching for Claire's hand.

Bo pulled out a chair for Claire and sat down while they all made their acquaintances. Then he made the mistake of looking around the restaurant. On the other side of the room, his vision snagged on Liz and Mike. They were expecting their first child if the rumors were true, which in Sweetwater Springs was fifty-fifty. A mix of emotions passed through him.

"I'm so glad you could meet us tonight," Ken said, pulling Bo back to his own dinner party.

Bo nodded. "Me too."

Liz had never been *the one* for him. He had come to terms with that during his time in Wild Blossom Bluffs. Perhaps he should walk over and thank them for that invitation to their wedding last year, because it'd led to an amazing night with the woman beside him. The *only* woman he had eyes for in the room tonight.

* * *

Claire had thought since this was a business dinner, that it would be tense or maybe a little stuffy. The Martins were probably twenty years older than her, but even so, Claire was having the best time. The older couple picked on each other in the most endearing way. And since Bo was paying, Claire helped herself to a steak with two sides of vegetables and a glass of wine. She didn't feel bad about it either. This was payback for last spring. They might have called a truce this morning, but she hadn't forgotten.

"It must be so rewarding to plan so many life events for others," Evelyn said, stabbing at a piece of shrimp on her plate and looking up at Claire.

"Oh, it is. I couldn't imagine myself doing anything else."

"I was a schoolteacher for thirty-one years," Evelyn said proudly, "and I loved every moment. If you love what you do and who you're with, life is always a party."

Claire was midway through lifting her glass of wine to her lips, but she paused to process that statement. "I love that philosophy."

"Well, it's true. I fell in love with Ken thirty-three years ago, and we haven't stopped partying since."

Ken Martin reached for her hand.

After that, the conversation turned to Bo's architectural proposal. The Martins loved all his ideas, and they seemed to love him too. Why wouldn't they? She hadn't been lying when she'd told him earlier that he was talented. He was. He was the architect behind the designs for so many of Sweetwater Springs' big businesses and houses. He was amazing.

By the time they left the restaurant, Bo and the Martins seemed like old friends. And Claire was totally and completely smitten with her date. Exactly like she'd promised herself she wouldn't be. But being with him was so easy.

He walked her out to the parking lot and, like a good gentleman, opened the passenger door for her.

"Thank you," he said, once he was behind the wheel. He pulled out of the parking lot and started to drive her home.

"It was no problem. I had a good time, and I had to eat anyway, right? Thanks for buying me dinner. Usually, the night before a wedding, we'd be doing a dress rehearsal. But nothing is the norm about tomorrow's ceremony." She was chattering away for some reason.

"Looks like we make a good team."

There was a smolder in his blue eyes when he looked over. Was she imagining that?

"Yes, I guess so."

"Maybe you could call me for all your catering and flower needs, and I could ask you to be my date for all my client meetings."

She knew he was only teasing. "I daresay, you'd grow tired of sampling food and picking out flowers." She cleared her throat. "I saw Liz and Mike. You were fixated over there for a moment at dinner."

She saw the muscles along his jaw tighten. "They didn't stay long, thankfully."

"Is it hard to see them together?"

"A little," he admitted. "Not because I still love her. Just knowing that they did things behind my back. Trust isn't an easy thing to repair." He sucked in a deep breath. "All for the greater good, I guess. They have a baby on the way, from what I hear."

Claire had heard the same. She reached a hand across the car and touched his shoulder, wanting to offer comfort. The touch zinged through her body. She hadn't touched this man since last spring. She'd made a point not to. Now she felt his hard muscles at her fingertips, and her body answered.

She yanked her hand away and turned to look out the window. "Not every woman would do that to you, you know."

"I never thought Liz would do that to me. Or Mike. So no, I don't know." There was an edge to his voice, making her sorry she'd even brought it up. He was obviously bitter about relationships now. No doubt that spilled over into his view on his dad and Rebecca's nuptials tomorrow.

They rode in silence for a few minutes, and then Bo turned on the radio.

Claire looked at him with interest. "Jazz? I would've pegged you for classical."

To her relief, the hardness of his face softened.

"I've always thought classical was boring. I played the saxophone in high school band."

"I remember. Do you still play?"

"I have the sax, but all the neighborhood dogs start howling when I put my lips to the mouthpiece."

Claire laughed. "I play piano. I had six years of lessons."

"Really? I thought we spilled all our secrets the night we spent together." His gaze slid over. There was a definite smolder there, contained only by thick-rimmed glasses.

He pulled into her driveway and cut off the engine. "I'll walk you to your door."

"How about a nightcap? I have wine. Or beer if you'd rather." What was she doing? She'd resolved earlier this afternoon not to take him home with her.

"I'm not sure you can trust me not to kiss you if you invite me in," he admitted.

Gulp.

Without thinking, she ran her tongue along her bottom lip, wetting it. Which was just silly because she absolutely was not going to kiss this man. While her mind was starting to make a rational argument for saying good night, her body was warming up for first base, maybe second.

Bo leaned just slightly and tucked a strand of her hair behind her ear. Then his fingers slid across her skin as he took his time with the simple gesture. Her heart pattered excitedly. Then she leaned as well, almost against her will. One kiss wouldn't hurt anything, right? One tiny, little...

His mouth covered hers in an instant, pulling the plug on her mind. Her thoughts disappeared along with everything else, except Bo. It was just him and her and this scorching-hot kiss. His hand curled behind her neck, holding her captive. Not that she wanted to pull away. Nope. She was close to climbing across the seat and straddling him at this moment.

He tasted like white wine from the restaurant. Smelled like a walk through Evergreen Park. Kissed like a man who wanted her every bit as much as she wanted him.

She heard herself moan as their tongues tangled with one another. She remembered this. How good he kissed. It was like a starter match lighting a fire that burned in her belly. He broke away and started trailing soft kisses down her cheek and then her neck. There was a slight scruff of a five o'clock shadow on his jawline. It felt sinfully delicious.

She tilted her head to one side, giving him access. Eventually, his mouth traveled to her ear and nibbled softly. That fire in her belly raged to a full-on hungry blaze.

"That nightcap sounds good," he whispered, tickling the sensitive skin there. "And I don't want to think about Liz and Mike anymore tonight."

Claire's brain buzzed back to life. That was exactly why he'd invited her back to his hotel room last spring. She was a distraction, nothing more.

She opened her eyes and pulled away just enough to look

at him. This was a mistake. There was no denying that she had it bad for this guy, but he wasn't emotionally available and she wasn't going to be used.

"Actually, I'm really tired." She averted her gaze because looking in his eyes, heavy lidded with lust, might sway her sudden resolve. "I'll see you in the morning. There are a few last-minute touches to do before the wedding. Thanks for dinner. Good night." She pushed her car door open, slammed it shut, and hurried up the porch steps as if running for her life.

But she was really running for her heart.

* * *

What happened tonight?

Bo sat out on his back deck and looked out to the garden. He'd turned on the fairy lights they'd strung earlier, giving the yard an ambient glow. Claire was right. It was a romantic touch.

He still couldn't decide if he was glad or disappointed that she'd slammed on the brakes to their make-out session. Going inside with her would have almost definitely led to her bed, and he didn't think Claire was the kind to have sex casually.

He'd been in a different place in his life last year. Liz and Mike's affair had plunged a knife through his heart, and he wasn't sure he'd ever be able to pull it out. It'd been hard to breathe for a long time after that. He'd dated casually, hooked up a few times, but he had no interest in anyone.

Until Claire. She'd sparked something deep inside him that was terrifying to him back then. The thought of allowing himself to have actual feelings for a woman felt like marching himself right up to Skye Point and preparing to jump off without a parachute. It was nuts.

But now...

He liked her. She evoked feelings he'd never experienced before. Not even with Liz, whom he'd planned to spend his life with.

Damn. He wasn't sure what exactly had happened tonight; all he knew was he needed to fix it. After tomorrow's wedding, there'd be no need to see Claire anymore. Not unless he climbed that proverbial mountain and forced himself to look off the ledge and jump. Getting into another relationship was a risk. Claire could hurt him even more than Liz had. But would she?

An hour later, he dragged himself to bed and flopped around restlessly until he drifted off. After what seemed like just a few minutes, he awoke with the chirping of springtime birds nesting by his window. A slant of sunlight hit his face, prompting him to sit up and shuffle down the hall. He made coffee, enough for two, and then showered.

Claire still hadn't arrived by the time he'd dressed and started preparing breakfast—also enough for two. A little worry elbowed its way to the forefront of his mind. Had he scared her off last night? He knew that she'd be here to finish the job no matter what. He trusted that she wouldn't let his dad and Rebecca down.

He trusted *her.*

That one thought stopped him momentarily in his tracks. His heart was more easily won than his trust, but it appeared that Claire had captured them both.

He continued walking to his office and opened his computer to scan his email. There was already a message waiting for him from Ken Martin:

Loved having dinner with you and Claire last night. Evelyn and I both love your plans for the mother-in-law suite we want to add on. We were unanimous in our agreement that you are the right man for the job. We'd love to work with you. We'd also love to have you and Claire over for dinner at our place again sometime soon. She's a keeper. A wise man wouldn't let her slip away.

Ken

Bo pumped a fist into the air. The deal was done. Success! He reread those last two lines.

It was good advice, and he planned on taking it.

Chapter Five

Claire was taking her time getting ready to go to Lavender Hill this morning. When she'd agreed to this business arrangement, she'd resolved not to let herself fall for Bo again. And who fell for a guy after only a few days anyway?

Apparently, she did. She wasn't in love with him, no. But she was long past lust.

Claire gave herself one last glance in the mirror. She hadn't put on the beautiful dress she'd purchased at Sophie's Boutique a few weeks back just yet. She still had work to do at Bo's house. Speaking of which, she guessed it was time to go.

She headed to her car, got in, and then, continuing to procrastinate, veered off toward the Sweetwater Café for a strong cup of coffee.

A few minutes later, Emma smiled up from the counter as a little jingle bell rang over Claire's head.

"Good morning, Claire," Emma said with all the warmth of one of her delicious hot cocoas. "You have a big event this afternoon."

"I do." Claire gave a nod. On the morning of a special event, she was usually buzzing with so much energy that she didn't even need to stop by the Sweetwater Café, even though she always did anyway. "Are you going to be there?" Claire asked.

"I wouldn't miss it. Rebecca is one of my favorite customers. I'm so happy for her."

"So you're not against the marriage because of the age gap?"

"No way. Not if she's happy, and I wholeheartedly believe she is." Emma was already preparing a cup of coffee for Claire per her usual specifications.

Claire fished her debit card out of her purse as she waited.

Turning back to her, Emma narrowed her eyes. "And you've been holed up for the last couple of days with Bo Matthews, I hear."

"Because the wedding is at his house," Claire clarified, handing her card over. "Not for any other reason."

Emma swiped the card and handed it back. "I wouldn't blame you if there was. He's hotter than that cup of brew you're holding. Don't tell him I said so though. He's not really my type."

Claire grabbed her cup of coffee and took a sip. Bo was *her* type. "No? What is your type?"

Emma shrugged. "I dunno. Chris Hemsworth, maybe."

"You do realize that he's a world-famous movie star, and that it's very unlikely he'll walk into your coffee shop, right?"

"Yeah, yeah. Just a technicality. It could happen," Emma said with a soft giggle.

Yeah, and Bo could realize he was falling for Claire too. Which would never happen.

Claire started to turn and leave, but Emma grabbed her forearm.

"I have to warn you," she said, biting down on her lower lip. "Your mom is here."

"What?" Claire looked over her shoulder, and sure enough, there was Nancy Donovan. How had she missed seeing her when she'd walked in? And why hadn't Emma warned her sooner? Not that it would've helped. There was only one way out and it was past her mom.

Claire turned back to her friend. "Thanks for the heads-up. I'll see you tonight." She took her cup of coffee and turned to leave. As she headed toward the exit, her mom's gaze flicked up and stayed on her. Her mouth curved just slightly in a sheepish smile. Then she lifted her hand and waved.

Crap. If Claire kept walking, she'd be the bad guy here, and that wasn't fair. Growing up, Claire was always the one trying to help her parents. She was the one victimized by their lack of attention and their shaming of her family's name.

Forcing her feet forward, Claire walked over to her mom's table and slid into the booth across from her. "I can only stay a few minutes," she prefaced.

Her mom nodded. Soft lines formed at the corners of her eyes and mouth as her smile wobbled. "I'm just happy to get to talk to you. How are you?"

Claire swallowed, wondering if she should answer that question truthfully. And if so, what was the honest answer? Work was great, but her personal life was all screwed up because she'd once more allowed herself to have feelings for Bo. "Swell. And you?"

"Better these days." Her mom molded her hands around

her own cup. "I'm working on things I wish I'd worked on a long time ago."

"Hindsight and everything," Claire said, hating how sarcastic she sounded. She blew out a breath as she looked around the shop and shook her head. Then she turned back to her mom. "Look, I'm sorry. I don't mean to be so rude."

"It's okay," her mother said. "I deserve it. I was hoping that we could work toward having some sort of relationship again though. Even if it's only five minutes every now and then over coffee."

Claire stared at the woman in front of her. Time hadn't been kind, mostly because of the way Nancy had chosen to live her life. "How's Dad?"

"Jail has helped him sober up. He's going to stay dry once he gets out next month," she told Claire with a hopeful lilt to her voice. "We're going to get a second chance to do right by each other. That's what we both want."

Claire sucked in a deep breath and let it go. It was hypocritical of her to expect Bo to believe his dad could change and settle down with Rebecca when she couldn't do the same with her own parents. It was easier said than done though. "I hope that happens, Mom."

They spoke for a few minutes more, and then Claire pushed back from the table and stood. "I really do have to go . . . But maybe we can do this again."

Her mom's brows lifted. "Really?"

"I'm usually here on Saturday mornings"—Claire shrugged a shoulder—"so maybe I'll see you next weekend."

"Yes. Maybe you will." Her mom reached for Claire's hand and gave it a quick squeeze, the closest to a hug that either of them was ready to give. "Thank you."

As Claire walked out of the coffee shop, she felt lighter. Maybe her mom would let her down again. But there was also the possibility that she wouldn't this time. Claire had always been an optimist. She never wanted to lose hope that things could change for the better.

There was no hope for Bo changing his mind about love and romance though. No matter how much her heart protested that maybe, just maybe, there was.

* * *

Claire had drained her cup of coffee by the time she pulled into Bo's driveway. She was surprised to find him outside setting up the chairs.

"Wow. You've been busy," she said, walking toward him. She kept her shoulders squared. Kissing him last night didn't change anything. She wasn't going to let it affect the task at hand.

Straightening, he looked at her. He was all hot and sweaty, with the same ball cap on that he'd been wearing at the coffee shop a few days before. "I promised to help, so I am. Ken Martin emailed this morning and offered me the contract, by the way."

Claire's smile was now sincere. "That's great, Bo. I thought he would. Last night went really well." Except for that last part.

Judging by the look in his eyes, he was thinking about that too.

"I'm, um, just going to call Halona and Brenna and make sure everything's on track. I'll use your kitchen for that, if you don't mind."

"I don't. There's coffee, eggs, and bacon in there too. I made plenty this morning."

It was official. Emma could have Chris Hemsworth, because he had nothing on Bo Matthews.

* * *

Claire was obviously ignoring him. Bo wasn't sure how to make things right, but he knew he wanted to. He wanted a lot more than that, and he was ready. Seeing Liz and Mike together last night at the restaurant had barely stung. In fact, he almost felt happy for the two of them. Yeah, they'd hurt him, but he knew they hadn't meant to.

Love didn't let you choose. He understood what Claire had meant by that now, because he was falling hard and fast for the sweet, smart, gorgeous event planner. *How the hell am I going to fix things with her?*

A delivery truck pulled into his driveway with SOUTHERN PORTA-JOHN written in large black letters on the side. Bo guided the guys toward the back of his house, where the porta-johns would be available to guests but not readily seen during the ceremony. After that, Halona Locklear showed up in a navy SUV with all the flower arrangements in the back. Claire came out of the back door to help her set things up.

It wasn't a good time to talk to her right now. Not when she had so many things to get done before tonight's wedding.

The next few hours were a blur of activity going on in and around his house. Brenna showed up with trays full of food. He helped her set up tables to display it all. A DJ showed up and set up a place to play music for the reception. The entire Ladies Day Out group showed up after that and helped Claire with a host of other things that he never would've considered. They set out tablecloths and large baskets full of party mementos for the guests. Pearson's and Rebecca's names and the date were written on little paper hearts attached to each favor.

"Aren't these the cutest?" Lula Locklear asked as she walked up to peek inside one of the baskets. "The ladies and

I were up all night making these." Lula was Halona's mom. She was often involved in the community, increasing awareness about her Cherokee Indian culture.

"They are," Bo agreed, unable to resist lifting his head and looking around to see where Claire was. He spotted her laughing with Kaitlyn Russo, the owner of the Sweetwater B&B. The sight of Claire happy and enjoying herself made his heart skip a beat. He longed to be the kind of guy who put that smile on her face.

"You are a man with the look of love," Lula said with a knowing nod. She followed his gaze to where Claire was standing. "She's such a nice girl. She needs someone who will treat her well." She gave him an assessing look as if trying to decipher if he was capable of being that kind of guy. *Was he?* "Maybe there'll be more weddings on Lavender Hill in the future," she said.

* * *

As the sun started to creep toward the mountains, the sky darkened, and guests started to arrive. Claire slipped on the beautiful satin dress she'd purchased from Sophie's Boutique and then headed outside to turn on the lights. The aroma of the food wafted in the air along with laughter and casual conversation.

Pearson and Rebecca would be on their way at any moment. Rebecca's obstetrician had okayed her to leave for two hours. That was enough time to greet guests, walk down the aisle, say their vows, and maybe even have a dance under the stars.

Claire sighed dreamily, imagining Rebecca getting the wedding of her dreams tonight.

Bo stepped up beside her, scrambling those happy

thoughts and feelings. "I need to talk to you. There's a problem."

She whipped her head around to face him. "What kind of problem?"

"Rebecca is in labor. The wedding has been called off."

"What?" Claire's lungs contracted as if the wind had been knocked out of her. "But she wants to be married by the time the baby comes. She needs to get here."

Bo frowned. "I just spoke to Dad. Rebecca's water broke when she was putting on her wedding dress." He grimaced. "It's not going to happen tonight. They can do it after the baby is born. She can buy a new dress and have it anywhere or any way she wants."

Claire shook her head. "The only thing she really wanted was to exchange vows before she gave birth." Claire looked around at all the guests, seated in wooden fold-out chairs. The scenery was perfect. There were even hundreds of stars speckling the clear night's sky.

Her shoulders slumped as she blew out a resigned breath. This was out of her control, and she knew it. "I guess we'll tell the guests the news and send them all home." She hesitated before looking at Bo. Disappointment stung her eyes. She didn't want him to know that all she really felt like doing was sitting in one of those chairs and having a good cry on Rebecca's behalf.

"You stay here. I'll take care of the guests," he said.

"You don't have to. That's my job."

"You did your job already."

"Not really. The wedding is off. I've never let a client down before. Ever." And now she wanted to cry on her own behalf.

There was something gentle in his eyes when she looked up at him. "Stay here," he said again.

She watched him walk off toward the crowd; then she turned to face the garden. She wasn't sure exactly how long she stood there collecting herself before Bo came up behind her. When she turned, he was standing there with Pastor Phillips.

Claire started to apologize to the older man, but Bo patted the pastor's back and narrowed his gaze at her.

"Pastor Phillips is ready to go to the hospital."

Claire scrunched her brows. "What? Why?"

"Because there's a wedding to be had, and we don't have much time. If Rebecca wants to be married before my baby brother gets here, then that's what we'll make sure happens. Assuming we beat the clock."

Pastor Phillips chuckled. "My wife was in labor for twelve hours after her water broke with our first child. I think we'll be okay."

Bo reached for Claire's hand. "You've never let a client down, right? Why start now?"

"You don't even believe your father and Rebecca should be together. Why are you doing this?"

"Maybe I see things differently now. Because of you."

Chapter Six

Claire grabbed the wedding bouquet before climbing into Bo's car. It was an assortment of purple irises and white lilies—exactly what Rebecca had requested. In fact, aside from wanting to marry before her baby was born, the flower preferences were the only other thing Rebecca had asked for.

After a short drive, Bo parked in front of the labor and delivery wing, and they hurried inside. Claire clutched the arrangement tightly as she walked beside him toward the elevator. Pastor Phillips had driven separately. Hopefully he wasn't far behind.

"What's wrong?" Bo asked. "You were talking as fast as I could drive on the way here."

Claire shook her head. "A hospital isn't exactly my favorite place. I watched my grandmother die here." And ever since, Mount Pleasant Memorial had carried nothing but bad memories for her.

They stepped inside the elevator, and Bo reached for her hand. He didn't let go once the door opened on the second floor. The feel of his skin against hers distracted her from the repetitive beeping sounds and the smells of disinfectant as they walked.

"Let's make a few happy memories here today, shall we?" he asked, giving her a wink that short-circuited all the negativity in her mind.

"There's nothing more joyful than a wedding. I've always thought so."

His smile wobbled just a little as they walked.

"I'm sorry. I guess weddings hold as many bad memories for you as hospitals do for me."

"I used to think I never wanted to go to another wedding again. But there's nowhere I'd rather be tonight than at this one with you."

Her heart fluttered. "Same. Even if it is at a hospital."

They stopped behind Rebecca's door, and Claire knocked softly.

A moment later, it cracked open, and Pearson Matthews peeked out at her. Claire had seen him many times over the years. His presence was always confident and commanding. Now he looked like a man juggling half a dozen emotions: excitement, fear, anxiety, exhaustion, confusion, joy.

"How is Rebecca feeling?" Claire asked.

In response, they heard Rebecca groan in the background.

"The baby is coming fast," Pearson said. "What are you two doing here?"

"You couldn't come to the wedding so we brought the wedding to you," Bo answered. "Do you think Rebecca is up for it?"

Pearson smiled at his son, a dozen new emotions popping up on his face. "I think that will probably make her really happy...Thank you, son."

Claire's eyes stung just a little as she watched the brief father-son interaction. "Great. Can we come in?"

Pearson swung the door open wider. "Becky, look who's here!"

Rebecca looked between Claire and Bo and then to Pastor Phillips, who stepped up behind them.

"Do you still want to get married before the baby arrives?" Claire asked.

"Yes." Rebecca shifted and tried to sit up in bed. She was wearing a hospital gown instead of a wedding gown. Her hair was a little disheveled, and the makeup she'd put on for tonight's ceremony needed a touch-up. Even so, she was as beautiful as any bride Claire had ever seen.

Rebecca flinched and squeezed her eyes shut, moving her hands to her lower belly. "But we better do this fast," she gritted out.

Pearson went to the head of Rebecca's bed as Pastor Phillips opened his Bible to read a short passage. Afterward, he looked up at the bride and groom and read off vows that they repeated.

Bo never let go of Claire's hand as they stood witness to the happy union. It was quick, but no less perfect. A tear slid off Claire's cheek as Rebecca said, "I do." Then Pearson dipped to press his lips to Rebecca's—their first kiss as man and wife.

Claire would've wiped her eyes, but one hand still carried the bouquet and the other was held by Bo. He squeezed it softly as he glanced over. There was something warm in his gaze that melted any leftover resolve to resist this man.

Rebecca pulled away from her husband and turned to her guests, which had expanded to include two nurses. "My bouquet, please."

Claire finally broke contact with Bo and handed the arrangement over.

"Okay, ladies. Arms up," Rebecca said. "Bouquet tossing time!"

"Oh, no. I'm already married," one of the nurses said with a laugh.

Bo stepped off to the side, leaving Claire and the second nurse in the line of fire. Claire usually removed herself from this moment at weddings too. Fighting with a bunch of single ladies over a superstition had always seemed so silly, albeit fun to watch. As the bouquet went sailing across the room though, Claire lifted her hands reflexively and snatched it from the air, much to the second nurse's disappointment.

"You're next!" Rebecca said with a laugh. Then she flinched again as another contraction hit her.

"Okay, that's it," the married nurse said. "I think your baby wants to join this party."

Rebecca opened her eyes. "Okay." She looked at Claire. "Thank you. For everything. This was absolutely perfect."

"You're welcome. But I couldn't have done this without Bo."

Rebecca looked at him with tears in her eyes. "Thank you too."

"That's what family is for, right? Welcome to the Matthews clan."

Pearson stepped over and reached out his hand for Bo to shake. He shook Claire's hand as well.

"We're going to give you two some privacy now," Bo told him.

"Don't go too far," Rebecca called from across the room. "Your baby brother will be excited to meet you."

Bo seemed a little stunned by the invitation to stay. He looked at Claire.

"I'm in no hurry to go home," she said. Nor was she in a hurry to leave Bo's side right now.

* * *

"That was amazing!" Claire said, leaning back against the headrest of Bo's car as he drove her to his home three hours later. "And your baby brother is adorable. I can't believe I got to hold a newborn who's only been on this earth for an hour. That was such a rush. And the wedding was perfect, even though we were the only ones in attendance."

He glanced over, feeling a sense of pride and accomplishment at helping to put that contented look on her face. "You pulled it off."

"*We* pulled it off."

From his peripheral vision, he saw her turn and look at him.

"You said it yesterday, and it's true. We make a pretty good couple." Her relaxed posture stiffened. "Team. We make a good team," she corrected.

"I liked it better the first way." He'd been waiting to talk to her all day. The hospital hadn't seemed like the right place, but now he couldn't wait any longer. He pulled into his driveway, parked his car, and then looked across the seat at her.

Her contented, dreamy look was gone, replaced by a look of confusion. It was just last night that they'd kissed in this very car, but it felt like a lifetime ago.

"I like you, Claire Donovan. I liked you last spring, but I was a coward. I'll admit that."

"Sounds about right," she agreed.

"I'd just watched my best friend marry the woman I thought I wanted. But I was wrong. I was so wrong. You're the woman I want, Claire. And I want you like I've never wanted anything in my entire life." His heart was thundering in his ears as he made his confession.

Her eyes became shiny for the hundredth time that night.

"The last few days have breathed new life inside me. I don't want to think about waking up tomorrow and not knowing if I'll see you." He ran a hand through his hair to keep from reaching out and touching her. "Claire, I want another chance with you. If you say yes, I promise I won't mess things up this time."

She was so still that he wondered if she was okay.

"Say something," he finally said.

"I'm hungry." After a long moment, her lips curved ever so slightly.

He cleared his throat and turned to look out at his yard. "Well, there's probably still some food left over from the reception. The guests each took some, but it'd be a shame for the rest to go to waste. I even think I saw Janice Murphy spike the punch on her way out," he said.

Claire gave a small laugh and nodded when he looked at her. "There's also a place to dance under the stars."

"The evening is set for romance," he agreed.

"So let's enjoy it and see where the night takes us. On one condition." Her expression contorted to something stern with just a touch of playfulness lighting up her eyes. "If it ends up leading somewhere nice, you have to promise you'll call me tomorrow."

He chuckled. "I promise that it will lead somewhere nice, and when it does, you might never get rid of me."

She looked up into his eyes and smiled. "I might never want to."

Epilogue

In the blink of an eye, everything could change. Or in Claire's case, one month's time. That was how long it'd been since she'd planned Rebecca and Pearson's wedding. It had all happened so fast, but everything had fallen into place perfectly.

Claire stepped out of the dressing room at Sophie's Boutique and did a twirl in front of the body-length mirror. The cotton dress was a deep rose color with tiny blue pin dots in the fabric. The hem brushed along her knees as she shifted in front of the mirror.

"That's the one," the shop owner said, stepping up beside her.

"I feel a little foolish. It's just our one-month anniversary, but Bo told me to wear something nice."

"One month together is definitely worth celebrating. Where is he taking you?" Sophie asked. "Any idea?"

Claire shook her head. "No." It didn't really matter though. It was the gesture that melted her heart like a marshmallow against an open flame. He was always doing little things for her to show her how much he cared. "Okay," she said, looking down. "This is the one. I'll take it off and let you ring it up for me."

"Do you have the right shoes?"

Claire laughed. She loved to shop as much as the next person, but she couldn't wait to get home and ready for whatever Bo had planned for them. "I do. But thanks."

An hour and a half later, Bo picked her up at her place and started driving.

"You're still not going to tell me where we're going?" she asked.

He was dressed in nice jeans with a polo top and a sport coat. She was almost disappointed to have to go out tonight because she would have rather been alone with him. They'd spent a lot of alone time together over the last month, and she wasn't sure she'd ever get enough.

"That would ruin the surprise."

She huffed playfully. "Fine. How's baby Noah?" she asked. He'd told her he was stopping by the hospital this afternoon. It had been all she could do not to invite herself along, but visitors were limited to family right now. She was just the girlfriend.

"A genius," Bo answered. "He takes after me."

This made Claire laugh out loud.

"And he'll be leaving the NICU tomorrow. The doctor says he's ready."

"That's wonderful news. I'm sure Pearson and Rebecca are so happy."

He nodded. "They are."

Claire blinked as she looked out the window, recognizing the route. Surely she hadn't gotten all dressed up just to go back to his place.

He turned the car onto Lavender Road and drove all the way to the end. After pulling into his driveway and parking, he turned to her. She blinked and kept her gaze forward. The fairy lights were turned on—they'd never taken them down—and a table was set up at the peak of the hill behind his house.

Bo stepped out of the car and walked around to open her door for her. Then they approached what he'd put together. There was a small vase of fresh flowers at the table's center, sandwiched between two candles, not yet lit. Another table was set up to the right with what appeared to be catered food from Taste of Heaven.

"A candlelit dinner under the stars." She turned and stepped into him, wrapping her arms around his neck and staring into his eyes. "All this just to celebrate one month of being together?"

He leaned in and kissed her lips, soft and slow. Nothing in her life had ever felt so right as being with him.

"No. All this is to tell you that I love you, Claire Donovan. I love you so much."

She blinked him into focus. A man had never uttered those words to her before, but they were music to her ears. She wanted to hear them again and again. "I love you too, Bo Matthews."

She laughed as he pulled her in for another kiss under the starry night sky. Then they had dinner and shared a dance before retreating to his room, where he repeated those three little words again and again.

**FOR MORE OF ANNIE'S SIGNATURE
SMALL-TOWN CHARM,
CHECK OUT THE REST OF THE
SWEETWATER SPRINGS SERIES!**

About the Author

Annie Rains is a *USA Today* bestselling contemporary romance author who writes small-town love stories set in fictional places in her home state of North Carolina. When Annie isn't writing, she's living out her own happily ever after with her husband and three children.

Visit her online at:
  http://www.annierains.com/
  @AnnieRains_
  http://facebook.com/annierainsbooks
  https://www.bookbub.com/authors/annie-rains

COWBOY REBEL
By Carolyn Brown

After a brush with the law, rancher Taggart Baker has decided to leave his wild ways behind, especially when he meets a beautiful ER nurse worth settling down for. But before he can convince her he's a changed man, his troubled past comes calling—and this time he won't be able to walk away so easily. Includes a bonus story by Annie Rains!

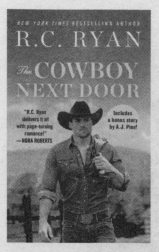

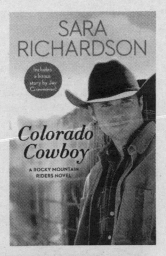

COLORADO COWBOY
By Sara Richardson

Charity Stone has learned to hold her own in the male-dominated rodeo world. There's no cowboy she can't handle...except for one. Officer Dev Jenkins has made it clear he doesn't look at her as one of the guys. He's caught her attention, but Charity doesn't do relationships—especially not with a cowboy. Includes a bonus story by Jay Crownover!

JUSTIFIED
By Jay Crownover

As the sheriff of Loveless, Texas, Case Lawton is determined to do everything by the book—until he's called to Aspen Barlow's office after a so-called break-in. The last thing he wants to do is help the woman who cost him custody of his son. But as threats against Aspen start to escalate, it becomes clear that Case is her last hope—and there's nothing he wouldn't do to keep her safe. Includes a bonus story by Carly Bloom!

Follow @ReadForeverPub on Twitter and join the conversation using #ReadForever.

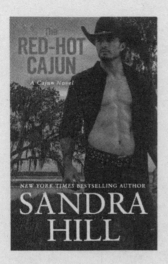

THE RED-HOT CAJUN
By Sandra Hill

Valerie Breaux vows she'll never give her heart to the Cajun bad boy, but when René LeDeux swears to get the girl who got away, things start to heat up between this feisty duo. It's never been steamier in the bayou than with two people this red-hot with desire...and more than ready for love.

THE LAST TRUE COWBOY
By Laura Drake

Austin Davis never meant to put his rodeo career before Carly, and this cowboy will do whatever it takes to win her back. But Carly's hiding a secret—one that will test the depth of their love.

Connect with us at Facebook.com/ReadForeverPub.

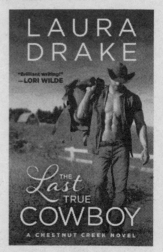